THE ... DARLINGS
AND PASSION'S CAPTIVES!

Bella heard a rap on the roof of the carriage and felt it start away from the inn.

She struggled with the sheet, pulling it off her head and preparing to do battle with the brigand who held her captive on his lap.

"YOU!?!" she sputtered.

"I think the words you are searching for are 'Thank you, David.'"

"Thank you! Why should I THANK you?"

The duke stared at her. "For rescuing you from that cad, for one thing."

"You must be demented. The only CAD I know of is YOU!"

Isabella Castillo-Sueras Alexander wasn't prepared for the duke of Exeter's lips capturing hers. Shock stilled her, then the fire engulfed her, heating her blood, coursing through her limbs, melting her resistance . . .

Praise for Sheila O'Hallion's *KATHLEEN:*

"Engrossing . . . a vivid, authentic . . . and ultimately joyful read."

—*Rave Reviews*

"As . . . romantic and lilting as an Irish bard's song."
—*The Romantic Times*

Books by Sheila O'Hallion

American Princess
Fire and Innocence
Kathleen
Masquerade of Hearts

Published by POCKET BOOKS

American Princess

Sheila O'Hallion

POCKET BOOKS

New York   London   Toronto   Sydney   Tokyo

This book is a work of historical fiction. Names, characters, places and incidents relating to non-historical figures are either the product of the author's imagination or are used fictitiously. Any resemblance of such non-historical incidents, places or figures to actual events or locales or persons, living or dead, is entirely coincidental.

An *Original* Publication of POCKET BOOKS

POCKET BOOKS, a division of Simon & Schuster Inc.
1230 Avenue of the Americas, New York, NY 10020

ISBN: 0-671-69398-0

First Pocket Books printing November 1989

10 9 8 7 6 5 4 3 2 1

POCKET and colophon are trademarks of
Simon & Schuster Inc.

Printed in the U.S.A.

American Princess

Chapter One

I simply cannot credit it," the elegantly clad Clarissa Stanisbury said to her cousin. As she spoke the horse-drawn victoria in which she sat was turning into Exeter Square.

Her companion, Henrietta Epps, Countess of Eppsworth, leaned forward, tapping the driver with her fan. "Slowly around the square, Joshua."

The driver yanked back on the reins, slowing the light four-wheeled carriage. Behind and below his high perch the two women glanced toward the massive facade of a huge stone mansion.

"What did you say she's called?" Clarissa's small dark eyes were alive with curiosity.

"The Terror of California!" Henrietta replied, relishing the words. "And she's to stay at Exeter House."

Henrietta's carriage continued around the cobblestone square, the railed garden in the center blocking their view of the mansion as the horse stopped in front of a tall Georgian townhouse. Identical Georgian townhouses lined the east, north, and south sides of the square. But only the massive Exeter House stood to the west.

"Her very own countrymen call her that, the Terror of California! Mark my words, Clarissa, the London season of

1

1881 will go down in history thanks to this American adventuress!"

Their conversation continued as the women were helped from the carriage by Henrietta's footmen. After they relieved themselves of their outer garments, Henrietta asked for tea and showed her cousin into the front parlor.

Patting her pale hair into place, Henrietta drifted toward a pair of delicate Chippendale chairs that flanked the mahogany tea table. Both chairs had a perfect view, out the large bow window, of the prepossessing facade of Exeter House. It rose beyond Exeter Square's garden with its black wrought-iron railings, the newly leafing plane trees, and the first tulips of spring.

Clarissa followed Henrietta, venturing a glance out the window. "What I cannot comprehend is why on earth Prince Henry invited such a creature to spend the season."

Henrietta settled her plump form onto the delicate chair. Even in her well-laced stays she looked matronly. "We're such old friends, you know. I was quite close at one time to the dear late princess." She smoothed her skirts. "The dear prince told me in confidence she's to arrive within the month. And she's here to find a titled husband. What else?"

Clarissa's delicate, lace-gloved hand went to her lips, a look of consternation crossing her face. "You can't be serious. A rich merchant is one thing, but she expects to capture a title!?"

Conversation was interrupted by the arrival of the tea tray. Clarissa's eyes drifted back toward the facade of Prince Henry's mansion as the butler withdrew and Henrietta poured. "Does he know?" Clarissa asked. "Does the prince realize he's inviting a fortune hunter into his home?"

"If the Prince of Wales can invite the King of Hawaii for a state visit, I suppose his cousin can invite whom he chooses. After all, she will be at Exeter House, not at Buckingham Palace."

Clarissa dismissed the Prince of Wales with a delicate sniff. "Bertie is always doing indelicate things. But as the queen has said herself, Prince Henry has ever been the soul of propriety."

"No male is the soul of propriety," Henrietta said.

"Clarissa, you spend much too much time in Kent. You are becoming positively countrified."

"It was so good of you to invite me to spend the season, dear cousin," Clarissa quickly replied. "I never forget what I owe to your kindness and charity."

"Yes, well, this season should be delicious. Entertained by the perfectly heathenish King of Hawaii and this savage from the Wild West. I do so hope she wears buckskins and feathers and whatever it is they wear."

"Good grief, is she a red Indian?"

"No." Henrietta sounded disappointed. "She's the daughter of some American adventurer. He married into a famous Spanish family who own Mexico or some such."

"So she is not after money, then?" Clarissa asked.

"They say she's practically swimming in it," Henrietta replied. "At twenty-one she had better be."

"Twenty-one and just coming out?" Clarissa helped herself to another biscuit. "The poor dear. She hasn't a chance."

"Unless Prince Henry thinks to possibly interest his own son in this heathen," Henrietta said artlessly.

Clarissa nearly spilled her tea. "Henrietta! He couldn't! He wouldn't!" She leaned forward. "Do you think he might?"

"Interest the Duke of Exeter? My dear cousin, in the last ten years every mother in England has tried, and *no* one has been able to snare the elusive David. He's spent his life enjoying the charms of the daughters while avoiding the grasps of their mamas. I hardly think his father can succeed where such accomplished campaigners have failed. David will hardly succumb to an aging heathen in buckskins!"

"Then why is Prince Henry trying?" Clarissa asked.

Henrietta smiled. "Did I say he was?"

"Yes. Well, you said—that is, you implied—I distinctly heard you say he planned on interesting the duke in this heathen."

Henrietta looked to be the soul of innocence. "I merely posited the possibility."

Clarissa scrutinized her cousin. "Henrietta, I know that look in your eye. What are you up to?"

"I can't imagine what you mean."

"You've had that look ever since we were children; it appears just before you get up to one of your outrageous pranks. Out with it. What devious little scheme are you hatching?"

"Dearest Clarissa, I'm crushed. I don't know what you can be speaking of." Henrietta gave one last glance to the mansion across the square before she rose to her feet. Her lilac-colored silk gown rustled becomingly as she moved toward the parlor door. "I really must rest before dressing for dinner."

When she reached the door, Henrietta looked back at her frustrated relative and smiled. "Have you decided what to wear to the Princess of Wales's salon?"

Clarissa put her teacup down and rose to her feet. "I thought perhaps the plum—"

"Oh, no! Much too drab." Henrietta studied her cousin's too-thin figure and soft brown hair. "I have a yellow gown that might do."

Clarissa looked toward Henrietta's overly ample form but wisely kept her thoughts to herself. Instead she said, "It's not until Wednesday next, in any event. There's plenty of time to make a decision."

"Ah, but you want to look your best. After all, the duke himself will be there," Henrietta said.

"Henrietta Epps, what *are* you planning?"

"Nothing, my dear. Absolutely nothing, I assure you."

"You'd best be careful," Clarissa said, already worried. "You can be too clever for your own good at times. Too clever by half. After all, you don't want to create a sensation over this creature."

"Why, Clarissa, pet," Henrietta cried delightedly, "how did you guess? That is *precisely* what I hope to do! I simply can't wait for this American to arrive!"

The American in question arrived three weeks later aboard Mr. Cunard's oceangoing steamer, the *Columbia*. However, she was not dressed in buckskins. Isabella Castillo-Suera Alexander wore a copper-colored silk traveling costume that made her ivory skin glow in the overcast morning light. Wisps of ebony hair strayed out from underneath a matching copper velvet bonnet, her waist-length hair twisted into an intricate braid beneath the velvet and tulle.

She was tall, her height and her perfect complexion inherited from the Alexander clan. But her ebony-black hair, shot through with sable and chestnut highlights, and her deep brown eyes came from the Castillo-Sueras.

She stood on deck, watching the crew furl the auxiliary rigging. Other men were just beginning to hoist the gangway into position.

The overcast London sky seemed oppressively close, the day gray and wintry. She was already homesick for the gentle warmth of a California March, for the huge vistas of Rancho La Providencia, where, as far as the eye could see, the land and the cattle and the people were her own.

From the two-foot-thick adobe walls of the thirty-room hacienda to the mountains purpling in the distance, from the joshua and eucalyptus to the fig and olive trees, to the new grapevines and orchards of oranges her grandfather Suera had planted, she missed it all.

"Bella? Isabella!" Connie's voice reprimanded from the passageway behind. *"Madre de Dios,* what are you doing?!"

"Trying to find a rowboat to row my way back home," Bella replied.

"Good girls do as their parents bid," Connie said with the air of someone who had given the same lecture a thousand times, all to no avail.

"Then you'd best find a good girl to do so!" Bella snapped. The gangway had been put in place, and Bella was moving toward it.

"And where do you think you are going?" Connie asked.

"Where you and Mama have been determined to send me—to London!" Bella declared, her words carrying back across the gangway.

"Bella!" Connie's charge did not stop. "Isabella Alexander! What will your mother say, you wandering about alone on the docks!?"

Bella looked back toward her duenna. Her stormy eyes were the color of darkest chocolate. "Mama said I would step foot on English soil if she had to die to insure it. Inform Mama she now has no need to die. I am already on shore!"

Bella turned away from her duenna, her nose wrinkling at the smells of wharfside London and the dirty Thames flowing sluggishly far below the double-roped gangway.

Consuela Maria Rivera watched Bella march across the narrow gangway toward dreary dockside buildings. The tall, proud girl looked out of place amid the dirt and squalor. Connie looked up toward the cheerless sky as if in supplication. She saw no help there; she thought about going after the headstrong girl and then thought better of it.

As her father had often said, Bella was a law unto herself. Connie's father had worked for the Castillo-Sueras as had his fathers before him. The Riveras had come with Don Miguel Castillo from Spain with the first Spanish land grants that deeded the new territories of the Californias to deserving Spanish aristocrats.

For almost one hundred years, since 1788, the Castillo-Sueras's fortunes had risen, riding out the departure of Spanish rule from California and the annexation by Mexico, surviving and profiting from the political battles that added, in 1850, the state of California to the United States of America. Thirty-one years later, the Castillo-Sueras aligned themselves with the powerful Alexanders, who had brought the railroad to the west coast of America, thus consolidating both their own fortunes and the fortunes of California.

"Well?" Dolores Castillo-Suera Alexander's low-pitched voice came from behind Consuela. "Did you find her?"

"She's gone ashore."

"Ashore? Alone!?" Dolores demanded.

Consuela shrugged. "She was forced to come, Doña Dolores. You know what she's like when she's forced."

Dolores Alexander stared down her family retainer. "I never, repeat never, want to hear that phrase again."

"I didn't start calling her the Terror of—"

"Consuela!" Bella's mother's voice stopped Connie's words, commanding respect in an imperious tone worthy of an empress. "We are leaving the ship," she continued crisply.

"Madre de Dios, momentito!" Connie lifted her black skirts and scurried back along the passageway to hurry the porters, muttering to herself the entire way.

The captain came toward Dolores Alexander and offered his arm. Nodding regally, Dolores accepted it. She stepped up onto the gangway, her black silk gown falling in elegant folds, her black lace mantilla fluttering in the damp winds that were blowing across the steel-gray Thames.

On the shore, Isabella watched the constant stream of carriages that came and went along the wharf of this busiest port in the world. Her every thought was on how to end this European trip quickly, her impatience showing in her expression and the tapping of her foot.

A large carriage, drawn by matched bays, slowed behind her, the driver bringing the horses to a sedate walk.

"Be careful!" Consuela called out. She hurried toward Dolores, who had almost reached Isabella's side. "These heathens will kill you without a backward glance!"

When she reached the dockside, Connie gave the driver of the coach a distrustful look. "We survived the railroad and the Atlantic Ocean only to die at the hands of a mad Englishman! I shall never be well again after that crossing. I can't face it again, I will die here," Connie told mother and daughter. "None have ever been asked to survive what I have been asked to go through."

"You did not travel alone," Bella told her duenna.

"Ah, but you, with the constitution of an ox, were well the entire journey!" Connie retorted.

A trail of seamen carrying steamer trunks and large wooden crates came across the gangway toward the three women.

"I shall be incessantly sick here," Bella informed her duenna. "Until I am once again at home."

"Isn't that rather premature, *querida?"* her mother asked. The wind had pulled loose a few strands of ebony hair, and Dolores reached toward her daughter, patting them back into place beneath Bella's copper-colored bonnet. "You've not even truly arrived."

Dolores Castillo-Suera had been a beautiful young girl

when Wallace Alexander asked for her hand in marriage. Twenty-two years later, she was a still more beautiful woman.

Raising a child in the midst of political upheaval and carrying on her husband's duties when he became ill had only added to her beauty and strengthened her innate courage. The strain of her husband's long illness had placed a sadness in her dark eyes that added an aura of mystery to her already striking features.

She wore the traditional black garb of the widow. But on her the black silks and satins made her dark looks even more dramatic. As did the smooth sweep of darkest brown hair that started in a widow's peak and was pulled straight back from her patrician face, twisted into a knot held by large tortoiseshell combs. Only the generous curve of her mouth and the lively sparkle that sometimes lit her large eyes belied the warmth that hid within her.

At the moment a fleeting twinkle smiled out at her only child as Bella stood, stubborn and resolute, ready to dislike everything she saw.

"I'm sure I needn't remind you of your pledge to Papa. He could not die easy without it," Dolores said mildly. She watched her daughter bite her lower lip.

"I promised to come. I promised to do as you asked. I did not promise to like it!" Bella's voice rose with frustration. "This place is exactly what I assumed! It is cold and damp and noisy and noisome!"

"All docks are noisy and noisome. You've seen the same in New York City." Dolores glanced at Consuela. "You'd best caution those men to be careful with the plate, Connie."

Trunks and crates were piling up around the women as they spoke. Connie moved toward the crates as the driver of the large coach came a little nearer Dolores and Bella. He lifted his cap to them, scratching his head and then turning to stare at Dolores.

"Mrs. Alexander?"

"Yes," Dolores replied.

"I'm Gideon, ma'am. Sent to bring you to Exeter House." He looked toward the alarming pile of trunks and crates that was still growing all around them.

"Another coach is expected, I'm sure," Dolores told him. "For the rest of our belongings. Or one can be sent for."

"Yes, ma'am, it can." Gideon replaced his cap upon his head. "It's a long stay you're planning, then."

Dolores did not reply. She turned toward her daughter. "I hope you're not planning on one of your little scenes, Bella."

Bella was affronted. "Scenes? Mama, how can you!?"

"How can I ask? Easily," her mother told her. "I've been privy to enough of them. But I assure you, there is no one here who will care. The crew will think you strange, the horses might be a little upset, but as for myself and Connie, it could not matter less. I merely intend to warn you that you will expend your energies for nothing."

"I have no intention of performing 'scenes' for the London populace!" Bella told her mother.

"I'm very glad to hear it," her mother replied mildly. "Now, shall we be comfortable in Prince Henry's coach while we wait for our things?"

Bella, with none too good grace, followed her mother toward the large black coach. "This trip is a horrid mistake," she told her mother.

"Don't say horrid, *querida*. It is such an ugly word."

The lane beside the dock was muddy and rutted from scores of wagon and coach wheels. The two women had to pick up their trailing skirts in order to move the few steps to the waiting coach. As they moved the seaside stench filled their nostrils.

"I shall hate it all."

"What did you say, Bella? I didn't hear you." Dolores was being helped into the coach by Gideon's young assistant. The boy stood by the coach steps, reaching a hand to help them inside, his eyes downcast.

Bella stepped up inside and plunked herself down across from her mother. "Nothing important to any but me," she replied.

"Nonsense. You know I care about everything you think and do. Sit up straight, Bella. It's not polite to slouch."

"I can't imagine why not," Bella replied tartly. "How I sit is of no concern to any but myself. And none at home seemed to mind me, no matter how I sit!"

"The only company you keep at home is with your horses," Dolores told her daughter. "And even they do not appreciate an ungainly seat."

"I warn you, I shall hate England and everything English! I do not want to be here!"

"Then it shall be a very trying season for us both," Dolores replied. She closed her eyes.

Bella watched her mother, suddenly feeling very selfish. She was the one who had promised her father this trip. Her mother had only promised to make it come true. Bella looked out the coach window. If only the land were not so bleak, so alien, perhaps she could carry out her promise with better grace. But she knew her father had wanted her to find a husband here, a husband worthy of her wealth and position.

The thought made her cringe. She had no wish for a foreign husband, titled or not. She did not want to live away from her home, from the sunshine and warmth that had accompanied her life until she had set sail for England.

She had given her word to her father to take this trip. She had not promised to marry. She would simply have to survive this unwelcome visit, and then she could return to her home and her friends.

Bella looked up to find her mother's eyes open again. And fastened upon her. Bella smiled a little, trying to make peace.

"I'll watch for the trunks, Mama."

Dolores returned her daughter's smile. Headstrong and flighty, she was a good girl at heart. She would see her duty and do it, her mother told herself. One day, Dolores amended the thought, sighing.

She closed her eyes, praying that day would come soon.

Chapter Two

David George Henry Michael Beresford, the Duke of Exeter, was eating a rather late breakfast in the small morning parlor of Exeter House. His six-foot frame was draped into an armed chair, the morning *Times* in front of him on the snowy lace tablecloth. A thick head of chestnut-colored hair and eyes of a startling deep blue were bent over the newspaper—silent witnesses of his Welsh ancestry.

Outside the mullioned windows behind him gentle spring sunshine warmed the view of yard and square. In Exeter Square itself it was the hour for servants to barter with tradesmen in front of the huge mansion and in front of the elegant Georgian houses on the other three sides of Exeter Square. Carts filled with dry goods, carts filled with food-stuffs or tools attracted the haggling buyers, the noise of their bargaining carrying back toward the four-story stone mansion in which David was eating breakfast.

The house around the duke held more rooms than anyone had ever bothered to count. Anterooms, drawing rooms, saloons, parlors, billiard rooms, libraries, tea rooms, coffee rooms, offices and servants' halls, kitchens, sculleries and stillrooms, gun rooms, music rooms, bedrooms, and dressing rooms. Huge, echoing dining parlors and smaller, more intimate breakfast parlors such as the one in which David was finishing his sausage and eggs.

"Hello, you must have been out rather late," Prince Henry said as he came through the doorway. His son's height and finely chiseled lips were duplicated in the prince, but there the resemblance ended. David's father had fair skin that tended toward freckles and reddish-blond hair. With his kind, rather absentminded-looking hazel eyes and pale coloring, he was attractive in an exceedingly English fashion. "We rarely see you eating at this hour," the prince told his son.

"I was in by three, which must have been quite a bit before you," David said. "I never heard you arrive."

"Ah, well—it was one of Bertie's long nights. We ended up with the cards and the brandy and the morning sun."

"Cousin Bertie seems determined to drive his mother to her grave," David said.

"The queen pushed him too hard when he was younger. Her uncles, including your own grandfather, I'm afraid, were a rather sorry lot. Dissipated, self-indulgent, the kind of royals who caused the French Revolution. She only meant to have Bertie become a good example."

"She meant for him to become his father, and he could never have become Prince Albert no matter what he tried. What he *is* doing seems to be making up for years of lost time at the gaming tables and in women's parlors," David said. "No matter what the queen says—or, for that matter, what his wife says."

Prince Henry studied his son across the breakfast table. "His marriage hasn't interfered with his nocturnal recreations."

"The Princess of Wales is the most understanding wife imaginable," David replied dryly.

"You might do as well," Prince Henry began cautiously.

"Do as well as what?"

The butler came forward to the table, pouring coffee as the prince grimaced at his son. "You know very well what I mean."

"Tate, I think I'll take coffee this morning," David interrupted.

The surprised butler carried the silver pot to the duke. Tate waited for the footman to bring a fresh cup and take away the cold tea before pouring. When the servants withdrew, David handed the *Times* across the table.

"I'm sorry, Father. You were saying?"

"I was saying that you simply refuse to discuss the subject of your marriage, and I can't understand it."

David was glancing through the pile of engraved calling cards and morning mail beside his plate. "I wasn't aware there was such a subject."

"Are you saying you shall never marry?" Prince Henry asked.

"I'm saying the entire matter bores me." Suiting action to words, he yawned.

"You'll be thirty-one this November, David. It's past time to think about it."

"You've said that every year since I turned twenty-one."

"Because I don't want to have to worry about it when you are fifty-one! You have a duty to your title and your family. The queen continues to ask each time we meet why she hasn't been asked to approve of some young lady. She can't understand your reluctance to marry and fulfill your obligations. And neither can I!" the prince said crisply.

"I faithfully discharge all my obligations to queen, to country, and to family, do I not?"

"Not the most important one of all! Securing the dukedom!"

"I am at the queen's disposal during the season. I oversee our northern holdings the rest of the year. Which you can't abide and had sadly neglected, I might add. Beyond that, I owe no obligations or explanations to anyone."

"Do you intend to be the bachelor Duke of Exeter? You might as well tell me the worst and let me prepare for our entire inheritance to be thrown to the four winds."

"Father. The Devonshire dukedom survived being handed from the Spencers to the Cavendishes. And Hartington's nearing fifty and still shows no inclination toward the married state."

"Harty-Tarty is not an example I want my son to emulate! As for your bringing up the two Devonshire dukes who were selfish enough to think more about their own pleasures than their family obligations, well, I think it's indicative of where this is all leading." The prince paused for emphasis. "You're slipping into a life of self-indulgence and dissipation!"

David grinned. "I'm not slipping anywhere at all, Father. At least not presently. There is nothing I do now that I have not done for years."

"My point precisely. Your life has no purpose unless you build for the future."

"I suppose my following cousin Bertie's example would give my life purpose. Marry some unsuspecting chit and then wander wherever my diversions—and my appetites—took me. Making her life miserable and mine a subterfuge. No thank you."

Prince Henry gazed across the oak table. "Are you by any chance a romantic at heart, David?"

"Heaven forbid!"

"Because you seem to be saying you expect marriage to be a happy estate. I'm simply saying, for the good of your line, it is a necessary step. Unless you want your dukedom handed over to John's progeny."

At the mention of his cousin the duke scowled. "If anything could convince me to marry, it would be the thought of those brats overrunning Exeter."

"Or John selling it off for gambling debts," Prince Henry added. "I'm serious, David. You *must* get your house in order before you endanger all who depend upon you." He watched his son stand up. "It's time."

David frowned. "You have succeeded in ruining both my breakfast and my good mood, Father. I am going riding."

Prince Henry studied his only child. "Are you going to think about it?"

"You've given me no choice," the duke replied ungraciously. He left his father to finish breakfast alone.

He was still out when Gideon returned with the carriage and his American passengers.

The ride through the gray London morning had done nothing to endear the city to Isabella. The noise and the crowds made her long for her own sweet green hills and the snow-capped mountains that towered above and beyond them to the north. She saw a thousand carriages on the narrow streets and longed to see her *vaqueros* galloping across the hills, working with horses and *reatas* to keep the numberless cattle in line. Shops and shops and more shops greeted her eyes instead of rivers that ran down from the high reaches, gorging out canyons where oaks and willows and sycamores gave shade.

Bella allowed Gideon's young assistant to help her step down from the carriage, joining her mother on the pavement in front of the imposing stone facade of Exeter House.

"Madre de Dios," Consuela breathed, "it is a castle we are staying at."

"Come along, Connie," Dolores Castillo-Suera Alexander commanded her servant, frowning at Connie's open-mouthed amazement. "Bella, stand straight. You are about to meet royalty."

"I can't very well stand at attention for months on end," Bella told her mother pertly.

Dolores ignored her daughter's words. She allowed Gideon to escort her up the wide, shallow steps toward the butler already alerted and waiting to greet them, four of his minions waiting behind him.

"Mrs. Alexander," he said with a slight bow, "I am Tate, the butler. Welcome to Exeter House."

"Thank you, Tate. This is my daughter, Isabella, and her duenna, Consuela."

The butler acknowledged them and stepped back into the vast main hall. "If you'll allow me to show you to your suite," he said smoothly, motioning to the footmen to unload the carriage.

"Is the prince at home?" Dolores asked.

"Yes. He assumed you would wish to freshen up before joining him in the blue parlor," the butler said.

"Please thank His Highness for his thoughtfulness."

As Dolores and the butler spoke, Isabella and Consuela followed them across the black and white marble floor and up the curving mahogany staircase.

The elegance of the lines of the marble-columned hall and

of the stairwell that curved up above it, the opulence of the forest-green velvet drapes below, and the artistry of the oil paintings lining the gallery above seemed cold to Bella.

The suite to which they were shown opened off the upper gallery into a large sitting room that overlooked Exeter Square. Isabella glanced toward the tall, narrow windows, their ruby-red velvet drapes swagged back and held by golden tassels.

Tate bowed himself out and Dolores reached to unpin her hat and pat her luxuriant hair into place. The doors to the rest of the suite were open, with two bedrooms to be seen beyond the sitting room. Unseen beyond each bedroom was a dressing room large enough to hold a single bed. A small trunk room for their luggage and a commodious bathroom completed the suite.

Consuela supervised the placement of the few trunks, boxes, and bags brought with them in the first carriage as a young maid brought a tea tray. The tray held pots of strawberry jam and orange marmalade with muffins, scones, and tea cakes, the pungent scent of Earl Grey tea filling the room.

Dolores poured tea as Bella drifted toward the windows, looking down at the wrought-iron-enclosed square. Early tulips and crocuses bloomed in the midst of new spring grass and spreading plane trees. Bella glanced idly at the narrow brick houses across the square.

"Bella, come have a bite to eat before we change."

Isabella turned toward her mother, unbuttoning her elbow-length gloves as she moved. "I'm not hungry, Mama."

"You will be by the time we go down to meet Prince Henry, and I don't want you showing off that ungainly appetite of yours. It's not ladylike. At least have a cup of tea."

Bella plunked herself down beside her mother on a fringed settee patterned in shades of forest, ruby, and sapphire.

"Nor is it ladylike to sit down that way, Bella. I hope you don't intend to behave like a hoyden when we meet the prince."

16

"Mama, please, please, listen to me. I could bear this whole trip, if only you wouldn't try to marry me off to some foreigner. I promise I will be everything you could hope for, wish for, I will be totally obedient, if only you will say I can go home with you."

"But *querida*, of course you can come home!"

Hope began to fill Isabella's eyes. "Do you mean it? Do you swear it?"

"Did you think marrying an Englishman would mean you could never go home? Silly child, I could never bear that. And your husband will be responsible for La Providencia; of course you will come home."

As her mother spoke the hope died out of Bella's dark eyes. Her jaw set into determined lines. "There is no Englishman alive that could handle La Providencia!"

"You've not met any yet, Bella." Dolores put her hand on Bella's arm. "You may be surprised."

Bella stood up. "I think I'll change, Mama."

"Bella—"

"Mama, please. I promised Papa on his deathbed that I would come. I am here. I promised to spend the season here. I shall. I promised to be polite and mind you. I will. More than that I cannot promise."

Dolores heaved an inaudible sigh of relief. "If you promise all that, I shall be satisfied. You have never gone back on your word, *querida.*"

Bella looked affronted. "Nor shall I ever!" Her imperious tone, the haughty angle of her head, her proud carriage all warmed her mother's heart. Dolores watched her daughter walk into the next room, thinking she could easily be a queen born. She would make a perfect princess or duchess or countess. And Wallace's dreams would be realized. He would have built an empire and handed his empire, along with his only child, into noble hands that would insure their safety and protection.

Consuela came toward her employer. "Your afternoon gown is ready, and your daughter insists she has no need to change."

Dolores stood up. "Humor her a little, Connie. This is all so hard on her."

17

"Hard on her! I shall age ten years before this is over. I can't take my eyes off her for fear of what she'll do or say next. She is, as usual, determined to have her own way, thanks to her parents' indulging her each and every wish since she was born!"

Dolores spoke mildly: "Her father was much worse than I in indulging her."

"Ha! And you say it will be hard on *her!* Don't waste your pity on Bella. Save it for ourselves," Connie said darkly. "Before this is over we shall need it much more than she, mark my words."

Consuela's warning followed Dolores as she changed and prepared to descend to meet the prince.

An hour later Dolores and Isabella were shown into the blue parlor, named for its sapphire-blue wallpaper patterned with tiny gold fleurs-de-lis. Prince Henry stood up, accepting Isabella's curtsy and smiling down at Dolores. She looked up into warm hazel eyes and smiled back. The prince had inherited the best features of his illustrious family. He was tall and slender with eyes that were both large and kind, the long family nose fitting the square planes of his face. He had escaped both the receding jaw and the family tendency to stoutness.

"My dear Dolores, it has been much too long between visits!" Prince Henry said.

Dolores laughed, a tiny peal of happy relief. "I am so glad you are the same, Your Highness, I—"

"Henry," the prince interjected. "You must call me Henry, Dolores, or I shall not be comfortable." He looked toward Isabella. "And this is the child."

Isabella curtsied again, unaccountably impressed by the imposing figure in his martial uniform. Heavy gold braid adorned his shoulders. "This is Isabella, Your—Henry," Dolores corrected herself. "Our daughter."

Prince Henry reached to kiss Bella's hand. When he straightened he smiled at her. "We met once before, but you were asleep in your cradle and could not possibly remember. You have grown up to make good the promise of your early beauty, young lady."

"Thank you, Your Highness." Isabella liked his eyes. She smiled back into them as he turned toward her mother.

"I can't tell you how glad I am to be able to finally repay, in a small way, the great debt I owe you," he said.

"Debt?" Isabella's question was spoken out loud. She lapsed into an unaccustomed confusion, earning a small smile from the prince and a very surprised look from her mother.

"Ah, yes, has your mother not told you?" Prince Henry asked. "Your parents saved my life."

"Hardly that," Dolores said.

"It is entirely true," the prince assured her. He led them to chairs. "Let me tell you the story, my dear Isabella. I was on a tour of your United States and was invited to the new state of California when I fell deathly ill on the road. Your father, who was with me at the time, acting as guide and host, immediately recognized the symptoms and ascertained that I had eaten tainted meat. He induced"—the prince hesitated, then went on—"the means by which my stomach was relieved of the poison and took me to your wonderful La Providencia, where your mother nursed me back to health."

Bella's eyes lit up. "You know La Providencia?"

"I know it and cherish it. I spent many long days exploring its arroyos and enjoying your fiestas and rodeos. I miss it still."

As he spoke Bella warmed to the man. And then, seeing her mother's satisfied expression, a horrible thought encroached. Surely her mother didn't intend to have her marry this elderly man. Why, he was her mother's age at least! Bella's eyes clouded as her mother and the prince continued to talk. Only her mother noticed Bella's unusual quietude.

As the two old friends talked Bella sat silent. After a bit she moved in her seat, standing when they looked toward her. "I find I am more tired than I thought. If you will excuse me . . ."

The prince rose, telling Isabella he understood perfectly. He turned back to her mother and sat down as Bella left the parlor and closed the door.

She moved with dragging step to the stairs, waves of

homesickness coloring her thoughts. In the suite above Consuela heard the sitting room door open and looked out from the trunk room, where she was unpacking the trunks and cases that had followed their arrival. "What's wrong?" Connie asked her charge.

Bella shook her head a little. "Nothing. I just felt a bit tired, that's all."

Connie watched Bella closely. The girl had never been tired in her entire twenty years. "What is it? What's wrong, *querida?* Tell Connie what it is."

"You know what it is," Bella said listlessly. "I want to be home. I don't want to be auctioned off like some prize cow." Her words trailed off. "And I haven't even heard from— home." She changed the last word.

Connie hesitated, one hand finding her pocket and reaching for a rather creased envelope. Her brow furrowed with doubt. "I don't know whether I should tell you—"

Bella turned back toward her duenna. "Do you know something?" She watched Connie. "Have you heard something? Did he write?" She saw the envelope in Connie's hand. "Is that from George?"

Connie held tight to the envelope. "Your mother would turn me out in the cold if she thought I was helping you keep in touch with that ne'er-do-well."

"It is!" Bella's eyes lit up. She danced toward Connie, reaching for the envelope. "It's from George! He *did* write!"

Against her better judgment, Connie let Isabella take the envelope and watched the girl waltz away toward the bedroom she had been given. As Bella shut the door Connie called out to her: "Just don't let your mother know what a fool I am!"

Bella heard the words as she closed the door. She held the letter tenderly, drinking in the dear handwriting on the envelope. He had written. He cared! He really cared. She had known it; no matter what her mother said, she had known it.

Her mother was against George because he was poor and had been an employee and because she thought him a fortune hunter. Isabella had known better, and now she had the proof in her hands.

She sank to the chaise longue near her bedroom window and tore the envelope open, hungrily reading the words:

Dear Bella,

I pray this letter gets to you. I have missed you dreadfully since your father banished me from the rancho; you know that. Our meetings are too few and too brief. I have just heard of your father's illness and passing away. For you, dear heart, I am devastated. But for ourselves, perhaps it is for the best. He was so against our friendship. Now I am determined to come to La Providencia and to implore your mother to let me call on you. Dearest Bella, I hope you still feel as you did the last time we talked. I hope you still have a small place in your heart for your most obedient of servants. I worship the ground you walk on and will do everything necessary to insure we can be together. Please let me see your dear face soon so that I may tell you all this in person. Send your letter to my address at the top of this page. I am in Los Angeles, only a little ways away, and I shall come immediately I hear you want me to. Dearest Bella, I want you for my very own. Please say you feel the same.

Your servant and your slave,
George

Isabella read and reread the letter before she heard the sound of her mother in the rooms beyond. Stuffing the letter down inside the cushions of the chaise, she looked up to see her mother opening the bedroom door.

Dolores looked concerned. "I was afraid you might be feeling truly ill, Bella."

"I'm fine, Mama. I was just a little tired."

Dolores came closer to feel her daughter's forehead and look into her eyes. Bella moved a little on the chaise, hiding the edge of the letter that peeked out from beneath the cushion.

"Are you sure? Your eyes look quite feverish. I think you should lie down. Perhaps it will be best if we have our dinner in our rooms tonight. I don't want you falling ill."

"Yes, Mama. Whatever you say," Bella said meekly.

Dolores watched her daughter. "You must be ill to be so meek. I shall inform the help." As Dolores started toward the door Bella called out to her mother, stopping her.

"Yes?" Dolores looked back at her daughter.

"You aren't considering marrying me off to the prince, are you?"

Dolores almost laughed. But seeing her daughter's woebegone expression, she stifled the laugh, telling her daughter no. "How could you even think so? He is a wonderful man, but he is much too old for you." Dolores saw Bella's relief. "Bella, did you really think that?"

"I didn't know. I—I wasn't sure. But I am truly glad, for I very much like the prince, Mama. I would hate to have to be mean to him."

"I certainly hope you will have enough sense and enough sensibility not to be unkind to our host," Dolores said primly.

"Yes, Mama," Bella said meekly.

Her mother was suspicious of the meekness, but she left the room, asking Connie if she thought Bella was coming down with something. Connie, worried about the letter, latched onto that explanation and elaborated upon it. The two women were discussing medicines and potions as Bella, alone in her room, reread the dear letter and prepared a reply.

Chapter Three

The Duke of Exeter spent the evening at Crockford's fashionable club, gaming with old cronies and toasting the midnight hour with a group of rakish ladies who would never be invited to Queen Victoria's Buckingham Palace.

They had, however, frequently been seen at Marlborough House with the Prince and Princess of Wales, as well as in the intimate environs of the infamous Marlborough Club in Pall Mall, which the Prince of Wales had created to the obvious dislike of his mother, the queen.

After a decade of experience, David George Henry Michael, Duke of Exeter, had come to the conclusion that an evening spent with some of the less reputable female members of society was infinitely more desirable than one with the simpering young fools who were constantly thrown in his path.

A striking-looking woman was next to the duke at the gaming table. Her abundant red hair was unfashionable by current standards, but her voluptuous figure and lazy good humor attracted a long list of suitors.

The duke threw the dice. Unsuccessful yet again, he turned toward Lady Winston, offering his arm and leading her toward a grouping of small gilt chairs across the room.

"I shall give up gambling, Adela, I swear it," he drawled.

"You'd best beware you are heard and then must make good your pledge," Lady Winston chided him, smiling.

David looked across the crowded gambling chamber. "My words will hardly be heard in this cacophony."

"One never knows when one will be heard . . . and understood . . ." Adela Winston paused for emphasis, her brow arching in response to David's direct glance.

David slowly grinned. "Adela, are you being coy?"

"Never," Adela replied. And she slowly smiled. "Not with you, my pet."

David looked across the room. When he spoke, his tone was low: "Are you free tonight?"

Adela glanced across the overcrowded room. "My lord and master appears to be in his cups. I might manage something." She gave David an arch look. "But then, you may not be free, from what I hear."

"I?" David was truly surprised. "What are you talking about?"

"Your house guest, my pet." Adela saw David's puzzled expression.

"The American?" David said, thinking of Dolores. "We were introduced this afternoon. And she's not my house guest. She's my father's. Every so often he has an irresistible impulse toward charity. What on earth would she have to do with our plans for the evening?"

Adela watched the enigmatic duke. She had known him since they were children, had known his family and his friends, and still did not feel she understood this tall man with the hooded eyes and patrician features. Speaking of Isabella, she continued, "I hear she is quite a sight to behold."

"She looked quite ordinary to me," the duke replied, still thinking of Dolores. "Quite nice looking for her age, actually."

"You make her sound ancient," Adela told him. "She's only twenty-one."

"Where on earth did you hear that? She's forty if she's a day."

Adela laughed. "Forty? What on earth are you talking

about? Be serious, David. You're deliberately misunderstanding me. I'm talking about the daughter, the one who's here to get a rich, titled husband." David groaned when he heard her words. "Henrietta Epps said she saw them arrive today," Lady Winston added.

"Does the Countess of Eppsworth actually do anything beyond peering out her windows?" David asked.

"Yes. She tells all she sees. Now don't keep me in suspense. What does she look like? The daughter, David, not the mother."

"I don't know. But she's sickly. I heard my father say she was keeping to her bed because of the rough passage."

Adela glanced around Crockford's ornate main room, smiling lazily when she saw jealous eyes upon her. There were many who would like to take her place as the duke's current love interest.

"She's probably afraid to come out of her room," he continued after a moment.

"That's unlikely, according to what I've heard. After all, she's called the Terror of California."

"Lord." David looked quite put out. "My father felt he owed their family his life because of some illness while he was in America. But bringing a fortune-hunting American into Exeter House is really a little too much gratitude." He reached for Adela's hand. "Enough of this nonsense, let's get out of here."

Adela gave him a swift swat with her fan, her merry peal of laughter insuring that others would look their way. She stood up, moving with affected care across the room. A friend came near, and she apologized, feigning, not too believably, a headache. She smiled weakly at the women around them as she allowed David to escort her from the overheated rooms.

They left behind discreetly wagging tongues and quite a few jealous ladies. Adela's overfed husband was still ensconced at the gaming tables, one of the few who didn't notice that they had left.

The next morning brought pale spring sunshine flooding into Exeter House's windows as the downstairs maids pulled open the scores upon scores of drapes and began their morning chores.

The upstairs maids moved quietly in the upper halls, dusting ornate gilt picture frames, sweeping the oriental rugs, polishing the mahogany gallery railings.

Consuela came up the servants' stairs carrying a tray of hot chocolate and dry toast. One of the maids opened the suite door and then closed it behind the Spanish guest.

Inside the suite, Connie herself had already opened the heavy velvet drapes in the sitting room, the morning sun warming the dark wood furniture. She moved to Dolores's bedroom door and tapped lightly, not waiting for a reply before opening it and entering.

"Good morning, señora."

Dolores stirred a little, yawning against her pillows. When Consuela threw open the bedroom drapes brilliant sunlight fell across Dolores's eyes. She closed them, one arm thrown across her face to ward off the light.

"It can't possibly be morning," Dolores said.

"It is, and the prince will be expecting you for breakfast. You told him last night you would go riding with him this morning."

Dolores sat up, stifling another yawn. "Why ever did I say that, I wonder."

"It might have something to do with drawing him out about his son," Connie said tartly. "And I have news of that quarter, too."

Dolores turned all her attention toward Consuela. "What is it?"

Consuela stepped back into the sitting room, leaving the door open between the rooms. "Come have some hot chocolate and wake up."

"Connie . . ." Dolores began, then she stopped. She knew her servant well enough to know it would do no good. Reaching for her satin-edged lace robe she stood up, belting it over her soft lawn nightgown as she marched into the sitting room of the spacious suite. "All right," she said ungraciously, "I'm here. Now tell me."

Connie poured the steaming chocolate into two cups, handing one to Dolores as she sat down across the small round table from the woman she had raised. "You won't like it," Connie warned.

"Consuela Rivera, I shall strangle you soon, I swear it." Dolores spoke over the top of her steaming hot chocolate.

Consuela took her time. "Prince Henry's son has quite a reputation with the ladies," she began.

Dolores dismissed the words with a wave of her patrician hand. "That's to be expected; he is thirty-one, handsome, rich, and a member of the royal family. Women would, of course, be attracted to him."

"And their mothers, in hopes of snaring the prize of the season as a husband for their daughters."

"If you're insinuating that I have any ulterior motives, Consuela . . ." Dolores let her words hang, her posture imperious as she sat up straight and glared at her employee. Grown men had been known to quiver at the thought of Dolores Castillo-Suera Alexander's icy wrath.

Consuela didn't seem perturbed in the least. "Put on your airs and graces with others, señora. I diapered you just as I have Bella, and I'm speaking plainly, woman to woman. He's a bad one."

"You don't even know him," Dolores retorted.

"I know enough to know I want nothing to do with him. And more to the point, neither should you. Nor should you allow him to have anything to do with our Bella."

"Good grief, you make him sound a total libertine!"

"He is," Consuela replied promptly. "He's the pick of the season, that's true. But he's been the pick of the season every season for the past ten years, and none has ever caught him!"

"None has ever pleased him," Dolores replied in a lofty tone.

"Plenty have pleased him, from what I hear," Consuela told her employer.

A shadow of a frown crossed Dolores's alabaster forehead. "What are you saying?"

"I'm saying he's adept at enjoying the daughters' charms while avoiding the mothers' grasp," Connie replied. "You'd be surprised what all the servants see."

Dolores put the cup of tea down. "I would never be

27

surprised what servants see," Dolores retorted promptly, giving an arch look to her own lifelong servant. "Nor at their putting the worst of interpretations on the most innocent of flirtations!" she ended crisply.

"Innocent is as innocent does . . . and the duke seems to be in the bad books of all the best families. They say he's a womanizer and a gambler and runs around with the most notorious set in London. When he isn't charming some young debutante out of her chemise."

"Connie!" Dolores's shock was real. "That can't be true!"

"No? Why? Because he has blue blood? Pierce his arm and the blood will run red enough, you mark my words. They say he's been lucky some father hasn't already come after him with his pistols and forced him to Gretna Green. That's a quick marriage, by the by. To save a young lady's virtue." Connie saw that her words had hit the mark. She continued more mildly: "Even if only half what they say is true, he's a dangerous one to have around our Bella."

Dolores contemplated Consuela's advice. "What you are really saying is that you think he is just the kind of man that Bella responds to."

Consuela shrugged eloquently. "After years of turning down all likely candidates, who did she decide to set her cap for? George Miller!" Consuela's pause was eloquent. "The most irresponsible young man any of us had ever seen. Until the duke," she ended darkly.

"Mama?" Isabella's voice came from the connecting door to her room.

"What's wrong, *querida?*"

"Nothing." Bella walked toward them, looking toward the pot of chocolate. "Is there more?" she asked Consuela.

"Come sit and share the rest," Dolores told her daughter, handing a cup over. "Did you sleep well?"

Isabella poured more chocolate into her mother's cup. "I slept abominably."

"You've complained about every bed since we left home," Connie told her.

"Yes, well, none have been the same as mine at home." Isabella looked around and then sank to a chair across from her mother and her duenna. "You both think I'm a terrible child who does nothing but complain, don't you?"

Consuela sniffed into the silence that followed Isabella's words. Dolores smiled at her only child. "We want what is best for you, Bella."

"I know, Mama. It's just that I'm never allowed to make my own decisions about what is best for me. I do have opinions on the subject, you know."

"You have opinions on every subject," Consuela replied tartly. "In the meantime, your mother has to dress for breakfast."

"And for riding in the park," Dolores reminded Consuela.

"Oh, Mama!" For the first time since they had reached England, Isabella looked truly enthused. "Can I come, too? Oh, please, I haven't ridden in such a long time!"

"You rode to the very day we left La Providencia," her mother replied. "And the answer is no." Dolores saw her daughter's crestfallen expression. "You would not be happy with this ride in any event, *querida*. It is a sedate canter in a manicured park, no more. It's not the kind of wild Indian ride you prefer. And it is sidesaddle to boot."

"Sidesaddle!" Isabella straightened up. "You can't be serious!"

"The English prefer their ladies to remain ladylike, even when riding horses."

"Ladylike!" Bella exclaimed. "How tedious! Besides, how can anyone remain ladylike while precariously perched on the side of a running beast? The whole idea is ridiculous!"

"Yes, well, they've done it for so long, they're not aware it's ridiculous."

"Then I shall tell them," Bella replied stoutly.

Dolores contemplated her daughter. "I think you would."

"No, Mother. You *know* I will," Bella said.

Dolores sighed. "You are a tiresome child, and I don't know why I put up with you."

Bella came to her mother's chair, kneeling down beside her and taking her hands. "You put up with me because I am so much like Papa, whom you loved very much."

Dolores allowed her daughter a small smile. "In your father the traits of stubbornness, foolhardiness, and total honesty were balanced by intelligence, humor, and compassion."

Bella pulled a face. "Am I stupid, then?"

"You're not, and you know it. But you certainly seem so when you cannot appreciate another's feelings. You have a great deal of intelligence but very little common sense, my girl."

"Are you mad at me, Mama?" Bella gave her mother a woebegone look.

"Only dogs go mad, Bella. I am not in the least happy with you at the moment. I fear you are determined to upset everyone you meet so that you may go home to that young upstart."

As her mother spoke Bella gave a quick, questioning look toward Consuela, who shook her head.

"Bella, Connie, what is going on?" Dolores looked from one to the other. "Have you been in contact with that man?"

"His name is George, Mother." Bella straightened up and then got to her feet. "George Miller."

"I know his name very well, Bella. And I know your father fired him."

"It wasn't fair! Daddy was angry at him for seeing me."

"Your father was angry because the young man gave his word and did not live up to it! That man wanted you to run away with him!"

"He loves me!" Bella burst out.

"He loves no one but himself. And he wants your money."

"That's not true!" Tears came to Bella's eyes. "You've never liked him. You've never given him a chance!"

"If he had stopped sneaking and had ever acted like a gentleman, I promise you, I would have!" Dolores stood up. Looking toward Consuela, she spoke slowly: "I sincerely hope no one is helping you keep in touch with him."

Bella tried to stop Consuela from speaking, giving her an intense look, but it did no good.

"There was a letter . . ." Consuela trailed off.

"May I have it, please?" Dolores held her hand out.

Consuela looked toward Isabella, who stamped her narrow foot. "I am not a child, and I won't be treated as such!"

"Isabella," her mother said, still holding out her hand.

Mother and daughter stood before each other, their eyes meeting and holding. Finally Isabella turned away, walking back toward her bedroom. Dolores followed her to the doorway and waited.

Bella reached within a small case and unwillingly withdrew George's letter. Looking up, she saw her mother still waiting in the doorway. With bad grace she came forward, thrusting it at her mother's outstretched hand. "I don't want to be treated as a child!" Isabella said again.

"Then stop acting like one," Dolores replied calmly. She opened the page, glancing down it and then handing it back. "He has no honor whatsoever."

"I love him!"

"You think you do, which is bad enough." Dolores hesitated. "Isabella, I have a proposition for you." She watched her daughter move away, sitting on the chaise longue. Isabella sat stiffly, awaiting her mother's words.

"My proposition is this," Dolores continued. "If you promise me you will not try to contact this man—hear me out—if you promise, and if you agree to be agreeable to the ladies and gentlemen you meet while we are here—if you give yourself the chance to like them, truly give yourself the chance—and you find none who catch your fancy, then I will consider allowing this person to call on you."

Isabella's gaze was penetrating, as if trying to see what lay behind her mother's eyes. "Do you mean it?" Bella asked.

"I have never broken my word. Do I have yours?"

Bella hesitated. "You want me to be nice to the people I meet."

"I want you to truly give yourself the chance to like them. I want you to compare the gentlemen you meet with this—man. And I want you to promise me you will not get in touch with him until we have left England."

"But that's months!" Isabella burst out.

"If he loves you, he will wait," Dolores replied.

Isabella bit her lip. Finally she nodded.

"Do I have your word?" Dolores asked.

"And you promise you will let him call on me, you will not send him away again——"

"If you truly give yourself a chance to like someone here," her mother repeated.

Bella nodded again. "Then you have my word."

"Say it," Dolores demanded.

Bella took a deep breath. "I will not try and get in touch with George until we leave England. And I will truly give the people I meet a chance to earn my affections. I promise."

"Very good," Dolores said quietly. "Now I must dress, and so should you."

"Yes, Mama," Bella said meekly.

When her mother left the doorway, Consuela came toward it, peering at her young charge. "If you give your word, you must keep it, *querida.*"

A brilliant smile lit Bella's eyes. "Ah, but Connie, I have just accomplished the impossible! Mama will let George call on me! I can be nice to *anyone* for a few months if I know I can go home to George. I have won!"

Consuela's look gave room for doubt, but she said nothing more as she turned away from the smiling girl.

Chapter Four

The girl who accompanied her mother down to breakfast with Prince Henry was a changed person. All smiles and kindness when she greeted the prince, she was totally agreeable to whatever her two elders decided about the day's activities.

"Are you sure you are quite well, my dear?" Prince Henry asked the girl he'd been told was called the Terror of California as she was seated at the breakfast table.

"Thank you, yes," Bella replied. "Why?"

He smiled. "I only meant you were rather under the weather yesterday, your mother said. The crossing, I suppose."

"I feel perfectly recovered," Bella replied.

"Good. Capital! Then I'm sure you'll enjoy getting out for a bit of fresh air. I understand you're quite a horsewoman," Prince Henry said pleasantly. "Your mother was telling me of your many accomplishments last night."

"My mother dotes on me and probably gives me too much credit," Bella replied.

The prince smiled across the table at Dolores. "I would trust your mother's judgment in anything," he said gallantly.

Dolores rewarded him with a small smile. "Now you are giving *me* too much credit."

"Your mother saved my life, Isabella."

"Hardly that," Dolores said.

Isabella gave the prince a sweet smile. "Please call me Bella, Your Highness. All my friends do."

"Then you must call me Henry."

"I couldn't! I mean . . ." Bella stopped, a little flustered.

The prince smiled. "You mean I'm such an old one, you wouldn't feel comfortable calling me by my first name?"

"No! I meant—it's just—"

He saved Bella's confusion by speaking over it: "It's quite all right, I'm certainly old enough to be your father, Bella. But I can't have you calling me Your Highness, or you will make me uncomfortable." He looked toward Dolores. "What about Uncle Henry?" he asked.

Bella looked toward her mother, unsure how to respond. But Dolores was smiling. "I fear it will confuse your friends no end, Henry. But it is certainly more appropriate than Bella calling you by your first name."

"It's agreed, then?" He looked toward Bella.

"It's agreed, Uncle Henry." The words sounded strange to her own ears.

"Capital! I've been thinking about something else, too. I've decided to give a ball for you."

Bella's eyes began to glow. "A ball for me?"

"Henry," Dolores began, only to be stopped by the prince.

"Now, you shall go to many balls and other events and diversions, but I think we should let society meet you both here first. In a proper setting for your beauty."

"Oh, I should love it!" Bella breathed the words.

The prince looked toward her mother. "You mentioned fittings and new garments to be purchased before you began accepting invitations. When will that be accomplished?"

"Within the week, I would imagine," Dolores said slowly. "But I don't want you going to such trouble."

"Nonsense. We've not had a party here since the last time I entertained Bertie. Since David's mother died, we almost never entertain in style. I shall rely on you both to insure everything is done properly."

"David's mother?" Bella questioned.

"My late wife, Ruth," Prince Henry answered.

"Ah, the mythical David," Bella said.

"Bella," her mother warned, but Bella only smiled at her. And then at the prince.

"I have heard you have a son, Pr—Uncle Henry. Will he then be my 'cousin'?"

"Of course he shall!" Prince Henry said with a large smile. "You must consider us family. And our home as your own while you stay. You haven't met David yet, have you?"

"No," Bella replied. "I fear he does not truly exist, except in your imagination," Bella teased.

"And mine," Dolores said. "I met him yesterday."

"So you said. I think you've both made him up, for he is never home."

"That's true enough," Prince Henry said, frowning. "He's home less and less these days." He looked toward Bella and banished the frown. "Perhaps you can convince him to spend more time with us."

"Perhaps," Bella agreed politely.

When breakfast was over and Bella had gone to retrieve her forgotten riding whip, Dolores stood alone with the prince in the front hall. She looked up to speak and found his eyes taking in her tightly tailored black riding costume. His eyes found her face and smiled.

"I have never seen black worn so well," he told her.

"You flatter me continuously, Henry. I—I hesitate to mention this, but I feel it might need saying." She tried to smile. "It's just that—well, Bella is such an impressionable girl, and she is really younger than her years, having lived on La Providencia, protected from the world at large, protected from—well—gentlemen."

"Yes?" Prince Henry said. He looked mildly interested but unsure what she was getting at.

"What I'm trying to say is that I hope she will find a nice young man who is, perhaps, not all that worldly. . . ." She trailed off as she saw recognition dawning in the prince's eyes.

"Are you worried about David?" he asked. "I mean, about his being interested in Isabella?"

Dolores plunged on. "Frankly, yes. From what I hear, your son is very—worldly."

The prince laughed. "He is that. And I must admit, I had a slight hope that they might hit it off when you first wrote and suggested this trip. I think Wallace may have had that in mind when he asked her to come. He liked David."

"Oh, I'm sure he's the most perfect—"

"Shush," the prince stopped her. "David's far from perfect. As are we all. But almost a decade has gone by since your husband was in England and met David. In that time David has been the object of many mothers' hopes. Too many. Believe me, he will be refreshed and most grateful you are not yet another."

Dolores truly smiled. "I meant no disrespect."

"Not at all. David is a handful. Wallace and I may have had passing thoughts about it, but I am afraid you are right. They probably wouldn't suit. And beyond that, I fear David is determined to retain his bachelorhood until his hair has long since turned gray."

"But the dukedom . . ." Dolores's concern was obviously genuine.

"Precisely. I confess I do not know what to do about it," he told her frankly.

Dolores shook her head. "Why do our children grow up determined to circumvent all our best plans for them? My daughter seems determined to throw herself and her inheritance away on a young man who has no scruples, no money, and no honor. Your son seems determined to let his inheritance slip from his fingers." She shook her head again. "I don't understand them. In my day these things were duties, and duty came before thought of self."

"Ah, yes. As in mine." Prince Henry sighed. "Is this young man the reason for your deciding finally to come?"

"He was the catalyst, I admit. In truth, Bella has been so set against this trip that I had allowed her to put it off ever since you first offered, four years ago. But she became involved with this George person. I mean, not really involved, obviously. But—well, smitten, I suppose, is the right word."

"And you are worried about her becoming more involved with this man?"

"Yes. Wallace didn't trust him. He worked for us for a short while, and Wallace found him lax and not necessarily truthful."

"Why on earth would she be interested in someone like that?" Prince Henry asked.

"Who knows what governs the human heart?" Dolores asked philosophically. "Perhaps mere arbitrariness."

The prince reached to take Dolores's hand. "I hope more than that governs our affections."

Bella came down the stairs to find Prince Henry kissing her mother's hand. "Mother?"

Dolores was blushing. She did not meet her daughter's eyes. "Shall we go?" was all she said.

"Of course," Prince Henry replied with alacrity. "Your wish is my command." He spoke with the tone of a practiced flirt, his inflection light, his words easily dismissed as mere banter by any who heard.

Isabella watched him carefully as they walked out toward Gideon and the waiting carriage.

Hyde Park was filled with the soft calls of birds and the steady clip-clop of horses' hooves. The morning had turned gray with quick-moving clouds and then began to clear. Now patches of robin's-egg blue appeared, the sun playing hide-and-seek with the clouds.

Prince Henry's horses were waiting when Gideon deposited them at the Hyde Park Corner end of Rotten Row and maneuvered the large coach with its royal coat of arms into a line of waiting drivers along the Carriage Road.

Prince Henry and his grooms helped the ladies mount, riding between Dolores and Isabella, his large bay prancing a bit against the sedate walk. Beyond them the water of the Serpentine glistened in the sunlight that was gradually spreading, the clouds dispersing as the day grew toward afternoon. Members of the ton, the high society, rode back and forth along the row, turning to nod and smile at acquaintances, or to pull off a bit for a small chat. The majority of riders were male; a few females were mounted on their own horses; more females were in light, high-wheeled carriages driven by their escorts. All eyes were decorously avoiding the Americans, and yet all would later be able to speak of what they wore, their demeanor, their equipage, and their ability upon their horses, remembering the least remark overheard.

"Quite different from La Providencia, isn't it?" the prince asked Dolores.

"Yes it is. And quite lovely," Dolores replied. "There is so much greenery. And everything looks so"—she searched for the right word—"so soft."

"I hoped you'd enjoy it. You didn't accompany your late husband on his trips to England. I've wanted to show you my country ever since you made me so welcome in yours," he told her.

"I did no more than any other would have done," Dolores protested.

The prince looked toward Bella. "Is your beautiful mother always so modest?"

"Yes," Isabella replied. "I'm afraid it's one of the traits I did not inherit." Bella gave her host a speaking look. "She is also always polite, even to impolite people. And impolite advances. I invariably say exactly what I'm thinking and ask the most inappropriate of questions."

"It sounds as if you have a great deal of your father in you," Prince Henry said mildly.

"No doubt," Bella replied pointedly.

"Bella." Dolores warned her daughter with her tone and her eyes.

Isabella smiled innocently at her mother, looking back to her mount as the black mare became a little frisky. Bella leaned to pat it and looked longingly at the wide fields beyond the waters of the Serpentine. "I really would like to gallop," she said wistfully.

"It simply isn't done."

"If I went through the fields there, beyond the trees,

couldn't I take off, just for a bit?" Bella asked. "I promise none will see, and I'll be careful."

"You really shouldn't," Dolores said. She looked to the prince for support.

He looked amused and indulgent. "If she really wants to, I can't see any harm in it. Can you?" He smiled at Dolores. "You told me she was a capable horsewoman."

"I'm not worried about her handling the horse, I'm worried about what people will think of her."

"I'm sure a little leeway is in order. I'm well aware of western riding, remember." He looked toward Isabella. "This sedate walk must seem very tame indeed."

Bella gave them both a winning smile. "I'll be ever so careful. And Mama, I promise I shan't make a display of myself. I just want to let my mare stretch her legs a bit. Say I may, please."

Prince Henry smiled at Dolores. "Say she may, please." He mimicked Bella's tone as best he could.

Dolores gave a little laugh. "It seems it's two against one. I suppose I'm outvoted."

"Thank you!" Bella replied fervently. "Thank you both!" Before her mother could change her mind, Bella touched the mare's rump with her riding crop and angled off the path, letting the horse have its head as they raced westward toward Kensington Gardens.

Along with many others, Dolores watched her daughter gallop away, then looked back at the prince. "I fear she may be making a spectacle of herself."

He glanced around them. "Perhaps many others wish to do the same and haven't the seat or the courage. In any event, I'm rather glad of the chance to talk alone."

Dolores arched her brow. "About what?"

"The past, the present, the future. Anything you choose, lovely lady. Anything you choose."

Bella rode between Hyde Park's trees, the mare cutting its own path through the grass, tacking away from the sedate confines of Rotten Row and its elegantly clad riders. The wind rushed by her, reddening her cheeks and bringing a glow to her face. She closed her eyes, drinking in the rushing air and spurring the mare faster.

At the western end of Hyde Park were the Kensington Gardens, where David was escorting Adela Winston to her carriage. He handed her into the phaeton and then mounted his gray, touching his gloved hand to his hat. "Please convey my best to your husband."

Adela smiled. "I'll tell him he was sorely missed at the cultural exhibit, shall I?"

"Tell him whatever you wish," David replied.

"I shall," Adela teased. She motioned to her driver and then waved at David as the carriage moved away.

David watched after her for a moment and then turned the gray toward the east end of the gardens and Hyde Park beyond, starting down the path at a sedate canter.

Blurred movement across the fields caught the corner of his eye. He looked toward it and saw a woman riding sidesaddle. The horse was galloping furiously, the rider unable to control it.

David urged the gray forward, cutting diagonally toward the runaway horse and rider. He whipped his horse harder, digging in his heels and racing to stop the helpless woman.

Bella didn't see the horse and rider coming toward her until they were on a collision course.

"Get away! Get *away!*" she yelled as loudly as she could, but he didn't hear the words.

"It's all right!" David shouted, his deeper voice carrying farther than hers.

"No!"

He pulled in alongside her and grabbed her reins, slowing both horses.

"How *dare* you!? What do you think you're doing?" Isabella demanded. "Who do you think you are?"

Disconcerted, David outright stared at her as their horses slowed and stopped. "What on earth is wrong with you? I've just saved your bloody life!"

"What's wrong?! You grab my reins and force yourself upon me and you ask what's wrong?" Bella glared at him.

"You're the American," David said slowly.

Bella still glared. "And if I am? Is that any excuse for abominable manners?"

David drew himself tall in his seat. "Madam, I could not hope to equal your own bad manners," he said in clipped tones. "I was merely attempting to rescue what I thought was a helpless female."

"Rescue? From what?" Isabella demanded.

"From a runaway horse!" He found himself nearly shouting at her and clamped his mouth shut.

"Runaway?" Bella shook her head. "I was merely giving her her head for a bit."

"You had no control over her," David said.

"I had complete control," Bella retorted.

"There is no way you could have had!" His voice began to rise again.

"I agree that you Englishmen punish your women by making them ride clinging to one side of their mounts, and I am perfectly willing to assume none of your women could possibly control this horse or any other, but I assure you I can, have, and did!"

She was glaring at him, stormy dark eyes meeting stormy blue ones. "I was told your countrymen call you the Terror of California," he said in clipped tones. "I now know why."

He dropped her reins in her lap and pulled his gray away from the black mare, riding off at a smart clip toward Rotten Row and the city beyond.

Bella patted the mare's mane and then turned back toward Rotten Row, urging the mare faster and faster until she flew by the odious man.

David, seeing her streak past him, took up the challenge and spurred his gray, matching her stride for stride as they raced toward Rotten Row and the polite society gathered there.

Bella leaned forward, urging the mare, determined to best the English fop who had insulted her horsemanship. As they drew near the others David's gray took the lead, her irritation growing by leaps and bounds.

He sped across Rotten Row, nearly colliding with a carriage and streaking out toward the carriage drive and the city beyond.

As the Duke of Exeter nearly overturned her carriage the Countess of Eppsworth peered out at the fast-departing rider and then nudged her cousin Clarissa. "My lord, he's riding as if the furies themselves are after him."

Clarissa giggled into her handkerchief. "He must be fleeing Adela Winston, determined to sink yet more teeth into him."

As Clarissa spoke and others close by murmured to one another, Henrietta saw horrified expressions appear on nearby riders as a black mare with a young lady aboard rushed straight toward the sedate stream of riders.

As people moved to clear her path Bella pulled back on the reins.

"It's she!" Henrietta exclaimed delightedly. "It's the Terror herself, and she's chasing the duke!"

Bella, unaware of the conjectures all around her, slowed her mare down to a brisk canter. She saw her mother and the prince up ahead, just making the turn back toward her, obviously unaware of the excitement behind them. Bella slowed even further, bringing the mare to a sedate walk as she passed other Rotten Row riders and came toward her mother and the prince.

"Are you all right?" Dolores asked, seeing her daughter's hardened expression.

"I'm fine. Except for meeting some odious man who insisted on spoiling my ride."

Prince Henry leaned forward, frowning. "Did someone have cheek enough to accost you?"

"He thought he was going to give me riding lessons!" Bella replied tartly. Deliberately, she took a deep breath and tried to smile at the prince. "He accused me of not having my mount under control."

"You?" Dolores laughed. "I think you were able to ride before you could walk."

"As long as he wasn't forward," the prince said.

"He wasn't forward. He almost had no manners whatsoever."

"What was his name?" the prince asked.

"He never introduced himself," Bella replied. "Nor were any with him to do so."

"Good grief, he must not have had any manners at all," Dolores agreed. "I think we should return to Exeter House, Henry. Bella looks a bit tired."

"I'm not tired in the least," Bella said. But she obediently followed them as they left the Row and handed over their horses to the prince's stablemen. She allowed Prince Henry to take her reins as she dismounted and followed her mother toward Gideon and the waiting carriage.

The prince remained mounted. "I shall take my leave and meet you later. I must look to some business in the city," he told them, touching his hat before turning away.

Bella was complaisant as she joined her mother in the carriage.

"Did you enjoy your ride, *querida?*"

"Yes, Mama. Thank you." Bella settled back on the cushioned seat. Thinking of George, she lost her frown, nothing able to keep her unhappy when she realized they would soon be able to be together.

Dolores patted her daughter's hand. "I'm glad it pleased you so much."

They arrived back at Exeter House just past one, Dolores following Bella upstairs to change. As they reached the upper picture gallery Consuela opened the door to their suite. "I thought I heard you come in."

A door farther down the hall opened and a man came toward them. As he moved Bella glanced toward him and then froze. "You!" She nearly shouted the word, shocking both her duenna and her mother.

"Bella!" Dolores said firmly.

David stopped in front of them, bowing slightly to Dolores and then smiling insolently at Isabella. He studied her from head to toe, slowly. "I see you've arrived back in one piece."

"You," she said again, her tone full of distaste.

"Permit me to introduce myself. I am David Beresford, Duke of Exeter, and son to your host, Prince Henry."

"David, what on earth is wrong?" Dolores asked.

But it was Bella who answered: *"This* is the man who accosted me in the park!"

"Accosted?" David glared at Bella. "I merely saved your bloody life, that's all!"

"David!" Dolores said, shocked.

He recalled himself. "I'm sorry, madam. I apologize for swearing in front of you." His blue eyes turned frigid when he looked toward Bella. "If you will excuse me—"

"With pleasure!" Bella retorted crisply as David moved toward the stairwell. He stopped for one brief moment, considering turning around and verbally blistering her. But he would not give her the satisfaction, he told himself. He continued on, leaving three silent women in his wake.

Bella saw the look on her mother's face. "I'm sorry, but that man is impossible!" Bella swept past Consuela and into the suite.

Connie waited for Dolores to follow. When she closed the hall door behind them, Connie smiled widely. "Well, at least we won't have any worries from that quarter. I don't know which of them dislikes the other more."

Dolores began to unbutton her riding habit. "You may think it funny, but I daresay it would be better if they did not dislike each other quite so much. It could be very uncomfortable living under the same roof."

"They won't see much of each other. He's never around, the servants say. They say he's seeing a married woman, *querida.*"

Dolores looked properly shocked. "No!"

Connie shrugged eloquently. "Never put anything past a man," she said. "Any man," she added. "Not a duke, not a king"—Connie gave Dolores a meaningful look—"not even a prince."

Dolores saw Connie's expression and found herself blushing. She turned away. "Please have our baths readied, Connie," she said. Then she turned back. "I don't want any more connection between Bella and George Miller. Is that understood?"

"*Sí, señora.*"

Chapter Five

The night of the Exeter House ball the mansion was lit by thousands of candles, the staff scurrying to and fro behind the green baize doors.

Dolores walked into her daughter's room as Bella was being helped into her ball gown. Consuela finished fastening the many back buttons and surveyed her handiwork.

"You look like a queen," Consuela told her charge.

Bella turned this way and that before a tall pier glass. Her glossy ebony hair was piled high upon her head, her oval face lit by large dark-chocolate eyes. Her cheeks were softest pink, her lips a deeper hue.

Beneath the comely contours of her face, the gown she wore set off her tall, slender frame. The silk dress was colored in the darkest shade of rose, set off by shell-pink ribbons and laces, cut modestly low in the bodice, nipped in at the waist, and falling in wide swirls to the floor.

In the mirror Bella met her mother's gaze and saw her mother's slow smile. Turning, she preened a little. "Do I look English, Mama?"

"You will never look English," Dolores told her daughter. Seeing Bella's downcast expression, she relented: "But you do look beautiful."

Isabella brightened. "Thank you, Mama!"

"Does it mean so much to you, *querida?*"

"Yes. I want them to like me, Mama."

Dolores smiled, her patrician features relaxing into a warmth seldom seen. "They will, *querida.* They won't be able to help it. And I am so very glad you want them to."

Bella watched her mother walk away. Turning back toward the pier glass, she studied herself, preening a bit until Consuela cut her short. "If you're finished admiring yourself, it's time to go downstairs."

"I wasn't admiring myself!" Bella said.

"And what would you call it then?" Connie asked.

Bella's smile was a little sad. "Gathering courage."

Consuela moved closer to Bella, her expression softening. "Are you worried about these people accepting you, *querida?* About how you look? There isn't a woman on this entire island who is as beautiful as you."

Bella's smile widened a little. "Connie, you haven't seen all the women on this island."

"No, but I've seen enough. Pale hair, pale eyes, pale skin, they've got no fire in their veins. You are worth a hundred of them," Consuela said loyally.

"They already call me the Terror of California."

Consuela grimaced. "They'd better not let your mother hear them."

"What had I better not hear?" Dolores asked. She was dressed in a high-necked black satin gown, its simplicity set off by a long strand of pearls that reached nearly to her waist. Her hair was pulled straight back from her temples and fastened into a chignon, the unfashionably severe style perfect for her long, well-molded face. "Well?" she questioned them. "Who is going to tell me?"

"It seems my nickname has followed me across the sea."

Dolores frowned. "Has someone called you that?"

"Yes."

"Who?" Dolores asked.

"That odious man who happens to be the Duke of Exeter," Bella answered.

Dolores thought of many replies but said none of them.

Instead she moved toward the hall door. "I think it's time we joined our host, Bella."

Bella followed her mother slowly, gathering her courage to face the roomful of strangers below. As they lifted their skirts to descend the stairs Bella whispered to her mother, "Will he be here? That odious duke?"

"It would be a slight to us if he was not," Dolores said.

Bella made a face. "If it's a slight to me, he'll not be here," she said. "Good," she continued, "that saves me having to be polite to him."

"Or vice versa," Dolores said mildly.

"He doesn't know how," Bella replied sharply.

The huge entrance hall below was brilliant with candlelight from a dozen large-branched candelabra. Men in full black evening dress escorted women in long velvet and silk, their gowns a rainbow of colors, their trains following them across the black and white entrance chamber.

Soft music from a string orchestra could be heard in the long gallery beyond, paneled double doors thrown wide. The long gallery traversed the entire center section of the mansion, more public rooms to one side, family rooms and servants' halls to the other.

The prince stood just inside the double doors, his butler bringing each arriving guest forward to be greeted. In the gallery scores of silver candelabra were placed on narrow tables that clung to walls covered with a Chinese paper in intricate tiny designs of gold and silver against a black background.

Oil lamps with painted Limoges porcelain bases added to the light and the heat in the room. Double doors on the far side of the long gallery were open to the wide terraced porch and the lawns that sloped away to the back of the house.

Dolores and Isabella came into the room, Bella glancing to the far end of the room, which was already filled with scores of people. In the musician's gallery above the orchestra was set up and playing, the entire center of the gallery cleared for dancing.

Along the far wall a huge mahogany sideboard was filled with food. It was supported by four gigantic paws and covered with a fringed cloth under the silver salvers heaped with hors d'oeuvres and a huge epergne heaped with fresh fruits.

Around the room other sideboards held more food, and still others held decanters of wines and brandies and stronger spirits as well as a massive punch bowl.

Isabella's mother touched her arm, directing her toward the prince, who was smiling as they approached. "Ah, the wait has been well worth it." He turned toward the room full of people. "Ladies and gentlemen!" As he began to speak the butler Tate motioned the orchestra to silence, the room quieting. "I have the honor of presenting Señora Dolores Castillo-Suera Alexander and her daughter Isabella." He looked down at Dolores. "And before you are hopelessly mobbed by suitors, I shall have your first dance of the evening." Before Dolores could demur Prince Henry reached for her arm and looked off toward a small chamber behind them. "David," the prince called.

Isabella's heart sank when she heard the name. The Duke of Exeter sauntered forward, a mocking smile on his face. He looked straight at Isabella as his father spoke.

"Isabella, this is my son, David."

"We've met," she replied in clipped tones, her heart hammering. She knew he was laughing at her; she could hear the words "Terror of California" as surely as if he'd said them out loud. She could feel her face reddening.

"Capital," the prince said. "Then I needn't introduce you."

"Believe me," David said, "there is absolutely no need."

"David will escort you for your first dance, Isabella," the prince said, smiling. "I'll warrant, with all the gay blades that are here tonight, he'll have to work hard if he wants to have the pleasure of a second."

"You have no idea how right you are," Isabella said under her breath.

"Bella." Dolores gave her a warning look. "This is your introduction to English society."

David bowed courteously toward Bella. Straightening, he put his arm out for her hand. She did not take it.

The prince was moving slowly through the crowded room,

introducing Dolores as they wended their way to the dance floor.

David's smile froze in place. "Take my arm," he said softly. "Or do they not teach you the amenities in the Wild West?"

"I know the amenities," Bella told him in the same low tone. "I simply have no wish to dance with you."

"Everyone is watching," he told her.

"Let them." Bella smiled sweetly at him and started to turn away.

She never made the turn. David reached for her slim hand, grasping it in his own large one and squeezing so hard she almost cried out.

"You may play these games with your American suitors, Miss Alexander, but you are not playing them with me." David spoke through gritted teeth, a smile still on his face. "You will *not* make me look the fool!"

"I'm sure you do enough of that yourself," Bella told him. He moved, and she was forced forward beside him. He bent his head toward her, his eyes never leaving hers, as if so enthralled he did not notice the people around them trying to catch his eye.

"How long are you staying?" he asked pleasantly.

Her own smile was forced: "Too long."

His laugh sang out, his words so soft none heard but Bella. "At last we agree on something."

They reached the orchestra, David glancing ahead and seeing the prince and Dolores waiting for them. Others were milling about, exchanging pleasantries and casting their eyes toward the American women.

David leaned down to speak close to Bella's ear. From a distance they seemed on quite intimate terms. "You have two choices," he was telling her. "You can show good manners and not disrupt my father's evening, or you can refuse to dance. Whereupon I will pick you up and carry you across this entire room to the terraces, where I will upend you over my knee and give you the spanking of your life!" His whisper was harsh in her ear.

Her eyes opened wide with shock and flew to meet his. "You can't mean it!" But she saw in his eyes that he did.

David looked up and smiled at his father, still holding Bella's hand. The prince nodded to the orchestra leader, the strains of a waltz beginning as he swept Dolores into his arms.

Isabella's mother smiled up into the prince's kind hazel eyes. "When I was a girl, the waltz was considered terribly wanton. Well-brought-up girls did not participate."

"And now it's totally accepted," Prince Henry told her. "Times change and change back, almost like a pendulum, I think."

As they danced he looked toward David and Isabella. "They move well together," the prince told Dolores.

"Surprisingly so," Dolores said, earning a puzzled look from the prince. She smiled. "Your son and my daughter met while riding this afternoon. And it seems they did not get along well."

"They seem fine now," the prince said.

Dolores did not trust appearances, but she said nothing more.

The rest of the assembly began to join the two couples on the floor, the ball truly under way.

Fresh night breezes came in from the open terrace doors and windows, cooling the overcrowded room. David held Bella tight in his arms, moving with practiced grace across the floor. "At least you can dance passably," David told her.

"Passably?" She reacted to his caustic remark before she could stop herself. "If so, we are evenly matched!" she told him.

He leaned his head back a bit, surveying her irritated face. "You have spunk, I'll give you that," he said grudgingly.

"I have a lot more than that!" she challenged.

"Do you indeed?" he asked lazily, still watching her flashing eyes. They were almost as dark as her hair, a dark chocolate color that could soften to syrup or freeze rigid. At the moment they were frigid.

"Don't be insolent," she snapped as the music ended.

He still held her in his arms as the music stopped. "I have never in my life been spoken to in such a way."

"Nor have I," she replied. "Will you let go of me now, or must I scream?"

His arms dropped away from her. She stepped back and turned, almost bumping into her mother. As the prince asked Bella for the pleasure of the next dance, David bowed toward her mother.

"Oh, I shall enjoy *this* one," Bella breathed to the prince, dancing away in a swirl of rose-pink skirts.

Dolores watched David. "If you would rather not . . ."

His smile was a little forced, but he was totally polite. "I hope you'll allow me the pleasure," he said, bowing over her hand.

She came into his arms, moving gracefully with him as peals of Bella's laughter began to be heard beyond them. "She seems to be enjoying your father's company," Dolores said.

"Yes," David said.

They danced in silence until Dolores spoke again: "I understand you met Bella while riding."

"Who? Oh. Yes," David replied.

"We call her Bella," Dolores added unnecessarily. "I also understand you two did not quite hit it off."

"That, madam, is a complete understatement."

"She seemed to enjoy your dance," Dolores said.

"She had no choice. Unless she wished to be spanked in front of the entire assemblage."

Dolores's breath caught in her throat, her eyes widening. She studied David's square-jawed face. "I believe you meant that. But what's more astounding, she must have believed it, too."

"She did," David replied.

Dolores's laugh surprised a startled look from the Duke of Exeter. Her merry peals brought many eyes toward them, including Bella's. "That's simply wonderful!" she told him.

A small smile edged David's mouth and eyes. "I'm glad you think so. Your daughter was less enthused."

Dolores smiled up at the tall man. "David, you have done the absolutely impossible. You have, for at least a few minutes, cowed my incorrigible daughter into doing something she did not want to do."

His smile widened. "Is she really as bad as they say?"

"Bad?"

"The Terror of California?"

Bella's mother frowned. "I don't like that appellation, David."

"I'm sorry," he said sincerely. "But I can certainly see that she has earned it."

"She's not a bad girl, David. She's merely been overindulged by her father and the servants. She is a little too pretty, a little too bright for her own good. And she has her father's stubborn temperament. And temper, unfortunately. If she had been born a man, all these attributes would be commended, but, unfortunately, they do not make a woman's lot any easier."

The music ended. David escorted Dolores through the crowded room toward the punch bowl. "If she had been more like her mother, she would have London at her feet," the duke said gallantly. "Instead of which, she'll probably have it at her throat."

"Perhaps you could be of help to us." Dolores's suggestion stopped David in midstride.

"I beg your pardon?" He looked as if she'd asked him to fly through the air.

"Perhaps you could keep an eye on her. As we say at home, ride herd on her a little. I'm sure your father would appreciate your helping to keep her in line."

"Madam Alexander, I would sooner wrestle elephants."

"It would be such a help. Of course, I wouldn't blame you if you weren't able to do it."

"Thank you." He sounded very relieved until she continued.

"It might be an impossible task to set for someone."

His brow furrowed. "Impossible?"

"You probably couldn't keep her in line for any length of time, anyway. Please forget I even brought it up, David. I'm sure you couldn't do it." Dolores watched him. "Don't give it another thought," she added lightly before turning away and heading toward the prince and her daughter.

She left behind a very aggravated young man. David felt irritated, and he wasn't sure why.

* * *

"Thank you, Henry," Dolores said, accepting a cup of punch from the prince. She looked toward Bella, who was nibbling at a fig. "Did you enjoy your dances, *querida?*"

Bella gave the prince a brilliant smile. "I enjoyed the last one enormously."

"Aha!" The prince smiled. "Then my son has not yet completely eclipsed me."

"Nor shall he ever," Isabella told his father firmly.

"Excuse me, señora." Consuela appeared at Dolores's elbow.

Dolores stared at her. "What is it? What's wrong?"

"May I speak to you for a moment? Alone," Consuela added pointedly.

Dolores started to refuse and then saw Consuela's determined expression. Apologizing to the prince, Dolores walked to a small anteroom beyond the long gallery. Racks held overcoats, capes, and men's hats, a footman tending to the wraps as they passed through.

"Excuse me, ma'am, may I help? This is the servants'—" The footman tried to stop Dolores, but Consuela pulled her through the green baize door and into a back hallway.

"Connie!" Dolores protested. "What on earth are you doing?"

"He's here," Connie told her employer.

"Who's here?"

"That George Miller!"

Dolores stared at Connie. "Here?"

"He tried to get a message to Bella. The footman brought it to me." Connie reached in a pocket and brought out a folded piece of paper. Dolores read it and then looked up.

"Dolores?" The prince peered through the green baize door. "Forgive me, but is something wrong? And what on earth are you doing in here?"

Dolores came forward. "Dear Henry, I may need your help."

While she explained the situation to the prince, in the long gallery Bella was surrounded by gentlemen. Glowing with the attention, she laughed and flirted and danced the night away, never noticing David's glances from across the room.

He stayed as far away as he could possibly get and yet, as Henrietta Epps pointed out to her cousin Clarissa, he did not leave. The fact that Adela Winston stood near enough to hear may have been part of the reason she continued to speak of David's obvious attraction to the American.

Henrietta didn't stop until Adela walked away.

"Do you really think the prince might be trying to interest the duke in that girl?" Clarissa asked.

Henrietta's attention was divided between her cousin and the scene across the room. Adela was stopping in front of David. "I think I'd like more punch," Henrietta announced, heading toward the punch bowl beside David.

"David, dearest, I feel positively neglected," Adela was saying as Henrietta reached for a cup of punch and handed it to Clarissa.

"Hmm? What?" He met her gaze and then looked off toward the dancing Isabella.

Adela tried to keep her patience. "I said I would like to take a turn around the terrace. It's much too warm in here."

"Oh," David said, his eyes not leaving the dance floor.

"David," Adela said more sharply, earning a quizzical glance from him finally. "Are you deliberately ignoring me?"

"I wasn't aware I was, Adela," he replied, turning his full attention toward her. "Would you care to dance?"

She hesitated, thinking about punishing him a bit, but then thought better of pushing him too far. She smiled and let him lead her to the floor.

"Henrietta?" Clarissa said.

"What?"

"What are you looking at?"

Henrietta smiled and turned toward her cousin. "The breakup of a romance, cousin. And the beginning of an absolutely delightful season!"

At the massive front door of the huge mansion a young man was moving restlessly to and fro, trying to see past the footmen to the crowded rooms beyond. Of medium height, the young man had light brown hair and dark, poetic eyes. His face had the classical features of a Byron, more pretty than handsome or manly.

Prince Henry came toward the door, his footmen standing back, ready to be of aid. "Young man, I believe you are George Miller?"

The young man stared at the tall aristocrat. "I beg your pardon?"

Prince Henry raised his quizzing glass, giving the man a particularly thorough once-over. "Are you, or are you not, George Miller?"

"I—I haven't the pleasure of knowing who I'm speaking to," he replied.

"Neither do I," the prince snapped. "But since this is my house and you are at my door, I suggest you reply to my question."

The young man looked uncomfortable and then managed an ingratiating smile, which did him no good with the experienced prince. "Forgive me, Your Highness. I have just arrived and fear my wits are not entirely about me. I am, as you asked, George Miller. I was so surprised anyone here would know my name that I almost lost speech for a moment."

"I had the benefit of this." The prince held the note out toward the young man.

George's gaze dropped to the paper. Unwilling, he let the prince hand it over. When he looked up his gaze was soulful. "I meant no harm, Your Highness."

"It is customary to call on young ladies of good family and leave your card. It is not acceptable behavior to ask them to sneak off to clandestine meetings."

"If you would let me explain—"

Prince Henry cut the American off. "I wish no explanation." The prince gave the young man another penetrating look. "You are not welcome on these premises. Is that clearly understood?"

George Miller saw the glint of steel in the older man's gaze. "Might I call tomorrow and—"

"No."

"But, sir! I mean, Your Highness! This is so cruel when you will not allow me a chance to explain or to even talk to Bella—we are close friends, she will want to talk to me if she knows I am here!"

"I have no idea of what correct manners are in the social circles you come from, young man, but you lost all chance of acceptance in polite society by your deplorable request. Asking a young lady to sneak behind her guardians' backs is beyond the pale!"

George Martin watched the prince walk back inside the brilliantly lit entrance hall, his frustration barely contained. He heard the prince inform his minions that George Miller was not to be welcomed into Exeter House under any circumstances whatsoever. If he were to become a nuisance by remaining by the door or returning, they were to call for the constable at once.

The last thing the young American saw was the impassive face of the footman who closed the front door, locking George Miller outside the thick stone walls that held Bella.

Chapter Six

*I*sabella floated up the stairs to her bedroom in the wee hours of the morning. The candles were guttering away in the tall hall sconces, the servants beginning the massive job of clearing away the remains of the party.

She had danced all night with one partner after another and had never after that first, miserable dance had to suffer the attentions of the Duke of Exeter.

He had disappeared hours earlier. Some plump woman who kept insisting to Bella's mother they must visit her house across the square had rolled her eyes at the mention of the duke's whereabouts. Lady Winston had left early, too, the woman had said, smiling wide at Bella.

She seemed to think the information might be of some concern and looked terribly disappointed at Bella's total lack of interest in the odious man's whereabouts. As long as he was safely away from her presence, she was content.

"Bella, stop fidgeting and let me unhook you," Connie said in the bedroom.

"I wasn't fidgeting, I was swaying to the music."

"What music?" Connie asked, hearing nothing but the night winds outside the draped windows.

"The music in my head," Bella replied. "I can hear it as

plainly as I hear you. Wasn't it lovely? Isn't the prince the nicest man you've met—excepting Papa of course? And did you see the Earl of Devon? He was most charming, and truly the most accomplished dancer. I allowed him three dances, which were two more than I allowed any of the others. Except the Austrian duke, of course, but he was so sweet and had ever so much to say about horses."

Connie worked on the hooks and eyes that trailed down Bella's back as her young charge waxed rapturous. "I'm glad you had a good time," the duenna said quietly.

Something in Connie's tone made Bella look into the pier glass. She studied the older woman in the mirror, seeing a worried expression that matched the tone. "What is it, Connie?"

Startled, Connie looked up, Bella staring directly into her dark eyes through the glass. Worry and a tinge of guilt looked back at Bella.

"What?" Connie said. "I don't know what you mean." Bella was turning around to face her duenna. "I'm not through unhooking you."

Bella faced Connie. "What's happened? What are you hiding from me?"

"Nothing—I—nothing. Your mother would slice me alive if I—I had to tell her, that's all. It's for the best."

Bella stamped her narrow foot into the thick oriental carpet. "Consuela Rivera, answer me this very moment or I shall never speak to you again!"

"You have to speak to me," Connie said practically.

"Then I shall never trust you again!"

The old duenna did not want to hear the words. Bella was more her child or her grandchild than an employer. Connie had raised both Dolores and Isabella, had spent her life loving and protecting them. "I had to give it to her!" Connie defended herself.

Bella stared at Connie, horror writ large on her face. "You gave her his letter!"

"Bella, *querida*, he is no good for you—"

"Leave me," Isabella said, her tone haughty and cold. "Leave me now. I want to be alone."

"Your dress—"

"I shall finish undressing myself," Bella told the older woman, whereupon she turned her back on the distraught Connie.

Connie delayed, trying to think of something she could say to the girl. Finally she turned away, her shoulders rounded, her face dejected as she opened the door to the connecting dressing room and left.

When she heard the door close, Bella threw her fan across the room, upset beyond measure that she would not be able to treasure his dear letter until she once again could see him, could tell him all would be well. Her mother had promised they could be together.

It was unfair of them to continue treating her as if she were a child! Bella reached behind herself, unhooking the last of the hooks and slipping out of the rosy ball gown. She laid it across the chaise, looking down at the cushions. They must have searched her room for it! How else would they have found it under the cushion?

They hadn't. Bella saw the tiniest line of white edging out from beneath the chaise cushions and reached for it. His letter was still here.

Confused, she looked toward the door Connie had closed, trying to make sense out of her duenna's words. Something else had happened. If George had gone to the rancho he might have found where she was staying, he might have written to her here.

Bella went to the dressing room door, prepared to cross-examine Connie if need be until she found the truth of what they were hiding from her.

The dressing room was empty and dark, as was the small trunk room beyond. Bella opened the door to the shadowy sitting room. One lamp, its wick turned low, gave off flickering light near the hall door, the dying embers of the fire in the grate adding more warmth than light to the room.

The sound of her mother's and Connie's voices, pitched low, came from Dolores's bedroom. Bella started toward the door and then stopped. Reaching down, she removed her dancing slippers before moving on tiptoe, as quietly as she could, toward the partially open door.

"You mustn't." Her mother's voice came through the

narrow opening, a sliver of light crossing Bella's forehead as she leaned nearer.

Connie sounded anguished. "She'll never trust me again, I know it."

"Bella is young. One day she will thank us beyond measure, Connie. You must put her words behind you; you had no choice. You could not have delivered that message to her without ensuring great harm to all."

"But she'll never understand," Connie replied, heartbroken.

"Yes, she will," Dolores said firmly. "One day she will see that young man in a true light and she will bless you for keeping her from an unthinkable mistake. Imagine, asking her to sneak away with him! Think about that and get angry, Consuela. Very, *very* angry! He treats our Bella as if she were a common street urchin!"

Bella's heart began to pound.

"The prince sent him away for good," Dolores was saying. "And good riddance."

Connie was more doubtful. "I don't think he's come all the way to London just to be turned away. I fear he will be outside in the square in the morning."

"Nonsense." Dolores dismissed the idea. "He wouldn't dare."

"Look at what he's already dared," Connie replied. "What if every time we go out he's outside? She's bound to see him, she's bound to find out he's here."

Bella's heart nearly stopped. *He's here!* The words hit her almost as a blow. George was here! He'd followed her all the way across the world!

"She'll not see him. I shall have the footmen check before we go out, if it will make you happy."

"I fear I shall never be happy again," Connie replied. "I can't stand to have her hating me."

"Consuela! You begin to sound as immature as Bella! Go to sleep. You must be exceedingly tired to prattle on so. You did what you had to, what you are trusted to do, and no more. Now go to bed."

Bella pulled back from the doorway, her heart stuttering

and then nearly bursting with the sudden enormity of unexpected happiness.

Her mother's voice was saying Connie would feel much better in the clear light of morning as Bella fled across the sitting room and into her own room.

She was closing the door as quickly and quietly as she could when Connie stepped back into the sitting room. The tiniest sound of a latch made the duenna look toward Bella's closed door. And then walk toward it, listening for a moment.

Light came out from under the closed door. Connie tapped on it softly before turning the knob. She opened it to find Bella, partially undressed and sitting on her bed, her head down.

"I want to be alone," Bella said.

Connie did not hear the trace of a happy lilt in her charge's voice. Guilt saw only a downturned head. *"Buenas noches, querida,"* Connie said softly, her own voice subdued and unhappy. "I was just checking to make sure you had not fallen asleep with your lamp on. I want only the best for you."

There was no reply. Connie turned away. As she pulled the door closed behind, in the narrowing stream of light that fell across the sitting room from Bella's bedroom lamp, a dancing slipper lay discarded on the carpet.

In the shadowy room she would never have seen it. Connie went to the lamp, raising the wick and reaching for the two slippers thrown aside halfway across the floor. When she straightened up she stared at them for a long moment before lowering the wick and taking them with her to the dressing room.

Within her own bedroom Bella lay back across the huge feather bed, a contented smile curving her lips. This wonderful evening of music and laughter had been capped with a dream come true. George was here, and somehow, like all the white knights in the fairy tales, he would come to rescue her.

The next day she was not so sure. She awoke to race to the windows that overlooked the square, hoping against hope

Connie's prediction to her mother would be true. Hoping he would be standing there in the square, awaiting her departure from the stone walls that held them apart.

She saw nothing but peddlers, servants, and the riotous blend of colors from the early flowers within the black wrought-iron grillwork. A statue stood in the center of the square, some long-gone Exeter ancestor astride a prancing horse. Bella watched it carefully for long moments, hoping he was hidden from her view behind it, hoping she'd catch a glimpse of him coming around it.

The arrival of morning chocolate and biscuits pulled her away from the window, her impatience to be up and dressed and away clipping her replies to Connie's questions about how she had slept.

Connie was watching her carefully. After finding the dancing slippers and enjoying the night's sleep Dolores had recommended, Connie did indeed see things differently. What she saw worried her greatly.

"You slept in your undergarments!" Connie accused.

"I was tired," Bella replied, heading toward her bath. "What has Mama got planned for us today?"

"I heard mention of paying call on some of His Highness's friends."

Bella smiled benignly. "That sounds splendid."

At breakfast Bella was the very essence of a dutiful daughter, earning her mother's approving glances as she even managed to make polite conversation with the odious duke.

Prince Henry was positively jovial, happy with the success of the party the night before and pleased his son was doing as he asked and taking an interest in their guests. "I must tell you, Dolores," the prince began, "David never eats this late a breakfast. It is your presence and your lovely daughter's." Henry gave a smile to Bella before returning his attention to her mother. "Nothing else would keep him home."

David's smile was polite. "Although I, of course, am most pleased the woman who saved my father's life is staying with us, I must confess last night's late hour is very much to blame for my tardy breakfast. I fear I am becoming quite lazy." He glanced toward Bella. "And, of course, her daughter," he added belatedly.

The prince was puzzled by his son's lack of proper social address; David was noted as the most gallant beau in London, his speeches to women always masterful, his words pretty and complimentary. This verged on being impolite.

Dolores was perceptive enough to see that David's intention was to bring Bella down a peg or two but was surprised by her own child when Bella did not rise to the bait of having been pointedly ignored.

She merely murmured, "How very kind," and went on with her meal of sausage and eggs and potatoes and toast and marmalade, further worrying her mother as the size of Bella's appetite could clearly be seen by the portions on her plate.

"I see you have a healthy appetite," the prince said to Bella approvingly, earning a startled glance from her mother. Henry's and Dolores's eyes met across the table, Dolores wondering if he had read her mind, Henry seeing only limpid eyes deep enough to drown one. "Most women these days seem to pick at their food as if they were birds."

"Vultures are also birds," David said blandly, his father nearly choking on his coffee at the words.

"David, what on earth are you saying?" the prince demanded.

"But he's quite right, you know, Your—Uncle Henry." Bella smiled prettily at the prince, totally unperturbed. "My father often said the same. I freely admit I enjoy my food and drink. And dancing, such as you allowed us last night, and all manner of physical pleasure."

"Isabella!" her mother's voice rang out, shocked.

Bella looked from the prince's rather startled expression to her mother's shock. She looked across the table at David as she continued: "I'm sorry, Mama, but it is perfectly true, after all."

"You have no conception of the implication of your words, *querida,* and on that head the prince and David will forgive your terrible choice of words. But I sincerely hope you restrain such comments in front of others."

"Why?" Bella asked. She saw David gauging her across

the table, assessing the depth of her understanding of the nuances of her statement.

"People could think you a bit—well—fast, my dear," Prince Henry told her, adding quickly: "Of course, we know the very opposite is true, but others—well, your mother is quite right."

David said nothing, his eyes alone asking his questions. But there was an appraising look in the eyes that were the bluest blue Isabella had ever seen. They looked as blue as the ocean pools at the western edge of her rancho did on a sunny summer day. They looked as deep as the outer depths of that same ocean. And as dangerous.

She reminded herself she did not like blue eyes.

"I understand we are to make some visits this morning," Bella said into the silence that followed the prince's words.

"Yes, I thought you might enjoy meeting Princess Louise. Actually she's the Duchess of Argyll now; she's married to the governor-general of Canada. She and John are just arrived in London from the colonies and are giving a garden party."

"It sounds lovely," Bella replied. "Doesn't it, Mama?"

Dolores shared a concerned look with the prince. "It sounds rather—public."

The prince's slight shake of his head might have gone unnoticed if Bella had not already been aware that the prince had seen George and sent him away. "Not at all," the prince told her. "It is merely for a few intimate friends."

Dolores spoke slowly: "Then I suppose it is suitable."

"Most suitable," David said, unaware of the intrigue around him.

David was not long to be kept in the dark. His father asked to see him for a few minutes in the morning room directly after breakfast. Upon hearing of the last evening's events the duke took his time replying. "Perhaps the American Terror has had more experience than we assume."

"Not at all, nothing could be further from the truth, I assure you," his father replied. "She's been as cloistered as a nun."

"This George Miller seems to have found his way into the nunnery," David said dryly. "And, Father, you must admit you have not seen her since she was a tiny child. You have no way of knowing."

"I knew her father and I know her mother. No, David, she is as ignorant of the baser passions as a mewing kitten."

"I might liken her to a tigress," David told his father, "but never to a kitten."

"The reason I brought up this matter at all," Henry continued, "is that I may need your help in ensuring, when we are out and about town, that this adventurer does not make his presence known to Isabella. We want nothing to disrupt their enjoyment of their trip."

"I rather doubt it would disrupt Isabella's pleasure," his son replied. "And Father, speaking man to man, do you know of any fool who would so compromise himself and his honor unless he were fairly sure of the lady's willingness to comply?"

"David, you have been mixing in the wrong female society. You would not trust the virtue of the queen herself."

The Duke of Exeter delivered himself of a wry smile. "I would most certainly trust the queen's virtue. But then, she is sixty-one years old."

David left to change for the garden party, leaving his father with a concerned look upon his face. The prince went back to the business of his morning mail wondering if there was any truth in what David was saying.

Chapter Seven

*B*ella could hardly contain her impatience to be away. She chose a bronze-green satin gown that was one of George's particular favorites and slipped his letter into her reticule, holding it close as she walked downstairs as sedately as she could manage.

Her mother sensed an agitation within her and exchanged glances with Connie. Both women stayed close to Bella as they descended the steps to the carriage portico at the side of the huge mansion. Prince Henry's bay was waiting for him, the duke's gray prancing a bit as it waited for its master. The men mounted their steeds, ready to ride beside the coach, and the women were handed up into the carriage. Bella tried in vain to catch a glimpse of the garden in the center of the square.

"Why was the carriage brought to the side?" Bella asked as they settled inside.

"Why not, dear?" Dolores returned.

Bella pressed her face to the small window in the door of the coach, straining to see out. She caught a glimpse of a man's form, but they were rounding the corner and gone before she could see clearly.

Dissatisfied, she sat back on the coach bench, her expression turning stormy.

"Are you feeling unwell, Bella? Would you rather not go?" Dolores asked.

"I'm fine, Mama," Isabella replied. "Perfectly fine."

"You don't sound fine," Connie put in from her seat across from mother and daughter.

Bella gave her duenna a speaking look and earned a flash of guilt from Connie's eyes. The duenna looked away first.

"I don't see why I could not ride with the prince and the duke," Bella told her mother.

"It simply isn't done," her mother replied.

"It seems to me these English women have no fun at all," Bella said tartly.

Kensington Palace was already full of laughter and champagne when Prince Henry's carriage arrived. The prince and the duke handed their mounts to waiting grooms and attended to the ladies.

The prince thrust David forward to walk alongside Bella. The duke noticed her continual glances toward the street beyond. "Are you looking for someone?" he asked quietly.

"What?" His question startled her, turning her glance toward him.

"I was merely offering my help if you were searching someone out," he said pleasantly.

Isabella considered his offer but could find no way to explain George to this arrogant Englishman and so turned her gaze down to the flagged walk they were slowly traversing. "I was merely curious to see the sights of London," she replied.

"Perhaps your mother will permit me to show them to you," David said.

Isabella's mood lightened. If she were out, it might be possible for George to contact her. Even the duke's company was not too great a price to pay for the chance to see her beloved George.

David found himself rewarded by shining dark eyes that smiled up into his. She was truly a beautiful wench, he told himself. Her lips were full and finely chiseled; eminently kissable. This American Miller was enjoying quite a prize, if such was the case.

Within the small palace Dolores and Isabella were introduced to the queen's daughter and son-in-law, and then to Prime Minister Gladstone. David spent some time with the liberal prime minister as Prince Henry took the ladies down the receiving line.

Bella was polite and subdued. She stayed close to her mother's side, which pleased Dolores; but Consuela, looking on from the sidelines, was less convinced of Bella's obedience. Connie knew the way Bella's mind worked. She was capable of lulling her parent into complacency so that she could slip away unhindered. Perhaps the unprincipled George had devised another way to get a message to Isabella.

David shared lemonade with Lord and Lady Winston, speaking of the upcoming horse races and avoiding Adela's obvious coy glances. Adela was doing what all women did once they were fairly sure of a gentleman's attentions: She was pushing the situation. They might say they merely wanted a flirtation, but they soon pushed for commitment. The fact of Adela's marriage to an aging baron did nothing to dissuade her from her pursuit of the eligible Duke of Exeter.

"You're going to the Marlborough tonight?" David asked Lord Winston in reply to something he said.

"He's gone every night for weeks," Adela supplied innocently.

"I've lost so much at Prinny's club, I have to keep going back to make it up, my pet," Lord Winston said. "David understands."

"David is so understanding," Lady Winston agreed, smiling provocatively.

David pretended not to notice. His gaze kept sliding toward Bella and her mother.

"David? David?" Adela finally regained his attention.

"Sorry, I wasn't attending," the duke said.

"We noticed, old man," Winston said. "You must introduce me to her."

Adela simmered, covering it with a smooth smile. "Yes!"

she cried with a little clap of her hands. "What a wonderful idea. We must of course meet the Terror of California, dear David. What a treat!"

Finding no way to decline, David paced beside the Winstons to where Dolores and Bella stood talking to Prince Henry and John Douglas Sutherland, the governor-general of Canada. When they turned he performed the asked-for introductions and then stood back, watching as Adela sized up the American heiress.

"We've heard so much about you," Adela began, and then she hesitated. Bella merely smiled politely, expectantly, forcing Adela to continue. "I trust that you are enjoying your stay in London?"

"Yes, exceedingly," Bella replied.

"Bella, my dear!" Prince Henry had a young woman in tow.

"Yes, Uncle Henry?" Bella replied, earning a surprised look from Adela and an arch one from David.

"This is Millicent Cavendish; Millicent, this is Isabella Alexander—I think you two young ladies must have a lot in common." He smiled at Bella. "Aside from your age, I sense you both are rather more interested in horseflesh than the usual young miss."

Millicent Cavendish would never be a beauty. Her mouse-brown hair was too long, too lank, her eyes too small, her nose too large. But the light of honesty shone within her pale blue eyes as she studied the equally tall Isabella.

"You ride, then, Miss Alexander?"

"I was taught English-style, but I must admit I prefer astride," Bella replied. Her mother began to object, but Millicent's eyes lit up.

"Oh, how I agree! What's your favorite mount?"

Bella didn't need to consider. "Toro. He's my gray Andalucian. Since he has such a mind of his own we named him after his bullheadedness."

"A quality you would easily identify," David said, smiling charmingly.

Bella's temper flared. Determined not to allow him to nettle her, Bella smiled at Millicent. "I named him Toro, which means bull, for this very trait."

"How appropriate," David interjected.

"Thank you," Bella agreed sweetly. "Wouldn't it be pleasant if we could be so specific in naming people?"

"Yes, it would," the duke replied.

"I simply can't stand the beasts," Adela put in. "They are so erratic."

"Erratic?" Millicent Cavendish apparently did not agree with Lady Winston.

"Terribly," Adela continued. "Always snorting, and so nervous."

"A good horse is never that way unless it senses fear," Bella defended. "Wouldn't you agree, Miss Cavendish?"

"I do agree, unless she's feeding them too much oats, of course. You must call me Millie," the plain girl said. "And I shall call you Bella, as your Uncle Henry does. I should love to go riding, if you have the time. I have a wonderful Furioso in London with me and an Arabian you might enjoy."

Bella warmed to the girl, truly smiling as they bent their heads together discussing the relative merits of barley and maize and bran mash.

Adela cast her eyes skyward, murmuring pleasantries with Dolores and watching David watch Bella. Prince Henry drifted away and near again, greeting acquaintances and friends, until he saw George Miller at the very edge of the gardens.

Seeing the American adventurer, Henry moved quickly toward Dolores to warn her. David saw his father's agitation.

"Is something wrong?" David asked his father.

The prince could not immediately free Dolores from the Winstons without making an issue of it. "He's here," the prince told David. Pulling his son a little away from Millicent and Bella, he stood with his back to Miller. "You see the slight one at the edge of the flower bed?"

David searched the crowded lawn, finally seeing George Miller through a space in the crowd. "Wearing a blue coat, yellow cravat?"

"Precisely. David, it is better if she does not see him."

"I don't know how we can manage that without manhandling either her or him out of here, thus creating a sensation while ensuring the two will see each other."

"Damn and blast!" the prince swore under his breath. "How could he possibly be invited here? How could he know she would be here?"

"I daresay he wasn't invited and didn't know until he followed us," David replied.

"You can't be serious!" Henry said. But his son's expression was very serious indeed. "What a bounder! No wonder Dolores and Wallace were so against the match."

"More to the point, why is your innocent young miss interested in such a person?"

"David, you've been in society much too long. You can no longer recognize virtue when you see it," his father told him.

"Possibly," David drawled. "I see it so rarely."

"Well, what is to be done?"

The Duke of Exeter smiled easily at his father. "I shall speak to him, shall I? I think I can get to the bottom of it."

The prince hesitated. Finding no other solution, he agreed. But he was frowning and admonished his son to go easily. And, whatever else, to avoid a scene.

George Miller was searching the opposite side of the garden, looking for a glimpse of Bella, of Dolores, or even of Prince Henry so that he could trace Bella and induce her to spend a moment alone.

"Have we met?" A voice behind George spoke, startling him. He turned quickly.

"I beg your pardon?"

David smiled, his eyes taking in every detail of the slender young man. He looked to be around twenty-five years of age, with eyes that looked much older. "Sorry. You're Canadian, I see. I thought you were someone else."

"No, American." The American's eyes were already back searching the crowd.

"Ah, I thought you must be with the governor-general's party," David continued. "May I help you find someone?"

The simple words made the American's attention return to David. "I beg your pardon?" he said for the second time. He looked secretive.

David smiled easily. "You seem to be searching for someone. Permit me to introduce myself. I am David Beresford, Duke of Exeter."

"George Miller," Miller said. He hesitated. "Actually, I am looking for someone."

"Ask away. I know everyone here. Except you, of course."

Alarm showed in George's face. "You're not about to throw me out, are you?"

"Why on earth would I want to chuck you out?" David asked.

"Nothing, no reason. It's just that I'm not used to all this title business and all. Do you know Prince Henry?"

"Intimately. He's my father," David said.

George opened and closed his mouth. "Oh," he finally managed.

"Do you wish to speak to him?"

"No! I mean, I was just—curious, you know, as to—as to where he was."

David turned, motioning with his head. "He's near the arbor." The duke watched Miller look toward the arbor and find the prince. David saw the moment when the man caught sight of Bella. In that moment the young man's eyes narrowed briefly, and then he caught himself and looked back at David.

"Thank you, Your Highness," George said.

"Actually, it's Your Grace," David replied. "But think nothing of it, chap. Glad to be of help. You're sure you don't want to meet him?"

"No, no, that's fine." George hesitated, wondering whether he dared chance using the Englishman. David looked bland, if not positively blank. "Who is the young woman with the dark hair? The one in green."

David glanced over as if unsure whom Miller might mean. "Isabella Alexander. Actually, she's a fellow American. Recently arrived and staying with my father."

"Oh, really?" George tried to sound nonchalant. "I—I think I might have met her before. I wonder if you could ask her if she remembers me."

David smiled. "Of course, old chap." David sauntered

away, feeling Miller's eyes on him as he moved. It had taken the young fool long enough to come to the point.

Bella and Millie were comparing notes on the relative merits of various bits when David came up to them and drew Bella away. She did not come willingly.

"What on earth is so important?" she asked impatiently.

"There's someone here who asked if you remembered him," David told her.

Bella heard the words, her heart leaping, but she was afraid to believe it. "Someone from the ball last night?"

"No, some Canadian, I suppose, from his accent. Or an American."

Her eyes widened, happiness leaping to her features, quickly followed by disbelief in her good fortune. "Where is he?" she asked.

David looked across the crowd. "He was near the flower bed, but I—ah, yes, he still is."

Bella glanced toward the flower bed, finding George's beautiful face. He was looking straight at her, the deep, brooding darkness of his eyes making her knees weak. He started to come toward her, but she shook her head no. Glancing quickly toward her mother, who was turned away, she looked back at him and smiled.

If he came near, her mother was bound to see, and that must not happen, she told herself. She must find a way to get word to him. And her only means was the duke himself. Doubtfully, she looked up at him. "Would you tell him I'm sorry, I don't remember?"

David stared at her. "I beg your pardon?"

"Please just tell him, all right? Tell him I have no idea who he is—unless he is the gentlemen I met in the city garden at noon. In New York."

"In the city—"

"In the garden in New York at noon. If he is, thank him for me. He returned a lost letter for me."

"How on earth did he manage that?" David asked.

"What? Oh, I mean I dropped it and the wind picked it up, and he caught it for me," Bella said.

"Why on earth don't you thank him yourself?"

"No!" Bella said. "That is, my mother does not like me talking to strangers. She and Connie are quite strict about it."

"Yes, I can see that," David said without inflection. He left to do as she bid, earning a puzzled look from Miller before he caught on and agreed that it was indeed he, and that he was glad she remembered.

It wasn't until they were alone, riding home, that the prince interrogated David about his strange behavior at the garden party.

"What did you think you were doing wandering between that adventurer and Bella? I saw you point him out to her!"

"Yes, I did."

"Why?" the prince asked.

"I wanted to see her reaction."

"Well, good grief, you *knew* what her reaction would be!"

"No, I didn't," David replied. "In any event, he is very definitely a fortune hunter. His eyes narrowed when he first saw her as if he were sighting a bird in the crosshairs before finishing it off. Hers, on the other hand, bespeak more than a passing intimacy."

"No!"

David shrugged eloquently. "I have some knowledge of women, Father."

"You have precious little knowledge of innocent girls!" his father shot back.

"She wished to arrange a meeting and thought to use me as the dupe to carry the message."

"At this rate, I assume you're going to tell me that is exactly what you did," his father said caustically.

"Yes."

Prince Henry groaned. "David, your head needs to be examined."

David smiled. "Possibly, but not because of this. Never fear, Father. I shall make sure to be on hand for the meeting. And I will find out for myself what game our American Terror is playing."

The West End traffic around them was thick with carriages and carts until they turned off Oxford Road. "Why are you doing this, David?"

There was a moment when David didn't answer, surprised by the question. "Honestly?" David thought about it. "I'm not quite sure," he finally replied. "I couldn't possibly be interested in her."

"Of course not," Prince Henry agreed blandly.

"Not possibly," David said emphatically.

"As you say," his father replied.

While the prince smiled to himself, considering the possibilities of his son and Isabella, David was glancing toward the railed garden in the center of the square.

At noon tomorrow it might prove to be an interesting place.

Chapter Eight

 "Something is wrong, I know it," Connie told Dolores for the seventh time that morning. "I can feel it in my bones, she is up to something. She's been fidgeting all morning."

They were in the ladies' downstairs morning room, noon sunlight streaming in toward the robin's-egg-blue walls and fragile Chippendale furnishings. Bisque figurines of shepherds and shepherdesses adorned a round table by the windows next to which Dolores was reading through a long document from Rancho La Providencia.

"I just know it," Connie said.

"Stop muttering to yourself," Dolores said, "I can't concentrate on the report from home."

"Wants to tour the house. Ha!"

Dolores looked up. "What did you say?"

"I said I don't believe for one moment Bella is wandering around drinking in the ambience of this house, or whatever nonsense she said this morning to the prince."

"Is he with her?"

The answer to her question stuck his head in the door as they spoke: "Dolores, do you happen to know where Bella is? I was called away by my estate agent before we had a chance to complete our rounds. I thought she might be with you." There was an edge of guilt in his voice as he remembered David's work the day before.

Dolores stood up, looking quite serious. "I think we'd best find her."

"She's not a prisoner, she tells me," Connie put in. "She doesn't need to be watched every blessed minute."

"Connie!" Dolores snapped. "That's enough. Let's find her, shall we? She may simply be lying down."

But finding her proved easier said than done.

While they went up to her room the prince sent for the butler. After enlisting the aid of his staff the prince retired to his study, where he could worry in peace and solitude about what his son was doing.

He would have been surprised to learn his son was at that very moment skulking between trees within the railed garden across the street.

David had ambled out for a morning stroll before eleven, slowly traversing each side of the large square, watching for any sign of the American Miller. Satisfied he had not yet arrived—in fact, unsure the man had the sense to figure out Bella's cryptic message—the duke crossed the cobblestone street and entered the arched gate at the east end of the gardens.

The black wrought-iron archway was lacy, the grillwork that surrounded the outer perimeter of the garden spaced wide, giving a delicate feeling to the iron fencing. David moved toward the small stand of plane trees, their broad branches in full leaf. In front of him, past the state of the third Duke of Exeter, the builder of the square, Exeter House towered in the western sky.

George Miller slipped across the north side of the square, entering the gardens by the north gate almost directly in front of David and only twenty feet away. The duke stepped back, using the tree trunks for cover.

The American crossed straight to the statue, staying behind as he peered around it toward the massive stone house. David removed his pocket watch from its vest pocket, carefully opening it. It had not quite gone half past eleven. He put it away, moving with silent grace, a little nearer the waiting American.

Bella was early. David saw her before George did. She slipped out around the side portico and headed directly across the street. Lifting her skirts, she ran forward, a little breathless and becomingly flushed when she came around the statue.

"Oh, George!"

"Dearest!" George reached for her, folding her into a passionate kiss.

Anger boiled up inside David and something else that felt strangely like jealousy. He watched the cad. The man's impertinence knew no bounds. The duke started forward, ready to pull the man away from her. Thinking better of it, he waited to see what Isabella would do.

"Dearest Bella, light of my life, I have risked all to come to you—I pray I am welcome."

Bella pushed him back a little, laughing up at him. "Does my greeting seem cold?"

"No, and I pray it means what I hope it does. That you have not changed."

"I have not changed, George. Nor shall I ever!" she declared. "And I have wonderful news! Mama has agreed that you may pay me court!"

For a moment he did not seem to understand the words. "What are you saying?" he asked.

"Isn't it a dream come true? She says if I stay here this season and am nice to all these English fops she wants to parade in front of me, when I come home we can see each other. She won't stand in our way!"

David's anger grew, rankling now at the American chit. English fops! She had just thrown herself into the arms of the sorriest fop she was likely ever to lay eyes on.

"But—Bella, that's months and months away!"

"Mama says if we truly love each other, our love will not only survive, it will grow in the time spent apart," Bella told him.

"But I can't wait!" George burst out. "That is, *we* can't wait—I've spent every penny I had or could borrow to follow you here!"

"And what a sweet gesture. You were trying to save me from being sold into a foreign marriage."

"Yes!" he agreed fervently. "But I have no money. I can't stay here for months with no money."

"I can get you money," Bella said airily, "enough to get you safely home. And then I shall return and we shall be together."

"No, sweetest heart, no." He grabbed her hands, going down on one knee in the grass in front of her. "They shall work on you, all of them—your mother, that prince, and his son—"

"His son is hardly going to convince me of anything," Bella said. "Nor are the others, as well you should know. I know my own mind!"

"I'm sure they want to arrange a liaison between you and him."

"Me and David? You must be mad! George, I can't stand that odious duke! We have nothing to fear from him. He was so dense he helped us without knowing it!"

"I implore you—if he did know, the others would, too, and they would cast me out as they did the other night, leaving me alone and destitute to die here in a foreign capital, without being able to see your sweet face again!"

"Cast you out?"

"The prince bodily threw me out and threatened me with prison if I so much as came near you."

"Prison!"

George Miller was warming to his topic. "The only way is to leave now."

"Leave?"

"Yes. Elope. Right this very minute!" Miller said urgently. Still kneeling at her feet, he leaned to kiss the hands he held.

"Elope." The thought stopped Bella.

Seeing her hesitation, George pressed on. "We can take the Great Northern Road to a place called Gretna Green. They will marry us there, and then none can ever part us again!"

"Elope." Bella took a step backward, but he held her hands fast. "I—it would break my mother's heart."

"She would learn to accept me and then to forgive us," George assured Isabella. "Say you'll come—come now."

"But I can't possibly. I couldn't do that to Mama. It would break her heart. And she and the prince have made all sorts of plans—they would be crushed if I acted so rashly. And Mama would be ruined in society. As would I."

George got to his feet, looking very somber. "Are you saying you care more about society than you do about our love?"

"No!"

"Well, then," George said.

"I must think—"

"There is no time to think!"

"Isabella?" The distant call of Consuela's voice came toward them.

"Now!" George said, prepared to carry Bella off, "before they see us!" Consuela was coming toward the south gate, searching the gardens as she moved.

"I can't. Meet me at Richmond Park, Sunday next—there's been talk of a picnic," Bella said, starting away. "I'll meet you there."

He grabbed her hand, stopping her. "Is there any way you can put together some money between now and then?"

"Yes. I'll manage, but I must go or she'll see you!" Bella ran around the statue and out of the garden toward the duenna. "I'm here—what on earth is wrong?" Bella called out, walking swiftly toward her servant.

Connie stopped where she was. She looked toward the statue and saw nothing, George moving quickly to let its marble girth hide him. What she did see, within the trees, was a glimpse of the Duke of Exeter as he moved to avoid discovery by George.

"Well?" Bella asked, arms akimbo and eyes blazing. "I am not a prisoner! I wanted some fresh air."

Connie allowed the girl to lead her back to the mansion, confused about what she had seen. When the two women had disappeared across the square, George Miller came out of hiding. He headed toward the north gate, his stride jaunty. He was whistling as he left the square.

David waited until the man was halfway up the street before he moved toward the east gate and his father's waiting carriage. "Joshua, we must make haste. I want to know where that man's headed."

"I thought you might want something a bit special, Your Grace," the old driver said from his box above the closed carriage. He opened the door in the roof of the carriage to be able to talk to the duke as they set out. "Seeing as you asked for the carriage and not your curricle."

"My curricle is too open. Secrecy is the key here. I want none to see us."

"Including Miss Isabella?"

"Especially Miss Isabella," David told his father's driver bluntly.

Ahead of them the American flagged a hansom cab.

David's lip curled. "Out of money, are we?"

"What's that, Your Grace?"

"The woman's a fool, Joshua."

"But a pretty one, Your Grace."

"This is purely curiosity, Joshua. Nothing else."

Joshua, wisely, did not comment. Several carriages back, Joshua kept the cab in view, giving the duke a running commentary on its whereabouts. Joshua jockeyed around tradesmen's carriages, around carts piled high with goods and sedate victorias, their falling tops open to allow their occupants a view of the lovely spring afternoon.

Joshua saw the cab stopping and slowed, bringing his immense gray percheron to the curb a short distance behind. The stallion stood almost seventeen hands high and weighed almost a ton, its graceful lines and movements belying its great size.

They were in Charing Cross Road, traffic heavy around them. "He's going into a little hotel, Your Grace, and the driver with him. Not a gentleman's hotel, it ain't," Joshua added.

The Duke of Exeter opened the carriage door. "Wait for me."

"I'll be doing nothing else. Your father would have me shot if I left you down here with the likes of this riffraff."

David grinned. Joshua had taught him how to ride when he was a boy and still thought of him as too young to hold his own. The bouts of fisticuffs the duke had continually won over the years at various men's sporting establishments meant nothing to Joshua when David reminded him.

"Begging your pardon, Your Grace, but fights as is at gentlemen's clubs, between gentlemen such as yourself, with Marquis of Queensberry rules and all, are all well and good. But a street brawl with the criminal element is something else again."

"You don't think I can hold my own?" David asked, grinning. He stood on the road beside the carriage.

"One on one, I'm sure you can beat any alive, Your Grace. Two to one, you'd give a good show. But with cowards who come five and ten to one, no, Your Grace, I don't."

David considered it. "Neither do I, Joshua. That's why I wanted you along. Two to ten we could do it," he told the old man.

Joshua sat a little straighter. "I'm not in me prime anymore, but I daresay I could whip a few still."

"Let's hope it doesn't come to that."

"Does your father know what you're about?" Joshua asked.

"In a way," David replied before he walked away, heading for the door to the ramshackle-looking hotel. In the street beside the door a sickly-looking young groom held onto the hansom's tired mare, fixing her feed bag.

The door led directly into a dingy pub. Battered wood tables and chairs sat on the straw-strewn floor, a long scarred bar taking up one whole wall. Behind it a bored-looking serving wench was waiting on George Miller and several others. She glanced toward David as he came toward the far end of the bar.

Definite quality, he looked to be as he came near, so she gave him a tired smile. "What's it to be, luv?"

"Ale," he replied, paying and taking it to a tiny table in the corner, his back to George Miller's back. The American stood ten feet away, laughing with a newfound crony.

"I was, I was, I tell you," George was saying as David sat down.

"Come away with you, laddie. You said you'd be gone to Gretna Green with a rich one by now."

George downed his beer and called for more. "And so I shall be by Sunday night. How far is Richmond?"

"Aye, is it Richmond this time? That'll cost you more, I'm afraid. It's a bit of a way for old Bess. I'll want me money up front, just in case it turns out like today, you understand. No hard feelings, but there's many a lad who'd like to catch a rich one and few that do."

"I have her caught and almost reeled in," George assured him.

"And what if her father comes after you?" the driver asked.

"She hasn't got a father. And if any others try, they'll soon back off. Once she's spent the night on the road with me, there'll be no choice for them but to accept our marriage. Damaged goods don't bring high prices."

The driver laughed. "And you'll enjoy the damaging, I'll warrant."

David ground his teeth. He stood up, walking outside before he spoiled all by confronting the wretch and challenging him to an immediate duel. This was the man who made Isabella's eyes light up as if Father Christmas had come before her in the flesh. The girl was not only stubborn and headstrong, she was incapable of telling truth from flattery.

Joshua visibly relaxed when he saw the duke walking toward the carriage. As David stepped inside he opened the tiny door in the roof. "I want someone to keep watch on this Miller. To let me know his every move until Sunday."

"Yes, Your Grace. Home?"

David was lost in thought "What? Oh . . . no. My club, Joshua."

The huge percheron brought the coach away from the curb. Wheeling around in the center of Charing Cross Road, it forced a light carriage to the side and a cart behind to stop before it made its turn and began the journey to the exclusive Mayfair Club.

Inside the carriage David looked grim. His every instinct told him to take the immoral cad apart limb by limb. But his reason told him it would be of little use unless he finished the American off for good. Upon which score not only Scotland Yard but his own father would string him up for taking the law into his own hands.

Isabella, of course, would believe none of it. She would hear him out, would hear every truth from his lips and brand him a liar to his face, then go on to waste herself all the more willingly on the bounder, in spite of all David's good intentions.

As he rode toward Exeter House David realized the only course of action that would avert tragedy was to let Bella walk into the trap and see for herself what came of it. A few hours alone with Miller should convince her.

Then again, it hadn't so far. But who knew how much time they had actually spent together and how much was merely a young girl mooning over a romantic intrigue? If her family had not been so set against the bounder, perhaps she would not have given him a second glance.

The more he thought about it, the more David was convinced his was the only sensible course of action. She must be allowed to make the mistake and then be rescued before real harm came to her. She must be with the bounder long enough to see for herself exactly the kind of man he was.

How to convince her mother and his own father was the problem. Neither of them would condone what he had done already, nor would they condone nearly throwing her to the wolf at the door.

David thought it strange that he should be able to so clearly see how to handle Isabella when even her own mother could not. Surely all could see she was a spoiled, stubborn, willful, overly romantic girl.

A beauty, of course, too. And it seemed the stories about hot-tempered, hot-blooded señoritas were true. At least in this case. Isabella had certainly not shrunk from the American's passionate kiss. She had run into his arms with abandon. Yet something about the man's attitude and remarks at the pub made David feel Isabella was truly the innocent his father had insisted.

She was obviously unable to judge the male character if

she could prefer a dangerous and caddish fop like Miller to someone such as himself. Odious duke, she called him. She would think him much more odious before he was through.

At Exeter House Isabella was being introduced to her new maid.

"This is Sally," Dolores told her daughter. "She will see to your every need and accompany you in your rambles."

Isabella glared at her mother. "Connie is quite sufficient."

Dolores turned toward the young maid. "Sally, please wait outside for a moment."

"Yes, ma'am," Sally said, a fierce blush burning her cheeks at the sudden attention. She had been the new tweeny at Exeter House for only four months, and already they were promoting her from helping Cook to being a ladies' maid. She curtsied awkwardly and left the room, her cheeks still burning so red they matched the fiery red of her tangled mop of curly hair.

Dolores spoke as the door closed. "Consuela has more than enough to do for me. She is no longer young, and we are asking too much of her."

"You want a spy to be with me always!" Bella burst out. She found her mother watching her carefully, the dark eyes trying to read Bella's own.

"Why should I want that? Is there cause for that? Do I need to do such a thing, Bella?"

"No, no," Bella said quickly. "I'm sorry, I just feel that—that you are hiding something from me," she ended up saying.

Dolores glanced down at her own hands, at the long fingers laced together and lying placidly on her lap. She looked back up to face Bella, her expression calm. "I fear it is the other way around. And has been for a very long time."

Bella bit her lower lip. "You know perfectly well how I feel about George."

"You have made yourself quite clear," Dolores agreed. "But you have not admitted to being in touch with the man your father banished."

Guilt made Bella uncomfortable. She was a straightfor-

ward girl, used to saying what she meant, unused to subterfuge and lies. Unhappily, she sat down on the footstool in
front of her mother's chair. "Mama, I love him."

"You do not even truly know him, *querida.*"

"Oh, but I do! Love knows in ways that others can't see!"

"It would have to, with one such as him," Dolores said
dryly.

"You've been against him from the very first," Bella
accused, and her mother nodded agreement.

"That's true. And one day I hope you shall understand
why. In the meantime"—Dolores stood up—"your new
maid is waiting."

"Mama," Bella said as Dolores went toward the sitting
room door, "I'm quite out of money. I need to have more."

"Already?" Dolores frowned.

"Yes, well, I've given a little largess to the servants, and I
played a bit of cards at the princess's garden party. I'll be
needing it for that, and I want to buy some trinkets while
I'm here, for myself and for the girls at home."

Dolores smiled. The Indian girls at home were a worth-
while project of Isabella's. She had been determined to
teach them to read and write and had done so well their
brothers were learning from the sisters.

"Remind me before we go out," Dolores said.

"Thank you, Mama."

Bella watched the new maid come back through the door.
It might not be so very bad not having Connie around after
all, she thought. If not for Connie, she could have spent
more time with George today. Isabella smiled. Sally might
be useful. And she could definitely be handled—a thing that
was not so easy to accomplish with Consuela. After all, Bella
told herself, she had no intention of running away; that
wasn't the way to handle things at all. And she couldn't very
well keep meeting George alone. With Sally there it would
be infinitely more proper. She knew she could cow this
young girl into doing as she asked and keeping silent about
it, an impossible task with Connie.

Isabella smiled again, even more warmly. With the money
she already had and what her mother would give her,

George would be able to leave for home and await her arrival. All would soon be well.

"Sally, I think I shall wear the yellow watered silk tonight. You'll find it in the next room. And ring for bath water and milk, please."

Sally gave a half curtsy and left as Bella leaned back on the chaise longue and closed her eyes, dreaming of the future. And George.

Chapter Nine

The week passed quickly, between balls, assemblies, and the opera. All of London was agog over the exotic American beauty and her equally beautiful mother.

Henrietta Epps was called upon at every party she attended to give a running account of the comings and goings of the two Americans who had invaded Exeter Square. Clarissa joined in, both women regaling their friends and friendly enemies with whatever tidbits they were able to glean from the Eppsworth servants talking to the prince's servants.

They passed the information off as firsthand knowledge, and the town was generally led to believe that Henrietta and Clarissa were not only constant visitors at Exeter House, but on the most intimate of terms with its occupants.

Happily unaware of the gossip all around them, Dolores and Bella, escorted by the prince, made the rounds of London society. The gossips' tongues wagged even harder as the duke joined his father, paying more and more attention to mother and daughter. The Duke of Exeter seemed to be turning up everywhere Dolores and Isabella went. He even accompanied them on their obligatory, but often boring, morning calls on the hostesses of the various parties to which they were invited, a process to which David had never before submitted. Wags made wagers as to whether he was after the mother or the daughter. Henrietta Epps merely smiled enigmatically, even a bit complacently.

During it all Isabella was sweet to everyone. Her mother complimented her upon her behavior and credited the duke's constant attendance for the change in Bella.

In a way, she was correct. David distrusted Bella's sudden change of heart and attitude, knowing full well she had secret plans. Across dinner tables and ballrooms he kept an eye on where and with whom she was, his father's worry ringing in his ears. David had thrust himself into the middle of Bella's affair, had gone against his father's wishes, and now felt responsible for keeping the girl out of harm's—and George Miller's—way.

By Friday afternoon Dolores decreed a long nap followed by a quiet evening. And so it was to an almost silent house that Bella woke after her nap.

Sally was asleep on her cot in the connecting dressing room; many of the other servants had taken the chance for a nap, too. The household chores began at six in the morning, with the valets and ladies' maids up before their masters and not to bed until after them. At the height of the season, with parties that lasted sometimes until dawn going on every night of the week, the servants took naps when they could.

Bella dressed herself, glad of the moment alone. Her mother and Connie slept on as Bella wandered downstairs, the house quiet. The distant sound of voices and movement in the faraway kitchens was muffled by the long corridors and the green baize doors between. Nearby, the only sounds were those of her own footsteps in the echoing marble main hall and the cough of a young footman who sat near the front door. Half-dozing, he opened his sleepy eyes at the sound of Bella's steps and then closed them again as she crossed far behind him.

Bella opened the door to the library, the book-filled room warmed by afternoon sunlight. Sunbeams streamed in past ruby-red velvet drapes to splash down upon the red-patterned oriental rug and the oak parquet floor. The room was filled with oak shelves of leather-bound volumes; the fireplace, with its marble mantel, and the tall windows were sandwiched between them.

A bouquet of tulips had been arranged on a round table in the center of the room. Comfortable leather chairs were placed around the library, small tables beside most of them.

Bella walked along one wall of books, fingering them as she read the titles. She pulled a volume of Sir Walter Scott from the shelf, taking it to a window seat. She looked out at the blooming gardens contained within the railings across the wide cobblestone street.

A nanny was walking a perambulator along the paved paths that wound through the gardens. She passed Henrietta Epps and her cousin Clarissa as they took an afternoon turn around the large center square.

Bella looked closely at a gentleman who hurried toward the gardens, her heart hoping for a moment until she saw it was not George. Sinking back against the cushioned window embrasure, Bella opened the book.

David walked into the library and was halfway across when he saw Bella looking up at him. "Sorry—I didn't mean to disturb you."

"You didn't," Bella answered pleasantly. "I'm merely whiling away the time."

"I thought all were asleep," he said, coming near.

"I was. I haven't taken a nap since I was six unless I was ill. But then, I've never been up so late so much in my life, either. How do you people stand it?"

"I beg your pardon?" the duke asked.

Bella smiled at him. "I'm fast becoming exhausted by all the parties and late hours."

David relaxed a bit, lounging against the corner of the embrasure opposite from where she sat. "I've never before heard a debutante complain about attending too many parties."

"Perhaps they're more used to all this."

"And you?" he asked. "What are you used to?"

"Truly? Rising at dawn. Riding in the first morning light, sunlight and fresh air and animals to tend to, and—"

"Tend to?" David interrupted.

She saw his surprise. "My father believed that, as his heir, I should be experienced in all parts of the management of the rancho." Seeing the duke's raised eyebrows, she bristled a little. "I assure you, I can handle a horse as well as any. And a calf as well as most. I'm not as strong as a man, but I can rope as well. I know more about grain and feed and cattle and orchards and wine grapes than any save my father."

David's eyebrows rose. "Your father had very progressive ideas about a young lady's education."

"He wasn't educating a young woman, he was educating the future *patrón!*"

"Sorry," David apologized. "How stupid of me."

Bella looked down at the pages of the book. "I wish we could spend more time outdoors."

"Yes, I can see you're quite used to it. Unfortunately, there are very few cows to rope in London," the duke replied dryly.

"I'd dearly love to go riding," Bella said. "Really riding, not that parade in Hyde Park. Perhaps a picnic somewhere and a long ride."

"It sounds delightful," the duke said.

Bella looked up, her smile widening. "Do you mean it? Could we do it?"

"I'm sure my father would approve of a picnic outing, if you would enjoy it."

"I'd love it! Oh, yes!" Bella enthused.

"I know a lovely place in Chelsea," David began, only to be quickly interrupted.

"Oh, no! I mean—" Bella recovered her composure—"I mean, I've been told Richmond Park is ever so beautiful. Couldn't we go there?"

The duke restrained a smile. "Oh? Who told you that?"

"I think it was Millie."

"There are many other lovely places you should see," David said, drawing it out. "Other people would tell you all sorts of other places."

"No! I mean, ever so many people have told me of Richmond Park. I feel as if I *must* go there—couldn't we?"

"Perhaps in a few weeks," the duke replied.

"Oh, surely we could go *this* weekend! It's been ages since I've been able to truly ride," Bella insisted.

David struggled to maintain a straight face. "This weekend . . ." He sounded dubious.

"If you said it would be a good idea, I know Mama would approve," Bella added. "And you are a very good horseman. I could see that in Hyde Park."

"When you were ready to throttle me."

"Oh, no, David—I mean—well, yes, I was a little upset—"

"A little upset?" David repeated. "Then I should hate to see you *really* upset."

"Then do as I say!" Bella said imperiously, her tone changing to one of supplication when she saw his expression change. "Please! You don't know what it will mean to me."

David answered slowly: "Perhaps I am beginning to."

"Oh, I hope so! Will you help me?"

"Yes."

Bella reached across the window seat, touching his arm. "Do you mean it? Do you truly mean it?"

David looked down at the delicate hand on his coat sleeve. It was devoid of rings, unlike the hands of every other female he knew. "I don't say things I do not mean."

"Oh, thank you, thank you!"

Isabella had brought up Richmond Park all week; she had used every opportunity to work it into the conversation. Now, close to her chance to see George, she smiled up at the man who had promised to help her.

David looked into her dark eyes and smiled back. "It means very much to you, does it?"

"Yes. That is, I shall be ever so grateful to you!"

"I will make it my business to convince Father and your mother," David promised.

"Wonderful!" she enthused.

"I shall have Cook informed to prepare a picnic for tomorrow."

"Wonder—" She stopped. "Tomorrow?"

"You want to go this weekend. Immediately, you said."

"Yes, but"—Bella cast about for an excuse—"but I thought we could go Sunday."

"Why Sunday?" David asked.

"Because—because tomorrow we are to shop for our ball gowns for the Prince of Wales's ball in honor of the King of Hawaii."

David shrugged off her words. "I'm sure that can wait."

"Oh, no! There will have to be alterations and all kinds of adjustments, and you can't always find precisely what you need immediately, and—and—it would be ever so much better to go Sunday."

David took a moment. "It sounds as if Sunday it is. If my father and your mother have no objections, of course."

"Of course!" Bella's dark eyes were shining with triumph. "And my mother shall have none, I promise you! But you must persuade your father."

"I shall do my best," David promised. He bowed and excused himself, leaving behind a rapturous Isabella.

Prince Henry was much less enthused when David talked to him over their after-dinner brandy. "I think it a mistake. Something could easily go amiss, and then where are we?"

"Father, I promise you, I shall ensure nothing untoward happens."

"She will see that cad. That is untoward enough, thank you very much. David, I think you are taking much too much upon yourself," the prince declared.

"Not so loud, they will hear you," David said.

Both the prince and David looked toward the closed sliding doors that connected the west dining room with the west parlor, where mother and daughter had retired after dinner. "I don't like it above half," the prince said.

"I know what I am doing," the duke told his father.

"I understand your point about her being too headstrong to listen to reason," the prince responded, "but I fail to see why we should put her in temptation's path. If she has nothing to do with him, there's an end to it right there."

"No, it's not. She will try at every opportunity to sneak away to see him, and even if we prevent it while she is here, what will happen when she arrives back in America?" the duke asked. "He will surely find a way around the women's guard, and she will truly be in danger."

Prince Henry studied his son's earnest face. "Why do you care what happens after she leaves?"

David stared at his father. "I—I don't, precisely. It's just that I would hate to see that bounder end up with your friends' lands, fortunes, and daughter."

The prince had to agree, at least with that sobering thought. But he was still of the opinion that Dolores should be privy to what was going on. Reluctantly, he agreed to say nothing for the moment. But he reserved the right to change his mind should circumstances warrant.

"You're sure you're not interested in the girl?" Henry asked.

"Perish the thought," David replied.

"I don't want you treating this situation as some kind of lark," the prince warned as he stood up. "We'd best join the ladies."

David followed his father into the west parlor, playing one game of whist before excusing himself and heading toward his rooms.

Upstairs he pulled the bell rope for his valet and waited impatiently for the man to appear.

"Ben," David said the moment the valet appeared in the doorway, "I need to see Joshua immediately and get his report on some work I assigned him. Then I need you to pack."

Ben was a middle-aged man with weary eyes and the beginnings of a paunch on his thin frame. At the moment he looked startled. "Are we taking a trip, Your Grace?"

"Yes," the duke replied.

"For how long?" Ben asked.

"I don't know."

"May I ask when we are leaving, Your Grace?"

"I have no idea," David told him, earning another startled look before the man left in search of Joshua.

Richmond Park was several miles southwest of London along the bank of the Thames. It had been enclosed by Charles I in 1637.

Late Sunday morning, Prince Henry's carriage pulled into the park through the main gate on Richmond Hill and proceeded to the top. A gray stallion and a chestnut mare were tethered to the back of the carriage, walking sedately along behind.

From the top of Richmond Hill the famous view of the Thames valley stretched out beyond and around them. Bella watched eagerly. She was the first one out when the carriage stopped, drinking in the fresh air and staring off beyond the trees to the river flowing below.

"Let's ride right away!" Bella said.

"Isabella!" Dolores stopped her daughter. "We shall take our time, we shall have our meal, and we shall see about the riding. You may help Connie and Joshua set up the food."

Bella began to protest but, seeing the firm look in her mother's eyes, thought better of it. She moved toward Connie as Dolores spoke to the prince.

"While David is seeing to their mounts, I want a word with you about this ride they've planned, Henry. I'm not at all sure it is such a good idea."

"Neither am I," the prince responded unhappily.

"Then perhaps you might mention to David that we would appreciate his being very careful not to let Bella away from his side or out of his sight during their ride. I should hate to have anything untoward happen."

"Dolores, I shall impress upon David your concern."

She smiled and thanked the prince before moving toward the white linen cloth the servants had spread under the wide branches of a hilltop tree. Wicker baskets of food and drink were being unpacked by Connie and Bella as Dolores came near.

Isabella ate very little, her eyes constantly surveying the people who rode and walked nearby. David lolled on the grass beside her, drinking champagne from a crystal goblet and watching Bella over the rim.

"The fresh air doesn't seem to have given you an appetite, Bella."

"What?" She looked toward the duke.

"Shall we ride?" he asked. He was rewarded by a huge smile. Bella bounced to her feet.

"Yes!"

Dolores looked up. "Don't go too far," she warned.

"Mama!"

The duke bowed toward Dolores. "I shall take good care of your daughter."

"See that you do," Dolores said pointedly.

Joshua untethered their horses from the back of the carriage, exchanging a look with the duke and nodding slightly.

The duke helped Bella mount the chestnut mare and then swung himself up onto the gray. They started off at a polite canter, Bella looking everywhere at once.

"I can see you are enthralled with the scenery," David said.

"Yes," Isabella said, surveying a group of riders coming toward them.

"I thought you wanted to really ride," David challenged.

Bella's attention came back to her riding companion. "I wouldn't want to show up my host," she said, smiling.

David returned her smile. "Why don't you try?"

She hesitated and then urged the mare forward, taking off at a gallop. David let the gray have his head, the two horses streaking down the hill toward the river side by side.

They slowed at the river's edge, reining in and cantering, strands of Isabella's long hair streaming back, loosened by the wind. She laughed, merry peals ringing out toward the water's edge. "That felt good!" she told David.

"Even sidesaddle?"

"Even sidesaddle!" Bella responded, still smiling. She patted the chestnut's mane, taking big, deep breaths of the fresh air. Her eyes strayed across the river and then back, glancing idly at the track ahead of them.

Her eyes widened as she saw George in the distance. David glanced ahead, seeing the American astride a black horse. He was following their path farther up the hillside, keeping pace with them.

"I think we should turn back," Bella told the duke.

"Already?" he queried.

She was bringing the chestnut around. From the corner of

his eye he could see the American stop and turn back up above. Bella began up the hill on an angle away from Miller, the duke keeping his eyes ahead and pretending not to notice her several glances toward the man.

They rode in comparative silence, David making a few attempts at conversation and receiving very little in return. Her horse could feel her nervousness, becoming a little skittish under her tightened hand.

They neared the carriage, Joshua shading his eyes and looking toward them and beyond to where Miller was coming slowly forward. Beyond the American a young man and his horse loitered near a parked hansom cab.

The duke slowed and dismounted. As his feet hit the path Bella spurred her horse on, wheeling to the right and riding straight for George Miller.

"Bella!" her mother called out sharply.

"David!" the prince yelled at almost the same moment.

The prince and Dolores both came to their feet, David remounting and starting after Bella.

She was streaking toward the trees, shouting at George to follow her. He tried to turn her toward the waiting hansom, but she was flying away, and he had to move fast to try to catch up. Looking behind, he could see the duke gaining on him. George spurred his horse, making it jump forward as fast as it would go. The young man near the hansom mounted his horse but remained walking it in seemingly idle circles near the cab.

Bella made for a spinney where a thick grouping of trees wove their branches together overhead. She disappeared into the thick trees and shrubbery of the spinney, George following her. The duke's horse seemed to lag behind, losing a little ground.

Breathless, Isabella smiled at George as he reined in beside her. "We must hurry!" George told her urgently.

"Yes, here." Bella handed over her reticule. "There's money to get you home."

"Home?" George shook his head. "No, I have a carriage, we can leave this instant!"

Bella's eyes widened. "It's not possible at all, George

dearest. Can't you see? They'd be right behind us! Besides, there's no need now. I told you, Mama says we can be together!"

George grabbed her hand. "I want you with me now! I *must* have you! I love you!"

She shivered becomingly. "And I adore you, you know that."

"Then prove it and come with me now!" George demanded.

"There is no way," she repeated, looking over her shoulder. "The duke is coming. Leave now before he sees you."

Torn, George glanced toward the hillside behind them and then back at Isabella. "They are lying to you! They will never let us be together!"

"My mother would never lie," Bella said. "Go, go! But write me!"

"I can't get through to you! I've tried and tried!"

"Then I shall write you! Where are you staying?"

"The Stag and Hounds in Charing Cross." Miller heard the duke's horse coming nearer through the thick underbrush.

"Go, go, dearest!" Isabella urged.

"I won't leave until I've talked to you!" he threatened.

"Yes, all right!"

The duke was calling out Bella's name, coming nearer. George Miller streaked away, Bella turning her horse and starting out of the spinney at a gallop in the opposite direction. When she saw the duke she cried out his name.

David had no choice but to pursue her. He smiled to himself, applauding her cunning. Catching up with Isabella, he grabbed the chestnut's reins, bringing it to a halt.

"Thank you, you saved my life!" Bella told him breathlessly.

David stared at her. "Isabella, please."

"The horse bolted, and I couldn't control it!"

The Duke of Exeter turned them back toward the top of the hill, Dolores and the prince visible far ahead, standing with their eyes shaded, watching as the two rode slowly back.

"I can't thank you enough," Bella continued.

"Bella, please don't." For the first time David looked truly grim.

"But you deserve my thanks!"

He reined in, halting the horses and staring at her, his blue eyes cold and hard. "Above all else, I hate liars."

Her own eyes flashed with sudden anger. "How dare you?"

"How dare *you* treat me with such contempt?" David snapped back. "Give me credit for something above total stupidity, at the very least!"

She glared at him and then turned to face forward, her chin lifted proudly. There was fire in her eyes, but she did not speak.

They began to move forward again, the air frigid and silent between them. David held the chestnut's reins the entire way, handing them over to Joshua at the top as the prince, Connie, and Dolores came near.

"*Madre de Dios,* what were you doing? What happened? Are you all right?" Connie asked.

"I'm fine," Bella said sharply.

The prince looked from Bella to his son. "What *did* happen?"

David spoke with a tight voice. "Miss Alexander says her mount got the better of her, and she could not stop its headlong flight."

Dolores stared at her daughter. "Bella, that is not possible!"

"I want to go home!" Bella said. "I am quite overcome."

Connie touched Bella's forehead. "I think you have a fever."

"Well, who wouldn't after nearly having her neck broken?" Isabella said. Seeing the duke's derisive expression, she found hot tears coming to her eyes. She didn't care what he thought of her, she told herself. She didn't care at all if he looked at her as if she were the lowest thing alive.

The tears convinced her mother. Dolores folded Bella close and looked at father and son. "If you don't mind, I think we should take her back as soon as possible. I know my daughter, Henry. She never cries. She is quite overset by all this."

"Did we bring smelling salts?" the duke asked caustically, earning a dirty look from Isabella and a questioning one from her mother.

"I hardly think smelling salts will be necessary," the prince answered. "Will they?" he asked Dolores.

David spoke before Dolores could: "One can hardly imagine what will be necessary next." His tone was cold. "If you will excuse me, I have just remembered urgent business I must attend to."

The others watched him ride off toward the London road until Bella started to move toward the carriage. Dolores walked with her, Connie moving to help Joshua pack up the wicker baskets. Dolores was worried.

"What happened between the two of you, *querida?* What caused all this?"

"He is a rude and obnoxious and horrible man!" Bella announced as she sat back against the blue velvet squabs of the large carriage. Tears began to spill down her cheeks unheeded. "I never want to see him again as long as I live!"

Dolores began to feel a little hope. A strong emotion— even a negative one—could grow into much more. She patted her daughter's hand and waited for the prince and Connie to join them.

Chapter Ten

At Exeter House Isabella went straight to her room. Dolores worried that something was very wrong with her daughter. Without a protest, Bella allowed Connie and her mother to boss her into changing her clothes and lying down, which worried her mother even more.

"I have never seen you lose control of your horse," Dolores said as Connie and Sally bustled about the room.

It was Connie who answered, "You've never seen her say no to food before either!"

"Was that all it was?" Dolores asked her daughter, her dark eyes searching her daughter's face. "Or was there something else? Did you see someone?"

Isabella was letting Connie fuss about the bedside. Her eyes did not meet her mother's as she replied in a low tone. "I was feeling quite faint," Bella said, comforting herself that she was not telling a lie. She had felt faint at the fear of not seeing George. She wasn't lying; she just wasn't answering everything her mother asked.

Connie told Sally to go fetch some broth and then shooed Dolores out of the room. Dolores left her daughter in the duenna's care as she went below to tell the prince all was well.

When Sally arrived back with the weak broth, Connie took it from her and insisted Bella drink some, threatening more gruesome medicines if she didn't obey.

"If you'd eaten earlier, you'd have had more strength," Connie said practically, "and none of this would have happened."

"I'm not hungry," Bella said listlessly. She closed her eyes only to see the duke's derisive expression again. He seemed to be looking straight through her. He had called her a liar. She wasn't a liar, she told herself, but her guilty conscience disagreed. As she fought with her conscience Connie left Sally to watch over her and went in search of Dolores to report on Isabella's progress.

Bella told Sally she would eat a solitary dinner upstairs. As she said the words she realized David would think her a coward as well as a liar. He would think even less of her than he already did. She didn't care a fig what he thought about her, she argued to herself; but it was not true, and she knew it.

Isabella Castillo-Suera Alexander was a very proud young woman. The thought that anyone would think her less than honorable rankled. She was honorable, one part of her brain insisted. She was protecting the man she loved, the man who one day would be her husband.

Her marriage to George was a foregone conclusion. She loved him, and therefore they would be wed. Bella didn't realize that whenever she thought of their marriage it was always in some distant future. She felt no need to rush into it. Her mother had been angry when she had first found out George had been meeting Isabella on her morning rides, that he had been shamelessly courting her without her parents' permission.

Bella had defended him, had defended their actions with the strength of their love. Dolores had told her daughter she didn't know the first thing about loving a man. She had said Isabella was in love with love, not with George. That love was not being courted and pretty words easily said and easily forgotten.

A fleeting doubt crossed Bella's mind, quickly squashed.

She wondered why she was remembering her mother's words now, and then she dismissed them. What she was really doing was avoiding the fact of the duke's sarcasm. His eyes had shown contempt.

Prideful anger rose within her. He might think what he wished, but she had protected George, and she would face the disdainful look in the Duke of Exeter's eyes and return it. He had never been so in love; he had no right to judge her actions.

"I have changed my mind," Isabella told the maid, her words ringing out in the long silent room. "I shall change for dinner. I shall eat with the others." The words sounded like a war cry. Or a challenge. Sally moved to help her mistress as Isabella girded herself for battle.

However, Bella marched regally into the dining room, her head held high, only to find David was out for the evening. Her composure slipped, and her mother was sure by dinner's end that Bella had truly been frightened by the unmanageable horse. At the time Dolores had felt Bella was feeling more wounded pride than anything else. It was probably good for the headstrong girl to have an experience now and then she could not control, but her mother's heart went out to her. Bella seemed so unhappy this night.

"You are very quiet tonight, Bella," the prince said, almost as if reading Dolores's mind. His hazel eyes perused Isabella kindly.

Dolores looked concerned. "You weren't truly hurt earlier, were you, *querida?*"

"I'm perfectly well," Isabella told them both. "I am just a bit tired. I think I shall retire early."

"A good idea," the prince said. "After all, tomorrow will be a very special day." Isabella's inquiring expression brought a smile to his lips. "It's a surprise for you."

Bella looked from her mother to the prince. But her mother looked surprised, too. "Henry?" Dolores questioned him.

He only smiled wider. "It's a surprise for both of you," Prince Henry told his house guests.

After Bella went upstairs the prince escorted Dolores to

the blue parlor where Fannie was already sitting, her supper long over, her knitting in her hands.

"What have you been up to, Henry?" Dolores asked as they sat down near the cozy fire. "It's all well and good to speak of surprises, but I've found in life it's generally better to be prepared for them in advance."

He laughed and turned to pour sherry into three small cut-glass goblets before sitting down. The ruby liquid shimmered as the faceted glass caught the firelight. "But I have everything planned for tomorrow," he told her.

Dolores watched the tall patrician walk across the room, handing a glass of sherry to Consuela, who accepted it a little self-consciously. She had never had a prince serve her before.

He was a good man, Dolores Alexander said to herself. A kind one, and a true friend. He reminded her a little of her late husband. Wallace had been tall, too, although wider, more hale and hearty than this reserved Englishman. They both had a quiet strength about them. And that most rare of commodities: Each of them had learned wisdom with their years. Another rare quality was that Wallace had never lost his fun-loving nature; it was a trait Bella had inherited.

And a trait Dolores saw gleaming in Henry's hazel eyes as he came near, handing her a goblet and sitting down beside her on the settee.

In spite of herself, Dolores found she was smiling back at the personable man. "Well?" she demanded. "Am I to be told?"

"Oh, yes," he said softly. And he stopped. The prince saw the lovely Spanish-American woman waiting for him to continue, her large, dark eyes curious. "Tomorrow I am going to ask for your hand in marriage."

"My—marriage?" She caught her breath, hearing Connie's sharp intake across the room behind them. "But— but—"

"Shhh." He put a finger to her lips. "I do not expect an immediate answer. I merely ask you consider the possibility."

"But my home is in America."

"You will have two homes, my dear. We can live there as

well as here, we can live in either. Or both. I want you by my side."

"Henry, I—I don't know what to say."

"Say nothing now, *querida*—did I pronounce it properly?" he asked, his smiling eyes seeking out hers.

She nodded, saying yes softly. Then: "I promised Wallace to bring Bella here to find a suitable husband for her—not for myself, Henry."

"Is the thought repugnant?" he asked, a little fear in his tone.

"No . . . not that."

"Good!"

"But—"

"No," he interrupted. "Wait. And think about it. Spending the day with you today, in the sunlight out at Richmond, I realized just how happy it makes me to be with you. To share things with you. I determined to tell you." He smiled ruefully. "I planned everything for tomorrow. A long drive alone in the park, just you and I—and Consuela as your duenna, of course." He glanced across the room and smiled before looking back at Dolores. "I planned a declaration of all the reasons and my feelings—but perhaps this is better."

"I am overwhelmed," Dolores said truthfully. "I had no idea you had any thought of me other than as a friend."

"Friendship is a good beginning to a marriage." He searched her eyes. "Although I confess I long for more than merely—friendship." His words were rewarded by a blush.

Consuela stood up. "Excuse me, señora; it is time to retire." The old duenna's voice was polite but firm. Dolores had not heard that tone of voice from Connie since she was eighteen and Wallace had first come courting.

Dolores stood up, the prince rising to his feet. "As Connie says," Dolores murmured.

Henry gave a slight bow toward the duenna. "I would never argue with Consuela's decisions on propriety," he said prettily.

Dolores did not at first recognize the slightly giddy feeling that was washing over her. It had been so long since she had flirted, she had almost forgotten the sweet mixture of feelings it evoked. She felt suddenly young and pretty again;

she felt a bit of power and a bit of fear, emotions she had long denied awakening within her.

Wallace had died over a year ago and for long years before had been ill and bedridden. She loved him mightily, had willingly nursed him herself until the very end. She had prepared him for his death, and she helped prepare his body for burial, steeling herself to let go of the man she had loved with all her heart.

When she buried him she buried her heart beside him. Or so it had felt until this moment when suddenly all her senses were alive again.

"Señora," Connie said again.

Dolores bowed her head, not wanting either of them to see the light in her eyes. "If you'll excuse me," she murmured, starting past Henry.

As she moved she allowed her hand to brush his, a spark coursing up within her as she felt his reaction to her touch.

He watched the two women leave the room and then turned back to pour himself more sherry. His hand was a little unsteady as he uncorked the decanter, and he stared at it, surprised. A smile curved the corners of his chiseled lips. She had given him a sign, he was sure of it. His heart began to sing within his breast, the sensations of youth flooding through him.

Upstairs Connie kept wise silence, leaving Dolores to her thoughts until her mistress was undressed and in bed.

"Is there anything else you need?" Connie asked. Looking at the woman she had helped raise, Consuela could see the change in her expression, in her eyes. Hope lived there for the first time in years, and it lit her from within. Dolores had been a beautiful girl and now was an even more beautiful woman. Age had not touched her yet, her early forties and the sadness of her husband's illness giving her mystery and wisdom that added to the clear-eyed and smooth-skinned perfection of physical beauty.

Now, with Prince Henry's declaration and the feeling of being desired again, of being admired, the bloom of youth was back on her cheeks and in her eyes.

Dolores was smiling softly at the old serving woman.

"You sustained me when I lost each of my parents, Connie. You helped me raise my child and bury my husband. What do you have to say?"

"It's not my business to say," Consuela answered.

"I value your opinion."

Connie's heart swelled. She loved Dolores as much as if she were the child Connie had never been able to conceive. In many ways Dolores was truly her daughter. "I think you should consider him."

Dolores's eyes lit up. "Do you?" Another thought clouded them. "But what of Bella?"

"Bella likes him, I'm sure. If by any miracle you were to be successful in interesting Bella in an English husband, it would be good for her to have you nearby," Connie said. "Besides, if you marry the prince, he can easily manage the rancho—something that this imaginary lord Bella might find might not want to do."

"I hadn't thought of that," Dolores said slowly.

"You've seen these Englishmen. Most of them look like young fops to me, but then what do I know? What I *do* know is that I haven't seen one who looked capable of taking over from the *patrón,* God rest his soul. Or of handling our Bella, for that matter. Excepting the duke, who doesn't want any part of her, as far as I can see."

"Life is so very strange, Connie. I have concentrated so much on Bella, I had even had small hopes about her and David—oh, I know. I see your expression. But I know my girl, and I have seen little things in his eyes, too. I have been so hopeful her father's plan would work." A shadow crossed her expression. "I'm afraid he may have judged all Englishmen by Henry."

Consuela tucked in the covers around Dolores. "The *patrón* would not want you to throw away the rest of your life thinking only of the past." She saw Dolores's surprise. "Now go to sleep, so I can," Connie demanded, cutting off the conversation before she ended up getting sentimental and making a fool of herself.

Dolores looked at her old duenna with so much love that Connie felt her eyes beginning to glisten with moisture.

"Go to sleep," Connie said gruffly. She wasn't about to lose control and sniffle in front of the girl she had raised.

Dolores watched Connie lower the lamp wick, her thoughts so jumbled she was awake almost until morning light.

In the bedroom next door her daughter tossed and turned all night, her dreams full of David's contemptuous face.

Monday morning's light found Bella out of sorts with herself, the world in general, and David in particular. With bad grace she allowed Sally to help her dress for breakfast, her irritation showing in her knitted brow and monosyllabic answers. Sally was quiet and cautious, not wanting to disappoint her new young mistress. If she did she would be banished back to being the tweeny and shuttling between the overbearing cook and the equally snobbish head maid. The tweeny was given all the dirtiest jobs no one else wanted to do.

While Bella ate a solitary breakfast in the upstairs sitting room her mother was already up and downstairs, a happy lilt to her voice as she rose to accept a morning call from the Countess of Eppsworth and her cousin Clarissa. The women sat to early tea and toast, discussing the upcoming week of social events. The prince made an appearance and then escaped to his study, unwilling to be caught in the snare of fashionable London's premier gossips.

They had been talking for a quarter of an hour when Bella came downstairs, wary at every step of finding David around the next turn. Tate bowed to her as she crossed the long gallery. "Your mother is entertaining the Countess of Eppsworth and Miss Stanisbury in the blue parlor," the butler told her.

"Thank you. I think I shall take a turn in the gardens."

"Shall I call your maid, miss?" Tate asked.

"Yes," Bella said listlessly. "I shall need rain clothing."

"Very good, miss." Tate went in search of the young maid and the clothing.

The morning was misty, a light drizzle covering Exeter Square in shades of gray. A footman helped both Bella and her maid into hooded oilskin slickers.

"You're sure you want to go out, miss?" Sally asked.

"We shan't dissolve," Bella said, heading out the open door.

Sally came quickly behind, scurrying across the street behind Bella. The maid took two steps to each one of Bella's long strides. Inside the gardens the ground was puddling with water, mud edging the flower beds. Bella kept her eye on the grass, crossing it instead of using the muddying paths. Past the center statue, under the tree branches, the light drizzle lessened, caught upon leaves high above and dripping much more slowly downward.

Bella walked and walked, Sally following faithfully just behind. As the hour lengthened the drizzle stopped, and Sally was hopeful at every turn that Bella would start back for Exeter House.

"Miss, aren't you tired?" Sally ventured.

"No. Oh"—Bella looked back at the young maid—"are you tired?"

"A bit, miss," Sally replied, looking a little fearful of earning Bella's wrath.

"We'll sit for a moment," Bella decreed.

"Here, miss?" Sally looked at the wet iron benches.

Bella was near the mounted statue. There was a thick stone ledge around it. "Here," she replied. Suiting action to words, Bella sat down upon it.

Sally eyed the ledge, sitting gingerly and staring at the row of Georgian homes that lined the north side of the square. The sound of other footsteps surprised the maid. She had thought only her own young mistress foolish enough to want to muck about in the rain. The fact that it had stopped raining did nothing to reconcile Sally with the situation. She knew it would start to pour in earnest at any moment, and they would be drenched.

They both would catch pneumonia, and she would be blamed for Bella's illness and probably sacked. Looking as gloomy as the day around her, Sally worried over the vision of the future she was building in her head.

"I tell you, I knew it all along." Henrietta Epps's voice came from the path on the other side of the statue. She and her cousin were walking slowly toward home.

"But what if she turns the duke down?" Clarissa asked.

"Mark my words, she will do exactly as her mother tells her. Can you imagine? An American duchess!"

Bella sat up straighter, shock registering as she listened to their conversation.

"They say she's already an American princess," Clarissa replied.

"Very fanciful, but, my dear, a real title is worth ever so much more than a fanciful one."

Bella stood up as the women passed nearer. She motioned to Sally to stand and then, her finger to her lips, warned Sally to say nothing. They moved around the statue counterclockwise, Bella keeping the bulk of the first duke's marble between themselves and the elderly women passing by.

"I wonder if her mother will stay on in England after they are married," Clarissa mused.

"I rather doubt it. I think it's rich, after David's escaping all these years, that his father and some American adventurer have succeeded where all the mamas in England have failed. The Duchess Isabella, can you imagine?"

Bella stiffened, her face turning to stone.

"Sounds so foreign, doesn't it?" Henrietta continued, the rest of their conversation lost as they walked farther away. "But he's on the point of offering. Did you see how happy her mother is? Trust me, Clarissa, it's a foregone conclusion."

"Can we go home now, miss?" Sally asked. She was frightened by the look in her mistress's eyes.

"Did you hear?" Bella looked horrified. "They never meant to have me go home to George, they never meant to have me go home at all! George was right!"

"I don't understand, miss. Can't we go home now?"

"Home!" Bella spit out the word. "They have had this planned all along. They intend to force me to marry that odious man!"

"Oh, no, miss!" Sally's eyes widened. "They'd never!"

"Oh, yes they would! You must help me, Sally!"

Sally leaned back. "I don't know how I can, miss."

"You must deliver a message. I must go back and write it this instant. Before it's too late!"

"Oh, dear, miss." Sally looked worried, but she liked the

idea of going back. "Who is trying to force this man upon you? Who is it they're trying to force upon you?"

"Come along," Bella said. She stood up, her resolution in her face and posture. "We must return at once!"

"Oh, yes, miss!" Sally agreed. She stood up and hurried alongside her tall young mistress back to the great stone mansion.

Chapter Eleven

Within Exeter House Dolores was talking to the prince and shaking her head. "I cannot quite credit that woman."

"I warned you," Henry replied. "She is the worst gossip in London. And that is saying something."

"She simply doesn't listen. She is bound and determined we've gotten together to force an alliance between your son and my daughter."

Prince Henry smiled. "Wallace and I did entertain that hope long ago, as you know." His smile widened. "But won't she be surprised if you find it in your heart to listen to my plea?"

Dolores blushed, answering only part of his words. "I told the countess I was afraid Bella and David felt an instant antipathy to each other."

"They certainly seem to have," the prince answered slowly. "But you never can tell what might happen."

Dolores tried to read his thoughts. "What are you saying? You can't still hold any hope in that direction."

The prince replied slowly: "And if I did?"

Bella came inside the front door. "Where is my mother?" she asked the footman.

"I believe in the prince's study, miss."

"Go upstairs and find me paper and ink," Bella said. "I shall be there directly."

The young maid watched the proud Spanish-American girl march toward the prince's study. Bella stopped outside the closed door, looking back and motioning Sally upward. The maid moved slowly up the wide stairs as the prince spoke inside the room. His words stopped Bella with her hand on the doorknob.

"I realize they haven't gotten along all that well as yet, but it's early times," the prince was saying.

"All that well?" Dolores's voice came through the wood. "Henry, they have been very nearly at loggerheads since first sight!"

"And yet they could suit quite admirably. And you must admit David is capable of handling her."

Bella's hand froze on the doorknob as her mother replied: "David is truly the first person I have ever seen who seems able to match her strength and temper, I admit that."

"All this talk of marriage is making your cheeks glow, my dear," the prince said.

"Henry," Dolores said, and then a happy peal of laughter came through the closed door. "I simply can't believe what is happening."

"Why not, my dear? People get married all the time."

Bella turned away, all her questions answered. It was true; David had already spoken to them about her! And they were even discussing it with others as an accomplished fact. By tomorrow everyone would know. By tomorrow, or even tonight, he would speak to her. He despised her, but he was still planning on acquiring her fortune. He was a cad of the first water! He was so despicable he probably thought he had no need to have Isabella's agreement, that her mother's agreement was enough.

And he was right. They could force her to do it. How would she escape them all? She had no rights under the law. Once he asked formally, she could not end it without risking not only her own disgrace but her mother's as well. If her mother gave her word, Bella would have to comply.

Bella was certain her mother at least had not done that

yet. She had sounded a little doubtful, answering the prince. She would not sell Bella away without at least talking to her first. Isabella fled up the wide stairwell; she could not let her mother speak to her. She must be gone! George had been right all along! They had no choice.

Bella flew into the sitting room. Sally had placed paper on a small writing table in the bedroom and was now picking up the clothes Bella has strewn around the room. Sitting down, Bella wrote quickly.

> *Dearest,*
> *You were right, I must leave or all is lost. Meet me across from the north portico as soon as it's dark.*
> *Your Bella*

She blotted and folded the note.

"Sally, you must take this at once, as fast as you can. Here's change for a hansom cab—"

"A cab, miss?" Sally's eyes grew round. "I've never been in a cab alone, miss." She looked frightened.

"Then it will be a new experience for you," Bella told the girl impatiently. "Now go quickly! Slip out the kitchens and run toward Oxford Road as fast as ever you can. You'll see cabs there. You ask to go to the Stag and Hounds in Charing Cross and ask for Mr. Miller."

"Mr. Miller?"

"George Miller. You must get this to him at once. Do you understand?"

"I understand, Miss Isabella, but I'm not supposed to leave you."

"I am ordering you to go. There'll be no problem," Bella promised.

"They'll sack me for sure, miss, when they see you gone without me."

"Then you must come with me. Where are your things?"

"My things, miss? In the dressing room."

"I shall pack for both of us while you're gone," Bella told her.

Sally stared at Bella. Reluctantly, she took the note Bella handed over. "You won't abandon me, miss?"

"Never!"

Bella hurried the girl toward the back stairs and the servants' halls below. Then, moving swiftly, she returned to their suite, rummaging through the trunk room for a small valise. She found it and then heard Connie in the hall outside. Bella slipped back into her own bedroom, moving quietly to pack a change of clothes.

There was a tap on her door after a few minutes. Bella thrust the bag she was filling beneath the bed. "Yes?"

Connie looked in. "I didn't know you were up here. I was looking for Sally to help me with some sewing."

"I sent her on an errand to the kitchens for some headache powder. I'd like to be alone," Bella said coldly.

Connie stared at the girl she'd known since birth. Seeing Bella's cold expression, Connie mistook it for pain. "I'll go hurry her, shall I?"

"No! Consuela, I am training the girl, and I can handle the situation properly all by myself! Or am I not even to be allowed to train my own servants?"

"All right, all right. I hope she gets back soon, that's all I can say," Connie told Isabella.

"So do I!" Bella snapped.

Connie shut the door with decided asperity. Bella reached for the valise and walked into the dressing room, looking about for Sally's things.

It was over an hour later when Sally slipped back into the house. On her way up the back stairs she ran into Connie. "Is she feeling any better?" the duenna asked the young maid.

"Begging your pardon?" Sally looked guilty of some dark crime. She almost cringed back from the Spanish maid.

"After the headache powders. Is her headache better?"

"I don't know, ma'am," Sally said. She sounded frightened.

"Well, go see, girl, go see! She was in a proper state earlier. We don't want her upset with us, now do we?"

"Oh, no, ma'am!" Sally dropped a curtsy to the older maid, hampered by the close quarters on the steps. She picked up her skirts and fled upward toward Isabella.

Bella was lying on her bed when Sally opened the door. "Oh, miss, are you ill?"

Bella's eyes opened. She sat up, reaching for the girl's hands. "I thought you were Connie or my mother. Tell me everything!"

Sally looked dubious. "Everything?"

Impatience looked back at the maid. "Hurry! Tell me what happened! Did you see him? Did you give him the note?"

"Yes, miss," Sally said slowly, "I did."

"What did he say? Did he send me a message?"

Sally handed it over. "I was just going to—"

But Bella was no longer listening. She tore open the note, reading swiftly.

> *Dearest Bella,*
> *I love you! I shall be in the side street by the north portico as soon as it's dark. Come to me, beloved.*
> *Your George*

Bella hugged Sally. "You have saved my life, and I shall never forget you for it. Never!"

"I hope not, miss, because Mr. Tate will kill me for sure if I stay here."

"You will not stay," Bella said boldly. "You will come with me and stay as long as you live!"

"Oh, thank you, miss! Does that mean I'm to live with Indians, miss?"

"Sally, what are you talking about?"

"They say as how you live with red Indians. And live in tepees," Sally told her employer.

"Nonsense! We have a thirty-room hacienda and all the land as far as the eye can see. And servants to wait on servants!"

Sally's amazement came out in her voice. "Oh, miss, truly?"

"Truly! Now, the next step is for us to act normal until nightfall," Bella told her maid.

"I don't know if I can." Sally very nearly wailed the words.

"Then you will stay far away from my mother and Connie. You will stay here with me," Bella said. "Nothing is going to stop our leaving this very night," she said firmly.

The afternoon was agonizingly long for Bella. She stayed shut up in her bedroom, reading when none were about, feigning sleep when any looked in to see how she was feeling. Sally sat by the bed, looking so concerned about her young mistress that even Connie unbent enough to tell the girl not to worry so, that Isabella was not as ill as all that.

Dolores and Connie were in the ladies' day room when one of the downstairs maids tapped on the door and entered. Dropping a curtsy, she moved to the windows as a footman came behind her, lighting the lamps.

"Begging your pardon, ma'am, we'll only be a moment."

"That's all right," Dolores said, standing up. She handed the last of her thank-you letters and calling cards to Connie. "I think we are quite caught up on our correspondence."

The two women walked out into the long gallery, heading toward the stairs so that Dolores could change for dinner.

"It's a nice change, a night or two at home," Connie said.

Dolores turned toward her servant, smiling softly. "You are almost developing an English accent, Connie."

"Me? Bah! Never. I wouldn't wish the way they talk on a dog."

"What would you think of spending part of each year here?" Dolores asked shyly.

Connie took her time answering. "I think I'd best stay at home and keep the girls in line. That is, if I ever get home. My poor stomach isn't ready to forgive me yet for coming across in the first place. It would surely turn on me forever if it thought I was going to keep doing such a horrid thing."

They reached the sitting room, Dolores looking toward Bella's closed door. "Do you think we should wake her?"

"No, señora. She looked peaked. I remember when you used to get those blazing headaches. I think we should let her sleep. We can send up a bite later."

"You're probably right," Dolores said. She yawned, covering her mouth with her patrician hand. "I think I shall make it an early evening myself. Prince Henry's declaration has quite overset me."

"You won't be hurt by a quiet evening. This next week looks to be busy from morning to night."

"Yes. Well, there's no help for it. To go to some and not all the parties to which we are invited is bound to slight someone, and we don't want to do that," Dolores said.

"I don't see why not," Connie replied grumpily. "Besides, if you say no to the prince's offer of marriage, we'll never see any of them again after we leave. Because mark me, *she* won't be staying on unless you do."

Dolores looked troubled. "You sound so very sure of that."

"As sure as I'm standing here. Bella will never pick one of those pale young Englishmen who've been following her around."

"What about David?"

Consuela looked as if Dolores was demented. "Especially not the duke! I can't imagine how you and the prince can even think about that. I don't know which dislikes the other more. There'll be no marriage in that quarter, señora. And you yourself have heard her gossiping about the others with that Millie girl. She'll have none of them."

Bella might have been heartened if she had heard Connie's words. But while Consuela spoke and helped Dolores dress for dinner, two maids in uniforms and warm-hooded cloaks slipped out the kitchen door far to the back of the north side of Exeter House.

They walked hurriedly along the pavement, their heads down until they saw the hansom cab waiting on the opposite side of the street. The taller of the two started across the street toward the cab, the shorter one quickly following.

George Miller stood looking toward the portico, waiting for Bella's appearance. A young driver held the reins, ready to urge the horses forward. "I don't see why your boss couldn't come himself," George was saying irritably.

The young driver found the American's accent funny. He grinned a little as he replied, "He doesn't tell me the why of things, sir. Only as how I should double-quick you anywhere you wanted to go."

George glanced at the two maids, seeing a fresh young English face clearly in the lamplight, the taller girl's face hidden. He ignored them until they slowed. "Get away from here," he said. "The cab's taken."

In an execrable attempt at an English accent, the tall maid said: "Blimy, guv, don't yer want some company?"

George Miller was not entirely in charge of his emotions. Nervous that Isabella had not shown up yet, worried that someone in the house would spot him or that Bella would see others and flee back inside, he wasn't in a mood to flirt. "I said get out of here or I'll call the police!"

Giggles answered his angry words, Bella slipping the hood off her head and astounding her beau.

"Bella!" George was thunderstruck, his consternation visible. He tried to recover, grasping her hands. "Oh, Bella, get inside!"

Joshua came around the square, he and a young stableman leading the prince's favorite Arabian back from his afternoon exercise. The boy saw the two maids step up into the waiting hansom. "Gor, lookee the ones as is playing at being rich, will you?"

Joshua's eyes narrowed. "I wonder whose maid can afford to traipse about in cabs, then."

"Aye, well, the short one's one of ours. The new tweeny, she is. Sally Boyd's her name," young Tim said.

The old stableman led the way past the cab and toward the stables in the mews behind Exeter House as the cab started away. Joshua was grinning at his companion. "And how be you knowing that's young Sally from this distance and all covered up? What you been up to, young 'un? And why is she carrying a valise, then? What have you done that's gotten her sacked?"

Tim blushed in the evening shadows. "I ain't done nothing," he told the old man. It was against the rules, and he wasn't about to get himself and Sally turned out of the house. "I just know her walk. And she's not sacked. She wouldn't be taking a cab if she were. She's delivering something for her new mistress, like as not."

"You know her walk from watching it enough, I'll warrant," Joshua ribbed him. They turned into the Exeter

House mews as the hansom cab left the square and headed toward the north.

Inside the cab Bella threw off her cloak entirely, showing George the uniform. "Isn't it horrid? Oh, it's not horrid on you, Sally, of course. In fact, you look quite fetching and sweet. But it's too small and too short for me. I'll warrant I look the fool!" She was laughing happily at the thought.

George held both her hands, telling her nothing could dim her beauty. But his gaze kept shifting to the real maid. "As soon as we reach the road we can let your maid out."

"Out?" Bella searched his face. "Why on earth would we do that?"

"Oh, miss! You said you never would!" Sally wailed.

"Hush, girl," George said sternly. His eyes went back to Bella. "Darling, we don't want any to know which way we're going or what road we're taking or what we're about. She can go back. By the time she arrives we will be away and safe."

"Nonsense," Bella said.

"They won't catch up with us," George told her. "Never fear."

"I should hope not. But George, I can't very well let Sally leave. It wouldn't be proper."

George started to speak and then thought better of the words. They were still too close to Exeter House, and he didn't want Bella bolting now when victory was so close. Trying to hide his irritation, the American leaned to kiss Isabella's gloved hand. "Whatever you say, my love. Your wish is my command."

Bella sighed, her pleasure filling the cab as she leaned back and smiled at Sally. "We are going to have an adventure, Sally!"

Sally looked much less happy. "That's what I was afraid of, miss." The young maid looked out at the city passing around them. It might have been her imagination, but she thought the traffic was already thinning out. She looked toward the dark hills ahead, wondering what was to happen to them and if she would be blamed. She should have said no. She should have told someone. She should have done something.

Tears welled up in her eyes. Bella saw Sally swipe at her eyes and reached across the seat for her hand. "Sally, whatever is wrong with you?"

Sally stared into George's eyes and swallowed. "Nothing, miss. I'm just happy for you, that's all."

"Well, good. Now dry your eyes and blow your nose. There aren't supposed to be tears shed until the wedding ceremony." As she said the words a pain smote at Bella's heart. Imagining what her mother would think, what she would feel, Bella lost her smiles.

"Bella, dearest heart, what is it?" George asked anxiously, leaning closer. He was ready to chuck Sally out of the carriage if she was giving Isabella second thoughts.

Isabella tweaked at the glove on her left hand, her eyes downcast. "I was thinking about my mother when she realizes I'm gone. She'll worry until she hears from us, until she knows all is well. I should have left a note." Bella thought about it. "But it wouldn't have helped her pain. She would still think I had gone against all reason. She is going to be terribly hurt."

"She has forced you to it!" George said dramatically.

"Oh, George, yes!" Bella turned to him. "When I tell you what I heard today you will see that I had no choice! I had to flee immediately before he spoke for me and she accepted, for I could not go back on my mother's word! He might have spoken tonight!" She shivered with the thought.

George helped her pull the wool cloak closer about her shoulders as she leaned back, excited and dejected by turns as she told him of the day's events.

At Exeter House the prince and Dolores had a quiet dinner with David, who arrived back late from his club. He looked to be out of sorts during dinner, rousing himself to nothing but the most desultory conversation when they retired to the parlor for after-dinner sherry.

In the kitchen Consuela waited for a cup of hot cocoa, getting to know the cook a bit. Idly, she asked where Sally was.

"Young Sally, miss?" the cook answered. "I've not seen her this evening." The rotund woman handed over the steaming cup of chocolate, placing it on the tray with the Spanish maid's help.

"I'd best see how my young mistress is and spell Sally so that she can have her dinner," Connie said.

Connie took the back stairs slowly, unused to the stairs of English houses. Out of breath by the time she walked down the upper corridor and entered the guest suite, she longed for the one-level haciendas of home.

Placing the tray of cocoa on a sitting room table, Connie tapped on Isabella's door, opening it as she spoke. "I thought you might . . ." No one was in the bedroom.

Connie glanced toward the open door to the empty dressing room and then crossed to the large bathroom, the beginnings of fear in the back of her mind.

The rooms echoed with silence. They were gone. Connie's heart stopped and then began to thud against her rib cage. Isabella was gone! *"Madre de Dios!"* Her voice rose loud in the silent room.

And then she ran for the hall, for the stairs and the parlor below where Dolores and the others sat quietly sipping their sherry.

Chapter Twelve

They're gone!" Connie's frantic words burst out as she stood in the parlor doorway. Three pairs of eyes turned toward her, startled.

David recovered first. He was on his feet as his father asked what on earth Connie was saying.

Dolores had turned pale, her hand going to her throat. "Connie—you can't mean—"

"She's run away!" Connie wailed. "She and the young maid, Sally. They're gone! That fiend must have gotten hold of her!"

At Connie's words the prince turned to glare at his son. "Well?" the prince thundered.

David gave his father a small smile. "There's nothing to worry about," he told them all.

"How can you say that?" his father asked, incredulous.

"Because I know where he's been staying and how to find him," David told his father.

"David!" Dolores looked confused. "How can you possibly?"

"I have not left things to the fates, dear lady," David replied. "I have insured that the man can do nothing without my being apprised of his actions."

The prince was nonplussed. "Are you saying you knew she was gone and said nothing?"

"No," David answered, "of course not. But I made it my business to know this Miller's plans, and there is nothing to fear."

"Nothing to fear?" Dolores stared at the younger man.

"After all, her maid is with her," David said.

"Her maid!" Connie spit the words out. "I knew not to trust that chit! She is too young by half, and too shy, and too easily led by the nose. Look what's happened!" The old duenna looked from one to the other in the small parlor. "Well?" she demanded. "Who's going after her?"

The prince began to move, his son stopping him. "There is no need, Father. I shall bring her back safe and sound. Never fear. As a matter of fact, one of my men is with them now."

"David, I don't like the sound of this at all," his father told him. "You say you didn't know she was gone, but you have a man with her. How?"

"I've had the man with Miller ever since he tried to contact Bella at the lawn party."

"What are you talking about?" Dolores asked David. She looked from him to the prince. "Henry, what does he mean, Miller was at a lawn party?"

Prince Henry looked unhappy. "It's rather a long story," he began.

Dolores was upset. "I demand to know what has been going on!"

"So do I!" the prince replied. He turned toward David, who was walking toward the door. "Where are you going?" his father demanded.

"To bring her back," David said. He almost sounded casual.

"Well, hurry, man, hurry!" the prince urged.

David stopped. "Father, Dolores, please listen to me. She must be protected, yes. But she must be alone with the cad long enough to see for herself his true colors."

"Alone with him!" Dolores was shocked.

"With her maid, of course," David said. "She will never believe us about him. He must prove his villainy to her."

"Sir," Dolores flared, "you are speaking of teaching my daughter a lesson by endangering her safety and her reputation!"

"Yes," David replied, "I am."

"By what right have you made these decisions without informing me? I am her mother!" Dolores told him, her dark eyes blazing.

"By the right of her future husband," David said calmly.

Connie nearly fainted. Dolores stared at him. The prince opened and then closed his mouth.

David continued speaking: "However, there is no possible way to marry her if she is still enamored of this cad Miller."

"I agree," Dolores interrupted, "but she must be protected from herself and her own foolhardy actions!"

David shook his head. "Forgive me, Dolores, but that is exactly what is wrong with her. She has been overindulged, overprotected. She has been so protected from the results of her own foolish actions that she has become ever more foolhardy—now to the point of endangering her reputation and possibly even herself. Or she would have been endangered, if I had not taken precautions."

"You are saying this is all for her own good," Dolores said doubtfully.

"He's right about one thing," Connie put in. "There's no way she'd believe us about that scoundrel."

"If he thinks he has her at his mercy, his true colors will come out," David assured them.

"You're quite sure this is the right thing to do?" Dolores asked the duke.

"It is the only thing to do," David replied.

None spoke for a long moment. Then Dolores turned to the prince. "Henry, do you agree?"

The prince struggled for an answer. "I'm not quite sure that any servant can protect her from that Miller. I'm afraid something could go amiss, and then it would not be in her best interests at all."

As Prince Henry voiced his fear Dolores turned back to his son. "David?"

"I am not trusting it to servants. I shall be there myself to insure she comes to no harm."

"Then you know where they are headed," Henry said.

"Of course," David replied. "He intends to take her to Gretna Green."

"My God!" The prince was horrified.

"What are you saying?" Dolores asked fearfully.

"He is attempting to elope with her," the duke told Dolores.

"No! But that's terrible. They may have been gone for hours! How will you find them? How will you catch up with them? They must have already boarded the train!"

"They are not boarding a train. Miller wants to ensure his privacy with Isabella. He is taking her by coach."

"My God," Dolores said, horrified. "Are you saying she is alone with an unmarried cad in his carriage?"

"No, Dolores, her maid is with her." David smiled. "And my own man has paid off the owner of the coach and is the driver. Have no fear; he has his instructions, and he shall only tarry at designated inns."

"Inns!" Connie was shocked. *"Public* inns?"

"David," Dolores implored him, "please leave now. Please see to her safety."

"Do you entrust her to me?" David asked.

"Yes, yes—please—"

"Dolores, I must have a free hand with her. You must trust me utterly. No matter how strange what I am doing seems."

"David," his father began, "I don't want you taking any chances with that girl's safety."

"I shan't, Father. But I must do it my own way."

"Yes, anything," Dolores said, "only please—hurry!"

David went to Dolores and took her hands. "Never fear, all will be well. And I shall send word as soon as the cad is sent packing. But we may not be back immediately. You must not worry. I know what I am doing."

With that the Duke of Exeter left the room, all three occupants of the small, cozy parlor watching his broad back as he walked away.

Consuela sat down hard, propriety forgotten as she stared up at her mistress. "Heaven help us all," she said, "the man is demented."

The prince rather agreed, but he kept his thoughts to himself as he moved to reassure Dolores. "I shall insist he be careful," Henry said before he left the room.

Markham, the duke's valet, was coming down the stairs, a valise in each hand. "Where is my son?" Henry asked the man.

"I believe he is speaking to Joshua, Your Highness."

The prince and the valet walked outside together, interrupting David's conversation with the stableman.

"Well?" the prince asked, and then he realized David's and Markham's mounts were ready and waiting. "What's this?"

David motioned Markham forward, the valet arranging the valises in the saddlebags. "I made the arrangements long beforehand, Father," David replied.

Henry stared at his son. "You knew she was gone at dinner, didn't you?"

The duke hesitated. "Actually, I knew before I arrived home this evening," he said honestly.

"David, you have been blasted high-handed about this! Why the devil didn't you say something?"

"Because they must have enough head start so that she thinks herself truly alone with him and well away from capture. Only then will his true intentions come out, and only then will she believe the worst of him."

"This is a dangerous piece of business!" Prince Henry thundered.

"I agree," David said dryly. "This situation was not of my making, Father. I am merely attempting the only plan that might work."

"Might?"

David shrugged. "Some females prefer scoundrels."

"Never! Never Dolores's daughter!" the prince told his son, David's brow rising quizzically at his father's choice of words.

"Is that how it is?" David asked his father, humor lighting his eyes. "I wondered about you and the señora."

"What we are discussing is your meddling, not my friendships," Henry told his son tartly. The prince looked away, his eyes straying to the Georgian row houses across the square. "That busybody is probably peering out even as we speak."

David allowed his father to skirt around his question. "I think I had best leave."

"Yes, you had!" Henry snapped. "It was your harebrained idea to let Bella meet the man, so this is your responsibility. Send word immediately you find her!"

"I shall, Father. And never fear. No harm will come to her beyond a scare, which will do her worlds of good."

"I pray you're right," Henry told his son. "And I trust that when you rescue her you will not put her into further danger."

The duke hesitated. "Whatever my plans, you need have no fear for her."

"David, I don't trust the sound of that." Prince Henry gave his son a piercing look, trying to read the prideful young man's attentions.

"Then, trust me, Father," David said simply. He smiled a little before turning away and rising to his horse. Markham was already mounted and waiting.

The prince watched them pull away before he went back inside toward the very worried Dolores.

While Exeter House's other inhabitants were concerned for her safety, Isabella was staring out at the moonlit landscape that passed beyond the hansom cab. The cob's steady clip-clop marched north along the great artery, passing little traffic now that they were well clear of the city.

"I can see only a few lights in the distance now," she told her riding companions. A heady mixture of freedom and naughtiness shivered up her spine.

Across from them in the large, covered hired carriage Sally looked from Isabella to the man who sat beside her. George Miller was impatient, and it showed. His expression was tense, his eyes cold when he happened to glance toward the maid whom he had not counted upon having with them.

The young driver had been rehearsed in his own role once they reached the first inn. And told of the dire results if he did not obtain what Miller wanted.

Miller himself was pulling out his pocket watch, frowning

when he saw the hour. "We should be there by now," he said out loud.

"Truly?" Bella looked a little alarmed. "I thought it was rather far."

"I mean to the first inn. It will be two nights, possibly three before we reach Gretna Green." George looked at the maid. "Where do we go once we are there?" he asked the girl.

Sally stared at him. "Me, sir? How would I be knowing, sir?"

"Never mind," he said irritably, "the driver will help. Although why we're not making better time, I don't understand."

"Wouldn't it have been quicker to go by train?" Bella asked.

George smiled. "They will expect that. They will use the wireless and try to find us, but we shall not be there!" He sounded very self-satisfied until he remembered the slow progress they were making. His thoughts brought back to the driver, George Miller rapped on the small overhead door, opening it with his cane. "Can't you move any faster, man?"

"Sorry, guv, she's an old one, and it's a long way. Don't want her throwing a shoe or sumpin' and getting us stranded out here, now do we?"

"Well, do what you can!" George said snappishly.

"Oh, I will, guv," the young driver said as George let the trap door fall shut. The driver leaned back on his high perch, smiling to himself. "I will indeed, your worship."

Tunelessly, he hummed to himself as he let the cob take her time down the dusty road, the way ahead lit only by the swaying carriage lamps.

Chapter Thirteen

*I*t was late when the hired carriage pulled into a darkened inn yard. The driver jumped down and stretched before reaching to pull down the carriage steps and open the door for the nobs inside.

"Here you go, then," the young man said. He reached a hand to help Isabella, Sally staying close behind her mistress as they stepped down.

A light shone from a low window near the front door of the small thatched-roof inn. George went past the others to pound on the door.

"Good gracious, George, you shall wake the dead!"

A bolt was slipped back within, the thick door opening to show a potbellied man staring out at them. His clothes were rumpled, as was his hair, his wide face framed by Dundreary whiskers. "Sorry, guv'nor, didn't hear you arrive."

"I don't know how you could help it," George said sourly.

The innkeeper heard the man's strange accent and looked past him to the coach driver, who made a face in answer. George was reaching toward the innkeeper, shoving something into the man's hand. Bella, behind and seeing to the driver and her bag, did not see; but Sally watched as the innkeeper looked down at his hand.

"I trust you have two rooms available," George said, winking at the man. "We need two, not just one," George said, his eyes never leaving the man's face.

The man stared at him and then nodded, smiling. He pocketed the money. "Ah, and it's sorry I am, but I've only one this night."

Bella reached George's side. "One will not do! How far is the next inn?"

"Much too far at this hour, my lady," the innkeeper said.

"Nonsense," she said crisply. She looked back toward the driver. "Don't bother to unhitch the horse, we must press on," she continued, earning a glowering look from George.

"We can't—" George Miller began, only to be cut off by Bella.

"We *must*," she insisted. "I cannot spend the night in the same room as an unmarried man!"

The innkeeper looked ready to change his mind, but the young coach driver spoke first: "I'm sorry, miss, but there ain't no way Bess can keep going tonight. She's plumb tuckered."

George relaxed a little. "There's no choice but to stay, dearest."

Bella made an impatient sound and moved toward the door, entering the low-ceilinged main room. "I suppose you're right," she said. "You shall have to spend the night down here."

George smiled. "Of course, my dear."

"Shall I see to some cold supper for you, sir?" the innkeeper asked.

"Bella, do you feel like having a bite of something?"

"We'd best." She eyed the corpulent innkeeper. "Is your kitchen quite clean?"

"Oh, yes, my lady."

"Well, then," she replied, "a bit of cold chicken and bread and some weak tea should be sufficient."

"Yes, my lady." The innkeeper bowed to her as she swept past him and toward the stairs.

"Now you may show me to my room," Bella told him. "I shall eat there once I've bathed. Sally, come along."

The innkeeper took the two women up the narrow wooden stairs, George staying below. Looking around himself, he rubbed his hands together, a half smile forming as he contemplated the coming night and the victory he would soon have. After this night, no matter what her mother attempted, she could not stand in their way. Once this night was over none would think to offer for Bella's sullied hand, least of all some titled Englishman. Men the world over wanted virtuous, blameless girls for their wedded wives, not young women with stained reputations.

George was standing near the inn's long scarred-wood bar, grinning wide, when the driver walked inside.

"And are we to bed down here, then, guv?"

"Do as you like," George said. "I shall be above before long."

The young man's eyes widened. "Is that how it is, then?"

George grinned, feeling quite the man of the world. "You'd best believe it. She may be a mite surprised when she wakes to find me beside her in bed, but I'll warrant she'll have no complaints before the night is over," George bragged.

The driver went behind the bar, reaching for a tankard. "Would you like me to draw you a spot of ale? For strength, guv?"

George shrugged. "Why not? I've got an hour or so to while away." As he spoke the innkeeper hustled down the steps as fast as his girth would allow.

"See to yourselves, then, lads," the man said, "me good wife is in bed, and soon your ladies will be, too."

A horrible thought flew into George's brain. He moved quickly to stop the man before he moved through the door into the kitchen. "Hold on there. You did see the maid to a room of her own, didn't you?"

"I showed her to the servants' room, guv'nor. There's only one other wench there, so they'll have plenty of room."

George relaxed a little and took a long swig from his tankard of ale. Moving to the front, he sat down on a wooden chair.

The innkeeper came back from the kitchen with the tray of food and tea. Taking it to the bedroom he had given Bella, he tapped on the door. Sally opened it, taking the tray and shutting the hall door in the man's face.

Bella was undressing, pulling a robe over her petticoats and looking around the room. "This isn't very tidy," she told the maid.

"The food's here, miss," Sally replied.

"Are you all right?" Bella asked. "You sound strange."

Sally bit her lip and worried about whether to speak her heart or to keep shut. "I can't leave you here alone, miss."

"What?" Bella sat down at a table, Sally bringing the tray to her. The maid helped with napkin and plate covers. "Sally, stop fussing about. Sit down and eat a bite."

"I couldn't eat a thing, miss!"

"You can and you shall. You must. I don't want you fainting away on me in the morning. We have a long way to go."

"A long way," Sally repeated, looking terribly unhappy.

"What is it?" Bella demanded.

Sally stared at the beautiful Spanish-American girl. "Oh, miss, I'm just so scared!"

"There is nothing to be scared of," Bella reassured her.

"I'm not scared for me! I'm scared for you," Sally wailed.

Bella stared at the girl in surprise. "Whatever for?"

"Miss Isabella, he has you all alone out here!"

Bella started to reply and then stopped. Seeing the girl's frightened face, she felt the stirrings of a heavy unease within her own heart. "I admit this is not a good situation," Bella began, "but George would never have put me in this situation on purpose." Sally didn't reply. She also didn't look convinced.

Bella continued: "This was my idea, after all. This was forced upon us by my mother and that odious duke!"

"He didn't have to go all alone to an out-of-the-way inn! We could have been safe on a train!" Sally burst out.

"He couldn't know there wouldn't be more rooms."

"Look outside! Look around you," Sally said. "There's no one about."

"Sally, it's the middle of the night!" Bella protested.

"What of the horses? If the inn were full, there'd be carriages and horses!"

Isabella considered the girl's words. She had absolute faith in George. But she had to admit to herself that the situation would look very bad were it to be known. Her mother would never approve of any of this, but she would be totally appalled if Isabella did not at least keep up the proprieties. George did not understand, that was all it was.

He hadn't realized the position he would have put her in if her maid had been left behind. He was so in love with her, he wasn't thinking about the practical considerations. It was always up to the women to ensure that all was proper.

"I see your meaning," Isabella told the girl. "Men oftentimes simply don't think about how things will look. They are engaged in more important thoughts."

Sally bit back the words that came to her tongue; she had seen more of men than Bella, and she wasn't blinded by love. She could see straight through the devious American man who was trying to ruin her mistress.

"There's not truly a problem," Isabella said. "You will simply sleep here with me tonight."

"Can we lock the door, miss?"

"Sally!" Bella's eyes blazed. "Are you casting aspersions on the man I love?"

Sally's eyes slid away from Bella's angered gaze. "I don't know, miss."

"Well, pray do not! I shan't hear it, and I shall order you out if you say one more word on this subject!"

"Yes, miss." Sally bobbed a half curtsy and moved to plump the thin feather pillows and bolsters on the bed. She pulled the covers down and readied it for Bella.

Isabella herself ate a few bites of chicken and sipped the hot tea. She thought about the end of this headlong trip, her stomach feeling strangely queasy when she did. Telling herself she was tired and it was late, she ignored the feelings and stood up, leaving the rest of the meal for Sally.

Isabella climbed into the lumpy bed as Sally began to undress and, belowstairs, George shared another ale and some very masculine laughter with the innkeeper. He accepted a third ale and then a fourth, building his courage for what was to come.

The young man who had driven the coach was outside. After taking one look at the room set aside for male servants, he had decided to doze inside the carriage, stretching out on the seat and waiting for the arrival of the man who had sent him on this adventure.

It was long after midnight when George Miller finally screwed up enough courage to make his way up the stairs to the room above. He had even thought of waiting until the next night of the trip, but the innkeeper had stayed up to urge him on and now watched, grinning, as George started upstairs.

"It's the first door at the top of the stairs. Get her good," the innkeeper called out in a loud whisper. "You should start out with a wench in the way you want to go on, lad. Don't let her get the better of you, or you'll have a deuce of a time later."

With the innkeeper's advice ringing in his ears, George squared his shoulders and headed toward the door at the top of the stairs.

Inside the room Bella slept soundly, tired from the day's excitement and strain. Sally lay on a pallet between the tall wooden bed and the small fireplace. A few embers still glowed but gave off no light.

The door knob screeched when George twisted it. Sally's head swiveled toward the door, her breath caught in her throat. It opened slowly; a lamp set on a hall table outlined George's figure as he hesitated in the doorway. Sally squeezed her eyes shut, praying he would leave, and then she could not stand the silence and the suspense.

She opened them to see George as he closed the door and crept forward toward the bed. He was removing his jacket and cravat as he moved, letting them drop to the floor.

Sally was so frightened she forgot to breathe. She prayed Bella would wake up, but this prayer was not answered either. When he began to unbutton his shirt the maid could stand it no longer.

Sally began to cough. Loud. Her first sharp sound nearly

frightened George out of his wits. He froze where he was. Squinting, trying to see through the darkness, he stood stock-still, afraid Bella was awakening too soon.

As it happened, she was awakening; she'd been brought awake by the sudden loud sounds that were continuing. Isabella reached for the bedside lamp and raised the wick.

The light blazed, Isabella sitting up to see George standing half-undressed and coming toward her bed. George saw Bella on the bed, staring at him with horrified eyes, and Sally on the floor, her eyes squeezed tight shut.

"George! What are you doing in here?"

"I—ah—I—" He fumbled for some kind of explanation. "I must be walking in my sleep," he finally managed to say.

Bella was still staring at him. "You aren't asleep," she pointed out.

George stood where he was.

"Your clothes are all over the floor," Bella said coldly.

"Darling!" George decided to try to brazen it out. He came toward Bella, seeing her shrink back against the headboard. "My darling, I can't stand to be apart any longer!"

The end of his sentence was punctuated by another loud fit of coughing. In that moment he would have gladly strangled the young maid with his bare hands. Bella moved off the bed and reached to touch the girl's forehead.

"George, you're being perfectly ridiculous," Bella told him with a good deal of asperity. "Sally, get up from there. There's a draft, and you'll catch your death." Sally allowed Bella to pull her to her feet. Avoiding the American man's angry eyes, the maid did as she was bid, letting Bella lead her to the bed and pull the covers up around her chin. The girl caught George's eye and gave another not-very-convincing cough.

A muscle worked in George's square jaw, his eyes ugly with irritation and anger. Bella ignored him as she helped her maid.

"There's nothing wrong with her, Bella. And she can't sleep in the bed with you!" George spat the words out.

"Of course not," Bella replied. "It would be most uncomfortable for her. She shall have the bed, and I shall take this extra blanket to the chair." Suiting action to words, she drew a fireside chair nearer the bed and sat down, wrapping the blanket around herself. "You may take the pallet, George. You'll need it downstairs."

"I'll wake the innkeeper and have him ready another room for you," George said. "You can't stay here if she is ill. You might catch her cold."

"There aren't any rooms. You heard the innkeeper. We can't very well throw someone out of a room in the middle of the night. Dear George, we must do as I said. You certainly don't want poor Sally to suffer more than need be."

Frustrated, George Miller glared at Bella. Then he reached to the floor and grabbed the rest of his clothing before coming around to grab the pallet.

As he started out the door, Bella called out to him, "It's perfectly dreadful that you must sleep below and not in your own snug room. But you know there's only this one room, so you must make the best of it below."

Miller ground his teeth. He would have to spend the night on the blasted pallet or risk having her know he lied. Or worse, having her find out he had paid the innkeeper to lie.

"Good night," he managed to say between clenched teeth before he closed the door and went back below.

After the door closed Sally sat up. "Miss, you can't stay in the chair all night."

"Oh, yes I can," Bella told her maid. She looked toward the closed hall door. "I think it's safer. But before I do, come help me push that table in front of the door."

Sally jumped up. "Oh, thank you, miss!"

"No. Thank *you,* Sally. I cannot understand what he was thinking of!"

"I can," Sally said darkly, earning a look from Bella, but no words came with it.

Downstairs the main room was cold and empty, the fire

long out. George threw the pallet in front of the fireplace and sat down upon it. It was hard. Swearing to himself, he lay back, feeling the chill drafts that skirted across the flagstone floor. He would probably die of pneumonia in this godforsaken country, he was telling himself when he drifted off into an uneasy sleep.

Chapter Fourteen

Morning's first light found the young coach driver snoring on the back bench of the hired carriage. His innocent dreams of cakes and ale were interrupted by a hand pressing his mouth closed just as he was about to take a long swallow.

His brain, foggy with sleep, told his eyes to open. Groggy, he stared up at a giant. His breath strangled, his brain cleared with his panic, and he saw clearly the features of the man who had hired him.

David released his hold, straightening up. "Good morning. I didn't want you to cry out and alert the good innkeeper too soon."

"Gor, you scared me wits outa me head!"

The Duke of Exeter settled himself on the bench the lad was vacating. "I hope you're awake, because you must listen very carefully."

The boy's eyes lit up. "I'll be all right, your worship. Just tell me what to do, and it'll be done."

The innkeeper's wife and daughter were stirring in the kitchen at the back of the small inn, starting the kettles for hot water and porridge. The daughter was as round and plain as her parents, with big hands and big feet as well as a big heart within her ample bosom.

She heard her father coming in from the yard. "I've already seen to the milk, Da." She spoke as she turned and, in the turning, saw a tall, thin stranger in the doorway. "Who are you?"

Her mother looked up from stirring the porridge. She kept the wooden ladle moving smoothly so that the porridge wouldn't stick and burn. "Good morning to ye," the girl's mother said.

"And good morning to you, madam," Markham said, the women hearing a fine, fancy accent. "I wonder if I could ask a small favor of you." The valet's eyes went back to the younger woman.

She was wiping her hands on her apron. "Such as?"

He looked a little hesitant. "It's like this, you see. My sweetheart's abovestairs. I have this note for her." He extended a small piece of folded and sealed paper toward the girl. "We were to be married, but her mistress wouldn't allow it."

The girl looked at the stiffly erect and very uncomfortable man. "I don't know if I should," she said, looking to her mother for direction.

The woman smiled at the ungainly-looking man. "I can't see where giving a girl a note is such a bad thing."

"Thank you, madam," he said fervently. "Thank you!"

The innkeeper's wife liked the way he spoke. None had ever called her madam before. "Go on with you, Lottie, do as the man asks and be quick about it."

Lottie took the note and moved off, Markham telling her mother he would wait in the common room out front. He thanked her again as he left, his relief obvious. The innkeeper's daughter came back, telling her mother he certainly didn't look to be the romantic type.

"Love goes where it's sent, and there's no way to tell who will be its victim," her mother replied.

Upstairs Sally was reading the note while Bella bathed. She read it twice and then stuck it deep within her pocket.

She sat down, surprising Bella when she turned around, asking for a towel.

"Sally? What's wrong?"

"I—I'm not sure, miss. Could I ask a favor of you, please?"

"Of course," Bella said a little impatiently. "What is it? What's wrong? What do you need?"

"It would be ever so much a kindness, miss, if you could fetch something for the stomachache from the innkeeper's wife."

"Sally, you're still feeling poorly, aren't you? Here, help me with these hooks and eyes and I shall run right down and tell them to prepare something. You can't very well ride with an upset stomach," Bella said.

A few minutes later Bella came out onto the landing. Below, George was drinking coffee with the innkeeper. Markham saw Bella coming down and turned his back, in case she might recognize him. He was facing George, and so he saw the American glance up and see Bella heading toward the kitchens in search of the stomach medicine.

George stood up, cutting the innkeeper's comments short and coming toward the door that led from the hall to the kitchen. Markham stepped in front of him, blocking the way. "Begging your pardon, sir, but I was wondering if you could help me with directions."

"No, I can't," George said, moving to step around the man.

"Just a moment, sir. I haven't explained where I need the directions to—"

"It doesn't matter!" George said testily. "I'm not from around here, can't you tell from my accent? Ask someone else!"

"Sir!" Markham insisted. With each move of George's, Markham stepped to block his path.

"Get out of my way!" George bellowed, the innkeeper coming near to stop a brawl.

In the kitchen the innkeeper's daughter was staring at the imperious-looking foreigner who was asking for her mother.

"She's in the henhouse," Lottie said, pointing out the back. Lottie watched the rich young woman sweep out the back door. Better that her mother deal with the woman than that poor Lottie have to take the abuse. She must have seen her maid's letter.

The henhouse stood next to the stables. Isabella lifted her skirts and crossed the yard, paying no attention to the hired carriage as it moved around the stables.

Clucking chickens and barnyard smells greeted Bella as she looked inside the large and lightless wooden shack. "Is someone there?" Bella called.

Light suddenly poured in from the other end of the henhouse, from a door opened and left ajar. Bella moved toward it, calling out. Beyond the door she saw the back of a large black carriage. She was ready to step outside when suddenly everything went dark.

"What—" She struggled against what had fallen on her, shoving at the sheet as a hand clamped down from outside the sheet to cover her mouth. Struggling with all the might she could muster, Isabella Castillo-Suera Alexander found herself being picked up and lugged outside.

She could tell she was outside because more light came through the sheet, and the air was fresh and clean. Battling all the way, Isabella was unceremoniously dumped into the waiting carriage, arms still around her, a hand still over her mouth.

She heard a rap on the roof of the carriage and felt the vehicle start away from the inn. Bella screamed and screamed against the foul hand that held her silent, small sounds escaping from his grasp.

In the inn, Markham saw the carriage moving around the side of the building and stopped the near-fist fight he had been engaged in with the American.

"Get out of my way!" George was screaming, his fist poised to flatten the other man's nose. Markham stepped back.

"If you're going to resort to fisticuffs, I don't know what to say," Markham said. Turning on his heel, he walked away toward the stairs, leaving a dumbfounded innkeeper and an enraged American behind him.

George moved quickly for the kitchen. The innkeeper, seeing his destination, asked if there was something he could get the gentleman.

Lottie looked up from stirring the porridge to see George Miller come through the door from the front. "You have the wrong door, sir. The dining room is—"

"Where is she?" he demanded.

Lottie stared at him. The maid must have slipped out. "I'm sorry, sir, I don't know who you mean," the girl said, red-faced.

"She just walked in here!" he thundered.

"Oh! Oh, you mean the lady, sir. She went out back."

The girl barely got the words out before the American was out the back door, calling Bella's name.

Upstairs the door to the room Bella and Sally shared was open as Sally finished packing. The maid looked up to see the duke's valet in the doorway. "What—"

"Hurry—there's no time to spare," the man said urgently. He took the valise from her and brought her out and down the stairs.

"But my mistress—"

"You're going to her," Markham told the girl without explaining.

The innkeeper came toward them, ready to stop them until his daughter called out to him from the kitchen doorway. "Da, they're the lovebirds!"

The man stopped. He watched Markham and Sally walk outside to waiting horses. "Have you ever ridden a horse?" Markham asked.

"No," the girl responded, eyeing the big brute fearfully.

"Well, you will now," Markham said practically. He lifted her to the saddle and swung up behind her, catching the other horse's reins and urging them forward.

"Where are you taking me?" Sally wailed, truly frightened.

"Look ahead up the road!" Markham commanded. "You see the carriage? His lordship has rescued your mistress."

"The duke?" she asked, and then she lapsed into silence. She couldn't imagine anything worse than having to spend another day and night with the horrible American man.

The American was at that very moment berating the innkeeper and all around as he saw the horses and, beyond them, the carriage disappearing down the road.

"I have to stop them!" he told the innkeeper.

"The coach for London is due within the hour," the innkeeper said.

"An hour! There must be a horse I can use—I'll buy it!" he told the man, pulling out the wad of currency Bella had brought him.

"Aye, perhaps there's a horse to be had."

"Move, man, move!" George insisted. He ran for his things as the innkeeper saddled a mare.

Inside the carriage whose cob had suddenly come to life this morning, Isabella felt the hand leaving her mouth as the carriage bowled down the road at a gallop. She struggled with the sheet, pulling it off her head and ready to do battle with the brigand who held her captive on his lap.

"You? Why you—you—" she sputtered, out of breath, her hair flying in sixteen directions, her dress wrinkled and missing buttons that had popped during her struggle.

"I think the words you are searching for are 'Thank you, David.'"

"Thank you! Why should I thank you?" Bella demanded.

The duke stared at her. "For rescuing you from the clutches of that cad, for one thing!"

"You must be demented! The only cad I know of is *you!"*

"How dare you?" David bellowed, affronted beyond measure. "I have ridden all night to save your reputation, not to mention your honor, and what do you say to me? You call me a cad!"

"I was perfectly safe, and you know it! George is my fiancé!" A vision of George entering her room the previous night flitted across her mind's eye, but she resolutely put it aside.

"Are you telling me he behaved like a gentleman?" David demanded.

"He is a gentleman!" Bella responded sharply.

"Ha! No gentleman abducts a woman from her family and carts her off to a clandestine marriage! That fortune hunter is no gentleman; he's just a little smarter than I gave him credit for—waiting for the ceremony before he consummates this nonsense."

"You would never understand," Bella told the duke. "You haven't a romantic bone in your body!"

"Oh, yes I do!" David said.

"Ha!"

David stared at her and then rapped on the roof, speaking to the coachman when he opened the trap door. "Take the next turning."

"But that's—"

"I know. Just take it!" David told the young man, and he let the door close. "You really look a sight," David said to Bella.

"I—!" Her outrage turned to fury. *"How dare you!"* She was still struggling to untangle her limbs from the sheet. "Unhand me this instant!" Obligingly, he spread his arms wide, grinning, watching as her mummy-wrapped body began to slide off his lap without the support. The more she struggled the more she slid. "Help me!"

"Certainly, my lady," the duke replied. "I was merely obeying your instructions," he told her with maddening logic. "You seem to be suffering a little confusion as to what you want from me."

"Help me get out of this mess, you pinch-brained, puffed-up popinjay, or by Jupiter, I shall make you rue you were born or hatched or whatever sorry process begat you!"

"Tsk, tsk, such language," David said placidly, "simply because I said your appearance was not all that it should be."

Bella's hand came up to slap the smile from his face, but he caught it before it reached its mark. "You, sir, are the most dastardly male I have ever had the bad luck to meet! You kidnap me from my fiancé, throw me about as if I were a bundle of carpeting, and then have the unmitigated gall to complain about my appearance!"

"In a bit of a tweak, are we?" he asked, holding her hand tight as it tried to move toward him.

"Tweak!" She very nearly croaked the word, her left hand rising and now caught by his right. She struggled against his grip.

The flannel sheet was twisted more and more tightly around her from her waist to her legs as she struggled in his lap. Her movements, wild with frustration and anger, were chafing her hips against his lap. He felt himself stirring. Their bodies, separated by the sheet and layers of clothing, were in intimate contact.

Her entire concentration was on her frustrated attempts to loosen his hold on her, and so she did not see the change in his eyes. His moods were mirrored in them. The stronger his emotions, the more dark his eyes became. At the moment they were deepest cobalt, his smile lost, his grip tightening on her wrists, chafing them as her hips and thighs moved against his own.

When he pulled her to him she struggled harder, her breast rubbing against his chest, increasing the tangled emotions that were now coursing through his veins.

She wasn't prepared for his lips capturing hers. Shock stilled her, her body frozen for one moment in time and then reacting, responding to the current that flooded through her. His lips seemed made of some kind of inner fire that burned in a way she had never before known existed. The fire engulfed her. It heated her blood and coursed through her limbs, melting her resistance.

The wild need David felt rising within him surprised him, his brain ringing out silent warnings. He felt the moment when Bella lost her anger, her sudden submission pushing him onward. His tongue invaded the sweet warmth of her mouth, forcing her lips apart.

Her body submitted to him even as her brain rebelled against her loss of control. The voice within told her she was being a fool, told her he was a cad of the first water, told her she would never forgive herself if she did not fight him with her last breath. But the voice was tinier and tinier, harder and harder to hear over the drumming of her blood that filled her ears.

Bella began to respond; her small tongue, tentative at first and then more and more aggressive, reached out to touch the very tip of his. His reaction was immediate, his arms crushing her closer, his hungry mouth more and more insistent. He felt himself spinning out of control and almost slipped over the edge.

From somewhere deep within he found the strength to pull away before he ravished her in the swaying carriage. The wrench of leaving her lips behind, of thrusting her arms from about him, made his movements harsh.

Bella's eyes flew open as the Duke of Exeter shoved her forcibly out of his arms and across to the opposite bench. Shock mixed into the longing neediness he had created within her. She stared at him, her eyes three feet away from his, their knees a bare twelve inches apart.

His voice was as harsh as his movements. "You'd best remove that sheet. It looks ridiculous."

If he had poured a bucket of cold water over her head, it would have been no worse. Isabella Alexander had lived for almost twenty-one years as the cosseted apple of every eye she saw. Her every whim had been indulged. The only important thing in which she had ever been crossed was her affection for George. And even in that, she knew she would eventually have her way.

And then this arrogant, odious, English duke rode into her life. Ever since that first morning he had gone out of his way to insult and upset her. Bella watched him now. His gaze was cool, civil, and uninvolved.

Her head rose, her chin held high. "I am waiting," she said.

The duke's brow rose slightly. "For?"

Her voice was frigid. "For an explanation of your inexcusable behavior."

"You fought too much," he said.

Isabella sat straighter. Her voice dripped sarcasm. "Please forgive me for having the termerity to resist you. I suppose your normal conquests behave differently."

"My . . . normal . . . conquests?"

"Don't look so smug, Your Grace!" Bella snapped. "You are a far cry from having any right to lord it over anyone!"

David's gaze flickered. He looked away from her, his face a mask. "It won't happen again," he told her.

"Is that your idea of an apology?" she demanded.

He gave no reply but stared her full in the face. "Any female who runs to secret assignations of which her family has disapproved, who runs from her mother's bosom to the arms of a man her mother has forbid to be near her, who kisses in public gardens and lies to steal a few minutes with her lover"—David saw Isabella's face turning as white as the flannel sheet—"in short, any female who has so lost all sense of propriety that she rushes headlong into illicit nights alone with her current lover can hardly expect other men not to consider her—shall we say—light?"

Isabella blanched, her face draining of what little color had remained. The worst of it was that what he was saying was the simple truth. If any outsider considered her actions, they would brand her forever ruined. The fact that he had reason to assume her less than innocent only angered her further.

"If you truly knew me, Your Grace, you would never dare make such assumptions," she told him coolly.

"Mark yourself lucky it was I that found you and not one of your London admirers. You would have much more to complain about at this moment."

"Why? Would this imaginary gentleman have been more high-handed than yourself? Would he also kidnap me?"

David yawned. "Would you want him to?"

"You are insufferable!"

"I've been told that before," the duke said.

"I'm sure you have!" Bella spit out the words. "May I know how long it will be before we reach London and I can leave your irritating company?"

"Eventually," David said.

Bella glared at him. "Eventually? What does that mean? Aren't you taking me to London now?"

"No," he replied. "I had planned on it, but I can see that you would only go running off again at the first opportunity."

Her voice was icy: "May I ask where you think you are taking me instead?"

"To Yorkshire," she was told.

"Yorkshire?" Bella repeated. "Where is Yorkshire?"

David smiled. "Where we are headed," he replied.

If George Miller had been five minutes sooner he would have seen the fork in the road where the carriage turned off the London road and headed east instead of south. As it was, George galloped for all he was worth down the London road, each mile taking him further and further from reaching Bella's side.

Chapter Fifteen

*T*hey rode for hours and hours, Bella's body beginning to rebel against the cramped quarters and the bumpy road. She watched the countryside flow past outside the carriage's small isinglass window.

The countryside was spattered with late-afternoon shadows; a lantern was already lit and hung on the tollgate ahead of them. Bella leaned closer to the window, seeing a heavily laden tumbril coming toward the gate from the other side. Drawn by an enormous carthorse, it was moving even more slowly than its normal pace as it came near the gate.

The gatekeeper came to the carriage door. "Frippence, please, your honor."

"Sir!" Isabella began, searching the countryman's simple face. "I need your help!"

The gatekeeper stared at her in shock and then pulled his eyes away, looking at the man with her as he handed over the ticket. "This'll get you through this gate and the next two besides, your honor," the man said.

"Sir!" she said more urgently, "I am being abducted against my will!"

"Abduction is usually against someone's will," David said mildly.

The gatekeeper looked only at David. "Is anything amiss, your honor?"

"No, nothing at all. But thank you."

"Yes, there is!" Bella insisted, her voice rising.

David smiled at the gatekeeper. "She has learned English tolerably well, don't you think?"

The gatekeeper looked relieved. "Ah, and that's what it is then, your honor! I knew she had a funny way of talking. I was afraid she was a little tetched." He tapped the side of his head. "If you know what I mean," he added.

"I'm not crazy!" Bella looked as irate as she sounded.

"A bit loud, she is," the man said.

"Don't talk about me as if I'm not here!"

The gatekeeper gave the duke a compassionate gaze. "These foreigners need some heap of taming, your honor."

"You obstinate country bumpkin!" Bella spat the words out as the man closed the carriage door. "I hope you rot in hellfire and damnation!" She saw David grinning at her.

"Wherever did you learn such colorful language?" David asked.

"From my father!" she snapped.

They turned off the road soon after the next tollgate, leaving the pike for wild, moorland country. And still they rode on and on. A cold white mist was lying heavily across the countryside around them. The sharp, sweet tang of the moors rose in the back of her throat, the moorland undulating into the distance around them as the twilight lengthened into night.

Bella turned to face her captor. "Have you planned to murder me?"

A muscle worked in David's lean jaw. "Not in the immediate present," he reassured her. "But it remains a comforting thought."

"How long do you plan to subject me to this bone-wracking ride?"

"Do you wish to stop?" he asked.

She gave him a withering glance. "I wasn't aware my wishes entered into this. But yes, I would gladly stop this headlong madness!"

David shrugged. "I had intended to press on to more

appropriate quarters, but if you insist, we can certainly stop. I believe there is an alehouse nearby where we could rack up for the night."

Her eyes widened with disbelief. "An alehouse? You expect me to spend the night at an alehouse? Alone? With *you?*"

"You were in worse straits last night," David told her.

"I was not!" she replied hotly. But her innate honesty reminded her of George's nocturnal visit. "At least I had my maid with me for propriety's sake," she ended, feeling a little defensive and fighting the feeling. "I wasn't asked to spend the night alone at an alehouse!"

"Nor I have asked you to," he reminded her. "You were the one who wished to stop as soon as possible."

"If I must choose between this carriage and a public den of iniquity, then I shall stay here," she informed him coldly.

He bowed his head slightly. "As you wish."

"My wish is to be returned to my fiancé," Bella replied crisply.

"If that is your wish, you shall one day obtain it," the Duke of Exeter told her. There was no inflection in his tone.

"Thank you." Her voice dripped with sarcasm.

"You are most welcome," he told her mildly.

It was long past nightfall when the carriage turned off the country road onto a long, winding drive. It led through a stand of beech, elm, and sycamore trees, clumps of wild rhododendron, and rambler roses climbing the hedgerows that fenced in the narrow road.

David was nodding off, Bella well and truly asleep when the carriage slowed and finally stopped. He came to a groggy wakefulness, his finger to his lips when the young driver opened the carriage door.

"Is she asleep then?" the boy whispered.

"At the moment," David said in a low tone.

The boy stared at her. "She's a loud one, Your Grace. I could hear her most of the way here."

David almost asked about the quiet time and then kept a prudent silence. His thoughts brought the memory of her in his arms, of the moment when he felt her let go, felt her capitulation to the feelings that were overwhelming her. And then felt the strength of her response, her reactions nearly overcoming his own senses.

He had come closer than ever in his life to being out of control, her abandon nearly undoing him.

"Your Grace?" the driver said. "We've arrived."

David heard the boy. He stared out at the sixteenth-century Tudor house that was filled with old-fashioned black oak and gilt furniture and his own youthful memories. Happy memories of his mother and Christmas holidays and riding the endless lands.

David put the memories aside, looking across at the sleeping Isabella. He reached for her, lifting her one-hundred-twenty-pound frame effortlessly. At six foot three he was seven inches taller and almost a hundred pounds heavier than the willowy beauty he once again held in his arms.

She stirred as he stepped outside, her cheek resting against the top of his shoulder. He walked toward the huge stone country house and the two servants who stood waiting in the wide oak doorway.

The woman was in her fifties, spare of frame and sharp of eye. A North Country woman, with keen eyes and an even keener brain, she stood with arms akimbo, watching her employer's progress from the hired carriage to the porch.

Beside the woman her husband watched, too. A little taller than his wife and just as lean, he moved forward to help.

"Welcome home, Your Grace."

"Thank you, Gibb, Mrs. Gibb," the duke acknowledged as he stepped up toward them. In his arms the sleeping girl stirred.

Mrs. Gibb looked stern. "And just what have you been up to lately?" Her eyes went pointedly to the girl in his arms.

David grinned tiredly. "Nothing, Mrs. G."

"Hmmmph!" was her only comment. She stepped back, leading the way inside the cold front hall as her husband saw to the carriage and driver. The hall was large and oblong, a long narrow passageway leading back toward a parlor at the back of the house. Off the dark passageway many closed walnut doors and one green baize door marked the other ground-floor apartments and the backstairs pantries and kitchens. At the far end of the narrow passage back stairs rose toward the upper floors; in the large front hall wide stairs with beautifully carved walnut railings rose upward, too.

"We only just learned you were coming, so the house isn't ready," the housekeeper continued in a lecturing tone. "You were always a bit reckless when you were young, Your Grace. I'd hoped you'd begin to settle down."

"Oh, but I have, Mrs. Gibb, I promise you," David replied in innocent accents.

Mrs. Gibb sniffed her disbelief. "So I can see by the bundle in your arms! You'll find a fire in your suite, but naught much else in the way of welcome. I suppose you want her in there?"

"I'll put her in my room, yes. Then you can make up another fire in one of the guest suites, where I shall spend the night, as chaste as you please."

Mrs. Gibb turned, eyeing him sharply, and then relaxed a little. "I don't much take to funny goings on in my house," she told her employer plainly. The fact that she worked for him did not deter her.

"This is a very special situation, Mrs. G.," the duke said.

"I can see that," she said tartly.

As they mounted the stairs toward the bedroom suites Bella's eyes opened. Dazed, it took her a minute to get her bearings. "Where am I?" she asked, her words a little slurred.

"Is she drunk, then?" Mrs. Gibb asked in scandalized accents.

"Nothing like, Mrs. G. She's very tired."

"Where am I?" Bella asked again, struggling against him a little. He held her tighter, making the landing and heading down the hall to the master suite's door.

Mrs. Gibb opened the door, giving the young woman in the duke's arms a good once-over. Dark-haired and -eyed, she was a tall girl, her features exotic. "What kind of speech is that?" Mrs. Gibb asked the duke.

"She's American," he replied.

"Oh, is that what it is?" Mrs. Gibb said. Her expression told of her distaste for the ex-colonists who hadn't had the good sense to stay under the protection of the crown. "No wonder," Mrs. Gibb said under her breath.

The housekeeper left as the duke crossed the Axminster carpet and deposited the girl on the huge four-poster bed against the far wall. The bed was massive, the posts carved to look like palm tree trunks with clusters of palm leaves at the tops.

Mrs. Gibb went downstairs to prepare a nuncheon for the duke and to tell her husband to light another fire. Before Mr. Gibb left the warm flagstone kitchen he was told to keep an eye on the two upstairs. Mrs. Gibb wouldn't put anything past an American, including setting her cap for the duke himself.

Mr. Gibb was of the opinion that the duke could take care of himself, but his wife clucked her tongue. If men wanted to be obtuse, it wasn't her concern.

Upstairs Bella was now fully awake. Deposited on the huge mahogany four-poster, she sat huddled against the pillows, trying to make sense of what was happening. Somehow she had believed he was only trying to frighten her. That he was taking some other roads but was in truth heading back to London and her mother.

Now, sitting in this strange house, hearing the North Country accents around her, she knew she was very far from London.

"Why are you doing this?" she asked the silent man who stood above her, staring down at her with a puckered brow.

"Why not?" he replied, his brow clearing. She saw humor lurking behind his eyes before he turned and left.

Isabella could not understand how he had found her. Or why he had abducted her instead of taking her back to London. There was no way for the duke to have followed them to the inn so quickly, but he had. How had he known where they went? There was none who had known where they were headed. She had not even known herself.

She couldn't understand why he hadn't taken her safely back to Exeter House until she remembered the morning's events in the carriage. Perhaps he truly thought her a loose woman, running away with George and then allowing the duke to take such liberties. Responding with such abandon, she admitted to herself, flushing scarlet with the memory.

If he thought her wanton, what must he be thinking they would do next? Bella jumped out of the bed, racing to the window and opening it. Unfamiliar land sloped away into the darkness, a forest of trees making the dark countryside even darker. There was no escape.

She turned to face her captor and saw Sally coming into the bedroom. "Sally!"

"Oh, miss, I'm so glad to see you safe!"

"Safe?" Bella looked indignant. "Look around you!" Her tone turned suspicious. "How did you get here?"

"It was Mr. Markham, His Grace's valet, miss. He brought me."

Bella stared at the young maid. "I don't understand."

"Cor, miss, nor do I, but I'm that glad to see you safe! That Mr. George, he was a bad one, miss. Out for only one thing, and I'm that glad we got away. I heard him with the innkeeper, miss. I saw him bribing the man."

"You lie! You are in the duke's employ!" Bella accused.

"Why, yes, miss—you know that I work for the prince," Sally responded, not understanding until she saw Bella's anger blazing out at her. "I—miss?"

"Leave me," Bella said.

"But I can't leave you alone—"

"Leave me!" Bella said again, her tone frigid. "I want no part of you."

"But miss, don't you want help getting ready for bed?"

"You are a traitor, and I want you nowhere near me!" Bella told the maid.

"Sally." The duke's voice came from the doorway. Both women looked toward him. "Please do as she says."

Bella turned her back on both of them. Folding her arms across her chest, she moved to the window and stared out at the inky landscape. Mists covered the countryside, the moon lost from view.

Dejected, her head down, Sally started toward the door. When she passed the duke she looked up at him woefully.

"Mrs. Gibb will see to your sleeping quarters," David told the girl.

After Sally left the room was shrouded in silence. David stared at Bella's back. "There is nothing to see at the moment, is there?" he asked. She did not reply. "Mrs. Gibb is bringing up some food. You must be hungry and thirsty."

Bella turned to face him, her arms still folded across her breast as if to ward him off. "Are you partaking of this feast with me?" she asked, her voice dripping sarcasm.

"Not unless you prefer my company to solitude."

Bella's expression answered before her words did. "I would prefer a horde of wild Indians to your company," she told him icily.

"I'm afraid I can't oblige at the moment. Short notice and all."

"If you are attempting humor, you are failing miserably," Bella told him.

He wanted to stride across the large room and grab her. He wanted to feel that tall, proud body submitting to him. He wanted her in his arms. He did none of it. Bowing his head slightly, he turned to go.

"One moment!" she called out, stopping him. "How long must I stay here?"

David answered deliberately: "Until you come to your senses and realize what that man is."

"You'd best send Sally for several trunks of clothing, for we shall be here until hell freezes over. Or until George rescues me from your clutches!"

"Rescues you from me!" David looked affronted. "I am rescuing you from him!"

"No one asked you to!"

"Yes, they did! Your mother is beside herself with worry over your behavior."

A glimpse of guilt could be seen in her eyes, quickly replaced by anger. "Then why did you bring me here instead of taking me to her? What do you hope to gain by bringing me here?"

David watched her. "I hope to convince you your fascination with Miller is a mistake."

"And how exactly do you plan on doing that?" Bella demanded.

"I'm not sure," David drawled. "Perhaps I shall make you forget him."

"How?"

"By making love to you myself," he replied.

Bella froze. "You wouldn't dare!"

"You didn't object all that strenuously in the carriage."

"How dare you! I was beside myself with fear!"

David smiled. "Bella, I doubt you've ever been afraid in your life, let alone beside yourself with fear of me."

Isabella drew herself up ramrod-straight. "If you were a gentleman, you would not bring up such subjects. Nor would you take pride in forcing me into such a socially unacceptable situation!"

"Tell that to your American Miller. He's bragged to everyone at the Stag and Hound as to his conquest of you!"

"You lie!"

"I never lie, unlike some people I could mention," David told her.

Isabella's cheeks flamed red. "And a gentleman does not bring up unpleasant subjects to a lady!"

"A lady does not careen across the country endangering herself and worrying her parent."

"What I do is none of your business! You'd best plan your excuses for when George rescues me. Nor will my mother think well of you for abducting me like this!"

"She has already given her permission," David told Bella.

"You mean she knows about this?" Bella was incredulous.

"She does," he told her. And he left.

"I don't believe you!" Bella yelled. She stared at the closed bedroom door and then ran to it to lock it. There was no key. As she stood there she heard something scraping in the lock from the other side. He was locking her inside! She grabbed the knob, twisting it to no avail. "How dare you!" she shouted.

His voice came through the thick planks: "I don't want to lose sleep fearing a dagger in the middle of the night."

"And well you should worry!" she shouted. "When I get

out of here you shall be sorry for all this, you big"—she searched for an epithet—"big ox!"

She kicked the door, hurting only her toes. There was no reply from outside. He was an aggravating, self-righteous, interfering, domineering male! She would never let him get away with this! Somehow, she had to get away.

An idea formed, and she ran to the window. She opened it as wide as it would go. There were no tree branches near enough to reach without leaping out into midair. There were no ledges, no trellises. Muttering to herself, she thought about making a rope from the bedding. She had read of it in one of the romance novels she devoured at every opportunity and thought at the time it might not be as easy as it sounded. Then again, it might be worth a try.

She scanned the ground beneath the window. It looked hard-packed. And then she saw the man below. It wasn't the duke. At first she thought it was the young coach-driver, but then she realized it was someone else. The man looked up at the open window, moving with a lantern and a kitchen chair to sit directly below and keep watch.

Two large tears gleamed in her eyes as she turned away from the window and sighed. She had read about such situations but had never thought she would be a victim. Throwing herself across the huge bed, she closed her eyes, her tired brain falling back to sleep.

She spent the night lost in dreams wherein she was caged in a dark and lonely castle waiting for her hero. But when her rescuer came she couldn't see his face. Throughout the night's dreams she tried to see behind the visor, trying to prove to herself that it was George.

Chapter Sixteen

In the morning Bella woke to a bleak dawn, raw and cold. She lay still, listening to the sounds of the unfamiliar countryside around her and longing for the California warmth and her own room. A cock crowed at the pale sunrise and cowbells clanged in the fields beyond her windows, the trees filling with chirping birds that seemed accustomed to the sharp North Sea winds.

The sharp tang of the nearby moors drifted on the freshening winds. It was a strange smell to one used to the dry desert air of southern California, mossy and damp.

Bella rose to dress herself, unwilling to ring for Sally's help. Because Isabella had her own maid, Mrs. Gibb had sent none of the staff to set the morning fire in her bedroom grate. The room was chill, the grate filled with long-cold ashes from the night before. Shivering, Bella looked across the room at the wilted maid's uniform she had worn since yesterday afternoon.

Near the wardrobe her small valise sat on the low table where Sally had put it before Bella ordered the maid out. As she stood in the middle of the large bedroom and shivered Bella regretted her harsh words to the girl. Even if Sally was a spy, at least there would have been a fire in the grate and clothing laid out.

As it was, Isabella, too proud to change her mind, had to ferret through the valise herself. She found a rumpled blue silk dress and tried to shake the wrinkles out of it. It was not only full of creases, it was much too light for the North Country weather.

While Bella worried over her clothing, Markham was shaving the Duke of Exeter. The valet's disapproving brow and continuing silence was beginning to irritate his employer.

"You have an aggravating habit, Markham, of saying more with your silences than most people can with words," David said impatiently. "Out with it."

"It's not my place to reprimand Your Grace. But, of course, if you ask my opinion . . ." the man trailed off, irritating the duke even more.

"I already asked!" David snapped.

"Well, since you ask, Your Grace," Markham replied, "I cannot understand why you are allowing Miss Alexander's maid to leave."

"I am merely doing as Miss Alexander insists," David replied testily.

"Begging your pardon, Your Grace, but you will be putting Miss Alexander in a most improper situation."

"*I* shall?" David shoved the shaving tackle away. Taking the towel from around his neck, he swiped at the remains of the shaving cream himself. "I didn't decide to ride pell mell across the countryside with an American adventurer!"

"No, sir. But at least she had the wisdom to keep her maid with her."

"I haven't brought Isabella here to ravish her, Markham!" David replied stiffly. He saw the doubt on the other man's face.

"Yes, Your Grace," Markham said slowly. "I'm sure the coachman was mistaken about what he heard—"

"Damn and blast the boy!" David yelled, "and damn and blast you! How dare you impugn my honor?" David was on his feet.

Markham remained calm. "You did ask what concerned me, Your Grace."

"Yes, well, now I've heard it! You may leave me."

"You might as well, Your Grace," Markham told the duke.

"Might as well what?" David asked irritably.

"Have your way with her," the man said practically. "Her reputation will be utterly ruined by this episode in any event, now that she is totally alone in an unmarried man's establishment. She shall go home in disgrace."

"She's not going anywhere," David said.

"I beg your pardon?"

"I'm going to marry her myself," David told his valet. He earned a look of utter consternation. And a moment of total silence.

"May—may I offer my congratulations, Your Grace?" the valet finally replied.

"Not yet, Markham. You see she loathes the sight of me."

"I don't understand," Markham said.

"Nor do I," David replied. "I've always been told I was the most eligible of catches. I don't understand why she can't stand me."

"Doesn't that place you in a rather . . . delicate position if you intend to propose?"

"It certainly makes it difficult," the duke agreed. "It is a rare quandary. If I take her immediately back to London, she will surely run away again. If I keep her here, she will probably never forgive me. But then again, she will be in no danger from that American adventurer."

"It doesn't sound promising, Your Grace," Markham said. "If I may be so bold, why have you decided to marry her?"

David sighed. "I'm not entirely sure, Markham. She is a trial and a pain, and she is much too independent. One never knows what she is going to do next. She is altogether too passionate about everything. I can't imagine why I want to make her part of my life. Why are you smiling?"

"Because, Your Grace, I think you have truly met your match." Markham hesitated. "But I still think the maid must stay for propriety's sake. You don't want your future wife's reputation bandied about London parlors."

"I suppose you're right," David said ungraciously. "I just don't trust the girl not to let Bella trick her into some strange adventure."

David had reason to worry. At that very moment Sally was outside Bella's door. "Miss, are you talking to me? Would you like a bit of breakfast?"

Bella flew to the locked door. "Sally! I thought you'd gone!"

"Miss, I know you said to go, but I can't just leave you alone all the way out here!"

"No, no, you're quite right. Is the duke about?"

"I don't know where he is, miss."

"Good," Bella replied. "Unlock the door, quickly!"

There was silence outside. Then: "I can't, miss. There's no key."

"Sally, listen to me. You must find the key—you *must!*"

"I'll try, miss," Sally said doubtfully.

Bella heard the maid's steps fading into the distance. She began to pace the room, gnawing at her lower lip as she tried to formulate a plan of escape. She had no idea where she was, so she had no way of getting word to George. The duke had mentioned the Stag and Hound; that must be where George had been staying in London.

Remembering David's accusation, her eyes hardened. How dare he accuse George of bandying her name about a tavern! He didn't even know George. He thought to make her distrust George, but there was no hope of that. She knew how much George loved her. He had followed her all the way across a continent and an ocean to ensure they would be together.

The scraping of the key in the lock turned her toward the door. "Sally!" Bella cried happily, and then she quieted, afraid of bringing attention to them. She moved quickly to the door.

It opened, but Sally was not alone. The duke stood in the doorway, smiling at Bella. "Good morning."

Bella turned her back on him. "I do not speak to kidnappers."

David motioned Sally inside. She carried a breakfast tray.

"I shall return in a few minutes," he told them both. Closing the door, he locked them inside the large bedroom.

Bella spoke softly. "You must help me escape," she told Sally.

The maid's round blue eyes were full of fear. "But how, miss?"

"I'm not sure yet. But I shall trick my way out of here, and you must have things ready for us."

"Things, miss?" Sally questioned.

Bella moved to the heavy cloak she had worn. She picked it up and began stuffing it in the valise. "Take this with you," she said, piling the borrowed maid's uniform on top, hiding the cloak. "Hide it somewhere downstairs where we can fetch it quickly when I get free."

Sally unwillingly took the case. "But where can we go?"

"We shall take horses and make for the nearest town. There must be something back down this road. We shall find a place to hide until we can find our way back to London."

"I don't know, miss," Sally said doubtfully. "And Mr. George, he was up to no good at the inn."

"He was walking in his sleep," Bella defended him. "Many people do that. It meant nothing. Nothing!" She grasped Sally's hands. "Sally, I shall marry George. No one is going to prevent me from being with the man I love. No one! Can I depend upon your help?"

Sally looked unhappy. "I shall try, miss, but I don't know if I can carry it off."

"Of course you can!" Isabella told her bracingly. "Now just take this when you leave, and then hide the cloak."

When the door was unlocked for her Sally did as Isabella bade, grasping the valise tightly.

David looked down at the case in the maid's hands.

"I need my other dress pressed," Bella told him quickly.

His eyebrows rose. "I thought you wished the maid gone."

Isabella eyed him coldly. "I realize she is your spy, but I must have someone to help me. Any servant you allow me will be your spy, so I might as well keep the one who already knows my preferences."

David watched her. "I don't trust you when you seem to cooperate."

"You won't trust me in any event," she told him, "and we both know it."

"Are you saying I should?" David queried with a rising brow.

Bella considered the question. "Where could I go?" she replied. "We are—what two days, three—from London. I have no choice but to stay until you allow me to go."

"That's altogether too reasonable," David said.

"I am not a fool, no matter what you think."

His brow rose again. "Perhaps then you would care to join me for dinner this evening."

"I must eat," she said ungraciously. "And I cannot abide being locked up here any longer." She hesitated. "I don't suppose you would allow me a ride." She saw his ironic smile. "Or at least a turn about the grounds? I need some exercise."

David bowed. "I shall, of course, be happy to escort you. And since you realize you are miles and miles from anywhere—and I might add the moors are a dangerous place to lose one's way; even natives have gone to their deaths trying to traverse them alone—since, as I say, you have come to your senses, I see no reason to keep you locked within here. Please feel free to use the house as your own."

"Thank you," she said coldly. Her hands were clenched together. Determined to hide her elation, she stared back at him stonily. "May I come downstairs now?"

"If you wish." David stood back, allowing her to precede him into the hall.

Bella glanced back at Sally. "Don't just stand there, see to my things," Bella told the girl. And turned so that David could not see, Bella winked at the maid.

"Yes, miss," Sally said unhappily, dropping a curtsy as the duke and Isabella walked away.

The North Sea winds blew fiercely around the huge house, rattling the windows and sneaking in through tiny cracks in the sashes. Outside the chill was accompanied with a wet mist as Bella walked out onto the porch with David. She stopped in her tracks, shivering.

"I shall find your cloak for you," David told her, heading back inside.

"No!" she said quickly, following him in. "I mean, I have changed my mind. I would rather stay indoors. I'm not used to your English weather."

David watched her. "Perhaps you might find a book to interest you in the library."

She seized upon the idea. "I should like that, yes. Thank you."

David led the way. Bella's brain worked feverishly to figure out a plan for her escape. She would need to get a horse, which would be hard to do when all were awake. So she must plan to leave late at night, when the stablemen and all others would be asleep. If she could get a good head start, she might be able to find her way to a village that had the wireless. And even a train station.

She had no money. The thought stopped her in her tracks, and David turned back to see why she wasn't following. She forced herself forward, following him into the book room. She could not board the train without money; she could not send a wireless message unless she could convince the operator to trust her long enough for George to reach her side and pay the man.

"I shall leave you to your reading," the duke said.

"Thank you," Bella replied. She moved toward the shelves of books as David hesitated a moment behind her and then left.

She fingered her brooch. A beautifully carved cameo was set into a solid gold filigree frame. Perhaps the wireless operator would take the brooch as security until George arrived.

A row of books on Parliament were in front of her, religious tomes beyond them. She looked on the higher shelves and saw novels, biographies, and a book on the history of Yorkshire.

She reached for the history, bringing it down and thumbing quickly through it. She found what she was searching for: a map of the county.

Smiling, she took it to a table, poring over it and memorizing the names of the towns listed. York itself, Bridlington, Great Driffield, Essingwold, Haxby; she had no idea of which she was near, or if she was near any of them.

Howardian Hills, The Wolds, the Vale of Pickering—she must find out which she was near and then get her bearings from the map. Looking about for a pen and paper, Bella pulled down a larger book from the shelves and put herself to work. She began to copy out a rough version of the map, ready to cover her work with the larger book if any came near the closed library door.

Chapter Seventeen

Sally found Bella in the book room later in the afternoon.

"Where did you hide it?" Bella asked.

Sally answered unhappily, "I put it in the hall, miss. Near the dining room there's a big hall chest. I put it behind there."

"Good. I shall take a look later and make sure it can't be seen."

"I don't see how it can help us, miss."

Bella took her time answering, unhappy about having to continue to fib. "Tomorrow morning at first light I shall explain it all," Bella promised. Sally nodded, leaving to see to pressing the maid's dress.

She told herself it was all the duke's fault and felt a little better. By morning she would be long gone. In the meantime, if Sally were reporting to the duke, he would think he could relax until morning light.

David Beresford was going to learn it would take more than the likes of him to best an Alexander. She comforted herself with the thought as she went back to work.

It was turning dark when Bella finished her work, blotting and then folding up the paper. She unbuttoned her bodice, tucking the folded paper down into it and rebuttoning quickly as footsteps came near.

Mrs. Gibb opened the door, bringing a lamp inside and putting it down. "Good evening, miss," the woman said in her thick North Country accent. "The master says dinner is to be served in half an hour." Mrs. Gibb peered intently at the exotic American beauty.

"Thank you," Bella said, feeling the questions in the housekeeper's close scrutiny. "I shall tidy up now."

"As you wish, miss. Shall I call your maid to your room?"

"Please." Bella moved toward the door. She could hear the slight sound of the paper rustling against the silk at her bosom. Moving as stiffly as she could, Bella prayed the woman would not hear.

"Are you through with the books, miss?"

"Yes—ah—I mean no. I think I would like to go through them tomorrow. Please leave them down for me. By the way, I see there are some very interesting tracts on local history on the shelves."

"Yes, miss. We've had our share of history around these parts," Mrs. Gibb said in a noncommittal tone.

"Truly?" Bella's interest was real, and it showed. "I would like to learn more about this particular area. What towns are we nearest? Where something of historical interest happened, I mean. I intend on asking the duke to show me the sights."

"I see. Well"—Mrs. Gibb's tone unbent a fraction—"I would guess you'd be wanting to see York itself, then. Henry the Second held the first English Parliament there. And there's Marsten Moor, where the Parliamentarians fought in the civil war. And there's Castle Howard, of course."

"It sounds fascinating," Bella told the woman. "How far is York from this moor? Could we make the trip in a day?"

"Oh, yes, miss. It's just down the road from Stramford Bridge and Dunnington."

"Stramford Bridge and Dunnington. It doesn't sound far."

"No, miss," the woman replied. She watched as Bella moved stiffly past her and then fled up the stairs, her hand to her chest.

Bella pressed the paper firmly against her rib cage until she was alone upstairs in the master bedroom. It wasn't until then that she let out her breath. She opened her dress, repositioning the map and placing it between her bare skin and her chemise instead of between the chemise and the blue silk of her dress.

Sally walked in as she rebuttoned her bodice, asking if Bella was ready for help with her bath.

"I just need my hair combed, Sally. I shall bathe in the morning."

"Oh!" Sally turned to her mistress. "I forgot your brushes are still in the valise." She moved toward the door to retrieve it.

"No!" Bella stopped her. "Leave it where it is. I don't want to take any chances on someone seeing it there and ruining our flight. You can just smooth my hair a bit and replace the pins. We can do that without my brushes."

At dinner David was pleasantly surprised at Bella's cooperative attitude. He complimented her upon it, and Bella shrugged.

"There's not much point in making this any more unpleasant than necessary."

"I agree," David said. He watched her as she tucked into her mutton stew. "I see you have quite an appetite. The north winds must be good for you."

"I always have a large appetite."

"I've only seen you eat like a bird," David told her.

"That's because my mother brings me snacks before meals and before we eat out. She says it is unfeminine to enjoy large quantities of food."

"Nonsense," David said. "I think it is very appealing."

Bella looked up then. "Truly?" She searched his eyes to see if he was teasing her.

"Truly. It speaks of passionate appetites."

She blushed, looking back at her bowl and losing some of her enjoyment of the food. "You are being very forward," she told him.

"Do you play?" he asked. "The piano," he added.

"Yes, tolerably well. Why?"

"We have a long night ahead of us," he said.

She watched him. "What do you think to gain by this? By holding me here?"

David had been asking himself that very question all day long. His moody expression took her by surprise, as did his words. "I hoped to keep you from harm's way and to give you the time to get to know me better."

"Why?" she asked.

"Why keep you from harm's way? Or why get to know me?"

"Both," Bella replied, curious to know his reasons.

"The first I have promised your mother, the second I had hopes might bring us closer together."

"Whatever for?" Bella asked. "I mean, you can't think that I—that you—that we . . ." she trailed off.

David's smile was tinged with irony. "I take it you find nothing appealing about either my looks or my character."

"You can't possibly say you find me appealing," Bella replied.

"I give you that I can't explain why I do. You are not all that much more beautiful than a hundred others, and God knows there are a thousand others much more docile and willing to please."

Stung by his honest appraisal, she retorted, "Perhaps you do what you accuse George of—seeking a rich wife."

David's gaze turned cold. He threw down his spoon and stood up. "If you think that, you are more of a fool than I thought." And so saying, he walked out of the dining room.

Bella was surprised by hot tears that suddenly stung her eyes, threatening to flow down her cheeks. She looked down at the heavy Flanders linen that draped across the dining room table and to the floor. Upon it sat her plate of lamb and potatoes, a goblet of ruby-red wine beside her dinner. She bit the inside of her cheek, determined not to cry. Reaching for the large napkin on her lap, she dabbed the Exeter-crested linen against the tears that were glistening in her dark eyes.

She had no idea why his words had so affected her. She did not care if he thought her a fool, she scolded herself. But her heart disagreed, and the tears would not go away.

Bella focused her thoughts on George. She had no reason

to care what this high-handed English lord thought of her. What she did was none of his business.

Music drifted into the dining room from somewhere down the hall, the soft tinkling sounds of a pianoforte being played in the distance.

The music continued as she forced herself to finish her dinner. She would need her strength for her daring escape. She gulped a healthy swallow or two of the red wine, feeling it warm her belly before she stood up and went in search of the music.

The old stone country house was large, the narrow hall seemingly endless as she followed the music to the very back of the house where a parlor opened off the passageway.

Within it David sat at the dark satinwood instrument, two Battersea enamel candlesticks on each side of the keyboard to light the black and gilt music stand. The duke's back was to the door, a Chippendale fire screen beside him. He was not aware she had entered the room; the notes of the Chopin nocturne were melancholy in the still room.

Bella moved around him to the fireside, sitting down on an overstuffed easy chair, closing her eyes and losing herself to the music.

When the music stopped she opened her eyes to find David watching her. "I didn't realize you were here," he said stiffly. "I must apologize for my poor performance."

"If you mean in taking me away from my love, you certainly should. If you mean your playing, you are being overly modest. It was beautiful."

David watched her. "Perhaps you would like to play."

"I should prefer you to play more, if you like," Bella told him.

He hesitated and then turned back to face the keyboard. Looking over his shoulder, he smiled a little. "May I trust you will not stab me in the back? At least until I'm through playing?"

Bella smiled in spite of herself. "A truce while you play," she agreed.

The music began again, Bella leaning back in the comfort of the big chair and the warmth of the fire. She drowsed, relaxing as David played a scherzo and then another nocturne, his own thoughts as far away from the music as hers.

A companionable silence spread between them when he stopped playing and came near, draping himself into a chair that matched Bella's own. He stared moodily into the fire, the flickering candle and firelight playing across his clean-cut features, shadowing the space beneath his eyes.

Bella realized she was staring at how handsome he looked. And how sad. The thought startled her into sitting up. "I'd best retire," she said in a much colder tone than she realized.

"If you wish," David replied, his eyes never leaving the leaping flames that crackled within the grate.

A long while after Bella had gone up to bed Markham came in to ask if the duke required anything further. David told the man to bring Sally to the parlor.

"What exactly happened in the inn, Sally?" David asked when he was alone in the room with the lady's maid. "Did this American Miller make advances toward your mistress?"

"Oh, sir!" Sally's eyes widened. "It were proper terrible what he did!"

David frowned, his brow knitting together. "What did the cad try to do?" he demanded.

"Why, sir, he bribed the innkeeper to say there was only one room available. I saw him with my very own eyes!"

David sat up straighter, almost spilling the brandy he held. "Are you saying he spent the night in her room?"

"Oh, no, sir, never! She said as how he would have to sleep downstairs. But he still tried, that he did. He came sneaking up the stairs and snuck into our room in the middle of the night, Your Grace!"

"He did *what?*" David exploded, scaring the little maid with his ferociousness.

Sally gulped. "He—he came into our room, and he—he started to undress! I made like I was sick, and I made noise coughing, and my mistress woke up and told him to stop where he was. I thought he was going to throw himself at her, I did!" Sally saw the duke's expression darkening even further. "Nothing happened, Your Grace," she reassured him.

"A great deal happened," David replied darkly. "She certainly knows he walked into her room and undressed!"

Sally nodded unhappily. "But she stopped him before he had his way, sir."

"She knows he is no gentleman," David said. "Leave me," he added after another moment. He turned to stare into the fireplace, and Sally scurried out, afraid of the look in his eyes.

A disappointment surprised him as it washed over him, turning him moody. There was no way she could have misinterpreted the American's actions. She knew very well he had intended on ravishing her on the spot. She had stopped Miller, a voice within David reminded him; she had not let him have his way with her. But David's expression was hardening as he stared at the flames.

Isabella was not repelled by the man's actions. She was still in love with him. No matter how badly he had acted, she still cared about him. She was still determined to have him as her mate.

David stood up, heading for the cupboard and pulling out a bottle of port. He had always prided himself on being a realist. Now he had to face the fact that Isabella must truly love the American Miller.

And if that was true, there was no point to any of this. He poured himself a healthy dose of the red wine. In the morning he would tell the boy to hitch up the carriage and begin the drive back to London. Once there he would tell his father and her mother that there was no sense in trying to keep Isabella apart from Miller any longer. He might be a bounder, but her heart and her mind were made up, and she was not going to change.

The depression he felt accompanied him all the way up to his bed in one of the guest bedrooms.

Bella's lights were out, but she was wide awake, staring at the moonlit ceiling. She heard his steps outside as he walked past her doorway and down the hall. Throwing the covers off, she reached for her high-button boots in the dark, listening carefully to the silent house around her.

Raising the wick on her lamp, she pulled the map out, looking at where she had marked off Stramford Bridge and the road that continued on through Dunnington toward York.

Reassuring herself, she pocketed the map and started on tiptoe to the door, listening for several minutes before she quietly tried it. He had been as good as his word. It wasn't locked. She smiled to herself. The duke thought he had her cowed by the distance and the unfamiliar territory. He thought she would fear the moors he had said were so forbidding that she should not dare attempt escape. And if Sally had told him anything, he would think she planned to take the maid with her. He would wait for the maid's next report.

In the morning he would learn the truth, Bella congratulated herself. He would find she had as good a stomach for adventure as any man had. And as much competence. Warming herself with the thought of the look on his face when they told him she was gone, she started down the hall. Moving cautiously, she listened for any sounds of movement around her. He would learn not to be so high-handed with her in the future, she told herself. The thought that her future did not include him did not cross her mind.

He was an obstacle to be surmounted and a meddlesome man who had to be taught a lesson. He had met his match, she thought. And she would tell him to his face one day in London. She would brandish her wedding band under his nose and make him admit she had bested him.

In the meantime, she had to make good her getaway.

Downstairs she heard voices and froze. They came from the kitchen, Mr. and Mrs. Gibb talking over a late supper of tea and bread and cheese. Bella moved slowly down the hall toward the dining room and the large lowboy that hid her valise, if Sally had kept her word. She reached down behind the thick oak cabinet, feeling in the darkness for her case, her heart beating loudly, fearing it would not be there. Finally her fingers found the valise.

She pulled it out, reaching for the thick cloak, every sound she made loud in her own ears. She froze when she heard movement beyond her. Crouching where she was, she dared not breathe, hoping the shadowy hall would hide her well enough. Footsteps came toward the green baize door across the hall from her and then veered off inside. The door did not open.

Bella quickly stood up, throwing the cloak around the shoulders of the thin blue silk gown. Racing as silently as she could, she fled toward the front door, in the opposite direction from the green baize door and the kitchens beyond.

It was locked, of course. She slipped the bolt back as gently as she could manage, opening the door and closing it carefully behind herself.

It was almost freezing cold outside, the early mist blown away by the strong winds. The sky was ink black, stars glittering like sharp-edged diamonds in the cold air.

Bella bundled the cloak more tightly around herself, her eyes searching the moonlit landscape for the stables. The sounds of a restless horse brought her near it, peeking around the front, making sure no one was stirring before she moved to open the door.

With only the splash of moon that came from outside to light her way, Isabella ran toward the tack room, reaching for a bridle and a saddle. The first one her hand reached was a lady's sidesaddle. She moved on, finding a row of men's saddles and picking the lightest. Heaving it off the wall, she carried the heavy leather toward the first stall, calling out softly to the horse as she moved. Reassuring it as she entered the stall, she reached up to throw the saddle over its back. She harnessed the animal, pulling the girths tight before removing the headstall and leading the gray mare to the mounting block.

Hampered by her dress, she swung herself up onto the horse and straddled it, tucking her wide skirts under and around her legs as she urged the mount forward.

Holding her breath, she made the yard and then dug in her heels, the mare taking off across the moonlit fields, heading west.

Inside the huge stone house Mr. and Mrs. Gibb were climbing the back stairs to their own bedroom, whispering to themselves about the duke's strange and unannounced visit and what it could mean.

The duke heard their steps in the distance outside his door. He was sitting in a high-backed chair in front of the bedroom fireplace, staring moodily into the flames, much as he had done below. When the steps faded away he stood up, suddenly restless. The moonlit view out his window was of fields that stretched away toward the western forest. He glanced outside and then his gaze focused. Something was moving across the moonlit landscape.

He walked nearer the window, squinting to make out the horse and rider streaking away across the fields. Heading into the trees. Bella!

David moved quickly, wrenching his door open and moving swiftly down the hall to the door to the master suite. He opened it, staring inside.

The bed covers were thrown back, the sheets gleaming ghostly in the shadowy light from outside. Swearing to himself, he bellowed for Markham, moving swiftly downstairs.

The valet appeared, sleepy-looking, from his small room beside the master suite. "Your Grace?" he asked David's back as the duke raced down the steps. Behind the valet Mrs. Gibb opened her bedroom door.

"What's wrong?" she asked.

The valet was running after the duke, catching up in the downstairs hall.

"She's taken off! I'm going after her. Wake the coachman and tell him to ready the coach for the trip south."

"To London, sir?"

"Where else?" David demanded. He grabbed a cloak from a hall tree and wrenched the front door open. "Tell him we'll leave at first light. As soon as I catch the blasted wench. There's no hope of changing her mind. She's beyond help!" The duke was saying more, but he was talking to himself, heading out across the yard toward the stables.

The valet was smiling as he went more slowly toward the stables to inform the boy they would soon be leaving. He roused the boy and then went in search of the maid, whistling tunelessly to himself. This had been a fool's errand, and he was glad it was soon to end. The American woman would mean nothing but upset and confusion if she were to share the duke's life.

At least the duke had come to his senses about making her care for him. Like was better with like, when all was said and done. Leave her to the American was Markham's opinion, and had been all along.

Chapter Eighteen

*B*ella rode through the night, finding her way back to the avenue that led to the closed and locked lodge gates. Praying she was going in the right direction, she turned off the drive, racing across the park to a farm track. In the distance she saw another gate and slowed as she reached it. It looked too high for the mare to clear.

It was unlocked. She could lean far enough to open it without dismounting. Closing it behind the mare, Bella hesitated, looking ahead. The moonlight was thin in the forested depths before her. Trusting to the mare's instincts to keep them safe, Isabella rode on into the trees.

Night noises began to intrude in Bella's ears, the sounds eerie and unknown as she rode away from the duke's lands. She was soon chilled to the bone, her legs bare between her shoes and the edge of her tucked-under skirts. Her teeth chattered as she rode on, determined to make her way back to George.

By now he would have found she was not in London and would be frantic with worry. She would summon him to wherever she was, and they would go on together to Gretna Green and not let anyone stop them!

Comforting herself with the thought of George soon rescuing her, she rode on and on through the silent countryside.

Behind her David was aboard a huge black stallion, racing across the fields toward where he had last seen her. He let the horse have its head, galloping in a straight line and praying she had not turned off into the marshes.

He entered the forest at the same time she was emerging from the other side, the moonlight gleaming down on the marsh meadows, the tang of the moors stronger and stronger.

Isabella slowed the mare a little, reaching for the folded map. Bringing it out of her pocket, she opened it, smoothing it and then trying to read the marks she had made.

The moonlight was strong, but the pen marks were barely dark enough to make out. If she was right, this would be the forest to the west of the duke's lands, and a town should be straight ahead.

The road wound through the countryside; the town looked to be in a direct line across the meadows before her. She halted the horse, deciding if she should continue on the winding road or take off across the fields. She was sure she was moving west, which meant she could cut across to the south and save time.

But if she were wrong, she would be going straight into the heart of the moorland and it showed no towns. She hesitated a moment longer and then urged the mare forward, staying on the road. She would be safest on the road, Bella told herself. A road had to go to some town sooner or later.

Behind her the duke reached the road and reined in briefly, looking back to the east and then taking off toward the west. She had been riding in a westerly direction; he didn't think she would double back. She had no reason to think anyone yet knew she was gone.

If she had a brain in her head, she'd stick to the road, he told himself. If she had a brain in her head, she wouldn't be doing anything this foolish, his own brain told him sharply. And if he had one, he would not have attempted to rescue her in the first place.

He raced onward, castigating himself for allowing this to

happen. If anything untoward befell her, he would never forgive himself. Nor would his father. Nor would Dolores.

Swearing softly to himself, he slowly gained ground until he was near enough to see her far ahead down the road.

She couldn't hear him yet, as the winds were rolling across the moors and marshland meadows and beating loud in their ears. Bella's horse was not galloping as fast as the black stallion, so David was slowly catching up to her.

Isabella did not hear the rider behind her until he was very close. She turned, looking behind, and stared at the rider making toward her. In the darkness of his hooded cape he was unrecognizable, a black figure on a black horse riding through the black night with only streaks of moonlight shining out from between the low scudding clouds that were crowding together overhead.

More frightened than she had ever been in her life, she urged the mare faster. Her breath was caught in her throat as she weighed her options. It might be David, but how? And if it was not David, if it was a stranger, he was out for no good at this hour, of that she was sure.

A stand of trees stood near the road to the south, the road ahead a smooth ribbon with no chance of losing her pursuer. Bella made her choice and turned the mare off the road, streaking across the meadowland toward the stand of elms.

Behind her David began to curse in earnest. He knew the treachery of the marshy ground she was heading into. He thought of shouting a warning to her, but wasn't sure she would hear. And even if she heard, she was stubborn enough to press onward.

His face a grim mask, he acknowledged to himself she would rather kill herself than stay near him. And he would not allow her to kill herself. Nor would he force himself upon her further. She was obviously totally smitten with Miller. So much so that she could even forgive his midnight advances at the inn.

Or perhaps she had merely sent him away because the maid was there to see. Perhaps Miller knew he was welcome in her bed. His jaw set into even more harsh lines as he turned the black off the road and rode in a diagonal line straight toward Isabella.

He was almost to her when the gray mare stumbled in the spongy undergrowth, pulling up short and balking. Looking ahead toward the cover of the elms, Bella was unprepared for the sudden movement and lost her seat.

David was almost beside her when she sailed into the air and fell toward the wet marshland meadow. "Bella!" David called out involuntarily, slowing the black and jumping off before it came to a full stop.

He ran toward her crumpled figure, calling out her name as he reached her side and leaned down to pick her up. "Bella!"

Her head lolled back when he lifted her, her eyes closed, her breath erratic. She was soaking wet, a foot deep in the cold water under the tall marshland grasses. Her arms hung limply as he held her close, soaking his chest in the process. One elbow seemed to jut out at an impossible angle. "Bella—Bella, wake up," he urged.

A low moan escaped her lips, but she did not waken.

"Sweet Jesus, please wake up," David was saying. His brain raced over possibilities. He carried her to the black, laying her across it on her stomach, her arms drooping down one side, her legs the other. He reached for the mare's bridle, feeling its legs as he led it out of the foot-deep water. He grabbed the black's reins and walked them forward, toward the stand of trees, testing the ground as he moved.

A small stone forester's hut sat just beyond the trees. It was used occasionally by hunters who were authorized to hunt his lands and poachers who were not. The land for miles around had belonged to his family for generations, every inch of it explored by the adventurous young boy he had once been.

It was dark under the trees, and David moved carefully, praying Bella had no broken bones. The cottage was a tiny one-room building with a thatched roof and soot-blackened fireplace.

It looked to be empty. Going slowly, the Duke of Exeter tethered the horses and moved to the broken door, looking inside, making sure no one was inside before he went back for Isabella.

He lifted her gently from the stallion's back, hearing her

low moan and cursing himself as he carried the wet bundle that was Isabella inside the tiny cottage.

Carefully laying her on the floor by the fireplace, David reached into his vest pocket for a match. Lighting it, he checked the fireplace, seeing one half-burned log and some small kindling. He put the match to the kindling, the wood sputtering a little and then glowing, slowly burning itself out.

He had to use almost all the matches he had on him before he got the fire started, the wood damp from the cold night air. He fanned the small flames until they leapt higher, finally catching the log and beginning to give out a little heat and light.

In the slowly growing firelight David moved to close the door that was half off its hinges. The wind no longer whistled through the cabin as he came back and knelt beside Bella.

"Bella—Bella, wake up. Please, wake up," David called out to her. There was no answer. He stood up, going out to the horses to make sure they were tethered securely and pulling the bag Bella had brought off the mare.

He carried it inside, shivering, with the cold air matting his wet vest and shirt against his chest. David hunkered down beside Bella, her prone body between him and the fire. Reaching inside the valise, he pulled out whatever cloth he could find. A shawl and a cotton chemise came out in his hands. He covered Bella's shoulders with the chemise and then lay down on the hard-packed earth beside her. Using his own body to warm her, he brought the shawl across them both, huddling near the fire and praying she would be all right.

He lay on the earth floor, holding her in his arms and thinking of taking her back. Until she was awake and could tell him what hurt, or until it was light and he could see her injuries, he was afraid to move her any further.

She moved a little, her head resting in the curve of his shoulder. David felt his arm going to sleep underneath her, but he did not move. Closing his eyes, he let weariness engulf him. Listening to the small sounds of the forest and marshlands around them, he could hear the horses moving a little restlessly, unused to being outside in the middle of the night.

The sounds from outside mixed with the sound of the wood burning on the grate. The heat felt good, slowly warming him as he fell into an uneasy sleep.

An hour passed and then most of another one before Bella stirred. Her eyes opened to see a fire slowly dwindling two feet away from her. Her head was aching, one temple pulsing as the blood flowed through it, a bruise already beginning where it had slammed into the damp ground. Her thick black hair fell around her cheeks, pins loosened and falling toward her shoulders.

Drowsy, her head hurting, her brain slowly registered where she was. David's arms were around her. She could hear his even breathing. She saw his hand thrown out toward the fire, his signet ring with the Exeter crest catching the firelight.

Isabella thought about pushing herself away from him and standing up. The effort seemed almost more than she could imagine, let alone attempt. Her eyes closed, her throbbing head nestled into the curve of his shoulder. He was a big man, even lying next to her own tall frame. She felt small and safe in his arms.

Safe, she repeated silently to herself. She wondered why as she drifted off into sleep. The fire cooled, the log glowing but giving off very little heat as the small hours lengthened toward morning.

The first fingers of dawning light stabbed through cracks in the cabin walls, very little coming through the grimy window. The fireplace was cold. David and Bella were asleep on the floor in front of it. Sometime in the night Bella's restless sleep had turned her toward David, whose arms held her tight as he still gently snored.

Bella woke first, her eyes opening to stare at David's sleeping face. In repose he looked to be the young boy he once was, the planes of his face smooth of all worry and anger, his eyelashes long and dark.

It felt as natural to lie in his arms as if she had always been cradled there, the gentle sound of his breathing calming something deep within her heart. Even the hard floor beneath her hip did not bother her.

Bemused, Bella studied his face. His eyes opened, blinking once as if unsure where he was. The startlingly bright deep blue of a California summertime sky looked back at her. She watched as his countenance lost its peacefulness and took on the worries of his waking mind.

"Are you all right?" he asked, his brow furrowing.

"I don't know," Bella answered truthfully.

David stared into the dark eyes that were contemplating him. His arms were full of her, her long slender body outlined against his own. Her breast was against his chest, her knees touching his thighs. He didn't want to move and break the spell.

Something in Bella's expression made him lean closer, bringing his lips to rest against hers. When they touched the feeling burned through each of them. David's arms tightened around her, bringing her closer. He felt her hands, one captured between them, the other reaching, tentatively, to touch his cheek.

The kiss deepened, Bella giving herself over to the sensations he awakened. Her submission brought a fierce and turbulent response from David. She gave in so easily, with such perfect attunement to his every touch, but the figure of George Miller loomed large in his brain, and anger mixed with desire.

She was not innocent. There was no coyness, no shyness, no fear. She simply leaned into his passion and matched it with her own. The feeling was heady, all control slipping away, David reaching to touch her breast.

A small sound escaped her, turning into a moan as he leaned down to press his mouth against the bodice of her crumpled blue silk gown. He was unbuttoning the bodice, and she did not stop him.

Her eyes closed, letting the storm he was drawing forth within her carry her away. Bella, for the first time in her life, gave over control to another human being. His hand was slipping inside her dress, caressing her breast through the thin silk chemise.

David stared at the outline of her breast through the thin white silk before pressing his lips to it. She shuddered, her body molding against him. He pulled back a little, the silk transparent where his kiss had moistened it over her taut nipple.

He couldn't take his eyes from her breast, couldn't think of anything past having her. His own body was shuddering with last attempts at control, his brain telling him to stop. He kept imagining her with the American Miller and despising the picture he saw in his mind's eye. He wanted to erase it, to erase Miller from her heart and her body and her brain.

He hated her for allowing Miller to hold her like this; he hungered for total possession of her. Bella felt the strength of his passion, the feeling so new to her she could not identify it.

She felt the edges of fear, but her fear was overshadowed, overpowered by the delicious feelings his hands and lips evoked. His head was bare inches from her almost naked breast. With the greedy innocence of a child who has first tasted candy Bella's free hand reached up to tenderly touch his cheek. She traced a pattern with her fingertips and then ever so gently pulled his head back down.

David's large hand pulled the chemise down, exposing one breast. His breath was ragged as his tongue flicked across the dusky pink nipple, Bella's body arching toward him. In that moment he lost control, his mouth coming down to devour her breast, his hands pulling the chemise downward, the silk ripping as her breast sprang free of the fabric.

His hands moved to her legs, grabbing the skirts and lifting them, plunging underneath them to reach for the silk that encased her thighs. She moved beneath him at his every touch, her response engorging him.

He sat up, reaching over her to pull her clothing off. Her fingers fumbled with the buttons of his vest and shirt, finally exposing the broad chest where his heart pounded against his rib cage.

She reached for him, her fingers playing through the hair

that matted his chest. She felt the clothes leaving her body as though it was the most natural thing in the world, watching, fascinated, as he rose above her and unbuckled his belt, thrusting his riding trousers down and off.

His flesh sprang free of the cloth, her eyes drawn down to stare at the shaft that thrust out stiff and hard from his body. She drew in breath, gulping the air down as her eyes flew up to meet his.

David stared down at her, his brain fogged with desire as he beheld the length of her tawny body. Her breasts were full and round, her body narrowing to the waist and then gently flaring to rounded hips and long, lean thighs.

He felt her reaction as he stared down at her smooth belly and the triangle of dark hair beneath him. He sat on his knees, straddling her legs, drinking in the sight of her. His flesh painfully erect, he came slowly down toward her, his tongue finding hers, his chest against her breast. Waist to waist, belly to belly, the thick shaft that had surprised her eyes now pressed against her thighs, weakening her limbs.

The pressure of his weight felt good, his body molding to hers, his lips kissing her mouth, her cheeks, her eyes, her ears, her throat as she moaned and reached for him, wanting him closer, kissing the side of his neck, biting little kisses into his shoulder as he moved against her, thrusting his hips against hers.

Her legs parted of their own volition, capturing him and closing again with the hardness that drove him onward rubbing against her inner thighs at every movement of their bodies.

"David—" She breathed his name more than speaking it, his reaction immediate, his body invading hers. She cried out at the sudden pain. He was too big, this was so intimate, she began to push up at him, to claw at him, to push him away before he ripped her apart.

He mistook her fear for unbridled passion, her fingernails clawing into the flesh of his back as an invitation, and even as he needed to devour her, his heart was cursing her wantonness, visions of Miller rising within him. He thrust them away, entering her more deeply, drawing back a little and then thrusting roughly deep inside her again and again. As he moved his brain registered the tightness of her body, the feeling of obstruction.

As he began to pour forth within her she cried out in sharp pain. In that one instant David realized what he was feeling, and Bella's body went past the pain, flooding with pleasure. She clung to him, wanting the miraculous feeling to continue, but he was rising up, pulling away from her.

They came apart as suddenly as they had come together, Bella still confused and wanting him close, wanting some completion she did not understand.

David stared down at her legs. At the proof of his treachery. Trickling red blood announced the fact of her lost virginity. "Oh, God," he said, his voice ragged with anguish. He forced his eyes upward to meet hers. "What have I done to you?" he whispered. "I thought you—I thought he was your lover."

Bella heard the words, her brain trying to impose order on her chaotic emotions. She wanted him back inside her. She wanted to slap his face. She felt as if he were now a part of her. She felt as if he were the most unknown of strangers.

In that moment her brain took over, scalding her with shame. He had thought she had done this with George and thus would allow him, too. He had thought her in love with another man and yet would take advantage of her.

She was naked beneath him. Hot tears welled up. Bella closed her eyes so that she wouldn't have to see his face. David saw her expression as her eyes closed. She was disgusted with him.

"I'm sorry," he began, and he stopped, the words inadequate. His own shame suffused his entire body, shriveling his desire, reddening his face. He moved away from her, reaching for his trousers and quickly dressing. "Bella." He called out her name when he turned back to face her. He was tucking his shirt into his trousers.

She lay as he had left her except that her one arm had gone to cover her breast while the other hand rested between her legs, protecting her nakedness. Her eyes were still closed, as if somehow she could will herself away from him.

"Isabella, please, say something."

Her eyes opened to stare into his. Say something, he asked. She didn't know what to say. Come back and hold me, fill me up and make me yours, get out of my sight and never let me see you again, apologize for accusing me of being wanton, kiss my lips, my breast again, make this all go away, make everything all right.

"Please," David said again in a troubled voice, his eyes searching hers.

She swallowed. Keeping her voice under control, her pride making her determined not break down in front of him, her words came out in a cold tone: "Would you please leave so that I can try to dress."

Her words hit his ears like smooth, hard stones. "Yes, of course," he managed to say, and then he turned away. His hand on the half-unhinged door, he hesitated, wanting to bridge the gap between them. Wanting to say something that would help. Finally he just walked outside, seeing to the horses as Bella sat up and tried to rearrange her clothing.

Her torn chemise was useless. She used it to blot the blood that stained her legs and dressed without it, her breast outlined against the crumpled blue silk. Bella reached for her shawl before she began to arrange her disheveled hair. Pulling hairpins out, she smoothed her hair straight back and tried to tidy it into a bun at the back of her neck.

A few tendrils still fell loose when she got to her feet. She felt achy from the hard floor and a little dizzy, a headache throbbing against her temples once she stood up. Bella reached to steady herself against the rough-hewn stones of the fireplace. Her legs felt weak beneath her. She took a deep breath and then another before straightening up and taking the few steps across the tiny room to the door.

The sun was high in the morning sky, shining down through the elms onto the cool Yorkshire morning. David looked up as she came through the door. "We have to get water for the horses," he said quietly.

"I'm ready."

"Can you—can you ride, or do you want to ride with me?"

"No!" she burst out. "I can ride," she told him.

David nodded, accepting her distaste. He moved to help

her mount, and she backed away, her reaction causing him pain.

"If you bring the mare here to the porch," Bella said, "I can mount by myself."

"Of course," he replied quietly, and he did as she asked.

He waited until she was safely mounted before he rose to the black stallion's back, following beside her as they started back.

They began and ended the ride in silence, David's expression more and more grim as he castigated himself for his actions.

Beside him Bella rode the gray mare side-saddle, her teeth gritted against the ache in her head and the aching in her body and her heart.

David saw only the side of her face, but what he saw made him feel worse than he had ever thought imaginable.

Chapter Nineteen

David and Isabella arrived back to find the household in an uproar awaiting word of the duke and his guest. Markham was told to get Miss Alexander's maid and to tell the coachman to prepare for an immediate departure for London.

Isabella was halfway up the stairs before Sally came running from the back of the huge house. "Oh, Miss Isabella! Are you all right? We were afraid you were lost on the moors."

"She was," David told the maid. He stood at the foot of the stairs. "I found her after her horse had wandered from the road."

"Oh, miss, you could have died!"

"I wish I had," Bella said in a low tone.

"What, miss?"

"Nothing." Bella walked toward the room she had left the night before with such high expectations.

David stood where he was, his frown keeping the servants at a distance. Mr. Gibb was of the opinion that his lordship was within an inch of giving the girl a proper and thorough melting. Mrs. Gibb wasn't so sure it was a spanking he was thinking of giving the girl. Markham, in the kitchen to fetch a pot of tea, went so far as to admit to the Gibbs that he was relieved the duke had decided to return the American girl to London before anything untoward happened.

Mrs. Gibb just shook her head, leaving the two men to share a quizzical glance. Markham finished fussing with the tea and left to deliver it to the duke.

"Is the carriage ready?" the Duke of Exeter asked when Markham let himself into the duke's room.

"Yes, Your Grace. There's not much to pack."

"What?" David looked up from his brown study of the cold fireplace.

"I said everything is ready. Would you like me to light the fire?"

"No, I want to be gone."

"Yes, Your Grace. Shall I see how long Miss Alexander will be?" Markham asked. There was no answer. The valet left the duke to his thoughts, heading out and across the hall to see to the women.

Isabella was already in the carriage, Sally sitting beside her, when the duke stepped up into the carriage and told the driver they were ready to leave.

The duke's dour mood made Markham decide to start the journey by sitting up above with the young coachman, away from the heavy mood inside the large carriage.

Sally, less lucky, stared at her boots, her head bent so that her bonnet hid her face. She already knew her mistress's ways well enough to know something was very wrong with her and could only think the duke had castigated Isabella something fierce.

Miss Isabella was not used to being turned off from her purposes, that Sally knew upon just a short acquaintance. She was willful and headstrong, else they wouldn't have careened across England with that American man.

Sally couldn't imagine what it had been like in this carriage when the duke rode away with Isabella. She was sure it was something the duke had never seen in his entire life. The head maid said the Eppsworth head maid had told her Miss Isabella was called the Terror of California. Sally peeked out from under her bonnet toward the unhappy-looking man across from them. She was sure from the duke's expression that Miss Isabella had given him a taste of the Terror of California.

"I assume you are determined to wed this Miller," the duke said after several bumpy miles had passed beneath the carriage wheels.

"Yes," Bella answered.

"I shall tell your mother."

Bella met his gaze. "You'll tell her what?"

"That you will not be happy apart from Miller." His eyes were moody. "I promise I will do everything in my power to ensure no one stands in your way."

Isabella looked at the guilt in his eyes. "All I ask is that you stop interfering with my personal life," she said stiffly.

"You shall have your wish," David told her quietly.

His words chilled Bella. He wanted to be shut of her once and for all. He felt guilt at deflowering her, and he did not want to face that guilt. Or her. She looked down at her own hands. He wanted to marry her off at the first opportunity, even if it was to the man he had been totally against yesterday.

She wanted to marry George, she told herself. At least now she would have one less opponent to fight. Perhaps even her mother would no longer disagree. Bella bit the inside of her lower lip, pushing back the tears that had hovered around her all morning. Her mother could hardly disagree now, Bella told herself honestly. Dreading the coming scene with her mother, she sat back against the squabs and closed her eyes. She didn't want to see David Beresford's face.

Sitting across from the two women, David heaped coals upon his own head. He had always taken what he wanted, but he had never violated anyone, let alone a young woman of good family. Any liaisons he had engaged in were with women who had had many men before and more afterward.

Even after all the years of good Queen Vickie's reign, human nature was what it had always been. It was simply much more secretive.

For a young man of substance and position to dally with women of easy virtue was regarded as one of the more deplorable attributes of the manly nature. Possibly necessary, but not something to be discussed in front of reputable women.

The fact that married women of impeccable lineage might themselves dally was unthinkable in polite society. When an illicit romance erupted into public knowledge the husband was to be pitied, the wife to be censured. Women were to be stronger than men. They were to be the bastions of society and propriety and to take their lead from their very determined queen. They were not to succumb to the baser passions, no matter the circumstances. They were to allow their husbands' marital rights in order to bring forth children. They were not supposed to enjoy the experience. It was a duty. Young daughters were told on their wedding day that in the night to come their groom might become terribly personal and do things which were disagreeable and hurtful. But as new wives they were to lie back and think of their duty to their husband and to England and let him have his way.

Unmarried girls of good family were totally off limits, totally virginal, and were to remain so until they died unless they married.

David had been brought up to believe that dallying with a bored married woman, who had already done her duty and delivered her husband his heirs, was one thing; to find a light of love or lady of the evening was another thing; but to besmirch the character, let alone the physical person, of a well-brought-up young woman was beyond the pale.

He would never forgive himself. And he knew she would never be able to forgive him. Bella must now despise him forever, as he richly deserved. He had not one word to say in his own defense. He had been so determined to wrench her from that American, he had been so intrigued with her, so jealous of her obvious familiarity with Miller, that he had jumped to conclusions. David stared out the small window nearest him. He had done what no gentleman could ever do: He had lost control of his emotions and harmed a female irreparably.

Whatever punishment his father and Dolores devised for him would never be enough to lift his burden. He quite simply could not forgive himself.

The fact that she obviously loved another, and that she still loved him, made his pain even deeper. He disliked the American adventurer intensely, and yet he now owed the man an apology. Whether Miller ever knew the truth of it or not, David himself did.

They drove until the coachman informed the duke they would have to stop for the night or buy a new horse, for this one would surely go no farther. The duke had him stop and hitch up the duke's own horse, letting the mare trail beside Markham's mount behind the carriage. The boy allowed as how they'd still have to stop sooner or later.

"Just get as far as you can," David said, dreading the night ahead.

It was late when they arrived at the Queen's Arms Inn, silence reigning in the carriage as Markham went in to make inquiries about accommodations.

The valet reported it was a little countrified but altogether it wasn't half-bad; the kitchen looked clean, and the rooms were warm. Markham helped Isabella and Sally from the carriage, the duke coming slowly behind them.

David ignored the innkeeper's invitation to partake of some refreshment in the coffee room and asked to be led to his room. Bella found she was not hungry either, leaving Sally to stare longingly at Markham for assistance.

"Excuse me, Your Grace," Markham said, "but if you wouldn't mind, I might order a bite for the maid and the coachman."

"Do as you wish," David replied.

"I'll just show you to your rooms, then, Your Grace," the innkeeper said, starting toward the stairs that led to the upper regions of the small inn.

"One moment," David told the little man. "Is there a private parlor down here?"

"Yes, Your Grace, through the door there, on your lordship's right."

David forced himself to face Isabella. "I would appreciate a brief conversation alone before I retire," he told her.

Bella's expression froze. "If you wish," she replied, and she followed him toward the doorway.

Markham went to order food for the other servants and

himself as David waited for Bella to enter the small parlor. He closed the door behind her, glancing around himself at the cold little room.

"There are a few things that need to be said," David began stiffly.

"I think everything has already been said. And done," Bella answered. She stood a few feet away from him, her hands hanging at her sides and balled up into fists.

David swallowed, his eyes darkening as he forced himself to speak: "Nevertheless, I must offer you my most abject apologies for my unforgivable actions." There was no reply. "I am not asking your forgiveness; what I did was unforgivable. I am merely asking your acknowledgment that you understand I am forever in your debt and will do everything possible to secure and insure your future happiness."

Bella's eyes clouded. "What are you saying?"

"Why, that I am determined to argue your case to your mother, and I shall insist my father allow Mr. Miller to call upon Exeter House and to escort you in public, so that his attentions may be seen as honorable"—David stumbled over the word, forcing himself onward—"and so that you may obtain your wish."

Anger blazed within Bella. "You were totally against him yesterday."

"That was yesterday," David replied.

"I see. Now I am worthy of no one better, is that it?"

David stared at the angry woman before him. "I thought that he was what you want."

"That's not the point!" Bella said sharply.

Nonplussed, David just watched her. "What is the point? I'm afraid I don't understand."

Bella didn't understand either, but she was not going to admit her mixed feelings to the coldly polite man standing in front of her. She thought of their naked bodies pressing against each other, of the size and solidity of him, her cheeks flaming with the thought. It had meant nothing to him, she could see that in his indifference ever since, his willingness to throw her toward George.

"Of course I want to be with George," she told him. "I love him as I always have and want to be his wife! If he will still have me," she added, watching him register the words, watching his discomfort and taking a perverse pleasure in it. He had stripped her bare, had reached inside her and then thrown her away. He deserved to feel shame.

"He will still have you," David was saying. "You need have no fear on that score."

"How could you know that?" Bella asked defiantly.

He answered slowly: "I know it." Frustration and shame were mixing with anger, and he forced himself not to say the words at the back of his tongue. George Miller wanted her money and her land; nothing would stand in his way, David wanted to tell her. He wanted to shout the words at her, to shake some sense into her and make her see she was throwing herself away upon an unworthy fortune hunter. He wanted to take her in his arms and make love to her, to make her forget the American, to make her react to him as she had in the cabin, uninhibited and passionate, drawing forth emotions from him the depth of which he had never before felt.

David's jaw hardened against the thoughts that were making his flesh react just standing alone in the same room with her. He could not be alone with her ever again, could not think these thoughts. He bowed stiffly and opened the parlor door. "I shall make sure you have your wish," he told Bella, his tone harsh with the strain of holding back all the conflicting emotions that were raging within his heart.

Bella marched out past him, her color high, her head set at a haughty angle. She sailed toward the innkeeper, commanding him to show her immediately to her room.

The balding little man glanced back at the duke and saw his curt nod. "Of course, your ladyship—this way, your ladyship."

Neither Bella nor David corrected the man's assumption that she was kith or kin to the titled nobleman who was gracing The Queen's Arms this night.

Sally saw Bella being escorted up the stairs by the innkeeper. She stood up, grabbing a breast of cold chicken. The maid left the coachman and the valet behind in the coffee room as she hustled after her mistress, catching up at the upstairs landing.

It wasn't until the innkeeper had bowed himself out of the small front bedroom that Sally saw the tears beginning in Bella's eyes. "Oh, miss, are you feeling poorly?"

Isabella Castillo-Suera Alexander stamped her slim foot against the thick wood planking. "I've never felt better in my life!" she told the serving girl, her eyes swimming in tears.

Chapter Twenty

*H*enrietta Epps and her cousin Clarissa were sharing their afternoon tea in the sunny front parlor of Eppsworth House when Clarissa spied movement across the square.

"My dear, isn't that the duke?"

Henrietta squinted to see better, shading her eyes and lifting the transparent front curtain for an even better look. "Why, so it is. And in a hired carriage. I wondered why he wasn't at the Lexington ball and—" Her words stopped, her intake of breath warning her cousin of important news.

Clarissa peered at the tall woman who was descending the carriage. "That's the Terror of California, isn't it?"

Henrietta dropped the curtain, staring across the mahogany table that was cluttered with gilt picture frames and china figurines. "Her mother and the prince told us she was unwell and keeping to her bed. She's not even in the house! She's been out, and here she comes back with David, who has himself been among the missing for days on end. Clarissa, something has happened!" Henrietta's eyes glowed with the possibilities.

"Do you think they might have eloped?" Clarissa said hopefully.

"I can't imagine the prince allowing it. Nor the duke doing it, for that matter. But why would both the duke and the American Terror be gone from town for—what, how long? At least from tea on Monday last." Henrietta's active imagination went into full gear. "What can have been happening?"

"Monday." Clarissa's excitement was barely repressed. "Henrietta, this is Thursday afternoon!"

"Have you seen to the mending of that yellow I let you borrow?" Henrietta's words seemed totally out of place to Clarissa until Henrietta continued: "You might ask Martha to see to it. Now. I think she mentioned one of the maids at Exeter House had a swatch of that exact shade of yellow."

"Of course!" Clarissa jumped to her feet. "I shall send her to Exeter House immediately!"

Henrietta went back to perusing the front of the huge mansion across the square, her brain spinning a hundred tales of what could possibly be transpiring in the hidden depths of Exeter House. A small self-satisfied smile played around her lips. Those who had so recently scoffed would soon be amazed.

Henrietta would have been disappointed if she had seen the almost silent homecoming across the square. Only Tate, the butler, was in the grand hall when the footman opened the door for the weary travelers.

Tate came forward to inform the Duke his father was in the study. And that Mrs. Alexander had retired within her rooms. The butler gave Isabella a disdainful look.

"Thank you, Tate," David said. His expression was even more sober as he shared a long look with Isabella. "I shall talk to my father," David told her. He watched Isabella hesitate and then walk away, heading for the stairs and her mother.

Tate took the duke's cape and gloves, David moving with obvious reluctance toward the study. Girding himself for an unpleasant interview, the Duke of Exeter hesitated at the closed door and took a deep breath before reaching to open it.

Upstairs, Bella opened the sitting room door to find

Connie dozing by the front windows, a pile of knitting in her lap. The sound of the door brought Connie out of her daydreams and back to the reality of midafternoon sunshine and the apparition standing in the doorway. Connie stared up at Bella, her first reaction almost reverent: "Bella! *Gracias a Dios!*" Connie's next reaction was more typical: "You have a lot of explaining to do, young lady!"

Bella offered no dispute. "Where is Mama?" she asked with an almost hopeless tone.

Consuela heard the strangeness in Bella's voice and worried even more. "Sweet heavenly mother, what have you done?"

Bursting into tears, Isabella gave Connie her answer. The old woman got to her feet, the forgotten knitting falling to the floor. "Oh, girl, girl—"

As Connie came toward Bella, Dolores opened her own bedroom door. "Connie, did you—" she got no further. *"Bella!"*

Dolores saw her daughter's forlorn expression, saw the tears coursing down Isabella's cheeks and read the truth in her daughter's eyes. "Oh, Bella—" As Dolores spoke she walked forward, taking her unhappy daughter into her arms. "You have ruined yourself, child. I can see it in your eyes."

"I'm so sorry, Mama," Isabella managed to say through her tears. "I never meant to worry you, I thought we would be all right and you would be happy for me. I never meant to let him do it!"

"Did he force you?" Consuela asked.

Isabella sobbed in her mother's arms. "It—was— terrible!" She choked on the words.

"Well, he won't get away with it, I'll tell you that!" Dolores said angrily. "Believe me, we shall see that he is punished for his despicable actions!"

Isabella let her mother lead her toward the bedroom she had run from Monday afternoon. As mother and daughter disappeared into the bedroom, Sally appeared in the sitting room doorway, valise in hand. Connie stopped the girl. "Go on, girl. If we need you, we'll call."

"But Miss Isabella will need me—"

"Miss Isabella has her mother and myself to take care of her. You certainly weren't able to keep her out of harm's way, were you?"

Sally looked fearful. "Oh, Miss Consuela, I couldn't stop her!"

Connie relented a little. "Not many can. Now go on, we'll call when we need you."

Sally did as Connie bade, her head bent forward dejectedly as she left the room.

In the bedroom, Isabella was letting her mother help her undress when Connie walked in with the valise. Dolores began unbuttoning the blue silk bodice as Connie reached inside the small case.

"*Querida,*" Dolores said as she uncovered Bella's bare breast, "where is your chemise?"

Connie was turning toward them, her face grim. "It's here." She held up the torn and bloody chemise.

Dolores blanched. "Good God, did he rip it off you?"

"Oh, Mama," Isabella said through her tears, "I can't talk about it, please don't ask me to!"

Dolores's eyes blazed with anger. "He shall pay! I knew he was no good, and so did your father!"

"My father?" Isabella stared at her mother. "You're talking about George? George didn't do anything! He wanted to marry me!"

"Bella, have you lost your reason? He convinced you to elope with him, he took advantage of your innocence, he ripped your clothing off you!"

"David ripped my clothing!" The words burst out of Isabella.

Dolores wasn't sure she heard correctly, but Consuela was very sure of what Isabella had said. "I knew it," Connie told Dolores, "I said it all along. I said not to trust that man either! I said he'd be up to no good!"

"Hush, Consuela! I can't concentrate!" Dolores watched Isabella. "What are you saying? Are you saying that David attacked you?"

Isabella's words were spattered with tears. "He threw a sheet over me and carried me off from George, and then he

202

kissed me in his carriage and took me to his estate in Yorkshire instead of bringing me back to you!"

Her mother listened to the words her daughter was crying over. "I don't believe it. David would never take advantage of anyone, let alone you—"

"Ask him!" Isabella burst out. "I ran away, and he followed me somehow, and he took me to a cabin because I was unconscious, and he—he—he thought I was George's mistress!"

"Why were you unconscious?"

"My horse threw me," Isabella said through tears.

"What horse? I thought you said you were in a carriage."

"That was Monday! Tuesday I sneaked out from his house late at night, and I was going to make my way to a town and get back to London and George, only he followed me."

"He followed you," Dolores repeated, trying to get the facts straight. "David took you from George Miller, and you ran away from David to get back to George."

"I love George!"

"So you ran off in the middle of the night, not knowing where you were or where you were going, and David realized you were gone, followed, and found you unconscious. Whereupon he rescued you once again."

"He didn't rescue me! He took me to a deserted cabin and he made love to me!"

"While you were unconscious?" Dolores asked, incredulous.

"We're lucky she's alive!" The words escaped Connie before she could stop them.

"No," Bella said, gulping for air and trying to stop the tears that streamed down her cheeks. "I woke up."

"And then what happened?" Dolores persisted.

"Señora! Isn't that enough?"

"Connie, be quiet, I'm talking to Isabella."

"But señora—"

"Leave us!" Dolores told Consuela.

Connie began to protest but then thought better of it. "I knew this trip would come to a bad end," she said darkly as she left mother and daughter alone.

Dolores watched her daughter. "Take a moment to compose yourself and then tell me exactly what happened, Bella."

Isabella gulped down tears. "He—kissed me, and he began to make love to me, then he—he stopped when he—when he realized"—Bella blushed, her words a bare whisper—"when he saw . . . blood. . . ."

Dolores's eyes closed. Bella felt her mother's pain and steeled herself against her mother's wrath.

A floor below them Prince Henry was staring at his son in utter disbelief.

"I deserve your contempt," David said.

His father's shock was plain. And still he did not speak. He had not spoken since David began to pour out the entire ugly story.

"Please, Father," David begged for the first time in his entire life, "please—say something."

The prince took his time. Shaking his head, he looked out across the side lawns. "David," he said, and he stopped. And then began again. "I don't know what to say. I can't believe you could have done such a thing. I don't know who you are. I don't know how you can ever make amends to either Isabella or her mother. I don't know how I can make amends to them."

David accepted his father's words. "Nor do I. There is no excuse for what I have done."

"Excuse?" Henry's voice rose. "By God, of course there is no excuse for such actions! I shall send for Dolores, and you will of course tell her plainly that you will make immediate plans to marry her daughter!"

"She doesn't want me, Father. She wants the American."

"You will do as you are told!" Henry thundered at his son.

"Father—I can't force myself further upon Isabella! She hates me now! She loves someone else! If I had not interfered, she would already be married to him!"

"Well, you did! And she isn't!"

"I have promised her I will help her attain her heart's desire. I have to help her, Father, I have to atone for the terrible wrong I've done her!"

"First you ruin the poor girl, and then you want to throw her to that fortune hunter?"

"No, I don't want to!" David controlled himself with difficulty. "I have promised to help her in whatever she wants," he replied, the words painful. "And what she wants is George Miller."

"Well, by God, we shall soon see about that!" the prince said, his expression forbidding. He stood up and reached for the bell pull, summoning Tate. "We shall see what her mother has to say."

If David thought the interview with his father painful, it was to pale by comparison with the moment Dolores Alexander walked into the study. Her dark eyes were full of pain and disbelief as they met and accused his. David found himself blushing and turned away, unable to meet her eye. Then, forcing himself, he faced her again, abjectly awaiting her wrath.

The prince walked to her, reaching for her hand. "My dear Dolores, I don't know what to say. I am so shocked at my son's behavior, I am lost for words. In large measure I feel responsible, since I convinced you to trust my son and he proved unworthy of that trust. I have never before been ashamed of him."

David reddened, but he did not defend himself.

Dolores's dark eyes stared fixedly at David as she spoke. "I would like to hear the story from your own lips," she told David.

"I have no excuses, señora," the duke began, only to be stopped by her raised hand.

"Please, do as I ask." She allowed the prince to escort her to a chair. "I have spoken to Isabella, and I have interviewed the maid Sally. Now I want you to tell me exactly what happened, from first to last. Beginning with how you found them."

The Duke of Exeter unwillingly moved forward, nearer Bella's mother. He stood in front of her, feeling worse than he had ever felt in his life. "After Miller first came here, I hired a man to watch Miller's movements in case he tried something desperate. I managed to get my man a position with a newfound crony of Miller's, a carriage driver who was being hired to help Miller in his plan to take—to elope with Isabella. I paid the carriage driver to have other business so that my man would drive the carriage, and I had told him the road to take and where to stop."

"Get on with it," the prince put in irritably.

"I want to hear all of it, Henry. Every last word," Dolores said.

David took a deep breath. "I arrived in the early morning and managed to get Bella—Isabella—to get her away from Miller and from the inn. She was—extremely upset—and I feared she would take off with him the moment she arrived back in London. I felt that a few days in Yorkshire would calm her down, and that she would begin to realize his behavior had been—less than it should have been."

"You are speaking of his coming to her room in the night."

David looked surprised. "She told you?"

"Sally told me," Dolores replied.

"Isabella did not seem to see his intrusion into her room as a problem," David said stiffly, "nor did she see anything wrong with any of the rest of his actions. She took her first opportunity to be away—it was sheer luck I saw her leaving."

"Leaving? Alone?" the prince asked.

"Yes. At night and toward the moors, which are extremely dangerous, as my father knows. I feared for her life, and I took off after her. When she realized I was following her she raced off the road. Her mare went into the marshes and threw her."

"Good lord!" the prince sputtered. "She could have been killed!"

"She hit her head in the fall and was unconscious. I was afraid to take her far, and we were near the old hunter's cabin so I—I took her there."

"Alone. Highly improper," the prince said.

"But possibly necessary," Dolores put in, "since Bella had again placed herself in danger."

David looked grateful for at least that much understanding. "I thought it necessary, at the time."

"Well, get on with it," Henry told his son. "Tell her the rest!"

David swallowed. "I tried to make her comfortable and await her awakening. It was very cold, and she had fallen in the marsh waters—I was afraid she would become chilled and ill. Therefore I—I kept her warm." He stopped briefly, seeing his father's frown. "In the morning she awoke, and I—I lost my senses. I have no excuses."

"Bella says you accused her of having been intimate with George Miller."

"She told me—" David began and stopped.

"Yes?" Dolores demanded.

David's voice lowered. "It doesn't matter what she told me. I misinterpreted it, and in any event, I have no excuse whatsoever. A gentleman should never lose control. I did."

"Why did you kiss her in the carriage?" Dolores asked.

David remembered her struggling with him, he remembered the vision of her in Exeter Gardens, in the American's embrace. He remembered her response and the wild need that grew from it. Remembering, he closed his eyes. "I have no excuse," he said in a low tone.

"You undressed her in the cabin," Dolores said.

"Good God," Henry muttered to himself, and he turned away toward a decanter of brandy.

"I tried to keep her warm. It was very cold, and she was soaked and shivering."

"By?" Dolores persisted.

David's reply was barely audible. "By holding her."

"You told us you wished to marry my daughter before you left. Does that mean that you loved her?"

David looked miserable. "My feelings, my wishes do not matter."

"They do to me," Dolores said crisply. "Do you still wish to marry her, David?"

"I promised her I would help convince you to accept George Miller."

"That's not what I asked," Dolores replied. And she waited.

Conflicting emotions wracked the Duke of Exeter. He

looked toward his father, knowing the prince would expect him to offer for Isabella. But he knew she wanted no part of him. He had forced himself upon her before. He could not make her entire life miserable.

If he said he would ask for her hand, Dolores would never consider Miller, of that David was certain. "She wants to marry Miller," David replied.

"You still have not answered me," Dolores told him.

David took a deep breath. "I do not want to force her into a liaison that I know would be repugnant to her."

"I see," Dolores replied. "I would like to speak to the prince alone."

The duke hesitated and then left his father and Dolores in the study. Outside Tate was hovering in the hallway. "Yes?" David asked, scowling at the man.

"Did you need something, Your Grace?" the butler asked, his face impassive.

"No."

"Very good," Tate said, turning away.

In the study, the prince was upset. "There's no choice in the matter," he said. "David must marry the girl."

"Henry, I don't think forcing the two of them together will accomplish anything other than misery. I know my daughter. And you should know your son."

"I thought I did," the prince said darkly. He watched the handsome woman. "You can't possibly be considering this Miller fellow."

Dolores looked off into the distance across the square, lost in thought. Musing aloud, she told him, "From what I can gather, David appeared on the scene a little too soon."

"Too soon!"

"Mr. Miller had just begun to show his true colors, but not enough to end Bella's infatuation."

"Good grief, Dolores—would you have had that cad have his way with her instead of David? I mean—that is to say—you know what I mean!"

Dolores gave the prince a small, sad smile. "I think I do know what you mean, Henry, but we are not dealing with the sale of oats. We can, of course, insist Bella and David marry, and at this point they will certainly both comply, if forced. But we are dealing with human emotions, and at this moment I must tell you, Henry, Bella does not even want to set eyes on David."

"Damn and blast the boy!"

Dolores sighed. "It saddens me that this had to happen, that he did not use more restraint, but I cannot blame him alone. If she had not gone off on this foolhardy venture, if she had not been acting the part of a wanton with this Miller, David would never have considered her so. I'm sure of that."

"That's no excuse for his actions!"

"I agree," she said quietly. "It is merely a reason."

"He cannot be allowed to get off scot-free!"

"Oh, Henry, I think your son is as far from getting off scot-free as my daughter is."

Henry came near the elegant woman. "You are truly a wonderful woman, Dolores. I don't know how you can be so calm about all this."

"I'm not calm," she told him. "I am worried and angry, and most of all fearful. Because I can no longer allow her other suitors to pursue their cases with her. It would be the worst of travesties if I were to do so and on his wedding night her husband were to find out the truth. He would surely cast her aside with the worst kind of publicity. No. I wouldn't put a man through that, and I certainly wouldn't put Isabella through such a farce."

"Then what is to be done?" Prince Henry asked.

"I am afraid I shall have to allow Mr. Miller to call."

"No! Dolores, you can't mean you will allow him to marry her!"

"Oh, Henry, I pray by allowing her to see him that I can prevent exactly that."

Henry's patrician features were clouded with concern. "I think you are playing with fire. I thought David was, and I should have put my foot down then. Now I see you making the same kind of mistake, and I must tell you so."

Dolores sighed. "I know I am, dear Henry. But I'm afraid there's no help for it. I know my daughter. The more I stand in the way, the more she is thwarted, the more she will want him. And at worst she will be properly married and not the talk of the town. George Miller will not care whether she is virgin on her wedding night or not."

"You can't be thinking of allowing him to see her!"

"See her?" Dolores laughed with bitter humor. "My dear man, I plan on throwing the two of them together! I even have the beginnings of a plan. But we must pray I am right in what I am doing."

Unhappily, the prince conceded her point. "It is your decision, and I shall stand by you, whatever transpires. But I must tell you I think it foolhardy to count on her seeing through the man before more damage is done. And I can't see giving poor Bella to that bounder." He took a deep breath, his frustration coming out. "I don't understand my son! He's never even been willing to talk of marriage, and here he is, proposing it on Monday, abducting her on Tuesday, having his way with her on Wednesday, and then giving her away to another man on Thursday! I tell you, I don't understand any of it. I thought he loved her."

"I'm counting on the fact that he does," Dolores said.

"What?"

Dolores stood up. Reaching out her hand, she squeezed his arm a little. "Just pray a little, Henry. Pray that I'm right and he truly does."

"I don't know what you're doing."

"Henry," Dolores said frankly, "I'm not entirely sure I know myself."

Henry's worried frown deepened as he watched Dolores walk out of the book-lined study.

Chapter Twenty-one

George Miller arrived at Exeter House promptly at eleven A.M. on Friday morning. A little unsettled that the Exeter footman had known where to find him, he was still more unsettled by the fact of the invitation to an interview with Dolores Alexander at Exeter House.

The butler was a smallish man with a disconcerting directness in his cold eyes as he listened to George tell his name and his reason for appearing again on the doorstep. The butler's gaze seemed to see right through the American. George felt as if he were being sized up as a man who was going to steal the family silver. "This way," the man said in a tone that was faintly contemptuous. He started away and then turned back, waiting for Miller to follow him down the wide hall. "In here," the butler added, again omitting the respectful "sir."

George was so nervous he didn't notice the omission.

The butler knocked on a closed door and then opened it, announcing: "Mr. Miller has arrived." The man stepped back, allowing George Miller to enter before closing the door.

The room into which George had been ushered was a small parlor decorated in cheery tones of lemon yellow and spring green. George glanced past the mahogany furniture, taking in very little of his surroundings as his gaze found the tall, patrician-looking man who was studying him from under hooded eyes. Recognizing him as the prince, George sketched a bow. "Your servant, sir. Your Highness," George corrected himself.

"Yes, well, I wanted a moment alone with you before the others arrive," the prince said.

"Yes?" George said with sinking heart.

"Your abduction of Miss Alexander was reprehensible."

"But sir, I mean Your Highness, you wouldn't allow me to see her!"

"A gentleman would have pursued the matter no further," Henry said stiffly.

"Love knows no rules!" George Miller replied dramatically. He earned a sour look from the prince.

"That is no excuse for not behaving as a gentleman should!" Henry snapped.

George tried to seem confident. "Is it any worse than abducting her against her will as your son did? He had no right to come between us!" the man ended passionately.

The prince brought a lifetime of control to bear and refrained from hitting the man in the jaw. "My son was asked by the girl's mother to ensure her safety." Prince Henry's voice was as cold as the north winds that blew across his Yorkshire estates. "You can hardly equate his helping Mrs. Alexander with your own actions, which put her daughter's reputation into jeopardy!" The prince heard his own words and, knowing what Miller did not, felt a pang of guilt. Miller had placed Bella in jeopardy of losing her reputation, but it was David who had ruined it forever if any became the wiser.

Henry was silent for a moment, both men still standing as the prince tried to decide what to say next to the man who was obviously the furthest thing from a gentleman. They had nothing in common except their manhood.

The parlor door opened as they faced each other, Isabella and Dolores entering. Dolores's step slowed, but Isabella took one look at George and then ran toward him. "Oh, George! You came!"

George let Isabella hug him, looking past her at the prince's scandalized expression. He glanced at Dolores next, something in her expression convincing him to pull a little away. "Of course I would come, darling. How could you doubt it? I have been beside myself with worry. But we must not allow our emotions to embarrass your mother." And so saying, George finally addressed Dolores. "Good morning, Mrs. Alexander. It was good of you to ask me to call."

"Good morning," Dolores responded in a neutral tone.

"George . . ." Bella was disappointed at his cool response. She wanted him to grab her, to rant and rave at the people who had ruined their plans. She wanted him to punch David in the nose. The duke, she corrected her own thoughts. He was only the odious duke, nothing more. But the memory of David's wild need to crush her near flitted through her limbs, making her heart uneasy. She searched George's face with fearful eyes. "What's wrong?"

"Nothing, my dear," George said formally.

Dolores reached for Bella's arm. "If we are to discuss this situation, Bella, I insist that the proprieties begin to be respected."

"Proprieties!" Bella began, only to be quickly cut off by her mother's next words.

"If you do not obey me, this interview is at an end!"

Isabella Alexander was a very stubborn young woman. But she knew her mother was even more stubborn, and she recognized the finality in her mother's tone. "Yes, Mama," Bella said, surrendering.

A little surprised at Bella's meekness, George stood where he was, watching Bella dutifully move to sit beside her mother. Fear began to clutch at him. He had always counted on Bella's defiance in his plans. "I—I'm sorry for any worry we caused you, Mrs. Alexander, but we had no choice," the man began.

Trying to hide her distaste, Dolores listened to the man's excuses for his inexcusable behavior. He ended with: "I tried desperately to catch up with Bella—I was left worried sick! I didn't even know who had abducted her!"

"You had no idea who had taken her," Dolores repeated.

"No, ma'am! It was done in such an underhanded and clandestine manner that I did not!"

"Underhanded!" the prince ejaculated, momentarily forgetting his anger at his son. He would have continued, but Dolores looked toward him, holding up one long-fingered hand to stop him. Turning back toward Miller, Dolores said, "So you thought some kidnapper had stolen her."

"What else was I to think?" George said insincerely, trying to sound wounded, aggrieved, and worried.

Dolores pressed on, her expression noticeably colder. "And thinking Bella kidnapped in a strange land, and knowing where I resided, you did not see fit to come to tell me she might be in mortal danger?"

George Miller stared at the woman. He was taken aback for a moment and then recovered. "Tell you? No—that is, I—of course—assumed that you had had us followed—"

"Which is it?" Dolores demanded. "You were beside yourself with worry over kidnappers or you assumed I myself was the culprit?"

"Not you!" he put in quickly, "but—well, your hosts."

Dolores glanced at Henry. "I see. So you thought our hosts had hired kidnappers."

"No!"

"Mother, please!" Bella started and stopped, seeing her mother's blazing eyes travel toward her and then back to focus on George Miller.

Miller took a deep breath. "Mrs. Alexander, as I said, I was at first beside myself with worry. And then I realized that you had probably been distressed by our actions, and your hosts, who had thrown me out bodily, were probably behind Bella's abduction and were bringing her to you."

"But she wasn't brought home," Dolores told the man.

He hesitated, sensing a trap. "I beg your pardon?"

"She was not brought home Tuesday," Dolores said very distinctly.

"I don't understand," George replied.

"Nor do I," Dolores responded. "Please enlighten me. I have been given to understand that the Duke of Exeter had been quite willing to help you see my daughter."

"He was the only one!" Miller said quickly.

"But you still assumed he was part of a plan to come after her and abduct her from your side."

"Well, he did!" Isabella burst in impatiently.

"Yes," George said belatedly.

"For God's sake, what is the point of this?" Prince Henry exploded.

Dolores took her time. "The point, Henry, is to see whether I will give my permission for Mr. Miller to escort Bella to Lady Groverston's ball this evening."

"Mama!" Bella's eyes widened in surprise. "But—I don't even want to go to Lady Groverston's!"

"You are going with me this evening, Isabella, and that is a fact. Whether Mr. Miller accompanies us is the only question."

George Miller came toward them. "Mrs. Alexander, I assure you, the only reason we defied you was our love for each other. Bella will tell you, too. If you give your consent to our marriage, we shall, of course, do exactly as you say!"

"That's blackmail, sir!" Henry sputtered. "You are saying you will behave like a gentleman if you are promised your reward!"

"Mrs. Alexander," George appealed to Dolores, ignoring the prince, "I love her!"

"If you love her so much, why did you allow her to be abducted and then never bother to cry an alarm?"

"Bella, tell them!" George urged.

Isabella looked from George to her mother. "Are you truly willing to accept George as my fiancé?"

"No," Dolores responded, seeing the hope fade on her daughter's face. "What I am saying is that I may give you permission to attend a few events together so that I then may make my decision as to whether this man is the proper spouse for you."

"I assure you, I shall be a model escort!" George cried, his eyes lighting with hope.

"You had better be," the prince said darkly, "or you'll have me to contend with!"

"But Mama, I cannot go! All will be talking— whispering—"

"Whispering about what?" George asked.

Dolores spoke before Bella could reply: "Bella has been among the missing and is afraid word will leak out about your endangering her reputation in such a foolhardy manner." Dolores gave her daughter a pointed look. "However, I have assured her there is nothing to be worried about. We have said she was ill and was being kept in bed for a few days."

"But the servants know better! They know I wasn't here, and they are bound to talk," Bella persisted.

"Whether they do or they do not, you certainly aren't going to be cowed by the gossip of your inferiors." Dolores stared at her daughter.

"Where were you?" George asked, his brow furrowing.

"Will—will *he* be there?" Isabella asked her mother, not hearing George's words.

"To whom are you referring?"

"The duke," Bella said.

"I have no idea," her mother replied placidly. "Why?"

Bella hesitated. Seeing her mother's disapproval and George's quizzical expression, she summoned up a tiny smile for him. "I—I just wondered."

"She is probably quite overset by all that happened," George told Dolores before smiling down at the seated Bella. No one had offered him a chair, the prince was still standing, and he was afraid to ask if he could sit. "I give you my word, Bella dear, I shan't let him come near you, nor even ask to dance with you. You have nothing to fear. Does she?" George asked her mother. "There is nothing for us to fear if we have your word."

"What about your word, sir?" Dolores asked him.

George Miller hesitated. "As to what, ma'am?"

"May we rely upon you not to attempt another abduction? May we rely upon your complete discretion? I want no talk of an engagement until I formally sanction it. I do not want London whispering about my daughter."

"As long as we know among ourselves," he began.

"Egad, man!" the prince blurted out. "Can't you give the woman a straight answer?"

George was irritated by the prince's attitude, and it showed. "I already have," he said stiffly.

"Very well." Dolores stood up. "If I have your word, I shall allow you a few minutes to talk. Henry?"

Unwillingly Henry followed Dolores out the door. He left it open, giving one last forbidding glance back at the American man.

In the hall the prince stopped Dolores. "I don't think it's proper for them to be alone."

"Neither do I," Dolores told him enigmatically.

Behind them the door to the parlor closed. "You see what I mean?" Henry asked her. "You can't trust the man!"

"I don't," Isabella's mother replied. "I am baiting a trap."

"For whom?" he asked.

Dolores smiled then. "For whoever walks into it, my dear Henry."

Inside the small side parlor George turned back from the door to face Bella. "Dear heart, we are going to be together at last!" He came toward her to take her in his arms, but she shied away from him. "What's wrong?" he asked.

"Nothing," she told him.

"Where did he take you? Why did he not bring you immediately here?" George Miller asked.

"He said they were afraid I'd only run away again."

George smiled. "And would you have, dear?" He reached to kiss her, and she pulled away again, worrying him. "Why do you move away from me? Sweetheart, you don't believe any of the things they say about me, do you?"

"Of course not!" Bella said quickly. "It's just that—so much has happened. And—well, there are things we must talk about."

"Of course, but I want to hold you, I want to kiss you and make you know how much I missed you."

Bella backed away from his touch. "You promised my mother to behave like a gentleman."

"She'll not know what goes on when we're alone, dear heart."

"But we'll know!" Bella told him, doubt rising in her eyes.

George saw the doubt and checked where he was. "Of course you are right, sweetheart. But you have to understand my feelings. I love you!" He looked a little worried. "You haven't changed your mind about marrying me, have you?"

"No!" Bella said vehemently. But she moved away to the windows. She fingered her linen handkerchief, plucking at the lace edging. "I haven't changed. Have you?"

"Never!" he told her. "I told you how much I love you."

"No matter what?" Bella asked, looking troubled.

"No matter what," he said easily.

She turned to face him, doubt filling her eyes. "You say that so easily."

"Because it's true!"

"But—could you forgive me if—if I did something— terrible?" Bella asked, watching his eyes so earnestly that he reached for her hands.

"You could never do anything so terrible I would stop loving you. As long as you love me and become my wife."

Bella smiled tremulously. "You really do love me, no matter what."

In answer he brought her hands up to his lips, kissing them. "If you'll let me, I'll show you how much."

"There are things I must tell you, George. Things you must know before you make your decisions."

"Make what decisions?" he asked.

Bella blushed a little. "To marry me."

"That decision has long since been made, dearest. And nothing could change it."

"You mustn't say that so easily," she told him again. "There are things that are unforgivable—"

"Nonsense," he told her emphatically.

The door opened behind them. George whirled around, glaring at the doorway as Consuela walked into the room. Ignoring his expression, she settled herself onto the settee and folded her hands in her lap, watching them.

"We would appreciate a moment alone," George said stiffly.

"You've had it," Consuela told him calmly.

George glared at her and then turned back to Bella. "Tell her to leave."

Bella looked from George to Consuela. "I can't," she said quietly. "It's best this way."

George strove to contain his irritation. "If you insist. But then I insist that I have all your dances this evening."

"I don't know if we can," Bella said quietly. "Anyway, I don't feel very much like dancing tonight."

"But why not?" he demanded. "Bella, your mother is finally letting us see each other! This should be the happiest day of your life!"

Bella tried to look deep into his eyes. "I want to have a hundred happiest days, a thousand! I want the day of my wedding to be the happiest day of my life, and the day my first child is born—"

"Our first son," George said.

"Isabella!" Consuela was truly shocked at the turn in the conversation. The old duenna stood up. "It is time to go."

"No!" George told the old woman.

"Yes," Bella said, turning toward him. "Mama is not against us now, and we must not make her so."

"She's not for us either!"

"No, but she's letting us see each other. Let's make her realize how much we love each other," Bella pleaded.

George hesitated. Ready to argue, he thought about his options, and about the last night they were together. He had almost ruined everything, and he had the feeling that the serious conversation Bella wanted to have was about that. It was probably the reason she had shied away from having him kiss her. "If you insist," he said with poor grace.

"I ask it of you," Bella replied. "And I shall see you this evening. The prince is procuring an invitation for you, and you will arrive with us."

The thought of being accepted into London's high society was entrancing to George, lightening his expression. He bowed toward Consuela and kissed Bella's hand one more time before he left.

Consuela did not speak until she and Isabella reached their suite upstairs. "I cannot credit it," Connie said as she closed the upstairs sitting room door.

Bella turned to face the woman who had raised her. "You can't credit what?"

"Well, if you don't know, you're a fool. And if you can't see through such an obvious one as that man Miller, I don't know what's gone wrong with your brain. That man is no more a gentleman than I am!"

"He loves me, and he'll love me no matter what!"

"Oh yes? He loves you so much he didn't even bother to report you missing."

"He knew who took me!"

"How? He could think he did, but how could he be sure? Heiresses are kidnapped all the time. How did he know you weren't in harm's way? He didn't even know you weren't here!"

"At least he'll stand by me when he learns what has happened to me," Isabella replied hotly, "which is more than you can say for a lot of so-called gentlemen!"

"Of course he will!" Connie countered with a sharp tongue. "He wants your money!"

"No!" Isabella shouted the word. Her mother opened the connecting door.

Dolores looked sternly from Connie to Bella. "Do you want the entire staff privy to your conversation?" Her words were angry but delivered in a soft tone that would not carry beyond the room.

Bella looked properly cowed, but Connie looked about to speak.

"Connie," Dolores continued, "I wish to speak to you. Bella, you should rest for an hour, and then I shall wake you to get ready for the evening."

"Yes, Mama," Bella said quietly.

Connie did not trust Bella's quiet attitude and told Dolores so once Isabella left. Dolores listened but said little.

In her bedroom Isabella began to undress. She almost didn't hear the soft knocking at her door that preceded Sally's entrance into the bedroom.

"I thought you might need some help, miss," Sally said softly, watching her mistress.

"I don't need any help," Bella told the girl.

"Oh, miss, please don't go blaming me."

"You told them where we were!"

"I never did! Miss, I couldn't have. I didn't know we were even going, or where, or anything! And I was with you!"

Bella heard the words and realized they were the truth. But her conflicting emotions did not want to hear them. "I don't need any help," she repeated. "Especially from one who does not like my future husband."

"Future husband? Do you mean the duke, miss? Or—oh, miss!" Sally's eyes rounded in shock. "Oh, miss, you couldn't mean that terrible man—the one who tried to sneak into our room in the middle of the night!"

"He's not a terrible man! George is a hero who wants nothing more than for us to be together forever!" Bella defended, tears rising to her eyes.

Sally rewarded Bella's words by bursting into tears of her own and fleeing the room. Bella stood where she was. Picking up a pillow, she hurled it toward the wall. "I don't care!" Bella said, the tears beginning to fall. "I don't care what anyone says! I hate that man! I hate him, and I always will! I love George!"

There was no one in the room to hear her.

Chapter Twenty-two

*L*ady Groverston's ball began promptly at nine P.M., with people arriving in a constant stream of carriages whose iron wheels clattered noisily over the cobblestones.

The ballroom of Groverston Hall beggared description. The centerpiece of an ornate Regency mansion, it had been built for an opulent age, and from its twenty-four-carat gold filigreed columns to its marbled dance floor it lived up to its status as one of the most stately of houses.

The Exeter carriage pulled around Berkeley Square toward the wide front portico of Groverston Hall. Joshua brought the matched bays to a stop, young Tim jumping down to help Mrs. Alexander and her daughter and the prince from the carriage. The young man hesitated at the sight of the American man who was so handsome he was almost pretty. George Miller waited for the others before he disembarked himself, very self-conscious in his newly rented evening clothes.

The American, not used to being helped, jumped down by himself, saving young Tim from having to make a decision about the unwelcome intruder. For unwelcome he was. Even Joshua, who had been with the family forever and had more fellow feeling than most, said as how the American was the worst of news for this family, and that was a certain fact. When Tim asked why, he was greeted with dark looks and ambiguous words about foreign devils who seduce good girls.

At the moment, the man of whom Tim and Joshua took a dim view was giving his arm to Miss Alexander and leading her forward, up the steps, and into Groverston Hall.

"He's up to no good, and that's for sure" was Joshua's opinion as he pulled the Exeter carriage into the queue that came close to surrounding the entire Mayfair square. Young Tim nodded vigorously, agreeing with anything his hero said. Tim had no family, at least none who wanted to know him, and Joshua had taken pity on the boy and said he might make a first-rate groom with the proper training.

Joshua had convinced Tate to give the boy a try, and young Tim would never forget the man who had given him his first three square meals a day. Two years later, young Tim was fast on his way to becoming the first-rate groom Joshua had predicted. How many extra hours the old man had taken teaching the boy, or why the bachelor Joshua had bothered, didn't come into the equation for either of them. Tim was grateful for the help, and Joshua was grateful for the companionship.

"I don't understand," Tim said to Joshua as they joined the queue and settled down to wait for the evening. "If he's such a bad 'un, whyever are the prince and the duke having anything to do with him?"

"It's blackmail, the way I see it," Joshua said. "It's all it could be. The man's got sumpin' on someone they're trying to protect."

Tim screwed up his brow in concentration. "Who could it be?" he asked, already feeling a little easier in his heart. He remembered Sally going off with the other maid in the hired carriage and had been afraid the American seducer of women might have been after his own Sally. Well, not his own yet, Tim admitted to himself, but at least he had a chance if a one like that didn't turn her head.

Henrietta Epps had positioned herself near the main doors of the ballroom, waiting for the Exeter party to arrive.

Finally spying them coming in, she started toward them, ready with a smile and small talk to do a bit of detecting. But she suddenly checked, shocked to see a stranger escorting the Terror of California. Coming behind the couple, the prince was beside Dolores. Henrietta's expressive blue eyes swept the people around the Americans; the duke was nowhere to be seen.

Moving backward a little, the Countess of Eppsworth nearly trod on the foot of the Prince of Wales's very dear friend, Lily Langtry. "Oh, I'm so sorry, Lily!" Henrietta couldn't contain herself a moment longer. "I just can't believe what I am seeing!"

Henrietta had always been known as the most reliable of gossips. Mrs. Langtry smiled at Henrietta, leading her on.

"Tell me, dear Henrietta, what is it that has you so upset?"

"I am quite beside myself," Henrietta said, Clarissa coming up beside her as she spoke. "What on earth can be going on between the Duke and the Terror?"

"Isn't it odd?" Clarissa put in, earning an introduction to the Prince of Wales's very dear friend.

"We were just saying," Henrietta continued, making a point of her acquaintance with the lady who was one of the current lights-of-love of the man who would one day be king of England, "it is passing strange that the duke is nowhere to be found now that the Terror has 'recovered' her health. I can't help but wonder where he is this night."

"If you mean the Duke of Exeter, he is already here," Clarissa said. She looked toward the man they were talking about. Startled, Henrietta followed Clarissa's gaze and saw the handsome duke with Lady Winston.

Henrietta clucked loudly. "Oh, my, would you look at that. I wonder if the American Terror has noticed yet."

The ladies' eyes all turned to peruse Isabella, who seemed not to know or care whether the duke was in attendance. The handsome young man none of the regulars had seen was leading Bella into a waltz.

As the eyes of the assemblage turned toward Bella she felt her color rising. She knew they were all talking about her, whispering about where she had been and who her new escort was. To a rich and bored society, even the suggestion of intrigue, mystery, or scandal was irresistible.

Isabella Alexander's pride came to her rescue. Her chin raised high, she leaned in toward George, obviously hanging on her escort's every word. Her smile widened as she laughed effervescently, looking the picture of happiness.

From all the way across the large room David could hear her merry peals of laughter. His heart frozen, he heard her obvious happiness and felt himself worsening by the minute.

"David?" Adela Winson touched his arm. "Weren't we just about to dance?"

"Sorry," he said. He led Lady Winston to the dance floor, his movements flawless as they joined the dance. Adela was smiling widely to friends and enemies alike as they whirled around the floor in time to Mr. Strauss's music.

Adela had heard the rumors about David and the American heiress, had heard that Henrietta Epps herself was pronouncing them an item. With David's disappearance all week and, of course, Isabella Alexander also being among the missing, Adela had feared the worst. She had been ready to face society with a stolid and imperious eye as the discarded mistress. But tonight had arrived, and she found she had no need.

David had appeared on her doorstep that very afternoon, begging her to attend the ball with him, and, as always, Winston was ready to allow any excuse that would enable him to escape society's functions and pursue his gambling and his boxing cronies.

Adela had put David through his paces for over an hour, had elicited apologies for his unexpected absence, for his not telling her he had to attend to Yorkshire duties, and later she chided him none too gently all the way to the ball about all the talk his sudden absence had entailed.

The Duke of Exeter knew exactly what polite society was surmising, thanks to Adela's barbed comments. His one thought was to save Bella's reputation and ensure her happiness. Which, David concluded as he danced and caught glimpses of Bella across the floor, obviously meant helping her marry the American. His heart felt leaden, his arms involuntarily tightening around Adela as he thought of Miller's arms around Bella. And what would come later.

"David, you're so aggressive tonight." Adela smiled up at him. "You seem positively ready to sweep me off my feet."

He deliberately relaxed his hold on her, forcing himself to smile at her, praying that all would be fooled, that none would find out the truth and blacken Bella's name. How any could look at his eyes and believe the farce he dared not think.

Adela was carrying off her part wonderfully. But then, she had experience. She was a much-admired lady and safely married; certainly none would ever believe the duke would do what her other suitors had not and cause a scandal by having her divorce to marry him. The queen had the right to approve marriages of all members of the royal family, a law upon which George III had insisted. Queen Victoria would never give her consent to the Duke of Exeter's marrying a divorced woman, let alone the much-gossiped-about Adela Winston.

As they danced David realized that, if he were to help stop the gossip about Isabella's whereabouts these past days, and his own, he must ensure the gossips would doubt their servants' whispered information. Society must see there was nothing whatsoever between himself and his father's American guest. They must be made to think he was actively pursuing another.

And Adela's company would not do. The only way was to pay court to a young lady who would be seen as a suitable mate, a possible duchess. Someone Prince Henry would obviously approve of, and someone who obviously would not merely be dallied with—therefore a young and unmarried lady. The fact of her existence would forestall all gossip about him and the American girl. Perhaps in some way it would make up a little for all the harm he had done Bella. It was a forlorn little hope. He knew no matter what anyone else ever knew or even forgave, he would never forgive himself. He had forced himself upon an unwilling woman.

"David, are you quite all right?"

"Yes, Adela, quite," the duke replied automatically, his thoughts going back to Isabella's naked skin and the wantonness of her first response to him. She had wanted him in those moments, he was sure of it. But then, she did not know where it all led, she had been innocent and unsullied. He had harmed her and destroyed his own peace of mind forever.

"You look as if you've lost your best friend," Lady Winston chided coquettishly. "And I know you haven't, for I'm here in your arms, darling."

"I don't like my name being bandied about," David said half-truthfully.

"Well, you shouldn't take quick trips to tend to your estates when your house guest is ill. You know how people love to talk," Adela answered practically.

"Yes, and I'm sick and tired of it."

"The only way people will stop talking about an eligible bachelor is when he is old or happily married, and you're in no danger of either," Adela told him, smiling up at his handsome face.

"You might be surprised," David replied.

The music stopped. Adela looked up into his moody eyes. "What is wrong with you tonight? I'm beginning to think something really is going on!"

"Something is," David told her, "but not with Isabella Alexander."

Adela almost lost her famous composure. With tremendous willpower she smiled at the people they passed as David led her back to one of the gilt chairs that lined the sides of the huge room. David draped himself across one as Adela smiled hellos at the Countess of Eppsworth and Clarissa Stanisbury. "So nice to see you, dear," Henrietta Epps replied, her pale blue eyes gliding toward the Duke of Exeter. "And you, David; we've missed you quite awfully this week." She gave a tittering little laugh. "The season simply isn't the same when you're not in attendance."

"I fear I shall be disappointing you further, then," David said.

"Really?" Clarissa said before she could contain herself.

"Whatever do you mean?" Henrietta continued, smiling widely. "Are you retiring from society? Or have you finally met your match?"

"You shall soon see," the duke replied. "But, of course, this is just between us."

"Oh, my dear, of course! I am flattered beyond measure that you would count me as a confidante. You can rely upon my discretion utterly!" Henrietta Epps very nearly rubbed her bejeweled hands together.

If David had felt less guilt he would have laughed out loud at Henrietta's words. He knew he could count on her to spread the word of something in the air. It would be across London by morning. He stood up, bowing to the three women. He sauntered across the huge room, threading his way through the crowds, aware of the three pair of female eyes watching his progress.

Of the three, Henrietta and Clarissa were the most avid. Adela's gaze narrowed as she watched David walk toward his father, her green eyes even greener as she waited to see him stop at Isabella's side. Her temper matched her red hair as she steeled herself, remembering his earlier denials.

The women waited with bated breath as David stopped beside his father and Dolores and nodded to Isabella and George Miller. After a brief interchange Prince Henry spoke to the American Miller and walked away with his son.

"What is he doing?" Clarissa asked.

"What you mean is, where is he going," Adela said waspishly.

Henrietta glanced at Adela before looking back toward the duke. "Adela, dear, do you know something we don't?"

"I know many things you don't, Henrietta," Adela told the busybody as she stood up. "Please excuse me."

"Of course, you poor dear. I'm sure you feel the headache coming on," Henrietta said insincerely.

Adela gave the countess a tight smile. "Darling Henrietta, how sweet of you to be so concerned for me. Believe me, I couldn't feel better!"

Clarissa watched Adela start across the room. "Do you suppose she is going to make a scene?"

"Adela? Never," Henrietta replied. "She wouldn't give us the satisfaction."

Their attention returned to the duke and the prince as the two men stopped beside Lady Cavendish and bowed.

"Good grief, he can't—" Henrietta began and then stopped.

As the two women watched, David spoke to Millicent Cavendish. After another moment speaking to her mother, David led the girl to the floor.

"I don't believe it!" Henrietta said.

"Do you suppose we've been wrong?" Clarissa asked, chagrined. "Lord, I don't want everyone laughing at us."

"Millicent Cavendish! She's too young, too plain, too insipid, too—impossible!"

"Well, he certainly wouldn't be paying attention to her unless he was serious. And he did say we'd soon see. And, Henrietta dear, she is most eligible. And her father is the greatest of friends with Prince Henry. David wouldn't pay attention to her and lead her on; she's a Cavendish!"

People around the room were divided between glancing toward Henrietta, toward Isabella and her very attentive escort, and toward the couple just beginning to dance.

"Shall we?" George was asking Bella.

"We can't leave Mama alone," Bella replied.

"Nonsense, dear," Dolores told her daughter. "I'm perfectly all right by myself."

"What is this about your being alone?" Prince Henry asked as he rejoined them.

"I was just telling Bella she could dance."

Isabella almost said no. When David had walked near she had almost left the floor and the room and the house. The only thing that kept her at the ball, and now propelled her into George's arms, was the thought of the watchful eyes all around her. Isabella was not going to give them the satisfaction.

"I'd adore it, George," Bella murmured, wondering why the words weren't true.

He took her in his arms, and all should have been well. It wasn't. But at least while dancing she was no longer shaking.

Isabella had been terrified someone would notice the state of her nerves when David came near. The duke, she corrected herself. He was not David, he was merely the odious duke.

She had felt faint when she realized David was coming toward her. She knew he was going to ask her to dance, and she knew she was going to say no. The entire time he spoke with his father, Bella steeled herself for the moment when he would turn toward her.

He never did. The moment he nodded briefly to her mother surprised Bella. When he had done the same to her, his eyes did not meet hers. He had been glancing somewhere past her. The snub went unnoticed by everyone but Bella.

And then he was gone. Isabella would not permit herself to look behind, to see at whom he had been looking. But when George led her to the floor she saw David leaning in to listen to something a very excited Millicent Cavendish was saying.

The Duke of Exeter and young Millicent were dancing, Millie's face flushed with pleased confusion. If David had told her the impression he wished to give, she could not have done better.

Every eye in the room was aware of the dashing duke and his innocent young dance partner. This was Millicent's first season, and to be singled out by the duke was a rare pleasure for any of the young debutantes. If he danced with her a second time this evening, all would be talking about it tomorrow.

The prince led Dolores to the dance floor, glancing toward his son and then toward Isabella and George Miller. "It seems David's plan is working," Henry said.

"I hope so," Dolores replied a little doubtfully.

"Young Millie seems glad of it, at any rate."

"Yes, and I hope the poor girl doesn't get her hopes up too high." Dolores spoke of Millicent, but she was looking at her own daughter over Henry's shoulder. "Or isn't hurt later when he doesn't offer for her."

The prince thought about it. "Well, you never know. He just might be serious. Then again, if you are right in your assumptions about our two stubborn children actually caring about each other, I rather doubt Millie will take it amiss. Her mother's a practical woman, and she certainly knows David well enough to assume he's merely giving Millie a wonderful first season. Young Millie's reputation will be quite made among all the young blades after David's paid attention to her. She'll be beating off suitors with sticks."

Dolores laughed at his words, light peals of merriment that began to prove to the assemblage that all was well with the residents of Exeter House. Several ladies seated near the punch table were of the opinion that Isabella had been living up to her nickname earlier in the week.

"Mark my words," one matriarch was saying as she watched the Terror of California, "she took to her room until her mother would let that young man escort her. They have an understanding."

"But he's an American. I thought she was here to find a titled husband," another woman put in.

"He's followed her here, and she's determined to wed him, it's as plain as can be." The woman looked across the room. "And Henrietta Epps has been pretending to be so close to them!"

"Bella, sweetheart, what's wrong?" George asked as the music ended.

"Why do you keep asking me that?" Isabella snapped, and she instantly regretted it. "Nothing's wrong," she said in a contrite tone. "I don't know why you keep bringing it up!"

"Bella, dear, how are you feeling?"

Isabella found herself almost face to face with Henrietta Epps. She gave the older woman a brilliant smile. "Just wonderful, Countess." Bella tucked her hand quite firmly into the crook of George's arm as they walked past the woman. "George, dear, I'm simply dying for some refreshment."

With her free hand Bella fanned her face, keeping up a chatter of small talk until they were well past the Countess of Eppsworth. Once away, Bella broke off her words in midsentence.

"What was that all about?" George asked.

"I'm sorry. Those two women we just passed are the worst gossips in London."

George heard Bella's words but still did not understand. "If I didn't know better, I would say your reactions had something to do with the Duke of Exeter. You have been acting very strangely ever since we arrived and you first saw him."

"That's ridiculous," Bella told him. "I couldn't care less where the man is or isn't." And then, contradicting herself, she added: "And even if I were, wouldn't that be understandable? After all, the man abducted me! It's no wonder I hate him, is it?"

"I'm glad to hear you say it," George said sincerely. "I'm not the jealous type, but some would say he is good-looking. And he obviously cares about you."

"Me?" Bella stared at her companion. "What on earth gives you that idea?"

"Bella, he wasn't against our seeing each other. He even helped us. But then he came on that wild ride to stop you from marrying me. Obviously his feelings changed when he thought you were out of reach."

"Well, I am out of reach!"

"Are you truly, sweetheart? I confess, I have feared the fact of his living in the same house with you."

Bella's eyes clouded. "Why? Why did you fear it?"

"Why, because he is there, with you. He can pursue his case with you at all the hours I am forbidden."

Isabella looked down. "There is something I have to tell you, George." She looked up. "But not here."

"On the terrace?" he suggested, smiling. "Then I can steal a kiss or two."

"No. I mean not here, tonight. Tomorrow. Come take me riding, all right? We can talk alone."

George smiled. "There is nothing I would like better. However, my finances are sorely straitened by all the expenditure this week . . ." He let the words trail off.

"I'll bring you more money," Bella said quietly.

"Oh, dearest, I'm sorry to have to ask, but if you could—"

"Of course." She dismissed the subject, her thoughts elsewhere.

"There is something I want to discuss with your mother,

Bella," George told her, sounding very serious. "I want to set a date for our wedding. The sooner the better."

Isabella heard his words through a haze of other thoughts. "Yes," she said in reply, "we should get back to Mama now."

Across the room David delivered Millicent back to her mother and father and accepted a cup of iced champagne punch with them. His eyes traveled the room, finding Bella as she moved toward the card room with a small group of people. She looked regal next to the others.

"What do you think about a bit of faro or cassino, David?" Millicent's father was asking.

"Yes, why not?"

David paced beside Millicent, walking just behind her father and mother as they crossed to the wide double doors that led to the card room.

The amount of attention the duke was paying the girl was unheard of for him and much remarked upon by the ladies around the room.

"He never dances attendance past an obligatory waltz," the mother of two debutantes was telling another.

"Adela may find her days numbered, poor dear."

"Do you suppose he really will settle down after all?"

"My dears," another matriarch put in, "he is the Exeter heir. Sooner or later he has to think about his family duties."

"But Millie Cavendish! My Edith is twice as pretty."

"Perhaps you should play a hand of cards, dear Faith. And take your Edith along. If his eye is traveling, you never know."

"Perhaps I shall, Alice dear."

"A capital party!" a man said as he lurched his cassino opponent in the room next door. With a grunt of triumph he stood up, giving place to Prince Henry. "The cards are going well this evening, Henry."

"Good, perhaps my luck will change." Henry turned to Dolores. "Would you care for a seat, my dear? A rubber of cassino?"

She smiled. "I can try, but I confess I am not much of a hand at games of chance."

"I shall teach you the ropes, as they say."

Dolores accepted the seat, gazing with interest across the green felt gaming table. Isabella and George stood nearby as Prince Henry adjusted Dolores's chair and then took one at her side and began to explain the play.

David saw his father at the next table over, deliberately avoiding looking toward Isabella and her American. The duke wanted nothing more than to leave the blasted party and get well and thoroughly drunk. He stayed and smiled and made pleasant inconsequential conversation. And he prayed he would never have to go through such a night again.

Chapter Twenty-three

⊱❦⊰

*I*t was almost four o'clock in the morning when young Tim awakened Joshua and told him their people were ready to leave for home.

David came with his father and the others. Having arrived with Lady Winston, who had left early, he unwillingly accepted his father's offer of a ride home. Any other course would have been remarked upon. He waited for the others to enter the carriage first. Not for the first time in his life David cursed the rigid societal rules by which he was forced to live.

He stepped up inside the carriage, his eyes going to Bella's against all his better judgment. Her eyes were as dark as night in the lamplit carriage. They looked full of pain, and his own mirrored that pain.

"Excuse me," George Miller said, breaking the spell of the moment. The American shifted his weight and moved closer to Bella. "Enough room now?" he asked the duke, who still hovered in the doorway, staring at Bella.

"Yes, thank you." David sat down next to his father, Miller directly in front of him.

The ride back to Exeter House was accompanied by small talk about the people at the party and the intricacies of the game of cassino. George entered into Dolores and Henry's conversation; the duke was lost in thought, not saying a word.

Dolores finally realized Isabella was as silent as the duke. "Are you feeling all right, *querida?*"

"I'm a little tired, Mama," Bella replied. She glanced across the carriage and saw David staring at her. She knew he was remembering the carriage ride when he kidnapped her from the inn. She could see it in his eyes. His lips were pressed closed. Bella looked away, not wanting to think about his lips or his arms. Or of the conversation she would have to have with George tomorrow. For she knew she had to tell him the truth and tell him quickly. Before she lost her nerve. Before he felt she had deliberately avoided telling him. If she lost his trust, they would have no basis for a happy marriage.

Connie and Sally were waiting up when Dolores and Isabella climbed the stairs and entered their apartments. Connie fussed over Dolores in one bedroom as Sally reached to help a tired Isabella out of her russet-colored satin ballgown in the other bedroom.

"And how was it?" Connie asked Dolores.

Dolores sighed. "I'm really not sure."

"Was Bella happy with her fortune hunter at her side?" Connie wanted to know.

Dolores shook her head. "I really don't think so, Consuela. I think she paid more attention to where David was and with whom he was than she did to George, who never left her side."

"Of course he didn't. I still say you're playing with fire."

"I know you don't approve, Connie. But I believe I'm doing the right thing. If Bella sees this George in the context of her own life and friends, I think she will have a change of heart. In fact, I think she is already having a change of heart and just won't admit it."

"She's gone too far this time, and you know it. The duke is out for nothing but a good time and makes no bones about it."

"Consuela! Are you saying he deliberately engineered a situation in which he could ravish her?"

Grudgingly, Connie admitted she didn't mean quite that. "But he's not about to marry, and mark my words, when he does he won't be marrying a girl he's had his way with!"

"We'll see," Dolores replied as Connie tucked her covers in around her.

Connie shook her head in exasperation. "You are bound and determined she marry a title, aren't you?"

"No, Connie. I wanted to do as Wallace wished. You know that. That's why we're here. But what interests me about David isn't his title."

"Well, what is it then?" Connie asked, her hands on her ample hips.

"He's as strong-willed as she. She might just have the chance of a happy marriage with him."

Connie minded her tongue, but her expression spoke volumes. She turned down the lamp and left, looking in on Isabella. "Are you asleep?"

"Not yet," Bella answered.

Connie walked into the bedroom, coming nearer Isabella's bed. "Did you have good time?"

"I had a terrible time," Bella answered honestly.

"What happened?"

"Nothing happened. Everybody watched me all night, and George danced every dance with me, and *he* ignored me and made a cake of himself over Millicent Cavendish and that red-haired woman whose name I never remember."

"Why do you care what the duke was doing?"

"I don't!" Bella said, contradicting herself.

"Young lady, are you sure you even know what you want?"

"No," Isabella replied, sounding miserable. "I'm so confused, I don't know what to do. Connie, I think I've ruined my entire life!"

"I could have told you about that George Miller, and I tried to. He's been up to no good all along, and he is just the fortune hunter your father said he was."

"No, he isn't!" Bella defended him. "It's not his fault everything's a mess, it's mine! And I have to tell him the truth tomorrow, and I'll probably never see him again!"

"You'll see him all right."

"You don't know that," Isabella said.

Connie reached to bring the blankets up around Bella's shoulders, tucking her in as she had tucked in her mother. "Oh, yes, I do. Nothing will stop him from getting your money."

"You keep saying that, but it's not my money he's after!"

"Isn't it? Oh, I don't say he doesn't want you, too. What man wouldn't? But if you had no money, there'd be no George Miller in your life."

"That's not true!"

"Are you sure? Have you ever tested him?" Connie asked.

"I have no need to!" Isabella said defiantly.

"The more I see of George Miller, the more he makes the duke seem like a prize beyond compare."

"You don't even like the duke!"

"Not for you, I don't. But at least he's more the man for you than someone who would sneak you away from your family and disobey your father's wishes."

"David Beresford is a stubborn, opinionated, hard-headed, stuck-up, stuck-upon-himself male who took advantage of me!"

Connie stared at the girl she had raised in disbelief. "No one has ever taken advantage of you in your life!" Connie replied tartly. "You can tell that to your mother or let the duke think it, but I know you, Isabella. Nothing happened you didn't want to happen, at least in the beginning. It's just like you to be so headstrong as to leap before you look."

"That's not fair!"

"You are responsible for putting yourself in such a vulnerable position, and you know it. Or you should! When you wander around the countryside acting like a brazen wanton, you can't expect to be treated like a lady."

"I can and I do!"

Connie clucked under her breath. "I've thought you a stubborn girl but never a stupid one before."

"How dare you call me stupid!"

"When people act stupid, they usually are," Connie told Bella tartly.

"How am I acting stupid?"

"Running away, for one thing," Connie replied.

"I had no choice!" Isabella said dramatically.

"And how much good did it do you? What did you gain?" Connie saw Bella's eyes slide away from her and continued: "Now you're going to make another mistake, and you're going to tell this man the truth and compound the stupidity!"

"I have to tell him!"

"You don't have to say one thing! He never has to find out."

"He'd find out in the marriage bed!" Bella said.

"Not necessarily," Connie told her charge. "You're not the first nor the last to be caught in such a scrape. There are ways of having things seem different than they are and the man never the wiser."

"I couldn't do that to him!" Bella said dramatically.

"But you can ruin the duke without a backward glance."

"Ruin—Connie, what are you talking about?"

"Don't tell me you think you're going to hand George Miller a club pointed right at the duke and think the man won't use it. I suppose you think he'll keep quiet about your little news," Connie said sarcastically.

Isabella was shocked at Connie's words. "Of course he will! He loves me! He won't say anything that could hurt me!"

"You give him this club over a rich man's head, over a duke's head, and you don't think he'll use it? Bella, I'm ashamed of you." Connie stood up.

Connie left the room, her words ringing in Isabella's ears all night. Bella tossed and turned, unable to sleep until long after the rest of the house was lost in dreams.

The next morning Sally woke Bella with a tray of hot chocolate and bread and butter and the news that George Miller was already waiting downstairs.

"What time is it?" Bella asked sleepily.

"It's just gone ten, miss."

"Ten?" Bella saw the look in the maid's eyes and sat up. "Mr. Miller isn't used to London society. He isn't aware that gentlemen don't call this early or call unannounced. I told him I'd like to ride today, and he's merely—anxious."

"Yes, miss. He said as how you weren't to forget what you

promised." Bella looked blank. Sally spoke again: "He said you'd remember because of all the expense this week."

"Oh . . ." Bella stood up. "Yes."

"Shall I draw a bath?"

"No, the basin is enough." Bella let the maid help her dress. "I shall wear my riding clothes."

"Yes, miss."

"But first go down and tell George to come back in an hour when I shall be ready. Go on before my mother goes downstairs."

"She's already downstairs, miss," Sally said. "I think she's talking to him now."

"Oh, dear, then help me hurry!"

Isabella fidgeted until Sally was through and then flew into the small parlor where her mother and George sat a quarter of an hour later. Both turned toward her. "Good morning," she said a little breathlessly.

Dolores stood up. "Good morning, *querida*. I shall tell Consuela you are ready for your ride in the park."

"Oh, Mama, please. We have to be alone. I—I have things I have to discuss with George—"

"Connie must go," Dolores said firmly. "However, if you should happen to take a stroll in Hyde Park, I will tell her to let you walk on ahead."

"English girls no longer have duennas."

"You are not English, Isabella," Dolores reminded her daughter before she left the room. "And that is not quite true. Properly brought up English girls do not go out with gentlemen alone any more than you are allowed to."

The moment Dolores left the room George came toward Bella. "Sweetheart!" he said, taking her hands in his and beaming at her. "Your mother says the decision is entirely up to you."

The sound of David's voice came from the hallway beyond. He was giving instructions to Tate. A little distracted, Bella smiled back at George. "What decision?"

"Bella, dearest! The decision as to when we may marry! She merely asks she be told first and allowed to make the necessary arrangements. Bella, you must tell her we want to be married immediately! Oh, my darling, I can't wait any longer!" And with that George swept her into his arms, kissing her passionately.

Isabella found herself pulling away from his embrace. "George, don't—" He heard her words but paid no attention, his arms imprisoning her. Bella felt the pressure of his lips and arms, felt him seek out her response. She couldn't give it.

He let go. "Bella, what's wrong?"

"Connie will see us!"

"Let her," George said, trying to draw Bella close again.

"You promised Mama we would behave properly. And— and I haven't been able to talk to her yet about your money."

George dropped his arms. "Why don't you go speak to her right now? I'll go out front and tell the servant to bring a carriage around while you talk to her."

Bella fell in with his plan, going in search of her mother. But before Bella found Dolores her steps faltered, the doubts Connie and her mother had voiced about George surfacing. They thought he wanted her money more than herself.

Test him, Connie had said, making it sound almost like a dare. Bella knew he would come through with flying colors. She knew he loved her. She told herself she had no need to prove the fact; she had more than enough proof. But the thought still nagged at her. And although she herself needed no proof, perhaps they did. Perhaps they would be reconciled to the marriage if they thought better of him.

"Bella?" Dolores came out of the upstairs sitting room to see her daughter stopped halfway up the stairwell. "Did you need me?"

Isabella looked up at her mother and made her decision. "No, Mama, I just wanted to say goodbye."

Dolores watched her daughter with sad eyes. "Bella, must I worry about whether you will return this afternoon or whether you will decide to take wild flight again?"

"No! Oh, Mama, no. I promise you, I shall not make that mistake again."

"Good." Dolores's voice softened. "I only want your happiness, *querida*. You know that, don't you?"

"Yes, Mama."

Dolores looked troubled. "If you are intent on marrying this man, if you think he will truly make you happy, I shall not stand in your way."

"Does that mean you've grown to like George?"

"No," her mother told her plainly. "I believe you are making a mistake. But if I cannot convince you otherwise, I do not want you to think you must run from me. I shall stand by you, no matter what your decision."

Isabella swallowed hard, blinking back tears. "Thank you, Mama."

"Now come along, it's not polite to keep people waiting." Dolores came down the stairs toward her daughter, linking arms as they descended the rest of the steps together. She kissed Bella's cheek before she released her and walked toward the morning room.

Bella stopped on the bottom step, watching her mother's proud carriage as she walked away.

"Excuse me." David's voice came from behind Bella.

Startled, she turned around, her cheeks flaming as she looked into his calm, cool gaze. "Sorry," Bella said. They stood facing each other for one brief instant until Bella stepped back.

"Thank you," the duke said as he passed by her.

Isabella watched him until he disappeared into the library, disappointment and anger welling up within her. It seemed anything and everything he did irritated her. He had missed most meals since they had arrived back, as well he should, she told herself angrily. When he was home his cool detachment irritated her beyond endurance. He should be on his knees begging her forgiveness.

"Bella?" George stood in the doorway. "Have you seen your mother? Are you ready?"

"Yes, I've seen her," Bella told him truthfully.

The late spring morning was warm, sunlight dappling the square as Bella joined George and Consuela inside the open carriage.

Young Tim had been given the job of driving them, the carriage taking off at a steady pace toward Hyde Park's shaded lanes. Consuela sat stoic and silent across from

George and Isabella, leaving them to speak of the party the night before and the one the coming evening.

George Miller looked a little impatient as he urged the driver to hasten his pace. Irritated with Consuela's obvious dislike, he spent the carriage ride wishing it were over.

The carriage finally turned in to Rotten Row, joining a score of other equipages and a dozen or more riders astride their own and rented mounts.

"Can't you go any faster, man?" George demanded when they proceeded at a snail's pace along the fashionable avenue.

"No, sir, I can't." Young Tim, having heard a bit about the American from Sally, and a lot more from Joshua's sour comments, was not about to take orders from the likes of him.

"It's meant to be a leisurely ride," Bella told George.

"Then let's walk a bit." George looked toward Connie as if expecting her to say no. "Your mother said we could walk alone in the park."

"Walk ahead," Connie corrected him. "Not alone."

"Whatever," he answered impatiently. "Bella?"

"Yes, fine, of course," Isabella told him. "Tim, will you please stop near the path to the Serpentine?"

"Yes, miss," Tim replied, and soon after he pulled over to the edge of the avenue, reining in his horse and jumping down to help with the carriage steps.

"Thank you, Tim," Bella said as she descended to the grass.

Tim smiled and tipped his cap to her before reaching to help the rotund duenna manage her voluminous black skirts down out of the carriage. He let George manage for himself. "I'll wait here, shall I?" Tim asked.

"Yes, fine," George said.

"Miss?" Tim queried Bella, ignoring George and earning a small smile, quickly gone, from Consuela.

"You might pull up a bit nearer the other end of the path," Bella told him.

George waited impatiently and then paced beside Bella, urging her a little faster than Consuela's sedate pace. When they were far enough ahead of the duenna to be able to talk in private, he slowed a bit. "Have you walked here often?" he asked.

"Not often," Isabella replied.

"I'll wager every man in London has been asking for your favor."

Bella smiled a false little smile. "Not quite all," she told him. Taking a deep breath, she hurried on: "There's something I have to tell you now that we're finally alone."

"How much did you manage to get?" George asked.

Isabella heard the question as if it came from a stranger. She turned wide, dark eyes toward him. "I beg your pardon?"

"The money—so I may stay on until we are married." George smiled as he spoke. "Oh, how I wish that were already accomplished. We almost managed it, sweetheart."

"Yes. Almost," Bella replied. "That's the beginning of what I have to tell you."

"How much did you get?" he asked, returning to the subject at hand.

He wasn't listening, she realized. His mind was on the subject of money, and he was not hearing her words. All the doubts that had been bedeviling her came back to haunt her. Isabella made a decision. Up until that very moment she had not realized she had already made her choice on the stairwell earlier. "None, I'm afraid," she told him quietly.

"None?" He repeated the word as if he had not heard it properly. "Did you say none? But how can your mother deny you spending money? You are the heir to La Providencia! She merely holds it in trust for you!"

"Oh, no, it's not like that at all," Isabella told the man she had dreamt of spending her life with, the man she had planned on calling husband. Ashamed at how easily the words came, she continued: "My father's will was very specific about my marriage. I don't inherit a thing."

"What?" George's consternation showed in every muscle of his face. Isabella saw the truth writ large across his features and still did not want to accept it. She told herself he would come through the test; he would, he loved her.

"Unless and until I marry—"

"Bella! What a fright you gave me!" He laughed and looked back at the duenna a little ways behind them. He lowered his voice. "You have nothing to worry about. We shall soon be married, and all will be yours."

"No, it won't," she replied.

"Well, obviously there is some provision made for your mother," George qualified. "We shall be so happy together, Bella. I intend to devote my life to making you happy."

"That sounds wonderful," she told him truthfully. "I couldn't ask for more. Where will we live?"

"Where? Why, on the rancho, of course. Where else could we live?"

"I imagined I should have to move to wherever your work took you."

"Darling girl"—he smiled down at her—"is that what's been bothering you these past days? Tell me the truth, I know something has been. You simply haven't been your old self. Well, never fear. I'm not taking you away from your home like one of these Englishmen might. You will live just as you always have, and I shall be at your side, running La Providencia."

Isabella looked doubtful. "I suppose Mama might hire you to work on the rancho, if that is what you wish to do."

"Hire me? Isabella, we will be *married*. It will belong to me! You and me," he corrected himself.

"No, it won't."

"What on earth are you saying?" George Miller demanded.

Isabella looked off toward the winding waters of the Serpentine, toward the distant trees. Unable to face him, she spoke in a low tone: "Why, just that I don't inherit one single penny unless I marry a titled Englishman."

"*What?*"

She forced herself to look into his consternation. "I thought you knew," she fibbed.

"Why didn't you ever tell me?" the American demanded.

"It's so unimportant. What does it have to do with us?" Isabella asked him.

"What does it—it has everything to do with us! How do you think we will live without your inheritance?" George demanded.

"Like anyone else, I suppose. I promise I will learn to be frugal and make ends meet on whatever you earn."

George Miller looked incredulous. "I can't believe it! How could you lead me on so?"

Isabella stopped walking. "What?"

"I've spent all the money I could borrow in order to come here! You owe me for the entire trip, not to mention the extra it cost for the trip north! Why, I don't even have passage money back, since I spent so much on the inn and the coach and all."

"I owe you," Isabella repeated the words.

"Yes, by God, you do! You should have told me you were poor!"

"I'm not poor," she said, seeing a flicker of interest in his eyes.

"Do you have another inheritance?" he asked.

"Yes, I do," she told him. "I inherited a love of honesty and industry from my parents, along with the sense to tell fair from foul, although I admit it would seem I have been willingly blinded. I inherited the ability to be able to be put down in my petticoat anywhere on this planet, and I would be able to pay my own way if I had to take in other people's washing!"

"Bella, be reasonable. I wouldn't be here if it weren't for you! I'm stranded!"

Consuela came up to hear the last of his words. And Bella's cold reply: "I shall endeavor to find enough money to repay you your expenses on my behalf." She turned on her heel, starting across the grass toward the carriage.

George watched her start away, Consuela giving him a dirty look before following Isabella. After a moment of hesitation he moved quickly after them, reaching Bella's side and taking her hand. "Dearest, perhaps there is a way around your father's will."

"There might be," Isabella told him, "but I don't intend to take it. If you will kindly let go of my hand, I shall say goodbye."

"But—"

She cut him off. "As to your repayment for money spent on my behalf, if you will come round to the servants' entrance at Exeter House tomorrow morning I shall have something left with Tate."

"The servants' entrance!" George said in shock. "I'm not a servant!"

"I'm afraid it will have to be the servants' entrance. You see, after today's conversation my mother and the prince will hardly allow you inside the front door. That is reserved for gentlemen," she told him sweetly, and she turned away, calling out to Tim. "We are ready to leave." Isabella looked back at George. "I'm sure you can find your own way back to where you're staying."

"You're just going to walk away and leave me here?"

"Yes," Bella told him, "I am."

"I insist you at least—" he began, only to be stopped by Bella's interruption.

"If you wish to see any recompense at all, do not try my patience too high, Mr. Miller! And above all, do not insist upon anything! You do not have the right." With a scornful glance she traversed the last bit of grass and stepped up into the carriage before Tim could lean down to help. "Connie, come along or we'll be late for luncheon."

Isabella put her hand out, both she and Tim helping the old duenna step up inside the open carriage. Consuela was seated with her back to the front, smiling triumphantly at George Miller as they started away.

Isabella did not give him a backward glance. She eyed Consuela when the older woman turned her attention back to her charge. "If you say one word, I shall scream and make such a scene as to put to shame anything I have ever done before in my life!" Bella threatened with blazing eyes.

"I didn't say a word," Consuela said. And she smiled.

Chapter Twenty-four

*B*ella marched into Exeter House and up to her room, Connie coming quickly after her. "Bella, he's not worth one tear," Consuela said as she closed the door between the hall and the sitting room.

Dolores was reading in a chair by the windows. She looked up, frowning. "What has happened?"

"My eyes have been opened," Bella told her mother. "You were right all along."

"Oh, *querida,* I'm so sorry." Dolores left her book behind on the fringed settee and came toward her daughter. "You must feel terribly upset."

Isabella shook her head. "No," she said, surprising even herself. "I don't!" She thought about what she was saying. "I don't at all! Isn't that odd?" she said, and she began to laugh.

"It's a nervous reaction," Connie told mother and daughter.

Bella looked from her mother to her duenna. "No," she said, calming a little, "you don't understand at all. I thought I was the most terrible person. Untrustworthy, letting a man I didn't care a fig about make love to me. I see your shock at my words, but you must imagine mine at my actions! I was in love with one man and letting another have his way with me! But that's not true! You see? I was infatuated with the idea of love, not with George, don't you see? I know that now."

Bella walked away from them, heading into her bedroom.

"Go after her," Consuela told Dolores. "She needs you."

"She seems fine—"

"Go to her," the old woman commanded. After a shared looked, Dolores walked forward, hesitating when she reached Bella's bedroom door.

"Bella?" her mother called out as she came inside the room. "Are you sure you're all right?"

Isabella was crumpled onto a window seat across the large bedroom. Silent tears rolled down from her large dark eyes. "Of course!" she said brightly. Too brightly. "Don't you see what I've done? I've gotten my very own way, as always!"

Dolores came closer as Isabella continued.

"I've gotten my very own way and lost what I truly wanted! What I was so stupid as to not even know I wanted. Isn't that a fine joke?"

"Isabella," her mother said softly, "we all make mistakes."

"Yes. But not like mine!"

Dolores found it hard to argue the point. "It isn't like you to give up on something you want."

"This is different," Isabella replied, turning her tear-stained face toward the curtains.

"How so?"

Isabella shook her head a little. "Because what I want includes another. And if he doesn't want me, there's nothing to be done about it."

"What makes you so sure he does not?" Dolores asked quietly.

"Everything!" Isabella told her mother. "Would you please leave me? I have the headache."

"Would you like a powder for it?"

"No powder is going to help," Bella said.

"We shall be right outside if you want us. Connie?"

Before Consuela followed her mistress, she walked over to

hug Isabella. "I've never known you not to fight for what you want."

"I don't want someone who doesn't want me." Bella's words were firm even though her jaw quivered a little.

"Someone who doesn't want you wouldn't go racing across the whole of England and get himself and you into such a lot of trouble," Connie told her young charge.

Left alone in the room, Bella stood up, looking around herself as if seeking help from the furnishings. She threw herself across the feather bed, burying her head in the pillows and finally letting the tears fall in earnest.

Her mother looked in later and covered her, telling Connie and Sally to let Bella sleep.

"What about her dinner?" Connie asked.

"She needs the rest more than she needs dinner," Dolores said. "If she wakes late, she can have something then."

"And what about the Mayfair Ball?" Consuela asked.

"I shall attend with the prince and make her apologies."

"They say it's one of the most important parties of the season."

"Connie, the situation has changed. If she and David do not come to an understanding, there is at least no longer the threat of George Miller. I cannot see any reason to risk her being hurt by letting any of the other young nobles pursue her. He would have to be told the truth, and then what? Her future would depend upon his discretion and his ability to rise above the facts of the matter. No. There is no point in forcing her to stay on in England at this juncture."

"Thank the Lord!" Connie said honestly. "Oh, Lord, that means another ocean voyage, doesn't it?" Consuela saw Dolores's expression. "And yourself? What about what *you* want?" Connie asked shrewdly.

Dolores sighed. "I haven't had the time to consider myself. I cannot stay on here; that wouldn't be fair to Bella."

"What about the prince, then?"

"If he doesn't wish to accompany us back to America, I see no future in it. Bella will never find a suitable husband here now. In California the style of living and the expectations are different. Pioneer men are interested in a good strong woman, a helpmeet. They are more practical about worldly matters, I think. And Lord knows, she's strong enough to make a good partner to a pioneering man."

"If she'll accept him."

"Yes," Dolores said. "There is that."

While Dolores and Consuela discussed Isabella's future, David Beresford, the Duke of Exeter, was partaking of an early supper at his club. Liberally washing down the roast beef and potatoes with red wine, he steeled himself for yet another night of farce.

He was to meet his father and the others at the Mayfair Ball. Having left Exeter House early, he had no idea of what had transpired that afternoon. In his mind's eye he saw Isabella on George Miller's arm yet again. It drove him to order another bottle of wine.

He had come very near to having Lady Winston's door slammed in his face when he had called earlier. She had agreed to see him for five minutes and, tight-lipped, told him in no uncertain terms what she thought of his conduct with Millicent Cavendish.

"That you dared to insult me in front of everyone in such a fashion!" she had ended, her eyes blazing as bright as her fiery auburn curls.

David soon lost what little patience he had left. "Adela," he said coldly, "I wasn't aware that I was your personal property."

"Of course you're not!" she very nearly shouted.

"Then why am I being subjected to this tirade?" he asked.

"More to the point, why are we even talking to each other?" she asked with acid in her tone.

"You are quite right," he told her stiffly, and he departed.

Adela was standing in the middle of her front parlor, shocked that he had not come to his senses and her knees, when her husband looked in. Lord Winston smiled at his wife. "Sorry, my dear, I thought I heard David about."

"He just left!" she said passionately.

"Really? Too bad. I wanted to show him the pair of bays I just bought."

"Clive, you shall have to accompany me to the ball this evening."

Clive Winston blinked. "Must I, my dear?"

"Yes, you must," Adela told her husband.

He sighed with the fatalism of the much-henpecked husband. He knew the futility of arguing with Adela. His mother said it was the strain of Anglo-Irish blood in her. There was no way to win an argument with an Irishman. The longer Clive had been married to Adela, the more he respected his mother's opinions.

Isabella woke later that evening, disoriented for a moment before the moonlit room swam into familiar shapes.

"Miss?" Sally's voice came out of the darkness, startling Bella.

"What?"

Sally got up from the window seat and came near, raising the wick on a bedside lamp. The light from the oil lamp was soft as it radiated out from the round, opalescent globe set into a brass bottom. "Would you like a bite of something?"

"What time is it?"

Sally looked at the clock above the fireplace. "It's almost ten in the evening, miss."

"What are you doing here? Where is my mother?"

"Your mother is out, miss. I told Mistress Connie I would watch for you to wake. She's taking a mite of a nap until your mother comes home. Are you all right, miss?"

Isabella lay back on the soft pillows, watching the girl. "I just might be, Sally. I think I have dreamt of a solution to my problem."

"Your problem, miss?" Sally said doubtfully.

"Yes. My problem. And I need you to do something for me." Bella saw the girl's fearful eyes. "It's very important."

"Will we get into trouble again, miss?"

"Very likely," Isabella told the girl.

"Oh, dear . . . what is it I'm to do?" Sally asked.

"I need you to secure a few things for me."

"Has this to do with the American gentleman, miss?"

"No, it has nothing to do with him," Bella reassured the girl, who brightened visibly at Bella's words. "Actually," Isabella continued, "it has to do with paying the Duke of Exeter back."

The clouds came back to Sally's eyes. "Will he get hurt, miss?"

"Not exactly," Bella replied. "Will you help me?"

Unhappily, Sally agreed to help. "What is it, then, that you're going to do to him?"

Bella studied the maid. "I'm not precisely sure, Sally. But whatever it is, he will richly deserve it."

"Oh, dear," Sally said softly. "I was sort of afraid of that."

"I shall need writing paper that is not from this house." Ignoring Sally's widening eyes, Bella continued: "I shall need to speak to Joshua in the morning, and I shall speak to young Tim, too, I think. Oh, and I must leave a note for my mother, and I must speak to the prince."

Sally stared at her mistress. "Are they all to be involved then, miss?"

"They most certainly are!" Bella replied. "Now go find some paper and mind that I don't oversleep in the morning. There is much to be gotten ready if I possibly can."

"Yes, miss," Sally said as she left the room.

At the Mayfair Ball eyes followed Dolores Alexander as she danced the night away with the prince and the duke, the duke giving one dance to Millicent, as he had the night before, and then none to any but Dolores.

What was it all about? The tongues around them wagged their questions. Henrietta Eppsworth tried to look enigmatic; her cousin Clarissa was less successful at it.

"Clarissa, for heaven's sake, stop looking like a whipped puppy," Henrietta commanded.

"I can't help it." Clarissa sniffled the tiniest bit. "I can see censure in all eyes."

"Nonsense. Something strange is going on, and I shall get to the bottom of it, never fear."

"I don't know," Clarissa told her cousin, "I just don't know what to think."

"Then stop thinking!" Henrietta snapped. "And for heaven's sake, smile!"

Clarissa tried to do as Henrietta commanded. Giving a speaking look to a retired admiral, she fluttered her eyelashes innocently when he arrived beside her and asked for the pleasure of the next dance. He was a full foot shorter than Clarissa and quite thirty years older, but he was a full admiral, and a baronet to boot.

"It's such a crush on the dance floor," Clarissa said demurely, fluttering her eyelashes the more at him.

"I shall protect you, my dear," the old man told her. He bowed to Henrietta and escorted a flushed and flustered-looking Clarissa to the floor for a stately quadrille.

Henrietta made a mental note to discuss with Clarissa the subject of permissible flirtatiousness at her advanced age and then went in search of sherry. Holding her head high, the Countess of Eppsworth sailed through the crowds around her, ignoring the eyes that cast knowing looks in her direction.

David left the ball early, escorting the Cavendishes to their carriage but declining their offer of a ride home.

"I have my carriage waiting," he informed them, and he stepped back, watching the Cavendish coach move off down the cobbled street.

David looked back at the mansion that was still full of people and noise and music and merriment. He felt like none of it. Telling himself he had done his duty and put in an appearance, he walked to his carriage, unaware that the tongues behind him assumed he had left with Millicent.

"Where to, Your Grace?" Tim asked.

"Crockford's, I think. Yes, Crockford's definitely."

"Aye, aye, Your Grace," Tim said, happy at the chance to do a little betting himself with the other drivers whiling away the night outside the gambling establishment. "And a fine night it is for a little winning of something or another."

The duke did not reply, and so Tim lapsed into silence, urging the gray forward and staying out of the duke's way until he delivered him to the club.

The sounds of revelry wafted out into the cold night air, Crockford's ablaze with light and laughter. The footman at the door bowed the duke inside, recognizing the regular patron. "Good evening, Your Grace. Looks to be a lucky evening tonight."

"That would be a welcome change," the duke said as he went past the liveried man.

"Davey, old man!" Clive Winston came toward the duke. "I see you got out early, too. Ready for a bit of sport, are you?"

"I thought I'd look in and see what was happening," David replied.

"Well, the faro's done me in so far, but I'm about to try my luck again. You could do me a favor and keep Adela occupied, old man. I know you like her company, and she's a regular jinx when she gets near me at the tables. Do me a good turn and take her off my hands for an hour or so, what do you say?" David listened to the rotund Lord Winston in silence. "Well? Can I count on you?"

"Clive, I'm not in the mood for polite conversation tonight. I'm sorry, forgive me."

"Oh, Lord," Clive sighed, "I suppose I'm for it, then. I'm doomed to lose all night long, thanks to your moodiness."

"Send her home," David replied none too patiently.

Clive looked surprised. "My dear David, have you ever tried to send Adela anywhere she didn't want to go?"

"Not lately," David admitted.

"I thought not. Oh, well, I suppose it couldn't last forever."

"I beg your pardon," the duke said.

Clive's round face wreathed into a melancholy little smile. "You and Adela. It's been ever so wonderful for me, old boy. Kept her busy and out of my hair. I suppose some of the gossip is true, is it?"

"Which gossip?" David asked stiffly.

"Why, that you're offering for some young wench or other."

"Is that what they're saying?"

"Oh, you know I don't hear much. Just the part that's been around the most. Lot of other nonsense, too, not worth listening to," Clive said.

"How right you are," David replied wryly. "Excuse me, I think I need a drink or three."

"All right, old man. But if you change your mind, I'll be in your debt."

"Clive, you really should pay more attention to your wife."

"She doesn't want me to, Davey. We're quite happy, bumbling along as we do. Since you've never been married, old bean, I won't disillusion you. Then again, perhaps I should. You see, I'm not the dashing blade some of you gents are. But I'm steady, and I've a reliable income, and I don't ask for much. Just my house run on time and my needs seen to and time for my gambling and my horses and my shooting. Not much more you can expect from a wife these days."

"Good Lord" was David's only comment. His visage was even bleaker as he headed toward a barman and ordered a brandy.

Several brandies later he was sitting in the lounge, nursing his drink and his irritation, when two gentlemen he did not know sat down behind him at a small table. They ordered their gins and sat back in the comfortable, man-sized lounge chairs.

"What a night," one said, and he yawned.

"Aye, and that's a fact. What was that woman's name earlier? The one who was introducing us to everyone?"

"Epps. John Epps's widow. From Kent, I believe."

"Ah . . . yes, I remember."

"How long are you staying in London?"

"Can't really, beyond tomorrow. Too much going on with the sale of the old manor and all the bits and pieces."

"Too bad, you'll miss the King of Hawaii."

"Something to see, I'll warrant. I'm sorry I missed that American adventuress, what's her name?"

"Spanish name, I believe."

"Amazing who gets invited into the ton these days."

"No more ton, old man. Frightfully egalitarian these days, you know."

"Hmmmmph."

There was a silence when they received their drinks, then one of them spoke: "Too bad to miss, from what I hear. The Terror of California."

David heard the words and found himself bristling. The men behind him laughed. "Did you hear she ran off with someone or other?"

"No! Really?" the other man said as David stood up and turned toward them.

"Quite a bit of talk about it, Stephen. Everyone in town knows she's no better than she ought to be, if you catch my meaning." The man glanced up to see a tall man with a wrathful appearance descending upon him.

"What—" the man began, but before he finished speaking David had him by the collar. Lifted out of his chair, the man was sputtering, his friend Stephen remonstrating with the big man whose hands were choking his friend.

"I say there, what do you think you're doing?" the man named Stephen shouted.

"How dare you!" the man sputtered as he tried to wrench David's hands away from around his neck.

"How dare *you?*" David demanded, the bottles of wine and all the recent brandy unleashing his anger and making his grip tighten around the man's scrawny neck.

"Let him go, I say!" Stephen demanded as others came close, a crowd forming around the three men.

"Not until he apologizes!"

"For—what—?" the choking man managed to get out in a strangled voice. "I don't even know you!"

"For speaking of a lady, a decent woman, as if she were a light frigate!"

"I know what I heard," the man defended himself, his windpipe closing over.

"I heard it, too," his friend Stephen put in. "It's the truth, and we'll say what we please!" David released his hold on the first man's neck and turned toward the second. "There's nothing you can do to stop us!" the man Stephen said boldly.

David proved the man wrong, his fist connecting with the man's jaw and sending him careening back against the chairs. "I can shut your mouth for good!" David told him through clenched jaws.

"Hold on there." Two Crockford employees came near, one of them speaking to the three men. "None of that in here, gentlemen." Then the footman recognized the duke. "Your Grace, have these men been bothering you?"

"Yes!"

"*He's* the one who started it!" The man who was nearly choked was still rubbing his neck.

The duke started toward the man as the two footmen reached for the stranger. "We'll take care of it, Your Grace," the first footman said.

The man called Stephen found himself being helped to his feet and out the door alongside his friend.

"You all right, Davey?" Clive Winston asked. "We heard the noise, and I thought I'd come investigate. Thought it was someone in his cups until I saw you were involved. Need any help?"

"Help? There's no help to be had!" David stared at Winston with moody blue eyes. He said no more, pushing past the men that had gathered round and stalking out toward his carriage.

Lord Darnley came near Winston. "I say, if I didn't know better, I'd say Exeter was in his cups."

"Davey?" Clive laughed. "Don't be daft. I've known the man since schooldays; never known him to go over his limit. Never! The absolute soul of control."

The man they were speaking of was striding toward his carriage, surprising Tim out of a nap. "Whoops! Sorry, Your Grace. Home?"

"No!" David roared. He jumped up beside Tim and took the reins. "I'll drive," he told the boy.

Tim could smell the thick aroma of good brandy and sat back as quiet as a church mouse. "Where are we going, Your Grace?"

"To get well and thoroughly drunk!" David said.

Tim sat back and kept his own counsel about the adventure. One thing he'd told Joshua earlier: things certainly had been dull before the Americans came to visit. Now all sorts of things were going on; the house was full of them. Dull as dirt the old place had been before.

Joshua had grunted, saying he liked it better the old way. Dull as dirt.

It was two hours later when Tim drove a snoring Duke of Exeter home. Just before dawn the air was chill. Even the birds were still asleep when Tim roused Tate to help him get the duke inside the house.

Tate was shocked. "What on earth happened? Did he take ill?"

"Ill with brandy and what not," Tim replied.

"Nonsense! The duke never overindulges," Tate told the boy.

"Well, mebbe he does, and mebbe he doesn't, but you asked what happened, and I'm telling you. He went off on a spree and dipped rather too deep, as can plainly be seen."

"Let me alone." David came awake, slurring his words as he pushed both men away. Staggering a bit, he made his way to the stairwell. Tate, concerned for the much bigger man's safety, followed the duke up the stairs. "Where is everyone?" David demanded loudly, his ears ringing, his head spinning.

"In bed, Your Grace," Tate said softly. The duke lurched a bit, and Tate prayed he wouldn't topple. He couldn't see how he could do much more than cushion the bigger man's fall. With visions of both of them tumbling down the wide stairwell, with poor Tate himself underneath, he continued up the steps behind the duke, his heart in his mouth.

Tate relaxed a bit when they reached the landing, David lurching toward his door and stumbling a bit. The butler reached around the taller man to open the door to his suite.

"Shall I send in Markham, Your Grace?"

"No! Leave me be!" David growled. He closed the door in the butler's face and made his way to a fireside chair. Tate, outside, worried about what to do and finally went down the hall to the servants' quarters and rapped on Markham's door. The valet opened the door after a few minutes, red-eyed and cross.

"Well?"

"Your master's just arrived, and he needs some seeing to."

"Seeing to?" Markham's brow rose.

"He's polluted," Tate said succinctly. "And I'm going back to bed!"

Markham disbelieved the news until he opened the door to the duke's suite. Across the room, in a chair before the guttering fire, the Duke of Exeter lolled back in a wing chair. He was breathing stertorously, his legs sprawled straight out toward the fire, his boots still on. One long arm was flung over the blue-patterned arm of the chair, a large, square hand grazing the floor.

Markham moved forward. Smelling the strong mixture of spirits on the duke's breath, his nose wrinkled. The valet reached to loosen the duke's cravat before removing his boots.

David stirred in his sleep, mumbling unintelligible words that sounded every so often strangely like "bell" or "bella."

Chapter Twenty-five

The next day the duke woke to the sounds of the maids sweeping the hall carpet outside his rooms. The sounds of their cleaning mixed with the thudding of his splitting headache, his temper evil as he came awake. He barked at Markham for making noise when the valet tiptoed in to check on his employer. The rest of the servants gave him a wide berth, only his father braving David's rooms to find out what was wrong with his only son.

"I have decided to ask for Millicent Cavendish's hand," the duke growled.

Prince Henry opened and closed his mouth, no sound coming out. Finally he sat down and repeated his son's statement.

"Yes, that's what I said," David said peevishly.

"May I ask why?"

"Why? I thought you, of all people, would be thrilled! You have been trying to marry me off for ten years!"

"Yes, well, but—why young Millie?"

"Why not?" David replied.

"David, 'why not' is hardly enough reason to marry someone. What has changed your mind about marriage? And why on earth are you considering Millie?"

"I'm considering marriage because I'm sick and tired of London and parties and balls and gossips and big mouths. I want to retire to Yorkshire and consolidate our holdings and forget everyone I ever met here!"

"I see," Henry said slowly. "And as for Millie?"

"As for Millicent," David corrected, "she is of good family, with good genes and a quiet disposition. She is young enough not to have been spoiled yet by society and its excesses, and plain enough to be glad of finding a husband at all. She will do as she's bid, and you will have your heirs!"

"I see," Prince Henry said again. "And what will you have, David?" the prince asked quietly.

"Peace and quiet!" David snapped. "Which at the moment are all I want out of life!"

Henry stood up, watching his son with sorrowful eyes. "I think you would be wise to think about this a bit before getting the girl's hopes up. Before committing yourself."

"I've thought about it long enough. Excuse me." David stood up. "I'm frightfully sorry, but I think I'm going to be sick."

Henry watched his son head for the water closet. The prince stood up, going downstairs to join Dolores and Bella for a light buffet luncheon on the side terrace.

"How is David feeling?" Dolores asked. "Connie said he got in rather late last night. Or early this morning."

"He seems to have been into his cups last night, and by the look of him, he's feeling the brunt of it."

"Henry, you look so worried." Dolores smiled. "After all, young men occasionally get up to a bit of something. His constitution will stand it, I'm sure."

"It's not the drinking I'm worried about. He's talking of offering for young Millie Cavendish," the prince told Dolores baldly.

Isabella dropped her fork, the clatter of the silver turning both parents toward her. "Sorry," she murmured, "so clumsy of me."

Dolores tried to read Bella's expression, but the prince was too occupied with his own thoughts to pay much attention. Turning back to their host, Dolores spoke quietly. "Has he then developed a *tendre* for the girl?"

"For Millie? No. Egad, if he had I wouldn't be so upset. After all, they say love will go where it's sent, but this isn't love. He talks of her as if he were buying cattle." Henry lapsed into silence.

Dolores stole a look at her daughter before replying. "Why has he decided on Millicent, then? Surely there are other girls."

"Excuse me, please," Bella told them both. "I—I have to see Sally about something."

"All right, dear."

"He said he wants a plain, biddable girl," Henry was saying as Bella stood up. "He wants peace and quiet." Henry was glum. "We had such high hopes, you and I." He glanced toward the retreating Isabella. "I can't credit it. David and Cavendish's young Millie, and Bella with that pipsqueak Miller."

"Oh, no," Bella told the prince from the doorway. "Not I."

"What? What's this?" Henry asked Isabella. "I thought you had decided on that head."

"Something happened between them," Dolores told the prince.

"What? Why didn't you tell me?" he asked them both.

"I was going to mention it to you later, after Bella had time to ensure she was making the right decision and wouldn't be changing her mind again," Dolores said.

Henry's expression brightened. "But that changes everything! If Bella's seen the light about that Miller fellow, what about David, then?"

"He doesn't want me, Uncle Henry," Bella answered before her mother could.

"We'll just see about that! He'll do his duty by you if I tell him to, by God, or I'll see why not!" the prince told her.

"No!" Bella looked alarmed. "Please, please don't force him to 'do his duty'! I couldn't live with the knowledge that he was forced to marry me."

"But my dear," Henry began, "when he knows you are free of other entanglements he'll *want* to marry you. He wanted to before he left to fetch you."

"He did what?" Bella stared at the man.

"It's true, *querida,*" Dolores told her daughter. "I was there. He was quite determined to marry you."

Isabella looked from one of them to the other, her brain spinning with the news. Finally a wide smile began in her eyes and spread across her face. "Then you both must leave everything to me!"

"Querida," her mother began, "I worry about you when you speak in that tone of voice. What are you planning?"

Bella smiled at both of them. "Don't worry. I had thought of a plan to get David's attention, but I was going to call a halt if he truly cared for Millie. But you say he doesn't!"

"Not a fig," the prince said in very definite tones. "I know the sound of a man in love, and David cares no more about that girl than he does about this table!"

"Henry, don't encourage her," Dolores said. "I know my daughter. She's up to some mischief."

"No, honestly, Mama. There's nothing to worry about now. I know what I must do!" And with that Bella skipped from the room, calling out to Sally as she ran down the hall.

"And don't run!" her mother called out after her. Looking back at the duke, Dolores sighed. "We'd best begin to pray, Henry."

"She said there was nothing to worry about," the prince replied.

"Yes, I know. That is precisely the reason I'm worried," her mother told him.

Sally was nearly dragged to Bella's room for her report on the status of her requests of Joshua and Tim. "Come along, now," Bella said, "tell me you've secured everything on the list."

"Not exactly, miss," Sally said unhappily. "You see, as to the last, they said as how they know of none and don't know where to begin to look."

Bella frowned. "All right, let me think." After a minute of heavy concentration she sighed. "There's nothing for it, I must do as I first thought and ask the prince for even more of his help."

"Oh, miss!"

"Yes, well, there's nothing else to be done. I shall swear him to secrecy! Let me know the moment he finishes his luncheon and is alone."

"Shall I go see now, miss?"

"Go, go," Bella told the girl. "I shall begin my notes, and you will deliver them at the proper times." Bella sat down at the tiny writing desk and bent forward over the writing paper, biting the end of her pen before dipping it into the inkwell. A small smile formed on her lips as she began to write.

An hour later Isabella had her private interview with Prince Henry. She was summoned to the south parlor, a room she had never seen. The prince was far across the large room when Bella was shown in by Tate. The butler's impassive features bespoke his disapproval of the American girl as he closed the door behind her. Nothing had been the same since the Americans had descended upon Exeter House. They were the cause of an upstart like that Miller being allowed in the front door at all, and they would wreak more havoc if they stayed on much longer. Their presence was taking its toll upon them all, in Tate's opinion. All the extra work was bad enough for the servants, but now their shenanigans were driving the duke to drink.

Henry turned toward the California heiress, his Hanoverian heritage never more apparent. He looked regal and very distant in her suddenly unsure eyes. "You asked to see me," the prince said, and he waited for her to speak.

"Yes." Bella came toward the slender aristocrat. "I need your help," she told him plainly. "I want to make things right with your son, and I need your help."

Henry brightened, his hazel eyes beaming at her. "Isabella, I knew you'd come around! You have only to say the word, and I shall insist that David drop this other nonsense immediately!"

"No!" Isabella told him, confusing him by the alarm he saw in her expression. "Dear Prince Henry, Uncle Henry, if you truly want to help us, you mustn't say one word about any of this to David!"

"Bella, I am completely baffled," the prince replied. "What are you asking of me?"

Bella smiled mischievously as she spoke: "When I answer, you must trust me that your help is absolutely imperative if my plan is to succeed!"

Henry looked worried. "Your mother is very concerned about what plan you are 'hatching,' to use her word. She says you have a tendency to get carried away."

"Oh, I hope to!" Bella replied, confusing him further. "Uncle Henry, you must trust me, please. This must be kept just between us until my plans are carried out. Not even Mama must know!"

"Bella, I won't lie to your mother," the prince said firmly.

"You don't have to! You simply must not say anything until tomorrow morning. That's not too much to ask, is it, dear Uncle Henry? Is it? Please say it isn't!" she implored.

"Oh, dear," Henry said. "I think I'm about to make a mistake."

Bella rewarded him with a brilliant smile and a kiss on the cheek. "I knew I could count on you!"

Upstairs David came out of his rooms, dressed in his riding clothes and a scowl. Snapping his whip against his tall black boots, he marched forward and nearly ran in to Dolores and Consuela.

"Sorry!" he told them stiffly.

"David, I was going to try to find a moment with you later, but if you could spare the time now . . ." Dolores said.

"I was about to ride," he began, and then, his face an impassive mask, he bowed his head slightly. "But if you feel it is urgent," he said, his tone telling her he hoped it was not.

"Thank you, David," Dolores said, smiling and ignoring his tone.

He hesitated one more moment and then gave in. "I am at your disposal," he told her unwillingly.

"Connie, would you fix up a bit of Wallace's old remedy for the duke?" Dolores asked as she placed her hand on the tall duke's arm. "We shall be in my sitting room." David allowed the patrician woman to draw him forward. He opened the door to her sitting room and waited for her to enter. She was still speaking: "My husband spent many years perfecting a concoction that he swore by on mornings when he had partaken of a little too much—revelry—the night before."

David gave her a brief smile that did not reach his eyes. "Am I that transparent?"

The older woman smiled. "Only to a wife who has rather intimate knowledge of that green-about-the-gills look," she reassured him.

Dolores motioned him to a chair as she sat down on the fringed settee, its intricate pattern of forest, ruby, and sapphire shades bright against her somber black dress.

"You said you had something to discuss?" David said.

She took a moment to compose her thoughts. "Yes. I'm really not quite sure how to begin. I don't want you to feel that I am being presumptuous, or too personal," Dolores said, trailing off as she saw his dark blue eyes take on an inaccessible look. "I wondered if you were aware that Isabella has broken off all contact with George Miller."

David stared at the American woman. "I don't understand."

"I think she finally saw through him," Dolores said. "And I want to thank you for your help in the unfortunate matter."

"Thank me?" His eyes widened in astonishment. "I cannot believe you even want to speak to me. Why should you thank the man who was a worse cad than any he tried to save your daughter from? I don't deserve your thanks, I deserve your hatred. And hers," he replied.

"Oh, but she doesn't hate you!" Dolores replied. "Nor do I," she told him. "I admit to being a little disappointed, however. In both of you. She should never have put herself into such a situation, and she is to blame for appearing to be—well, loose."

"She was in love!" David defended Bella. "People in love are capable of great folly."

Dolores began to look worried. "She was not in love with George Miller, David. She is very young emotionally, she has been perhaps too sheltered, and he was the first man who paid court to her. The romance of the forbidden situation appealed to her, not the man himself."

"She very nearly married the man himself," David replied.

"That would have been the ruination of her fortune, her future, and her life. So you see, in spite of your own rather rash actions, I do still owe you thanks."

The duke's brow furrowed. "You are a very unusual woman, Dolores. And a most unusual mother as well."

"Thank you. I take that as a compliment."

"It is," he told her. "You have none of the social falseness that mars most of the people in our society." He gave her a wry smile. "I find that refreshing."

"And my daughter?" Dolores asked. She was rewarded by seeing his expression close over.

"I owe your daughter a debt I can never repay," David said.

"You had said you wished to marry her before the unfortunate incidents up north. I assumed that meant you were in love with her."

David stood up. "Perhaps I was being as rash as your daughter was. I have come to see in recent days that many things I thought I wanted are not good foundations for my future responsibilities."

"Must you go? Connie will return soon with your potion. I promise you it is magical."

"Dolores, I am extremely uncomfortable with this conversation."

"I do not mean to make you uncomfortable, but I felt it was important you know that Bella is no longer involved with Miller."

"For both your sakes, I am glad."

"Is that all you feel? Gladness for us?" Dolores tried to search out answers in his eyes. "I thought my daughter might mean something more to you still."

David hesitated, conflicting emotions struggling within him. In answering her he told himself he was being absolutely honest. "I have said I learned many things about myself throughout this—this experience. The most important one is that I have recognized the need my father has been trying to convince me of for a decade. My life is not only my own; there are many dependent upon me. I intend to live up to those obligations of family and fortune."

"I find that commendable," Dolores responded. "But I don't see the connection between my question and your response."

"Your daughter is a remarkable young lady, Dolores. The wife I need, however, is an unremarkable lady. Someone who will share my burdens, someone dependable who will do her duties and who will not fight me at every turn. Someone who will not try to rule me or compete for control. Someone malleable."

"Someone like Millicent Cavendish," Dolores put in.

"She is young without being riotous. She is honest, reliable, easy to please, and eager to please me."

"Totally unexceptional and unremarkable," Dolores commented.

"Yes," David replied.

"Does the girl herself know of your evaluation of her?"

David hesitated. "She soon will," he replied.

"I hope when you speak to her, you do not speak in quite these accents, David. There is no female alive whose heart is so stalwart she would be able to hear such comments about herself and feel pleased."

"I hope to make her happy," David said.

Dolores sighed. "I must say in all honesty Bella is none of the things of which you speak. She has a willful nature, that you already know. For all her goodness of heart and intelligence, she has always been a handful and resists control of any sort."

David felt his heart become leaden within him. "Dolores, that is precisely the problem. I now realize I would have made as bad a husband for Isabella, albeit in a different way, as would Miller. Your daughter is a high-spirited racehorse, Dolores. What I need is a steady, dependable workhorse."

"Good Lord, David!" Dolores stared at him in horror. "Please, whatever you do, never be this honest with poor Millie!"

"Millicent will understand, I am sure. She is a plain girl

with plain ways." He stopped. "Of course, if you and Bella feel I should pay the price of our—of what happened"—he floundered—"I stand ready to do anything to lessen my obligation to both of you. Including marrying her, if that is your wish," he said stiffly.

"No," Dolores answered truthfully. She looked sad. "No. I would never wish a loveless marriage on my daughter."

Consuela tapped on the door before opening it, holding a tray with one mug on it. The duke took the mug, swallowing without stop until he had finished it and put the mug back on Connie's tray.

"Thank you," he said to them both. "If you will excuse me," he continued to Dolores, "I must be off."

Connie did not speak until the duke was out the door and halfway down the stairs. "Well?" she asked her employer.

Dolores sighed. "Connie, I'm afraid Bella has truly wrecked all hope of David's seeing her in any light other than as a total madcap."

As Dolores voiced her worries to Consuela David was heading out toward Joshua and his waiting mount.

"David—one moment," Prince Henry called out. He came down the hall toward his departing son.

"Father, is it important?"

The prince hesitated. "I—ah—was just wondering how you were feeling."

"I'm feeling fine!" David said, his pinched features belying his words. "I need to clear my head before I see Millicent this evening."

Prince Henry watched his son stride toward the front door. A footman opened it just in time for the tall man to pass through without breaking his stride.

The footman looked back toward the prince. Henry shook his head and walked back down the hall toward his study as the man closed the thick mahogany door.

The Duke of Exeter rode away from Exeter House on a chestnut Arabian, while within its huge confines Prince Henry tried to focus on his estate books, Dolores allowed Consuela to rub her neck and commiserate, and Isabella recruited Sally's aid in her plan to win the duke back.

"Are you sure we're doing the right thing?" Sally asked Isabella.

"Sally, we're doing the *only* thing!" Isabella told her maid in ringing accents. "I've only one chance now to find out the truth and to make things come out right!"

"Yes, miss," Sally said unhappily. "Only the last time you were so intent on something, it didn't turn out so good."

"This will be different!" Isabella made the statement seem like a command.

Chapter Twenty-six

David arrived back in Exeter Square as the afternoon sun was setting in blazing splendor behind the massive facade of Exeter House. Joshua was not there to greet the duke; it was young Tim who came forward to take the chestnut around to the stables.

"Where is Joshua?" the duke asked.

Young Tim didn't meet the duke's eyes. "He's around about somewhere, Your Grace."

David did not notice Tim's discomfort. Taking the steps two at a time, the Duke of Exeter disappeared into the house, determined to make good his decision and talk to Millicent's father before the night was out. David felt sure Cavendish would be delighted at the prospects for his daughter and would agree that David could broach the subject to Millicent immediately.

Something in the back of David's mind told him he was deciding on a wife in the same way he decided on a purchase of farm equipment, but he brushed the thought aside. His conversation with Dolores earlier had convinced him he was right. Isabella's mother did not want her daughter burdened with a husband she did not love; she had said as much. There was no way he could atone to Isabella for his inexcusable behavior. But he could regain a bit of his father's trust by getting his life in order, by settling down as his father had wanted for so long. He would marry and present his father with Exeter heirs.

David Beresford, Duke of Exeter, surveyed the shambles he had made of his life by his rash actions and told himself he wanted no more upheaval disturbing his peace and quiet. He was not going to end up a rake or a common drunkard over *any* woman, no matter how dark her eyes or how much she had affected his heart. He would get over her. He would make himself get over her.

He thrust aside the memory of Isabella's eyes soft with longing, forced his mind away from remembering her naked form; her comeliness had made him act the cad. Her continuing appeal to his senses had made him strike out at strangers and pollute himself with too much brandy and whatever else he had tried to find solace in the night before.

He was not going to end up a pathetic roué, debauched and miserable. He would marry Millicent and make the kind of life everyone else had. His father had been right all those weeks ago. He had been a romantic about marriage, thinking to wait and marry only for love.

Markham was tidying up the duke's suite of rooms when David entered. "Good afternoon, Your Grace."

"What's good about it?" David asked sourly.

Markham ignored his master's irritation. "A letter was delivered for you," the valet told David. Reaching toward a silver salver, he thrust it toward the duke.

David glanced at it as he passed the man. "Later" was all he answered. "Draw me a bath, Markham. And lay out the new suit from Weston and the rubies. I want to be at my best tonight." As Markham helped the Duke of Exeter get ready for the night ahead the wind came up outside, the skies beginning to cloud over.

Neither Markham nor the duke remembered the letter until David finished dressing for the evening. He studied his appearance in his bedroom pier glass. The perfectly tailored black jacket was smooth across his broad shoulders, a ruby-colored Venetian waistcoat and ivory-colored cravat surmounting his ivory silk shirt. Black breeches and tall black boots, polished with a champagne shine, completed his attire, along with a large ruby stickpin that held his cravat in its impeccable folds.

Markham gazed from the top of the Duke's thick, curly chestnut-colored locks to the toes of his shining boots. "You do look a treat, if I may say so, Your Grace."

The duke grimaced but otherwise did not reply. His gaze caught sight of the silver salver and the letter upon it. Bored, he reached for it, using his thumb to prize open the sealed paper.

Ranleigh Gardens. Upon peril of your life, stay far from it this night.

"What the devil?" David threw the note down.

"Disturbing news, Your Grace?" Markham asked.

"No news at all!" David replied. "Just some damned nonsense."

"From whom?"

David picked the paper up. "It doesn't say."

"How odd," Markham said.

"Yes. Curious." David frowned. "Come to think of it, it's not only curious, it's really quite a challenge!"

"Your Grace would be wise to heed the warning," the valet told his employer.

"I'll heed nothing!" David replied hotly. And with that, he left his rooms and clattered down the stairs toward his waiting carriage. "By God," David muttered to himself as he raced down the outside front steps, "no one is going to threaten me!" Joshua opened the door for him. "I see you're back," David said.

Joshua looked nonplussed. "I—yes, Your Grace." The old stableman waited for the duke to dress him down, but David merely stepped up inside the carriage as the lowering skies began to drizzle.

Joshua climbed up top as David sat back inside, his mind racing over the possibilities. Who would send him such a warning, who would threaten him so? He thought of all those whose paths he had crossed, all who might wish him harm and throw down such a gauntlet. And of who might know of it and try to warn him. Or send a threat just as a prank.

There were many who envied him, possibly even those who sought the rich Cavendish heiress's hand and wished him evil for escorting her. Whatever they were up to, the wording, the warning, the writing, and the paper had been of the finest; it was no fool who had issued the challenge.

Nor was it the work of a stranger.

It was probably some young fool in his cups who had been boasting of besting the renowned Duke of Exeter's reputation with fisticuffs or swords and been put to the laugh by his cohorts.

Curiosity gnawed at the Duke of Exeter as he sat back inside the carriage and let it carry him forward through the wet streets toward Devonshire House and the waiting Cavendishes.

"Ranleigh Gardens?" Millicent said, her words accented by a shiver of excitement. "They're thought quite risqué, are they not?"

"Only a little," David replied. "And I shall be by your side."

Millicent Cavendish smiled trustingly up at the handsome duke. "With you at my side, dear David, I fear nothing and no one."

A little uncomfortable with her innocent accolade, David turned to her parents. "Shall we?"

"Of course, David," the duchess replied. "Just give us a moment to see to our wraps." Millicent's mother left the room.

Her husband sighed. "What do you say to sharing a glass of port while we wait, David? We shall be kept a quarter hour, mark my words. My good wife's idea of 'a moment' is elastic, to say the least."

David followed Millicent's father and accepted a small crystal glass filled with the ruby-red liquor. "Thank you, sir."

"You've never called me sir before; no need to start now, David. We're almost of an age, within—what, seven—eight years of each other, aren't we?" Millicent's father asked, and then he continued, laughing: "If you'd married as young as I did, you might already have a daughter of Millicent's age yourself."

"Not unless I'd married at thirteen," David said dryly.

Cavendish laughed again. "Now what's this about you two going to Ranleigh Gardens? They're not exactly proper. And it looks as if it will soon be pouring."

"We shall be inside the rotunda listening to the orchestra. Ranleigh is not as it once was. If it's not proper, it's certainly no longer improper."

Cavendish smiled. "I would say more against it, but my wife is bound and determined to see for herself. So I shall have to trust you to take good care of Millicent until we meet you there. I must put in an appearance at the engineering exhibit at the Prince Albert first, but we shan't tarry there. We shall meet you as early as possible."

"I shall ensure nothing untoward or risqué is allowed," the Duke of Exeter reassured Millicent's father.

"It's a mixed crowd that goes there, but you've no need to reassure me, David. I know you to be a complete gentleman."

Visions of Bella in the woodland cottage rose behind David's eyes. He turned away from the other man, unable to meet his gaze. "No harm will come to her," David repeated. "In point of fact," David added, "there is something I want to discuss with you concerning Millicent."

The sounds of the women returning interrupted their conversation. Millicent floated into the room cloaked in a sky-blue velvet cape, looking very young and very shy.

"I'm ready," she said in tremulous accents, looking at the Duke of Exeter from under her pale lashes.

"We shall meet you there directly," her mother reassured them both. "Where shall we meet?"

"Perhaps near the organ?" David suggested.

"Yes, Millicent will enjoy the music until we arrive," Millicent's mother said, coming toward David and reaching out her hand for him to kiss. "David, I am a bit nervous about your destination, so I am counting on you to keep a watchful eye until we arrive."

"Mother, we shall be completely safe."

"Now, Millicent, the truth must out, and David must know. David, dear, you must ensure my girl's tender sensibilities aren't unnerved by this rather rakish excursion."

"I shall ensure her safety," David replied as they left. They were escorted to his carriage by two footmen holding up oversized umbrellas to protect them from the worsening weather.

Once they were safely inside Millicent leaned forward to wave back at her mother and then sat back, sighing happily. "I am so glad you thought of this excursion. I have been absolutely dying of curiosity about Ranleigh for ever so long."

"I'm glad you approve," the duke replied.

Millicent was slightly nearsighted. She leaned forward to peer directly into her escort's eyes. "I must ask you something most important, David." Her soft words were almost drowned out by the rain that thudded down upon the carriage roof.

"Yes?" was all David vouchsafed.

"This may not seem ladylike, but I must ask you a personal question. I have the feeling that you are on the point of speaking to my father and offering for me. If I am wrong, please, please forgive me. But if I'm right, I hope you will reconsider and not say anything rash this evening when they arrive."

A bit of coughing interrupted David's response. "Sorry," the duke finally managed to answer.

"Oh, dear, I didn't mean to make you uncomfortable."

When he fully recovered his voice, David stared at her. "Are you telling me not to offer for you?"

"It's just that it's not as if you truly cared about me, after all. You do see what I mean, don't you?"

"I don't see at all, and I think this conversation is most unseemly, Millicent. If the topic were to be raised, it should be raised with your father first."

Millicent was not to be deterred. In her own simple way, she was ready and willing to pursue what she desired. "Oh, no! That is most especially what I do not want! Please don't talk to Papa! I'm sorry you're shocked, but my generation feels things differently perhaps than yours."

"My generation! My dear girl, I am only thirty-one years old!"

"Precisely," the eighteen-year-old Millicent replied. "After all, isn't it better to be honest than to be seemly? I mean—that is, you're not saying you do care about me, are you?" she asked.

"Millicent, I would hope that you would already know that I care."

"Oh, dear," she replied, her shoulders slumping a little. "That's entirely too bad."

David was thoroughly confused by her reaction. "I beg your pardon? I mean, I thought—that is, I hoped you had some feeling for me as well."

"Oh, I do!" she reassured him. "But not as a prospective husband, if you see what I mean."

"Not as a prospective husband," David repeated.

"No. I can see I am shocking you, and I assure you that you are most desirable and eligible and all. I mean, you know that, and so do I. But that is really the point, isn't it?"

"Millicent, what on earth are you trying to say to me?" David interrupted impatiently.

"Just that you are altogether much too handsome and much too much sought-after to marry someone like me. I'm sure I would never be quiet and content. I would always worry about who should catch your eye next, and all the ladies would be so jealous of me and trying to catch your eye, and that is no way to be married. Don't you agree?" Millicent asked hopefully.

David stared at the young woman across the shadowy depths of the carriage as they traversed the wet London streets. Rain was pounding on the roof. Wounded pride made his bearing stiffen. "I assure you, I am not such a fool as to wander the streets and gutters of London now, let alone as a married man. I would never so humiliate myself or my wife."

"But that's ever so much worse," Millicent told him. She

bent forward, imploring him with every look and movement. "Don't you see, David? I would feel so terrible knowing you wanted to pursue others and were denying yourself on my account."

"I don't behave in that way unmarried!" David nearly shouted. With terrific determination, he controlled himself. "Are you saying you would want me to seek out others?"

"No. I'm simply showing you how impossible our situation would be if you insisted on marrying me."

David was incredulous. "Are you turning me down?"

Millicent smiled sweetly at the duke. "Oh, David, I can hardly do that if you never offer for me, can I? After all, you can have your pick! You don't really want me."

It took him a moment to answer. "You are telling me you don't want me to ask your father for your hand."

"If you could see your way clear to not doing it, I would be eternally grateful. Because if you do ask, my father will most certainly insist I comply, and I'll have to say yes because he'll tell me you're the biggest catch I would ever get. I would have to say yes, and then we'd both be just miserably unhappy." Millicent ran out of breath. She stared at him hopefully. "I wouldn't want you to be unhappy for the rest of your life."

"Thank you," David said stiffly.

Millicent reached one gloved hand to his arm. "You know it's the truth. David, you're not in love with me."

"That's not the point," David said sharply.

"Maybe not for you. But it is most definitely the point for me."

"Millicent, I warn you, love is the worst foundation for a strong marriage. Love is not a foundation at all. It is a quicksand wherein you lose your way and your honor and possibly your very life if you do not squash it!"

"Lord, you make it sound horrid!"

"It is!" he insisted vehemently.

The young girl scrutinized the thirty-one-year-old duke's face. Even set into hard, forbidding lines, it was handsome. "Dear David, who is it that you have loved so very much and who has hurt you so?"

279

"No one!" he snapped. "I'm not in love with anyone!"

"Yes, David," Millicent murmured.

"You sound as if you don't believe me, but I assure you, the farthest—" David began, but the carriage came to a sudden halt. "What the devil is going on out there?" The windows showed only a dark landscape. David raised his silver-tipped walnut walking stick to the small trap door in the roof and lifted it up, dribbles of rain seeping inside the carriage from the coachman's wet seat above. "Joshua, where are we? Why are you stopping?"

The tiny door slammed shut with no answer, the carriage lurching forward. Millicent was thrown off her seat and into David's arms as the horse galloped forward down the dark road. The rain hissed under the fast-moving wheels. It sprayed up, spattering mud high on the sides of the carriage.

"Oh, my!" Millicent's breath was shocked out of her.

"What the devil is he doing?" David helped Millicent to the seat beside him before rising to force the trap door open. "Joshua, what the blue blazes is going on?" the duke demanded as he forced the trap door open.

"We're running from brigands, Your Grace!" Joshua shouted, the carriage careening madly down the wet and bumpy road. Millicent Cavendish hung on for dear life to the seat beneath her, the duke nearly thrown in her lap by the sudden jolt of a large-sized bump.

"Thieves!" Millicent cried out. "David, what shall we do if we can't outrun them?"

The duke was swearing steadily to himself. He had no weapons upon his person. He looked around the carriage for something, anything to use and ended with the walnut walking stick. Upending it, he grabbed it from the bottom, weighing the value of the thick silver-encrusted knob.

"Damn and blast the swine, they'll have a fight for it, I promise you that!"

"I don't want to die!" Millicent wailed. "I haven't even met the King of Hawaii yet!"

"Don't turn hysterical," David ordered. "Just do as I say and you'll be all right."

The carriage was slowing, the duke moving back on the seat, out of sight from the nearest door. "Lock the other door!" he whispered fiercely. "Hurry!" he urged as Millicent fumbled with the latch. *"Hurry!"*

"I am!" she wailed. Fumbling a moment longer, hearing his muttered epithets across the seat, she finally shot it home. "It's locked," she told him, "but they'll break it down!"

"Not if they try this side first," the duke said through gritted teeth.

The carriage stopped. Millicent held her breath and closed her eyes. "Oh, I so wanted to see the King of Hawaii when he arrived," she said again, this time in a tiny voice. She began to pray silently that she would survive this adventure.

While Millicent's short life ran before her eyes, David was preparing for battle. The carriage door nearest him opened, a sheet of cold rain pouring inside the compartment. David began to pray in that moment, hoping Millicent wouldn't open her eyes and look toward him, giving away the fact of his existence. If the robbers thought they had a lone female, they would relax, and David would have his one chance to save them from tragedy.

Millicent was not a problem. Her hands were to her face, covering her closed eyes as she tried to pretend none of it was happening. All she could think about was her mother waiting for her at the Gardens. She'd never even gotten to see Ranleigh Gardens.

Nothing but icy rain came through the open carriage door, chilling the air inside. Damn and blast them, David railed to himself. Why were they hesitating?

Scraping sounds came from the other side of the carriage. Someone was trying the other door. Millicent stiffened, her hands still covering her face as soft, despairing moans began to escape her lips.

The sound of a gunshot made David stiffen and Millicent gasp. "Don't shoot!" Millicent called out in a faltering voice. "Oh, please, don't shoot me! My father will give you money!"

Grateful she had not given him away, David was swearing under his breath at the girl. Telling robbers where they could get more money was asking for them to kidnap her. She was a little fool, but he was much more worried by the gunshot than by her stupidity. If there was more than one of them, if they all had guns, he had very little chance of saving the situation.

If he could surprise them, if Joshua was not hurt and could urge the horse forward at David's command, David might stand a chance of surprising the gunman and breaking them free.

"Stand down!" a rough voice called out. "Stand down or we'll shoot up the carriage!"

He said "we'll," David told himself. There's more than one. As he sorted out the ramifications of this information he heard Millicent again calling out to the robbers.

"Don't shoot! I'm coming out," Millicent Cavendish yelled. "Please, don't shoot!" Making good her words, Millie started for the open door.

"Don't do it!" David hissed, but she paid no attention.

"I'm here! Don't shoot!" she said again, sounding very fearful as she started out of the carriage. Her teeth started to chatter from her fear and from the cold rain that began to soak her hair and her velvet cloak as she stepped outside.

David cursed the girl's stupidity, ready to grab her back inside but unable to hold her back without making himself a target and destroying any chance of helping her. For the first time in his life David found himself irritated beyond endurance at the female of the species. Millicent's lack of courage brought both herself and her defender into mortal danger, her rushing outside into the arms of her abductors effectively hamstringing David from even trying to save either her virtue or her life.

In that moment he wished it were Isabella in the carriage and not the mild Millicent. Isabella's fiery self-defense was what was needed now. She would not have willingly given herself over to any enemy.

"Step down," the rough voice called again. It sounded gravelly, rough, as though the robber had a thick cold.

David heard it and waited. They couldn't know another was inside unless Millicent had told them. Even if she had, he might have a chance if they came in one at a time.

He waited.

"David!" Millicent's voice came from outside. "David, please—throw down your arms! They're going to hurt me!"

The duke began to swear under his breath at the stupidity of the girl, but he could not ignore her plea. He didn't know who they were or how vile they might be. She was safer with him, even unarmed, than she was alone. He at least would fight. He thought of Bella. Bella would give such thugs a run for their money. "All right!" he called out.

"Throw out your arms!"

"Not bloody likely," David muttered to himself as he moved forward. Aware that they knew he was inside, David moved forward, presenting himself in the open doorway. "I have no weapon!" he called out. The walking stick was behind him.

A masked man came out of the shadows of the overhanging trees, an oilskin cloak hiding most of his form. With a lethal-looking pistol he motioned the duke out of the carriage into the dark, rainy, deserted roadway.

The man came closer, still brandishing the gun. Under the rain cloak a long greatcoat that boasted several shoulder capes could be discerned. A wide-brimmed and greasy hat was pulled low across the brigand's brow, a muffler knotted at the throat and obscuring the man's mouth. Even without a mask the cutthroat was effectively masked from view. The deadly pistol and spurred boots only added to the menace of the man's stance and attitude.

David stayed in the carriage doorway, swiftly calculating his options. The robber came through the muddy tracks, nearing the carriage. The duke retreated inside, reaching for his walking stick.

The robber was still coming forward, pistol in hand. He was left-handed, David saw. The brigand reached the carriage steps and then put his booted foot upon the lowest one and stepped up.

David reached behind himself, holding the walking stick tight and imprisoning it within his clenched fist as he brought it up, out of sight from outside.

The robber's head and upper torso entered the carriage,

and David struck, the stick hitting the man's gloved hand, the pistol discharging. Urgent voices called out excitedly, asking if all was well, if any were hurt, what was happening.

David grappled with the robber, the muffler coming loose and then the greasy hat pulled off as the robber called out as loud as he could: *"Move!"*

The carriage lurched forward, David still grappling with the robber in the dimly lit interior. As the carriage put on speed David saw two things clearly. He saw another gun leveled at him, and he saw the robber's face.

"Bella!" David shouted in startled tones. "What in bloody hell do you think you are *doing?"*

Isabella Alexander was favoring the left hand David had very nearly broken in grappling the pistol away from her. But she kept the other pistol, the one in her right hand, trained on the duke. "I assumed you'd have something up your sleeve; that's why I led with my left hand. This one"—she motioned with her right hand—"is the one you should be wary of. And if you think I won't shoot, you'd best think again, because you're sorely mistaken!" she told him.

David stared at the young woman whose virginity he had taken, the girl who had destroyed his sleep before that night in the Yorkshire cabin and who had invaded his dreams ever since.

"What is the meaning of this? What do you think you are doing?" he demanded.

"Kidnapping you," Bella replied. Favoring her left arm, which still stung from the blow from David's cane, she sat down across from the Duke of Exeter. Water dripped off her cloak as she glared at him across the dimly lit carriage. A small oil lamp flickered soft light from its sconce near one door. The opposite lamp had blown out when the rainy winds had invaded the open carriage door near it. "Luckily," she told him, "I came prepared for your aggressiveness."

"My . . ." He stared at her. "I beg your pardon?"

"And well you should!" Bella told him sharply. She picked up the other pistol, waving both guns. "I came in here assuming you would flail out at me, ready for your futile attempt!"

"Futile, madam?"

"Futile!" she snapped. Leveling the pistols at his chest, she repeated the word: "Futile, Your Grace!"

David stared at her. "You must have lost all your senses."

"I've lost none."

"I can overpower you at any moment," David said, ignoring the pistols aimed at him.

"Only if you wish to chance not only my largess but that of my partners."

David thought about it, thought about whoever was urging the carriage onward, whoever was riding on top or alongside. "What do you think you are doing?" the duke finally asked. "Whom have you got in your employ?"

"As I said, I am kidnapping you," Isabella replied, earning a blank stare.

"You can't possibly be serious," the duke told her. He stared at the flashing eyes that alone seemed familiar in the figure dressed in a man's cape, hat, and trousers. She sat across from him on the damp leather seat, staring back at the incredulous nobleman. "Not only am I serious, but so is this pistol." Bella waved the lethal-looking pistol at him, its ten-inch barrel deadly-looking.

David Beresford stared at the American girl who was dressed as a brigand. "This is ridiculous," he told her. "What do you think you will gain by this farce?"

"Satisfaction," Bella said.

She looked perfectly capable of cocking the pistol she held, capable of blasting a large hole through him. David knew he could overpower her. He was less sure he could do it before she mortally wounded him. Bella was no whimpering Millicent. "Satisfaction is usually demanded by a lady's protector and involves a duel at dawn," the duke told her. "Or so I've read," he continued, drawling the words and sounding much more at ease than he felt.

"I am my own protector," Bella told him. "And we shan't be waiting for dawn."

David stared at her. "You are the one who had the note sent, aren't you? The note about Ranleigh Gardens."

"Yes." She smiled. "I knew if you were given a dare, you would not be able to refuse the challenge."

"I should have known," David said darkly.

"Take off your boots."

David wasn't sure he had heard her correctly. "I beg your pardon?"

"You'll be begging for more than my pardon if you don't do as I say," Isabella said in a swaggering tone, hugely enjoying herself. "Take off your boots!"

Chapter Twenty-seven

"What did you do with Millicent?" David demanded.

"I sent her home," Bella replied.

"How many confederates do you have?"

"Enough."

The carriage came to a stop an hour later, rain pouring down hard but lessening on the carriage roof as it came to rest under the branches of a stand of trees. The Duke of Exeter was leaning back against the corner of the carriage, not even bothering to look out at the darkened countryside.

"Are you, by some sad mischance, thinking of holding me for ransom or some such?" David asked the woman whose beauty could not be hidden in her borrowed men's clothing.

"I hadn't thought of that," Isabella told him truthfully. "But now that you mention it, I rather think your father would say poor loss and write you off. I don't think he'd pay enough ransom to make the crime worth it."

"The crime? Excuse me, which crime are we speaking of?"

"Blackmail," Bella replied. "As you suggested."

"What about kidnapping?" David asked. "Isn't this a crime already?"

"You didn't think so when you kidnapped me! Besides," she said, smiling, "dead men tell no tales."

The duke sat up straight, becoming fully alert. "You don't mean actual harm! I realize I owe you more than mere apologies, but you can't seriously want to take my life!"

"Can't I?"

David's own guilt unmanned him more than anything she could ever say or do. "Have you then hired people to do the deed? You certainly will not pull that trigger yourself."

Isabella opened the carriage door, jumping out and motioning the duke forward. "I'm not quite sure, but soon we both shall know." She held his boots in her hand.

David peered out through the rain at the dark cottage a few feet away. "Where are we?"

"That's no concern of yours," Bella told him. "Your only concern is in doing as I ask. Which is to get out of that carriage."

"You have my boots," he told her.

"Yes, and I intend to keep them. You'll not get far in this rain, cloakless, in evening attire, barefoot, and hours from anywhere," she replied.

Every fiber in the duke's body bade him rebel against any female ordering him to do anything. But a combination of self-preservation, curiosity, and guilt propelled him forward. He stepped down, his stocking feet feeling the cold, slippery, wet wood of the carriage step, the ground below muddy and even colder.

"I feel ridiculous," he told her.

"An unnerving feeling, as I remember," Isabella replied.

David reacted to her words, Bella unable to see his disquiet through the rain and the darkness around them as she motioned him forward into the cottage.

"You know where to go and what to do," Bella called out to someone.

David caught a glimpse of a man, his shape familiar despite his voluminous cape. David allowed Bella to motion him inside, his black stockings soaked through as he felt his way across the stony yard and up onto the unevenness of the plank-floored porch.

"Inside," she told him, poking the gun at his back.

"Be careful," he snapped, "or that may just go off by accident! Pistols are not to be toyed with!"

It was clammy cold inside, and pitch-black. Bella reached down, feeling for something.

"What do you think you're doing?" David asked, coming closer.

"Stay where you are!" she said. Then, thinking better of it, she changed her mind. "Better yet, go on inside."

"I can't see a thing."

"Good!" she said. He stepped just inside and stopped. Bella picked up the oil lamp that had been left waiting. She threw matches toward David, the gun trained on him. "Light one."

"Light one? I can't even *find* one," he complained, but he bent down and ran his hand across the rush-covered plank floor. "Ouch!"

"What is it?" she asked.

"A sliver," he muttered, irritated, as he found the matchbox and struck a match. The inside of the cottage flared into brief light. "Hand me the lamp," he said none too nicely.

Bella did, the gun still trained on him. He lit it, a rough stone fireplace visible in the yellowish light. It filled the far wall of the one-room cottage. The only furniture was a narrow pallet drawn near the fireplace and a scarred wood table beside it.

David looked down at the rush-strewn plank floor that was cold and rough against his soaking feet. The freezing wind blew against the uneven window sashes, finding chinks in the molding and sending fingers of icy air drafting in to disturb the rushes and chill around their feet.

"This is probably filthy," he said.

"Probably," Bella replied easily.

"Where are we?" the duke asked. "It looks vaguely familiar."

"You have a wide acquaintance with peasant cottages?" Bella replied.

David grimaced. "All peasant cottages look alike, is that what you're getting at? Thank you for reminding me of the obvious." He set the lamp on the small table and watched Bella look around for another. She found it near the fireplace, the small room glowing in the flickering, yellowish lamplight.

"Now what?" David asked his captor. "Even if you don't shoot me, I shall probably catch my death from the bloody cold!"

"There's wood and more matches in the fireplace. You may light the fire."

"Thank you so much," he answered sarcastically. Moving to the fireplace, he balanced against the rough stone mantel as he reached down and took off first one wet stocking and then the other before seeing to the fire.

"It will surely smoke," he warned. "Everything in here is damp. And God knows what debris is up this chimney. What's that?" he asked sharply as he heard sounds outside.

Bella glanced out the small window at the departing carriage. "That's the only means of transportation leaving this place and returning to London."

"You can't be serious!" He stared at her, the storm unleashing a bolt of lightning that brightened the fields beyond the window for a moment.

"Do you need instructions on how to start a fire?" Bella asked maddeningly.

"No!" He turned back to his task, Bella rubbing her arms a little, cold despite cloak and jacket.

Some of the wood was a little green, but David finally got the kindling to burst into flame. The fire licked up around the edges of the two logs. "You'd best pray the chimney isn't blocked," David told her as he stood up. "This place looks to have been deserted for quite some time. How did you find it?"

"My associates found it."

"And how long have you been acquainted with underworld figures?" he asked sarcastically.

Bella did not reply. Unclasping the cloak from around her neck, she threw it across the room toward him. "Put it on," she said.

"You need it more than I. You're farther from the fire, after all."

"You'll need it soon enough. Put it on and then undress."

"What?"

"Put the cloak on and then undress. Hand me your clothing as you take it off."

"You can't be serious!"

Bella stamped her booted foot. "I wish you would stop saying that! If I were an ordinary robber, you'd have been done to death already out of my sheer impatience with you!"

"I am most frightfully sorry, Miss Alexander, but I am not used to being abducted, I am not used to finding out that people who have been given shelter in my own home are crazed criminals, and I am not used to having a lady force me, at gunpoint, to undress! And speaking of ladies, how do you know you can trust your associates to deliver poor Millicent safely home? Especially after she blathered on about her father ransoming her."

"She'll be long since safely home," he was told.

"Really?" David asked sarcastically. "I suppose you're counting on honor among thieves."

"No, I'm not," Bella replied.

"Thank you for that, at least!"

"You are welcome. Now—I am totally serious," Bella reassured him. "The cloak—and then your clothes."

A glimmer of doubt crossed his mind. David gauged her. "I don't take orders from anyone, particularly not at gunpoint," the duke said. "If you want me to undress, you will have to undress me yourself," he told her finally.

Bella's gaze was locked into his. "Do it," she said, raising the huge pistol.

The duke's eyes never left Isabella's. His peripheral vision took in the menacing gun. "Do what?" he asked.

Bella hesitated. "Take off your jacket," she told him finally.

The Duke of Exeter delayed. "No."

She waved the pistol at him. "You are in no position to say no!"

"As I said, if you want me to undress, you shall have to undress me," David said.

"I am not foolish enough to put down this gun or to come near you with or without it until you are safely in such a condition as to be unable to run away. Now, that can be accomplished by your removing your clothes, or it can be accomplished by a well-placed bullet in one of your legs. I assume you would prefer the former." Bella raised the gun. "And don't tell me I wouldn't do it. Would you have thought I would have done any of what has transpired this evening?"

He thought about it. Everything, including what was now happening, was unthinkable. He watched her eyes as he removed his exquisitely tailored black evening jacket.

"You may put the cloak on," she told him. "And then remove your vest and shirt."

He made no move toward the cloak. Slowly he unbuttoned first the ruby-red velvet waistcoat and then the creamy-white shirt beneath it. Watching her face, he reached for the ruby stickpin and undid his cravat. "Pity there's no mirror here. I have no idea how I shall manage to reorganize my cravat later. Or do you intend to bury me naked?"

"I hadn't thought about it," Bella told him.

David pulled the cravat from his neck and dropped it to the floor on top of his jacket. He took off the waistcoat, folding it carefully on top of the slowly increasing pile of clothing. His shirt came next, the top of his white long johns the only covering left on his chest.

A shiver ran through Bella as David bent to place the shirt on the pile. She took a step nearer the warmth of the fire, watching his broad shoulders as his arms folded the shirt. The muscles of his back rippled underneath the white cotton long john. He straightened up, staring at her defiantly. "More?" he asked.

"More," she replied.

He reached to his waist, unbuckling his belt and pulling it off. Unbuttoning his trousers, he saw her eyes flicker. He pulled off the black breeches, the white cotton long johns his only clothing. When he straightened up he smiled. "There."

"You're not done," Bella said.

"Obviously I am not going to roam the countryside in the pouring rain, dressed only in my underwear!"

"I have no idea what you are capable of, but I'd wager you will think twice about running off naked."

"What do you intend to do with my clothes, burn them?"

"Yes."

He stared at her. He felt ridiculous standing half-naked in front of a completely dressed female, no matter how outlandish the female's costume. Half-naked and kidnapped! "What do you intend to gain from all this?"

"We'll talk once I have your clothing."

He took one step toward her, the pistol rising in her hand. David gauged her eyes. He could not believe she would actually shoot him. Then again, Miller had deserted her. Perhaps even because of what had happened. Perhaps she had confessed her fall from grace, and he had rejected her. A delicately balanced mind might go over the edge at the thought of her entire life being ruined by the foolishness of her own decisions and the unforgiveableness of his.

Miller's leaving her, the fact that she could no longer expect an offer of marriage from any of the men her mother would deem suitable—it all could have unhinged the high-strung girl. She was known as the Terror of California; perhaps she had done other outlandish things. In any event, she was certainly used to having her way. She was used to being sought after, not discarded, not set aside and reviled.

He stopped moving toward her. Bending down, he picked up the cloak. He fastened the clasp around his neck and then turned it half around so that the opening fell across his back. Without a word he reached beneath it and began unbuttoning the long row of buttons from neck to crotch.

Bella moved near the pile of his clothes.

"It is a shame to burn such fine material," he told her.

"You won't miss them," she replied.

He squirmed beneath the rough cloak, pulling the long johns off his shoulders and chest and then shoving them down his flanks until the cotton puddled at his feet.

"Step back," Bella ordered. He pulled one foot and then the other out of the material, stepping back toward the fire, his posterior warmed by the fire as the cloak swung open a bit behind him. In front of him Bella was scooping up the long johns from in front of his bare feet and ankles. He watched her move toward the fireplace.

"Bella—you can't be serious!" he protested as she walked

forward. He watched, astounded, as she tossed the clothing onto the fire. The logs blazed up around the material, burning brighter for long moments in which the Duke of Exeter watched every stitch of his clothing go up in flames.

"I don't believe it," he said, staring at her in horror. He was now sure she was truly demented.

The ruby stickpin slipped from her fingers, hitting the plank floor with a tiny tinkle. She leaned down to the rushes, picking it up. In that moment David made his move, grabbing for the pistols.

She struggled against him, one of the guns going off as David grabbed them away from her. The shock of the sound stopped both of them. Each of them froze, staring in horror at the other, afraid of what might have happened.

The relief they felt at seeing neither had been wounded was quickly replaced by anger. Bella scrambled to get her hands on the nearest pistol, David determined to stop her. Her hands clawed at him, grabbing the rough cloak and trying to pull him back from reaching the pistol first. The clasp broke, the material falling down around his shoulders and hampering his arms. He shoved at it, trying to push the material out of his way.

Bella grappled with him, bending toward the gun as he turned to block her. The cloak fell off at their feet as she reached toward him and grabbed his flesh.

The shock stiffened his entire body. Bella's breath caught in her throat as she felt him hardening in her hand.

David felt his flesh engorging and willed himself to stop. But her hand was still holding him. "You have to let go," he told her in strangled tones.

His hands went to her shoulders, ready to push her away. But Bella reached for the top button on the thick peasant shirt she wore. And unbuttoned it.

"What are you doing?" he asked, his voice skipping over the words, his breath coming hard. "We can't do this," he said.

"There is no reason not to now," she told him, her voice throaty.

"Why are you doing this?" he asked in a whisper.

She unbuttoned another button. And then stopped, looking down at her own hand. David's gaze traveled from Bella's face to the creamy skin that was visible between the edges of the partially opened shirt. And then down to the hand that held him captive, his desire given undeniable proof by his stiff, erect hardness.

She let go of him. Bella stared at the curly hair of his chest, at the narrow hips that ended in two massively muscled thighs.

"Why?" he whispered.

"You started to make love to me," Bella whispered back. "You never finished."

He had no words. David was so involved in a mixture of embarrassment and desire he had no words. Bella was surprised at the thudding trip-hammer her heart had become. Now that she had reached her plan's objective, now that she had spoken as she had planned, her own audacity and forwardness made her blush. He could easily think her beyond redemption before this night was over.

Praying she wasn't wrong, Bella's hand went back to the man's work shirt she wore under the heavy frieze jacket. Her eyes on his, she slowly began to unbutton the rest of the buttons. She watched his gaze move from her eyes to her throat. She felt his hands fall away from her shoulders when she reached to take the jacket and shirt off in one movement.

Her own white silk chemise clung to her body, outlining the firm, round breasts that were seared into his memory. She slipped out of the thick work boots and the dark trousers, still watching his eyes.

Dressed only in the thin silk, garters, and stockings, she stood in front of him and waited.

David stared down at the clinging silk. His flesh was painfully erect, reaching out of its own volition toward her.

Bella waited, her breath caught in her throat. If he turned away, if he made no move toward her, all was lost. She waited, each of them aware of the sounds of the other's breathing, both fighting the pounding of their own blood.

David reached for the shoulder straps of her undergarment, hooking his thumbs through them and then stopping, searching her face until she opened her eyes and looked up at him. Their eyes locked and then, carefully, he pulled the straps off her shoulders.

He slipped the silk down to her waist, exposing the hardening pink nipples of her breasts. Sinking to his knees, he knelt in front of her on the rush-strewn floor. Gently he took one pink nipple into his mouth, rolling his tongue across and around it as he slipped the chemise off her waist and down her legs.

Bella's eyes closed again. She leaned in toward him, feeling his hands travel up her legs to cup each buttock as he kissed first one breast and then the other.

He brought her to the floor, reaching for the cloak and spreading it like a blanket before bringing her down upon it. Stretching her out in front of the fireplace, his hands traveled lightly down the length of her, feeling her body shiver in reaction. His hand went between her legs, her eyes flying open at the invasion.

Forcing himself to move slowly, he reached to cover her mouth with his. His hands were touching exquisitely sensitive flesh, her body moving with the feelings he evoked, caught up in the wonder of what he made her feel. Feeling her response, he thrust his tongue against hers. Bella's arms went around him, her hands pressing on the small of his back, pulling his body dangerously close to hers.

He tried to go slowly, but she moved beneath him, her hips rising to press themselves against his swollen flesh. David groaned, letting his weight fall toward her, feeling his body invade the space between her thighs.

Bella stiffened, fearing the sudden pain of their night in Yorkshire. But David moved slowly, rhythmically against her until he felt her thighs relax. He reached to widen the space between them, using his hand to help her accept him.

When the tip of him entered her she shuddered, the movement nearly undoing him. He wanted to plunge deep inside her, but he steeled himself, forcing himself to slow his movements. She reached up for him, her hips coming off the cloak, her arms pulling him down.

David bruised her lips with his own as he entered her. He

could bear it no longer and thrust deeper. Prepared for the moment of pain, Bella felt only exquisite pleasure as he plunged within her, opening the center of her being and making it his.

"Bella." His voice choked with emotion, he spoke against her mouth. "I love you."

He heard her repeating his words, heard her soft words end in a moan as he pulled a little away and then thrust deeper and deeper, again and again, over and over, deeper and deeper.

Nothing he had ever felt prepared him for the sensations that coursed through him as they found each other's rhythm and reached out toward each other.

The rain poured down outside, thrumming on the cottage roof, blanketing the world in wetness as man and woman came together in front of the stone fireplace.

Bella let his body teach hers, let him take control of her entire being, flowing with him until she could no longer stand it.

She began to cry out, her body shuddering in involuntary paroxysms as he poured forth inside her, their bodies one.

Bella clung to him, neither of them wanting the feelings to end. "Oh, David, I was such a fool. . . . I loved you, and I didn't even know it. And then when I did know it I didn't want to admit it. I thought I'd lost you. David, oh, David, I love you so much. . . ."

He moved to rest on his side, bringing her with him, his body still within hers as he cradled her in his arms.

"I thought you hated me. I almost asked Cavendish for his daughter's hand. I thought you would never forgive me. Why didn't you say something?"

She snuggled close, content just to feel the strength of the arms that held her. "If I had said something you would have felt duty-bound to say yes to anything I asked no matter how you really felt. I had to know how you truly felt."

"By kidnapping me?" he asked. He pulled back a little to see her face, and their bodies parted. A small sigh escaped Bella before she replied.

"By getting you off alone, by surprise, so that you would

be honest." She reached down to hold his slackening flesh. "I needed to find out if you truly wanted me, too." She giggled softly. "I couldn't very well walk up to you in the parlor or somewhere and grab you like this, could I?"

David laughed. "Good Lord, you are incorrigible!"

The sound of a carriage arriving outside startled him. David sat up. "What's happening now?"

Bella sat up, too, reaching for their clothing. "You'd best be dressed before they enter."

"What have you done now?" he demanded. "Who is outside?"

Bella smiled. "It should be Tim or Joshua with my maid and a preacher."

"What?"

Bella's smile widened as a fist pounded on the cabin door. "Well, you do have to marry me now, don't you?"

David stared at the dark-eyed beauty whose tousled hair gave ample evidence of their situation even as they hurriedly buttoned their clothing. "You are positively mad," he told her as a man dressed in clerical garb opened the cabin door. David had never before seen the man in his life. And one look at the man's face was proof he had never been greeted with a sight such as was now before him. The man stopped in his tracks, gaping at the disheveled man and woman who were still buttoning up their attire.

Behind the man dressed in clerical garb were not, however, Tim and Sally. The prince and Dolores walked in and checked, their eyes widening in astonishment at the sight of the two young people.

"My God!" the prince said. "David, what have you done *now?*"

"It's not David's doing," Dolores reminded his father. "It's Bella's!"

The prince simply stared. Behind them Consuela was the last to walk inside. She took one look at the disheveled pair before the fireplace and gasped. "Didn't I *tell* you?" she demanded of her companions. "I knew they were up to no good!"

It was hard to tell which of the people in the room was the more shocked.

"I think I should leave you to your family—problems," the minister said. Dolores reached out to stop him.

"No, Father. As you can see, we need you most urgently right here! Connie, please wait with Tim outside."

"This is most terribly irregular," the minister said, turning toward the prince.

"Yes, it is," the prince agreed. "But you can surely see the necessity of our presence. And especially of yours, reverend Father."

"I'm not quite sure—" the minister began, only to be interrupted by Bella.

"You may not be sure, but you must do your duty. This man has taken my honor and my virtue twice over, and now you must make me his wife!"

"Twice over," the man of God repeated, horrified at the woman's bald statement of fact. "But marrying people against their will—"

"There's nothing for it," David told the man, "she's right. You must marry us. Even thought it's against both our wills."

"Against both—" The priest was at a loss for words.

"David!" Henry interrupted. "You may be enjoying this, but it is cold and damp outside, and we have to ride back through this beastly weather all the way home. Therefore, please shut up and let the man get on with it."

"Highly irregular," the minister said again.

"And when we've done being their witnesses, they can be ours," the prince said.

"*What?*" Bella, David, Dolores, and the minister all chorused the single word.

Prince Henry smiled at Dolores. "When your daughter insisted I get the special license for them to be immediately married, I decided I might as well get two."

"Who—I beg your pardon?" The reverend looked from the prince to the woman standing beside him and then to the demented pair on the floor.

"My father is marrying her mother," David explained helpfully.

The churchman thought about running outside and fleeing the scene. These were obviously mad people, positively insane. However, the prince was handing him the signed legal consents and a very large bill along with them. And it was raining unmercifully outside. And they were a very great distance from London and his own little parish.

"I suppose I shall have to," the minister said in shocked and even slightly aggrieved tones.

And so he did.

Chapter Twenty-eight

The formal ball the Prince and Princess of Wales gave in honor of His Majesty, King Kalakaua of Hawaii, was held at Marlborough House. Queen Victoria, as usual, was not in attendance.

The little queen's widowhood had long since ended any pleasure she might once have had in parties and balls. The Prince and Princess of Wales—Edward and Alexandra, known as Bertie and Alix to their friends—had taken on the lion's share of the social burdens of the monarchy.

If the truth were known, there were other reasons the queen did not attend gatherings at Marlborough House. She did not approve of many of her son's friends.

The queen was concerned that her grandsons would be contaminated by the society in which their parents delighted. She had clear memories of her riotous uncles, each seeming to outdo the others in bad taste and debauchery.

Neither did she approve of the money her son spent on all manner of follies, including the new ballroom he was having built at Sandringham.

And to top all of it off, the Prince of Wales had gone against the queen's express wishes this very night. She had asked him to cancel the ball because of the death of her greatest friend, Arthur Stanley, Dean of Westminster. Stanley had been more than any bishop or archbishop, the queen had told her son, and she deplored her son's heartless frivolity in arranging the funeral a day earlier than intended so that he could attend the Goodwood Races.

The queen was almost the only member of the royal family not in attendance at the ball. The aristocrats who were privileged enough to be invited along with the royals were slightly disappointed in the exotic Hawaiian king who, although dark-skinned and -haired, was dressed in perfectly presentable evening attire and seemed to conduct himself with the gravity one would expect of a king.

"It's too disappointing," Clarissa Stanisbury said unhappily from her vantage point a great distance from the royal threesome.

Henrietta Epps smiled. "The evening won't be a total loss, Clarissa dear. Look who has just arrived."

At the huge double doorway to the ballroom a uniformed royal servant was announcing David and Isabella, the Duke and Duchess of Exeter, and Prince Henry and Princess Henry.

The buzz of gossip reached all the way to royal ears, Princess Alix as curious as Henrietta and Clarissa about the newly married foursome. "Bertie dear, you must invite them over. I heard they got married in a hayloft."

"I r-rather d-doubt it," the Prince of Wales replied. He spoke wonderful German and charming French but somehow seemed least comfortable with his own language, a slight stutter occasionally coloring his comments. "Not H-Henry's style at all, m'dear."

"I shall present them, Your Highness, shall I?" Lady Antrim asked the Princess of Wales.

"You had best, unless you want me to die of curiosity!" Alix told her, and then she exploded into the sudden, infectious laughter those around her knew well.

Lady Antrim stepped down from the raised dais where the Prince and Princess of Wales and the King of Hawaii sat on thronelike chairs and wound her way through the crowded room toward the newcomers.

A matronly-looking woman was talking animatedly with

Prince Henry and his bride. "Oh, you will have to be presented to the queen herself. She will insist. And I can tell you what it will be like, my dear Dolores—I hope you don't mind my calling you that—"

"Please do, and please again tell me all you can. Henry says I shall have to see Her Majesty alone, and I must tell you, the prospect is frightening."

"Actually, you and Henry will go in together. Henry will present you and then leave you to have a few minutes' private conversation. It's all very formal at the palace. Very. First off, you must not cough, no matter what urge you feel. Secondly you must not sneeze." She saw Dolores's widening eyes and smiled. "I am quite serious. It is considered completely unseemly. Then, too, you might give her a cold or something worse, heaven forbid. Thirdly, you must not on any account stir either hand or foot. If, by chance, you are unfortunate enough to be stung by a bee or sit on your hatpin or whatever you can imagine, you must not say one word, and you must not move to remove it. You must bear whatever pain without wincing. If tears come to your eyes, you must not wipe them away."

"You jest!" Dolores said. "Bella, are you listening?"

"Yes, Mama." Isabella's hand was firmly gripped by her husband's.

"I do not jest, nor does the queen. She demands meticulous attention and the most proper respect." The woman continued, "If your tears flow, you must ignore them as if they weren't there. If blood were to gush forth, you must not move to stop it. No matter what, in other words, you do not stir." The woman smiled at Dolores. "However, Mama said if you have a pain that is just nearly beyond endurance, you may bite the inside of your cheek for a little relief. As long as the movement cannot be seen from the outside, of course."

"Oh, my," Dolores said. "Tell me, how many succumb in the middle of their presentations and have to be carried out?" She looked into her new husband's warm hazel eyes. "And dear Henry, how many die and none know until it is time to leave?"

Lady Antrim arrived to find the small group laughing. Henry introduced the woman to his wife and daughter-in-law. Lady Antrim glanced curiously at the tall, dark-haired American who stood beside the prince's son while they spoke, their hands entwined.

She was the beauty all had said, especially in the gown she wore that night. Made of starched stiff satin and colored a deep shade of old gold, the gown left her ivory shoulders and the top of her bosom bare except for the thick filigreed necklace of gold encrusted with pearls that banded her neck.

Matching gold and pearl earrings shone lustrous against the background of her thick upsweep of darkest ebony hair.

Introductions over, the small group moved toward the dais, a hundred pairs of eyes upon their progress across the floor.

The Prince and Princess of Wales sat talking with the King of Hawaii as Prince Henry's party drew near. Bertie glanced toward the group coming toward the dais and smiled.

"Cousin Henry—it's good to see you. Let me present you to the King of the Sandwich Islands, dear boy. Or as you Americans say, Hawaii." The prince smiled at Dolores and Isabella. The Prince of Wales made the introductions and then pulled Henry a bit aside as the others spoke politely with the foreign king.

The Prince of Wales spoke in a low tone to his cousin: "Mother is quite p-put out with you, Henry. When she gave you special dispensation, she had no idea you intended to go forward in such an unorthodox fashion." The Prince of Wales glanced toward Isabella and then looked toward Dolores, his gaze lingering there. "Although I certainly can understand your wish for haste. And I must tell you, you have helped me no end."

"How so?" Henry asked.

"I've been in Mother's bad books for months. You see, among all my other faults, I did the unforgivable at the requiem mass for Emperor Alexander II of Russia."

Prince Henry grinned at the man who would one day be king. "I was there, Bertie. You fell asleep."

"Yes," the Prince of Wales agreed, "but I did it standing up!" Both men laughed in spite of themselves. "Mother was told the whole sordid story. The all-night party the night before. You remember, Henry—you lost every game that night. And at the mass they even reported my taper tipping down and guttering away on the floor while all others were held high."

"Lord, Bertie, she must be truly upset."

"Aye; she even wanted me to call off this ball because old Stanley died. And I'm not just in her bad books, either. We had dinner at Lady Spencer's while you were away, and my brother-in-law was beside himself because I gave the king precedence over him. Can you imagine? I told him, brother-in-law or no, he was merely the German crown prince, and a king had to take precedence, no matter where he was from or whom he ruled!"

"Quite so," Henry agreed. "I am beginning to understand why you are so happy with my family's recent doings. I daresay it will take some of the pressure off you for a bit."

Bertie nodded vigorously, grinning at his second cousin.

"Bertie." Alix came near, bringing the others. "We must lead the royal quadrille."

The Prince of Wales sighed. "Duty calls," he told them. And then he nodded first to Dolores and then to Isabella. To David he smiled wide. "You and your father have certainly complicated our family tree. However, with you finally off the marriage mart, perhaps some of the younger bucks will finally have a chance." The Prince of Wales smiled at Isabella. "I s-shall insist upon a dance with the beauty who finally captured your heart. But why on earth you settled for my ne'er-do-well cousin I am at a loss to comprehend."

Isabella flashed the Prince of Wales a brilliant smile. "He has hidden charms, Your Highness."

Bertie laughed and turned toward his wife. "Alix, you are going to adore our newest family members."

The Prince and Princess of Wales led the King of Hawaii and Lady Antrim to the floor, beginning the royal quadrille and officially opening the dance.

Across the room the Countess of Eppsworth was beside herself with pleasure. "Clarissa, I told you we would be vindicated. He who laughs last, laughs best. And could you ever see anything better than the view before you? The King of Hawaii and the Terror of California, talking together! Don't you just adore it? And to think we did it all!"

"Oh, Henrietta," Clarissa replied, "I hardly think *I* had anything to do with it."

"Well, I know *I* did. I told you before they arrived I was going to arrange something between the American Terror and the duke. And I helped do just that!"

Clarissa looked off toward Prince Henry and Dolores. "If so," she said, "you got more than you bargained for."

Henrietta laughed. "That's true enough!" She spied Millicent Cavendish and her parents. Henrietta dragged Clarissa over to them. "My dears, how are you? And Millicent, how sweet you look tonight."

Millicent smiled at Henrietta. "Thank you. I feel— wonderful!" Her eyes went toward David and Bella as she spoke.

"Truly?" Clarissa asked.

Millicent saw the direction of Clarissa's gaze and smiled wide. "Oh, my, yes! You know, I was Bella's very first friend when she first arrived from America. We share a love of horses. And, I must tell you, I helped the success of her plans to capture him!"

"Really?" Henrietta's eyes grew wide. "You must tell me all."

Millicent's mother politely intervened, stopping her daughter before she launched into a little too much explanation. Bringing Millie away from the notorious gossips, she handed her daughter over to the young earl who was politely flirting with Isabella.

"Millie dear, this is John Hargrove. He's been badgering your father for an introduction." And with that, Lady Cavendish turned away from the young people.

"Henrietta—there's Adela Winston," Clarissa was saying across the room.

"Poor thing," Henrietta replied insincerely, "she had to bring her own husband."

Henrietta watched as the first dance ended and the Prince of Wales led the newest Duchess of Exeter to the dance floor, joining the first waltz. The Prince of Wales was an accomplished dancer, his shyness leaving him as he whirled the young Isabella around.

David offered his arm to Alix but was told one dance in the shoes she was wearing was quite enough. She would much rather sit and talk and hear of the wonderfully scandalous courtship firsthand.

Henry drew Dolores into the dance, the sounds of the music welling up around the partygoers as the candles blazed from countless wall sconces and the food and drink flowed from tables full of ornate serving dishes, manned by scores of footmen dressed in royal livery.

At the end of the waltz the Prince of Wales turned to Dolores, and Prince Henry smiled at his new daughter-in-law, leading her into the next dance.

David made small talk with the Princess of Wales, his eyes continually wandering toward his new wife's progress across the dance floor. Isabella was surrounded by admirers, one tapping Prince Henry's shoulder and cutting in, another cutting in, and then another and another.

Able to stand it no more, David excused himself from his royal relative, moving across the dance floor to cut in himself. Princess Alix watched him with sparkling eyes. Leaning toward Lady Antrim she spoke softly: "He is very passionate and jealous about her, isn't he? How delightful."

"Did you truly dress as a brigand?" a young earl was asking Isabella when David drew close. The young man's eyes were full of admiration. "Weren't you frightened?"

"Frightened?" Isabella laughed merry little peals of mirth. "Why should I have been frightened? *I* was the brigand!"

The duke tapped the young earl on the shoulder, but his words were for Isabella. "If you don't know why, none can explain it to you."

Isabella gave her new husband a saucy smile. "Aren't you even going to try, David?"

"I'd try if I were you, Exeter," a laughing male voice told him from somewhere near.

David did not look pleased. His voice lowered. "You are flirting outrageously."

"I am not!" Isabella defended herself. "I am merely

having fun!" And so saying, she smiled coquettishly back at the young earl. "Aren't I?"

"My lady, I would agree with anything you said," the earl said gallantly.

"You'd best watch out, David; she might decide to abduct someone else next time," a friend of David's joked.

The Duke of Exeter was not pleased by all the comments around them. "Shall we?" he said, attempting to waltz Bella away.

"She's a fiery one, Exeter," a voice called out.

Another man tapped David's shoulder. David attempted to ignore him but was tapped again. "I say, I'm trying to cut in, old man," David was told.

David scowled at the man. "She's through dancing," he said.

"But I'm not!" Isabella replied.

"Oh, yes you are," David told her through gritted teeth. "You're coming with me," David said to Bella.

"No!" she replied loudly enough to be overheard.

David spoke very carefully to his new wife: "You will come with me now. I will not stand here and be made to seem a laughingstock."

Isabella's chin rose, a stubborn tilt to it. "You can't make me," she told her new husband.

"Oh, yes I can," David replied. Suiting action to words, the Duke of Exeter reached for his wife's waist.

"What do you think you are doing!?" she demanded as her feet were leaving the floor. "Put me down!"

"Not bloody likely," David said as he lifted her higher and slung her over his shoulder.

The crowds around were staring. The orchestra was still playing, but all eyes were on the newlyweds.

"Oh, dear," Dolores said as she looked toward her daughter. "Bella's up to something again."

Prince Henry merely met the Prince of Wales's raised brow with a small smile. "He can handle her, Dolores," Henry told his wife, and they began to dance. Other couples around them, realizing they were staring, began to resume their dance.

"Put me down!" Isabella demanded. The crowded room was treated to the sight of Isabella being carried off the dance floor over her husband's shoulder. "Don't you *dare!*" she shouted, her fists beating against his back as she heard titters of laughter around them.

Princess Alix was so shocked she outright stared. And then began to laugh uproariously as David gave his wife's satin-covered bottom a slap and marched out the terrace doors. A few other titters here and there were heard before the glass doors closed.

One of the people laughing was a very amused Lord Winston. He wiped his eyes as he spoke to his wife: "Oh, Adela, David has finally met his match!"

Adela's smile was disdainful. "Shocking behavior," she said. "Come along, Clive, I want to dance."

"Again, dear?" he asked dispiritedly. He gave a large sigh as he escorted his lovely wife to the dance floor.

Outside cold night air greeted David as he carried Isabella across the terrace. She was still beating on his back and trying to kick him, all the laughter inside still ringing in her ears.

David continued across the stone terrace to the steps and the wide expanse of lawns beyond. "I said put me down!" she demanded fiercely.

"I'll put you down when I'm good and ready!" David told her.

"Put me down this instant!" Bella shouted at her husband.

Much to her surprise, he did. He brought her off his shoulder and dumped her onto the damp grass.

"Let me up, I'll get grass stains all over my gown!"

David followed her to the ground, covering her protesting mouth with his own.

Shocked, she responded to his urgency and then tried to push him away. "David! Stop it! Are you crazy?"

"Of course I'm crazy! Look whom I married!"

"What?" Bella demanded.

"Anyone who would marry the Terror of California has got to be crazy!"

"How *dare* you!"

"How dare *you* create such a scene!" David demanded.

"I shall make all the scenes I please!" she told him defiantly.

"Fine! Then so shall I!" her husband promised. As he spoke he moved to pinion Bella's arms against the ground.

"David, what are you doing? We can't! You can't! Not here!"

"I can and we shall," he promised her, "right here! If you can make scenes, I can better them and really give them all something to talk about!"

"But they'll all see! David, please, I'm sorry—I was just teasing—I won't make scenes any time I please. I didn't mean it."

"You were not teasing. You did mean it, and furthermore you were being a willful brat!"

Bella swallowed. "I was being a willful brat," she agreed.

He straightened up a bit, staring down into her alarmed eyes. "What did you say?"

Bella tried to smile a little. "I said you were right. I was being a willful brat."

"And you will behave properly?"

"Yes," she told him.

"You will do as I say?" he asked.

"Yes, David," Bella told her husband meekly. "Anything you say."

"Why?" he demanded.

The tiny smile hovering around her lips widened. "Because you're bigger and stronger than I am." He moved back, letting her sit up. "And because you're even more stubborn than I am," Bella added impishly.

David began to grin. "I'm glad you've figured that out," he told her.

"I've known it all along," she told him. Bella held out her hand imperiously. "Now get up and help me to my feet before we're seen like this."

He hesitated one more moment and then moved to get to his feet. Reaching back, he took her hand and lifted her up.

As he did, Bella grinned wickedly. "If I hadn't known how stubborn you are, I wouldn't have had to kidnap you."

David drew her near, kissing her soundly. "Nor I you," he told her when their lips parted.

"Let's go home," she said.

"Not yet. First we shall go back inside and you shall dance with your husband."

"Yes, David."

"And no others," he warned.

"Yes, David. No others," Isabella said obediently.

David stopped, turning her toward him and eyeing her suspiciously. "I mean it. I want you to pay no attention to anyone else for the remainder of the evening."

"I shall do exactly as you say," she replied.

Not sure he trusted her obedience, he held the door open for her, and they walked back inside. "Whatever you want, David," Bella said meekly as they passed Henrietta and Clarissa.

Seeing them, Bella smiled innocently at the expressions of disbelief on the women's faces. A moment later the Duke of Exeter drew his wife into his arms. Music welled up around them as they joined the other dancers. Their bodies began to move in perfect harmony.

As David whirled Bella around the floor he brought her closer and closer. Bella's arms were around David's neck. She kissed him, her lips parting, her tongue reaching to enter his mouth and touch his own. She felt his reactions, luxuriating in the feeling. Then slowly she released him, looking up at him with glowing eyes.

The Duke of Exeter stared down at his wife's laughing eyes. "And you said you would behave!"

"David, do you think we might leave early?" the Duchess of Exeter asked her husband meekly, only her eyes still dancing.

"We may have to," he said into her ear. "Else all will see my ardor."

Bella giggled. "Serves you right," she told him as they danced on after the music stopped.

The Prince of Wales motioned to the orchestra, music swelling up again. "I had to tell them to continue," the Prince of Wales told his wife. "It was obvious the young couple were not about to leave each other's arms."

Dolores and Prince Henry watched their children's progress across the floor. "You see? I told you everything would be all right between them," Henry told the new princess.

"Oh, yes, Henry dear," Dolores replied, smiling. "You were absolutely right. My daughter has finally met her match!"

The prince reached for his bride's hands, bringing them to his lips. "As have I," he told her before he kissed them. "As have I."

The prince led his bride to the dance floor, joining in the waltz, as did Adela and Clive Winston and Millicent Cavendish and her young earl.

While David and Bella were lost in each other's arms, outside Marlborough House Joshua and Tim were recounting to the other carriage drivers the events that would one day be stories told to children and grandchildren.

At Exeter House, a much less romantic Tate gloomily informed the staff that between Yorkshire, London, and California they would be stuck with the Americans and all the extra work for the rest of their lives. Sally grinned wide, telling the butler she was going to learn to be a cowgirl when they were in America.

And upstairs in the Exeter mansion, Consuela Rivera sat happily alone, preparing for the months ahead.

She was knitting little Exeter-crested booties.

Jude Deveraux

America's favorite historical romance author!

The James River Trilogy

- [ ] COUNTERFEIT LADY 67519/$4.50
- [ ] LOST LADY 67430/$4.50
- [ ] RIVER LADY 67297/$4.50

Enter the passionate world of the Chandler Twins

- [ ] TWIN OF ICE 68090/$4.50
- [ ] TWIN OF FIRE 68091/$4.50

The Montgomery Saga Continues

- [ ] THE TEMPTRESS 67452/$4.50
- [ ] THE RAIDER 67056/$4.50
- [ ] THE PRINCESS 67386/$4.50
- [ ] THE AWAKENING 64445/$4.50
- [ ] THE MAIDEN 68886/$4.50

The Falcon Saga

- [ ] THE TAMING 64446/$4.50

• • • • • • • •

- [ ] WISHES 64448/$4.50

POCKET BOOKS